Summer in Tuppenny Bridge

Sharon Booth

Storm
PUBLISHING

Ebook ISBN: 978-1-80508-034-3
Paperback ISBN: 978-1-80508-036-7

Cover design: Debbie Clement
Cover images: Shutterstock

Published by Storm Publishing.
For further information, visit:
www.stormpublishing.co

Also by Sharon Booth

For my best friend Julie with love and thanks.
I owe you cake. Lots of cake.

xxxx

Chapter One

Summer Fletcher padded into the kitchen of the flat above The White Hart Inn, rubbing her freshly shampooed hair with a towel.

Her mother, Sally, who was standing at the window, staring down on the pub car park, didn't look round as she said, 'That's better, love. Have you put your clothes in the basket?'

Summer grinned. 'Don't worry, I haven't left them on the bedroom floor.'

'Good lass. I'll wash them later.'

She sounded distracted, and Summer frowned. 'What's up with you? You can't be nervous, surely?'

Her mum finally turned to face her, and Summer saw anxiety in her eyes. She wondered why she'd be in such a state about a visit from Rafferty's daughter, since her mum and Frankie had always got on.

Frankie, or Francesca to use her full name, was the only daughter of Sally's fiancé, Rafferty Kingston, and the youngest of his children. She'd grown very close to Summer's mum when Sally went to stay with the Kingstons at Mill Cottage in the Norfolk Broads, back when Rafferty was still married to Elizabeth, Frankie's mother.

Sally Fletcher, it seemed, could do no wrong in Frankie's eyes, and she'd jumped at the chance to spend the first half of her school holidays in Tuppenny Bridge, so Summer couldn't imagine why her mum was so worried about her imminent arrival.

'Frankie should be here any minute,' Sally said, as if that answered the question.

'I know that,' Summer replied, amused. 'That's why I was herded into the bathroom to take a shower and get changed the minute I got home from Whispering Willows. You're not usually so fussy. What's really bothering you, Mum?'

Her mum sighed and sat down at the table. 'It's been ages since I saw her.'

'Not that long.' Summer sat beside her, still towelling her hair.

'Nearly a year!'

'But you've spoken to her by video, haven't you? Besides, this is Frankie we're talking about. She's like your best pal, isn't she? Followed you around like a shadow, as I recall.'

'It's different now,' Mum explained when she voiced the question. 'Before, I wasn't about to marry her dad. How will she feel now I'm practically her evil stepmother?'

'Evil?' Summer burst out laughing as she dumped the wet towel on the table. 'As if! You haven't got an evil bone in your body and Frankie knows it. Mind you,' she added mischievously, 'you might have your work cut out. She's not a little girl any more, is she? She'll be, what... thirteen, fourteen?'

'She was fourteen in January,' Sally said.

'Well, there you go. If anyone's likely to be evil it's Frankie. Nothing worse than a fourteen-and-a-half-year-old girl. I should know.'

'Oh, give over.' To Summer's relief her mother laughed, the anxiety leaving her face. 'You were my little angel. You both were—you and Billie. I was very lucky with both my daughters. You're right, you know. I'm sure Frankie will be fine. I mean, she's known about me and her dad for more than six months now so I'm sure she's got used to the idea. And I'll bet she's ever so excited about the wedding. What girl wouldn't be?'

Summer could think of lots of teenage girls who wouldn't give a fig about a wedding—she had, after all, been one of them—but thought it best not to say so. Her mother was nervous enough.

She took her comb from the pocket of her jeans and began to untangle her long, chestnut hair.

'Can't believe she's fourteen already,' she said. 'You know, I don't know why Rafferty didn't just let her get the train. Elizabeth offered to drive her to Norwich, didn't she? Train to Peterborough, on to Northallerton, Rafferty could have picked her up at the station and it wouldn't have taken long to bring her home from there.'

'It wouldn't have saved Frankie any time, though,' her mum said. 'Besides, there was no way Rafferty would let his teenage daughter travel all that way by herself on a train, and neither would I.'

'Fair enough.' Summer glanced at the clock on the wall beside the door. 'I hope they're here soon. I'm starting my shift downstairs in forty minutes.'

'Are you up to it, love?' Her mother's eyes crinkled with sympathy. 'You've already had a long day at the sanctuary. I can get cover for you if you need it, you know. You only have to ask.'

'Mum, we've had this conversation. You work just as many hours as I do.'

'But it's physical labour at Whispering Willows,' her mother pointed out, for the thousandth time.

'So is working in a pub! Anyway, you wouldn't offer to cover Chloe's or Nick's shifts if they were working part-time in a horse sanctuary, would you?'

Her mum looked sheepish. 'I suppose not.'

'Well then. If it's good enough for your other bar staff it's good enough for me. Shall I put this towel in the washing machine?'

Her mum nodded. 'You might as well. I'll put a load on this evening when we're all settled. Oh, I hope Frankie likes her room. I've put fresh flowers in there for her, and it's a nice view of the green...'

'Were you this worried when I came to stay at Christmas?' Summer asked, amused.

Mum gave her an embarrassed look. 'Probably worse.'

'Blimey. Poor Rafferty. He must have the patience of a saint.'

'He does. Why else would he ask me to marry him?'

Summer put her arms around her, and her mum held her tightly, despite the wet hair.

'He's lucky to have you and he knows it. And if it's any consolation, I can't wait for the wedding. It's going to be amazing.'

Her mum deserved the very best after all. She'd had her heart broken so many times by Summer's cheating dad and yet, somehow, she'd still found it in herself to put her trust in Rafferty. Not that Rafferty was anything like Summer's dad, but even so. Summer thought her mum was brave to have faith in another man. She wasn't sure she could be so courageous.

As she pulled away she saw tears in her mother's eyes, but at least she was smiling.

'It is, isn't it? And isn't it brilliant that Zach agreed to marry us in church, even though we're both divorced?'

'The perks of being mates with a vicar.'

Summer shoved the towel in the empty washing machine and slammed the door shut just as her mum called, 'I think they're here!'

She straightened and tucked her still damp hair behind her ears before following her mum through to the hallway.

They heard footsteps on the stairs, and the sound of a suitcase being bumped up each step. Summer gave Sally a sympathetic look.

'Deep breaths, Mum. This is Frankie, remember? Everything will be fine.'

* * *

Frankie, Summer thought, was like a different girl. It was rather disconcerting to see her sitting on the sofa, sipping Diet Coke through a straw between bursts of conversation, which covered just about everything that had happened to her over the last year. It was as if she'd forgotten they'd spoken at all since the last time she'd stayed in Tuppenny Bridge, and all her news was pouring forth in a torrent.

Rafferty and Mum barely got a word in edgeways as Frankie chattered about her school, ('I'm going to be in year ten in September, can you believe it? And they still won't let us drop maths!') about her amazing friend, Phoebe, ('I really wanted her to come with me, but her parents have dragged them all to Ireland to stay with her granny for the summer.

Phoebe's outraged!') and about her home life, ('You should see Mum trying to be nice to Bingo. It nearly kills her, but she daren't say anything. You know what she's like about dog hair, and Bingo is *such* a hairy dog. It's hilarious!').

Summer risked a look at her mother and, as she'd suspected, Sally looked dazed. Even Rafferty seemed bewildered about who this child was, and he'd had a five-hour journey from Hoxbridge to get used to her.

She wondered how he'd reacted when he'd seen his daughter. Frankie didn't look anything like the young girl Summer had last met in person. Then she'd been a thin, freckle-faced child, with strawberry-blonde hair that she usually wore in a ponytail. Well, she'd certainly filled out since then, with curves in all the right places, her freckles buried under layers of foundation. The strawberry-blonde ponytail had been replaced by blue space buns. Not only that, but she'd had her nose pierced and was now sporting a gold stud. Summer couldn't imagine how Rafferty had coped with such a huge change.

'Your hair looks, er, lovely,' Mum said, giving Rafferty a sideways glance. Clearly she'd been wondering the same thing. 'What a gorgeous shade of blue.'

'Do you think so?' Frankie beamed and patted one of the space buns. 'Thanks. Do you like my nose piercing?'

'Very, er, distinctive,' Mum said.

Rafferty eyed his daughter doubtfully. 'Is it even legal to get your nose pierced at fourteen?'

Frankie laughed. 'Yes, of course it is. Mum said it was okay as long as I take it out for school. She even came with me and gave permission.'

Mum and Rafferty exchanged surprised looks.

'She did?'

Frankie nodded. 'Oh yes. She's been really nice to me

6

lately. Lets me do anything I like really.' She leaned forward, as if imparting top secret information. 'You know what I think? I think it's since she found out you two were getting married. She knows how nice Sally is, and now she's going to be my stepmum, Mum's got competition. I reckon I could ask for just about anything and get it.'

Seeing her dad's horrified look she added hastily, 'Not that I would. But it's proper funny seeing her falling over herself to keep me happy.'

Given Elizabeth had practically ignored Frankie for years, while lavishing all her attention on her sons, Summer couldn't really blame her for making the most of it now.

Rafferty clearly wasn't so sure.

'And that extends to letting you dye your hair blue? Won't the school have something to say about it?'

'Oh don't worry about that, Dad. It's a semi-permanent from the supermarket. It'll wash out by the time I go back to school. Chill out. It might be pink at Christmas.'

'I'm sure that'll look lovely, Frankie,' Mum said, sounding far from certain about it. 'Now, shall we get you unpacked and settled in your room?'

'And I'd better get off to work,' Summer said, getting to her feet.

'Are you going to Whispering Willows?' Frankie asked.

'At this time? No, I've got the evening shift in the pub,' Summer said. 'I'm back at Whispering Willows the day after tomorrow.'

'Could I pop over?' Frankie sounded surprisingly keen. 'I'd like to see the place again. Do you still have those ponies we saw when we visited?'

Summer smiled. 'Sure. You'd be very welcome.'

She shared the relief she saw on Rafferty's and her mother's faces. Behind the blue space buns, the make-up, and the nose stud, Frankie was still there somewhere. Maybe a few weeks in Tuppenny Bridge would remind her of that fact.

* * *

Ben Callaghan rested his head in his hands and closed his eyes briefly, shutting out the image of the letter on his desk.

Another increase in Jamie's school fees. How could they justify a further three per cent on top of the already extortionate price they were charging? A quick calculation told him how much more he'd be paying from next year. Thank goodness he didn't have to send his younger brother as a boarder.

He knew what Clive would say right now if he showed him this. *You know the answer. You could solve all your problems in one fell swoop.*

He was right, too. Ben glanced around his study, noting the shabby wallpaper and threadbare carpet, the scratched surface of his desk, and the plaster coving with the broken corner piece that irritated him every time he looked at it.

If he sold Monk's Folly he could pay Jamie's school fees, clear his credit card, find a smaller, lower-maintenance home for himself and his family—somewhere the council tax wasn't so high, and the gas and electricity bills wouldn't make his eyes water, even when the family had shivered their way through the winter, wrapping themselves in layers of clothing rather than turning on the central heating.

There had to be more to life than this, surely? He had a good job working for fellow vet Clive Browning at Stepping Stones. He should be comfortable, earning more than enough to pay a small mortgage and his utility bills. But this house...

Ben pinched the bridge of his nose, feeling a headache

coming on. He'd never have a penny while they remained here. This house was less a home and more a prison.

There was a tap at the door, and he switched on a smile as his mother entered the room.

'I brought you a coffee,' she said, handing him a mug. 'I thought you might need some refreshment since you've been in here such a long time.'

'Thanks, Mum. I appreciate that.' He glanced at his watch, surprised to find that it was almost nine o'clock. Where had the evening gone?

'Is everything all right, Ben?' His mother glanced at the papers on the desk and Ben hastily folded the bills and letters and shoved them in his top drawer, aware that she'd had a tough day and probably wasn't up to yet another discussion about the state of their finances.

'Fine. Just sorting the accounts, that's all.' He noticed the sad look in her eyes. 'How are you feeling? I'm sorry I couldn't be with you today.'

'Oh!' She shook her head dismissively. 'You had work to do. Clive couldn't possibly spare you, and what could you do anyway? Still, I'll admit it was awfully sad to see Mr Eckington leave. It'll be strange, seeing Daisyfield Cottage standing empty now he and his wife have both gone.'

'Did he seem upset to go?' Ben asked hesitantly.

Mr Eckington had worked at Monk's Folly for longer than Ben had been alive. His wife had also worked at the house, and even though they'd retired fifteen years ago they'd remained a fixture of Ben's life. Ben had many happy memories of visiting them at their home from being a young boy.

Sadly, Mrs Eckington had died the previous year, and Mr Eckington's health had gone downhill so fast since then; their daughter had decided it would be better all round if he moved in with her.

Today had been the big day and Ben was sorry he hadn't been there to see him off, although he'd popped into their pretty little cottage on River Road the previous evening to say his goodbyes. It had been sad to hear Mr Eckington insist that the move was only temporary, and he'd be home as soon as he was on his feet again, while behind him his daughter shook her head, denying the possibility.

'I suppose nothing stays the same forever,' his mother said sadly. She moved towards the window and gazed out across the overgrown land that had once passed for a garden. Since Mr Eckington had retired, their lawn had vanished under long grass and a jungle of weeds, which Ben would attack now and then when he remembered or had the time.

He watched his mother, wondering what she was thinking. He felt a sudden hope that maybe she was looking at the state of the place and thinking it was time to do something about the way they were living. She must surely see how shabby Monk's Folly looked, and she had to know why Ben had done nothing about it.

'Mum...' His voice trailed off. Could he really put the suggestion to her? 'Mum, I—'

'I was thinking we could plant some roses,' she said thoughtfully. 'Brighten it up a little. We really should have got another gardener after Mr Eckington retired. After all, we're highly visible here, being up on the hill. It would make a much better impression if the garden was sorted, don't you think?'

Ben massaged his temples. 'Mm. Mum—'

She turned away from the window and scanned the study as she rubbed her arm. 'You know, this room needs decorating,' she said, as if she'd only just noticed how drab it looked. 'It was such a warm, welcoming room when your father used it. He'd be sorry to see it in such a poor condition. We'll pick out some wallpaper, Ben. What do you think?'

Ben couldn't put into words what he thought. Did she really think a bit of wallpaper would make a difference to this place? She knew the state of their finances, so she must know they couldn't possibly afford a gardener, or even spend money on decorating. Who did she think she was kidding?

She nodded, answering her own question. 'Yes, that's what we'll do. You shouldn't have to work in such ugly surroundings. You deserve better and so does Monk's Folly.'

He stayed silent and she gave him an appealing look. 'Everything is all right, isn't it, Ben?'

He wanted to scream at her that no, everything wasn't all right. Her stubborn refusal to leave this place, her determination to carry on here as if they still had money to spend on it, and her wilful refusal to let him take Jamie out of public school was pulling them all under. He felt as if he was suffocating under the weight of so much responsibility.

And yet, she'd lost so much already, and Monk's Folly was all she had left to cling to, with its memories of his dad and older brother, Leon.

His own feelings didn't matter. Somehow he had to find a way to keep the roof over their heads.

'Everything's fine, Mum. I was just about to go downstairs actually. I'm a bit peckish. It seems like ages since we had dinner.'

Her smile returned. 'Wonderful. I'll see if Jamie's hungry too, shall I? We can all eat supper together and watch that documentary you were so keen to catch about the penguins in the Arctic.'

'Antarctica,' he said, smiling.

'Yes, that's right.' She hurried towards the study door, clearly relieved to have something to do. 'I'll go and tell

Jamie. He's been up in his bedroom for hours playing those silly computer games of his. A break will do him good, too.'

The door closed after her and Ben leaned back in his chair and sighed. At least, he thought, there was a comfortable sofa in the living room. This old chair was as hard as nails. He'd been so wrapped up in his financial worries he hadn't noticed how uncomfortable he was.

Roses! As if planting roses was going to make any difference to their precarious living.

He sighed, imagining Clive's voice begging him to take Jamie out of St Egbert's and send him to the local state school in Lower Skimmerdale.

He could imagine his mother's reply to that. As far as she was concerned Jamie had a bright future ahead of him, and that meant giving him the best education money could buy. To her that was all that mattered.

She didn't seem to recognise how much pressure she was putting on Ben. Or if she did, she didn't care.

Ben headed downstairs, mug of coffee in his hand, thinking he really couldn't blame her.

Chapter Two

Set on the lower banks of the River Skimmer, Tuppenny Bridge was best known as the home of Georgian artist, Josiah Lavender, for its thriving twice-weekly market, and its annual sheep fair, which took place during the last week in September.

When the market wasn't on, the square became the town's main car park. There were no parking meters, although there was an honesty box near one bench with a suggested parking fee of fifty pence. Surrounding the square were various cottages and businesses, all built of sandstone, with stone slate roofs and sash windows.

Just outside Market Place was the Church of All Hallows, and before that, across the road from The White Hart Inn, was the large, square house that was All Hallows' Vicarage.

The Corner Cottage Bookshop, which stood on the corner of Little Market Street and faced the market place, was a solid stone building, with a single, large bay window to the left of a glass front door. Upstairs, there were just two small windows. It would have looked quite stark, but for the pink and white striped canopy over the window, the pink rambling roses that climbed the stone walls, and the fantastic display of books behind the glass.

Summer had already grown fond of the shop, not least because of her friendship with Clemmie Grant, whose aunt, Dolly, was the owner.

Clemmie was dealing with a customer when Summer pushed open the door and walked in. She took a moment to look around her and breathe in the calming air. She'd never been a massive reader, but it was funny how soothing she found this shop. It was probably her favourite of all the shops in the little market town.

Although the main room was quite narrow, it was impressive. Painted in cream with oak shelving, it felt warm and welcoming. It was also longer than it appeared from the outside. At the end of the room was an archway into another room, where there were more bookshelves. A sign above the arch read, 'Children's Books'.

To the right of the room, a glamorous spiral staircase—the sort Summer had only ever seen in films or TV until she'd moved here—snaked its way to the first floor, and a sign on the wall nearby proclaimed that there were more books upstairs.

Clemmie finished serving and beckoned Summer over as the customer left the shop.

'He's just spent eighty-seven pounds on books!' she said, her eyes sparkling with delight. 'Can you believe that? Eighty-seven pounds! I might shut up the shop and go home for the rest of the day.'

Summer laughed. 'I'm sure Dolly would love that. Where is she anyway?'

'She's nipped to Bridge Bakery to get us two vanilla

slices. Aw, if we'd known you were popping in we'd have got you one, too.'

Summer leaned on the counter. 'It's okay. It's not that long since I had lunch.'

'Has Frankie arrived?' Clemmie asked. 'Has she settled in okay?'

Summer couldn't help but smile. 'Yes to both questions, but I think she's practically given Rafferty a nervous breakdown.'

'Oh heck. What's she done?'

Briefly, Summer explained the change in Frankie since the last time she'd seen her, and how grown up she looked compared with the little girl she'd been then.

'Honestly, it was a shock to me, but to Rafferty... Well, he looks scared to death of her. I don't think he knows how to handle this sophisticated young woman with her blue hair and nose stud. I don't know, it's quite sad really.'

'Sad? How old are you? You're twenty-three, Summer, and here you are shaking your head and moaning about the kids of today.'

Summer laughed. 'It's not that! I quite like her new look. It's funky. No, it just made me wonder about Dad. How he felt as Billie and I grew up.'

Clemmie tilted her head in sympathy. 'You miss your dad, don't you?'

'I suppose I do,' Summer said. When her parents had split up, around two years ago, she'd initially lived with her dad in the East Yorkshire town of Bemborough, but after visiting her mum at Christmas she'd moved to Tuppenny Bridge permanently in January to live with her and Rafferty, having been assured by her dad that he would manage perfectly well without her. 'But we speak regularly and he's doing well, so that's the main thing.'

Dolly—a short, curvaceous woman with a dark bob and silver fringe—pushed open the door of the bookshop and hurried in, a broad smile on her face.

'I must have known you were coming,' she said cheerfully, waving a paper bag at Summer. 'I bought two extra just in case. I'll put the kettle on, and we'll have a vanilla slice each to celebrate.'

'To celebrate what?' Summer asked.

'Life, my love. Life,' Dolly said cheerfully, and hurried into the kitchen at the side of the shop.

Summer looked at Clemmie in surprise.

'What was all that about?'

'It's her birthday,' Clemmie said. 'She's fifty today. We've already had buck's fizz for breakfast and pink balloons tied to the kitchen chairs. She does love a birthday, and this is a special one so you can imagine.'

'Oh, bless her. I'd have got her a card if I'd known.'

'She won't mind. She's got dozens of them taking up every available inch of space at home. You know how sociable Dolly is.'

That, Summer realised, was quite true. Dolly had lots of friends and was very outgoing. She was resolutely single though, declaring men only spoiled your fun and women should please themselves, not some boring fella. It was funny really, given that Dolly was a successful romantic novelist, whose wartime sagas were dearly loved by readers. Her heroines were often as soppy as Clemmie, but Dolly herself had no time for all that *hearts and flowers stuff* as she called it, and saved any romantic thoughts she might have had for her characters.

Dolly returned a few minutes later with a tray bearing three mugs of coffee and three small plates, each holding a vanilla slice, one of which had a birthday candle stuck in the icing.

She insisted they sing 'Happy Birthday' to her, which they did, with some embarrassment, while she beamed at them.

'Just blow out the candle before the icing melts,' Clemmie advised, and Dolly did so with gusto.

'Here you go. One vanilla slice each. Wet wipes for afterwards,' she said, pointing to a packet on the counter. 'No sticky fingers in my bookshop please.'

'Well, I'm really glad I popped in now,' Summer told her. 'Happy birthday, by the way. I can't believe you're fifty.'

Dolly paused, a vanilla slice halfway to her mouth. 'Fifty? I'm not bloody fifty! Who told you I was fifty?'

'Aren't you?' Clemmie asked. 'I could have sworn you said...'

'That's next year!' Dolly shook her head. 'Let me get my head around forty-nine first, for God's sake. Oh bugger, another customer,' she added, as the bell above the door jingled.

Summer had just taken a bite of her vanilla slice, and custard was oozing all over her fingers. Her cheeks bulged as she stared in horror at the man approaching the counter.

Ben! Of all people!

She frantically chewed as she reached for a wet wipe to clean her fingers, then cast a desperate look at Clemmie, who burst out laughing and showered the counter with pastry crumbs.

'I'm sorry about this, Ben,' Dolly said, giving her niece a stern look. 'Not very professional, I know. It's my birthday you see and—'

'Oh, happy birthday.' Ben held up his hands. 'Honestly, it doesn't matter.'

He was quite pink and didn't seem to want to look at Summer at all. Probably too disgusted by her hamster-like face she thought miserably, as she finally swallowed the vanilla slice down and stood wiping her fingers, even though she'd already cleaned them.

'I've got another one in the kitchen if you'd like to join us,' Dolly said.

Clemmie gave Summer a sly look. 'Ooh yes, and I'll make you a coffee,' she said. 'You'd be really welcome, Ben.'

Summer glared at her as her face burned with embarrassment. Honestly, the only times Ben had seen her she was in filthy jeans and muddy wellies, and never looked nice. Today, she was wearing leggings and a decent top, and she'd had to ruin the effect by stuffing her face with pastry and custard. Typical!

'That's really kind of you,' he said, sounding as if he couldn't think of anything worse, 'but I need to get back to the surgery soon.'

'What can we do for you, love?' Dolly asked, pushing away her plate and trying to look professional.

'I, er, I just wondered if you had this book in stock?'

Ben pulled out his phone and began fumbling with it as Dolly waited patiently.

'It's here somewhere,' he said, tapping frantically on the screen and scrolling for what felt like ages. 'I know I put it on here.'

He glanced up and his eyes met Summer's for a moment before he cleared his throat and continued searching.

'Ah, here it is!' He couldn't have sounded more relieved as he held up the phone and showed it to Dolly. 'Do you have this?'

Dolly arched an eyebrow. 'Well, fancy that! Didn't have you down for a lover of Regency romps, Ben. Just shows you. You never can tell.' She winked at Summer and Clemmie.

Poor Ben looked mortified. 'It's for my mother. She saw a review of it in her magazine the other day and said it sounded good. I thought I'd get it for her. It's not her birthday yet but I thought I'd buy it now before I forget all about it. I never know what to get her.'

'I haven't got it in stock,' Dolly said, 'but I can certainly order it in for you, love. No problem.'

'Really?' Ben smiled. 'Thank you. That's great.'

'No worries. I'll give you a shout when it comes in.'

'Thanks, Dolly. Er, I'd better be getting back to, er, work. Bye.'

He gave them all an awkward wave and hurried out of the shop. As the bell jingled again, Summer's heart sank. What a humiliating encounter that had been! Why, oh why, had she said yes to the vanilla slice?

'Well, that was enlightening,' Dolly said cheerfully.

'I know!' Clemmie said. 'Do you think the book really was for his mother, or do you think Ben's a secret romantic?'

Dolly gave them both a knowing smile. 'I think,' she said, 'probably both.'

* * *

Ben hurried through the market place, his face still burning as he replayed the embarrassing scene in the bookshop. Trust him to walk in when Summer was there! And then to mess up the simple task of finding a screenshot on his phone! Really, he despaired of himself sometimes.

His pace slackened a little as he remembered Summer standing at the counter, eating a vanilla slice. She'd looked so adorable, with flakes of pastry on her lips and custard on her fingers. It had been good to see her in something other than wellies and jeans, too. Not that she looked bad in wellies and jeans. Far from it. Summer was so pretty she'd look good in anything.

He mentally shook his head then groaned inwardly as he saw Eugenie Lavender hurrying towards him, dragging her two Yorkshire terriers, Boycott and Trueman, behind her.

'Ben, dear, how lucky that I've bumped into you,' she said, beaming at him.

'Hello, Miss Lavender. What can I do for you?'

Ben was always polite to her, even though she could be a bossy old gossip at times, and certainly had delusions of grandeur. Her ancestor had been the famous Georgian artist, Josiah Lavender, and Miss Lavender owned his old home in the town, which she'd turned into a successful museum dedicated to his life and art.

Unfortunately, that seemed to be enough to convince her that she was responsible for the welfare of Tuppenny Bridge and its inhabitants, and she made it her business to find out as much as she could about what was going on, with the willing assistance of her best friends, Rita and Birdie Pennyfeather.

Since Miss Lavender was seventy-nine, and the Pennyfeathers were eighty-one, no one liked to tell them to mind their own business, a fact they all used to their best advantage by snooping around and taking bets on the residents' lives. It was probably, people often speculated, a pretty lucrative sideline.

'I was wondering if I could book the boys in for their boosters. It must be that time of year again, and I wouldn't want their immunity to wane.'

She beamed fondly at the Yorkshire terriers, who ignored

her as they scanned their surroundings, ears pricked, eyes alert.

Ben nodded. 'Just call the surgery, Miss Lavender. Jane will make you an appointment, no problem.'

'Oh, but you're here now,' she said. 'You can book it for me, can't you? Just telephone me when you've got it sorted.'

'But if I've got to telephone you anyway you might as well just call the surgery in the first place!'

Miss Lavender patted his arm. 'Thank you, Ben. I knew I could rely on you. Now,' she added as she walked beside him, 'how is your mother these days? It's a long time since I've seen her out and about. Is she keeping well?'

She gave him a sympathetic smile and he hoped she couldn't see the anxiety in his eyes as he assured her that his mother was perfectly fine, and that he'd pass on her regards.

Miss Lavender drew to a halt and peered up at him. 'It doesn't do, you know, Ben. It's been far too long. I fear she's got into the habit of hiding away and wallowing. You must be firmer with her. If not you, who will?'

Ben had no words. He stared at Miss Lavender, wishing he could think of a casual reply, but he had a feeling that even if he *could* find the words he wouldn't be able to say them without giving himself away.

'Of course, she went to Katherine Pennyfeather's baby shower before Christmas,' Miss Lavender said thoughtfully. 'That was a good start. But here we are at the end of July, and I fear she's reverted back to being a recluse.'

Ben nodded dumbly, then bent to fuss over the Yorkshire terriers, hoping she'd change the subject.

'I wonder,' Miss Lavender said, 'if you've ever considered selling Monk's Folly?'

Ben closed his eyes in bliss at such a wonderful thought, then he straightened and said regretfully, 'It's Mum's home.'

'Of course it is, but your father left it to you. And do you ever worry that perhaps it's rather isolated for her? It's all right for you and Jamie. You come into town to work, and Jamie goes to school each day, but your mother is across the river in that big house all alone. Perhaps she'd get out and about more if she lived on this side of the Skimmer. A smaller house, maybe. More manageable. Fewer memories...'

'I really do have to get back to work, Miss Lavender,' Ben said, walking away. 'I'll get Jane to make you that appointment and she'll call you later today.'

'As you wish, Ben,' Miss Lavender said, shaking her head gently. 'As you wish.'

Chapter Three

It didn't surprise Summer in the least when Joseph Wilkinson, the owner of Whispering Willows, failed to remember Frankie—at least initially. It had, after all, been two years since Frankie and Summer had visited the sanctuary together, on a brief excursion to Tuppenny Bridge while holidaying on the East Yorkshire coast.

In his mid-sixties, he gave the impression of being much older somehow, so it was no wonder he eyed Frankie's heavy make-up, designer ripped jeans, blue hair, and nose stud rather dubiously.

'I remember there being a little lass with Summer,' he said, rubbing his chin. 'But that can't be you, surely?'

'It is,' Frankie said, sounding proud of the fact that she'd changed so much since she'd last visited Whispering Willows that he couldn't believe she was the same person. 'I've grown up a bit since then.'

'By heck, you're not wrong there.' He gazed down at her white trainers and shook his head. 'You shouldn't have worn them,' he told her. 'They'll be ruined. It's going to rain within the hour, you mark my words. Haven't you got any wellies?'

Frankie admitted she hadn't but shrugged off his worries. 'I've only come to have a look around. I won't be doing any mucking out or anything.'

'No,' Joseph said. 'I don't suppose you will. Time was we'd have chucked jeans into the dustbin if they had all them holes in them.'

He winked at Summer who suppressed a grin.

'I'll keep her with me, Joseph,' she said. 'Don't worry about a thing.'

'Just see that she's careful,' he said, digging his hands into the pockets of his old cardigan. 'I'm not insured for visitors, so if she gets into any trouble it's on her own head.' He smirked and pointed to Frankie's nose stud. 'And stay away from magnets.'

As he turned and headed back towards the house, Frankie pulled a face.

'Well, he's funny, isn't he? Not.'

'Oh, that's just Joseph. He's got a heart of gold,' Summer said.

'Are you sure? He hides it well.'

'If it wasn't for men like Joseph, I'd have no faith in humans at all,' Summer said. 'Think of all the good he's done; all the horses, ponies, and donkeys he's saved from neglect and cruelty. How can you doubt it?'

'I suppose so.' Frankie gazed round the stable yard, her nose wrinkling. 'It's gone downhill since I last visited. It's a bit of a dump really, isn't it?'

Summer followed her gaze, her heart sinking as she viewed Whispering Willows through Frankie's eyes. It wasn't, she supposed, the most welcoming of places. The grey, stone house and outbuildings looked bleak, even in the

July sunshine, and there was no mistaking the peeling paint-work, the missing hinges and sagging doors of some of the looseboxes, and the general air of neglect about the place.

It was supposed to be a sanctuary for equines in need, but to be honest it looked as if it needed rescuing itself.

'We keep everything as clean and dry as we can,' she said, keen to defend Whispering Willows from any criticism. 'We don't use most of the looseboxes, but those we do are in decent condition, and the occupants are cared for exceptionally well. Most of the horses live out, and the paddocks are tiptop.'

It must, she thought, cost a fortune to keep the fencing intact, fix gates, and make running repairs. Not to mention the cost of feed, vet's bills, the farrier, and insurance.

She glanced over at the house itself. Once, so Joseph told her, it had been a grand family home. Generations of Wilkinsons had lived there, and there'd been servants and carriages and parties.

Now there was just Joseph, a house in need of a lot of loving attention, and a dwindling income that couldn't provide either the house, the stables, or Joseph himself, with everything they needed.

'Has he always lived alone?' Frankie asked, as she followed Summer across the yard to the stable block.

'Not always. His mother died when he was quite young,' Summer told her, unbolting the door of one of the best looseboxes. 'Then his dad died, and his sister left home.'

Frankie frowned. 'What's that noise?'

They entered the loosebox and Summer carefully closed the door behind them.

'Whoa! What's with the trendy coat?' Frankie stared in amazement at the pony who was eyeing her back with some curiosity. He was wearing a rug that covered most of him,

25

complete with a hood with two holes which his ears poked through. 'He looks like Batman.'

'Don't make fun of him. He's had a lot to put up with, haven't you, Barney?'

'Aw, I'm not making fun of him. Just surprised, that's all. What's up with him? And what's with the electric ceiling fan? Bit posh for a stable!'

'He's prone to sweet itch,' Summer said. 'He has a reaction to the saliva from midge bites, and it can be really nasty. So, from March onwards he has to wear this rug, and he's stabled between four p.m. and eight a.m. with the fan going all night to keep midges away. They're rubbish at flying and can't fight the air current. It was Ben's idea. He's so clever.'

Frankie narrowed her eyes. 'Who's Ben?'

Summer tried to sound casual. 'Oh, just one of the local vets. Ready to go out now, Barney?'

'He doesn't look as if he's suffering,' Frankie said.

'That's because Joseph acted before the midges started biting. Prevention's better than cure with sweet itch. In fact, there is no cure, so if you can stop the midges getting to the animal in the first place that's the best you can hope for.'

'So are you going to let him out now?'

'Yes, but first I'm going to put some barrier cream on the areas not covered by the rug. Ben recommended it.'

'Did he?' Frankie smirked, making Summer wish she'd never mentioned him. Funny how she couldn't seem to control her mouth sometimes. She'd found Ben's name slipping into her conversations far too often lately, and always promised herself she wouldn't make that mistake again. And yet...

Frankie watched as Summer worked. 'So does he wear that rug all the time?'

'Yes, I'm afraid so. Between the first of March and the

end of October anyway. It's for his own good, and it's comfortable for him. It's lightweight, don't worry about that. When we bath Barney with his special shampoo the rug goes in the wash, and we put a clean one on him.'

'Poor thing.' Frankie fondled Barney's ears. 'What sort of pony is he?'

'He's an Exmoor. Native ponies seem to be particularly prone to sweet itch for some reason.'

Frankie leaned against the stable wall. 'So, doesn't he see his sister any longer?'

Summer paused, confused. 'Who?'

'Joseph.'

'Oh!' Summer laughed. 'You threw me then. Er, no, I don't think he does. At least, he's never mentioned her.'

Summer put a halter on Barney and led him outside.

'We'll take him to the field up on Harston's Hill. It's open and exposed, so there's plenty of wind blowing and less chance of midges attacking.'

'Don't you think it's strange, though?' Frankie said as they walked, the Exmoor pony plodding patiently by their side. 'About Joseph, I mean. If this sister of his is his only living relative, why do they have no contact with each other?'

Summer shrugged. 'I don't know. All sorts of reasons, I guess. Maybe she lives abroad, like Billie?'

'Or maybe she hates him? Or he hates her?' Frankie laughed. 'Maybe they're like me and Ellis—happier apart.'

'Oh, Ellis!' Summer wrinkled her nose in distaste at the mention of Frankie's brother. 'Have you heard from him?'

'Hardly anything. We hear more from Beau,' she added, referring to the young man who was a distant cousin of her dad's. Ellis was currently sharing a flat with him in Devon, where Beau worked as a dentist. 'That's how we know Ellis is okay, really, because he never bothers to ring

Mum, and when she tries to ring him he's usually out. Or Beau says he is. Funny how his mobile's always switched off.'

'Unless he wants something, I guess?'

Knowing Ellis of old, Summer suspected that the only time he would bother with his family was if he needed a handout. He'd been thoroughly spoiled by Elizabeth, given his own credit card from an early age and free rein to buy whatever he wanted. He was immature and selfish, and Summer thought it sounded as if he hadn't changed much, not bothering with his own mother.

'To be fair,' Frankie said, 'he hasn't pestered her for anything, which you've got to admit is unusual for Ellis.'

'Unless your mum just hasn't told you.'

'No, she would have done. She's always complaining how she hasn't heard from him, and he could be lying dead in a ditch somewhere for all she knew.'

'But Beau would let her know if that were the case,' Summer said.

'I suppose so. I don't know how Beau puts up with him,' Frankie said with a sigh. 'It was bad enough living in Mill Cottage with him, which is a big house. Beau's got a flat! Can you imagine living in such a small space with Ellis all year round?'

Beau, Summer thought, must be an angel. Still, at least Ellis was actually working now, which was something she thought he'd never do. He was a talented pencil artist and seemed to be making a decent living selling his drawings and associated merchandise.

She knew he had a website, and a shop on Facebook, and supposed she ought to check it out now and then, but worried that if she did Ellis would somehow find out and assume she was interested in him. He'd had a huge crush on her a couple of years ago and had been convinced she'd feel the same way about him, given enough time.

There wasn't enough time in eternity for that to happen, Summer thought. He just wasn't her type.

An image of a gorgeous vet with light brown hair and blue eyes flashed through her mind, and she pushed it away, blushing, as if Frankie could read her thoughts.

'He'll be at the wedding, won't he?' Frankie said, her tone of voice making it obvious that she was as unhappy about that as Summer was.

'If he turns up,' Summer said. 'There are no guarantees with Ellis, are there?'

'Fingers crossed then. Do you think Joseph and his sister feel the same way about each other as me and Ellis do?'

Summer hadn't given it much thought. She'd just assumed, on the rare occasions it crossed her mind, that Joseph's sister lived too far away for them to meet up. Or that she was busy, or they'd simply grown apart. Maybe she'd been rude not asking Joseph more about his life. Then again, it might be ruder to pry. Tricky.

They turned Barney out into the field on Harston Hill and watched fondly as he cantered off to join his companions.

'I hope they don't pick on him for looking like Batman,' Frankie said.

Summer laughed, then looked up at the sky. 'I think Joseph was right, you know. Look how grey the sky is. Rain's on its way. Come on. You and I are going to go back and muck out the stables.'

'In these trainers!'

'Okay, okay. I'll muck out the stables and you can make me and Joseph a nice cup of tea. But next time you come, you'll have to dress more appropriately. That's assuming you're going to come back, of course. Maybe it's too much for you, now you're a sophisticated young woman with more important things on her mind than rescued horses.'

Frankie gasped. 'Of course I'll come back! What do you think I am?'

Summer put her arm around her. 'You're the same old Frankie, thank goodness. And soon,' she added as the realisation hit her, 'you'll be my stepsister.'

'Oh, wow!' Frankie beamed. 'I never thought of that. I've always wanted a sister.'

'Good, because in just over a week you'll have two.'

'Billie will be my stepsister and my sister-in-law,' Frankie said. 'How confusing is that?'

She was right, Summer realised. Her older sister, Billie, was married to Frankie's older brother, Arlo. It was through them that the two families had met. Now Billie and Arlo were living in Australia, but were coming home for Mum and Rafferty's wedding. Summer couldn't wait to see her sister again.

'Best not to think about it,' she advised Frankie. 'At least, not without a cup of tea to hand. Ooh, and while you're at it, how are you at making bacon sandwiches? If you want to be Joseph's friend for life, that's where you start. Trust me.'

* * *

'I take it everything went well?'

Ben looked up and smiled as Clive entered the consulting room at Stepping Stones.

'Absolutely perfect. Lad's just gone to recovery. Hopefully, he'll behave himself from now on.' He finished typing up the notes on the castration he'd just performed on the Labrador, then leaned back in the chair and yawned.

Clive grinned. 'Coffee?'

'Love one.'

Clive opened the door and called out to Jane, the receptionist. 'Could you bring a couple of coffees in here when you've got a minute, please?'

He shut the door again, and Ben shook his head. He should have known his boss wouldn't make the coffee himself. That would be the day. It wasn't that Clive was a bad boss, or a bad man, come to that. He just didn't think sometimes, and it wouldn't occur to him that Jane already had enough to do.

'It's okay, I'll make it,' he said, getting to his feet.

Clive followed him across the waiting room to the kitchen. Ben assured a harassed-looking Jane that she didn't have to worry, he'd see to the coffees, then closed the kitchen door behind them. He flicked on the kettle and reached for four mugs.

'Four?' Clive frowned.

'Me, you, Jane and Hannah,' Ben pointed out, referring to the veterinary nurse who was currently settling Mr Cobb's Labrador in the recovery room.

'Oh, right.' He sounded surprised, and Ben suppressed a smile. 'So, any progress?'

Ben spooned coffee into the mugs and frowned. 'With what?'

Clive shook his head. '*With what*, he says. With Summer Fletcher. Who else?'

'Oh.' Ben's heart sank as he took milk from the fridge. 'I haven't seen much of her lately,' he said, deciding the embarrassing encounter at The Corner Cottage Bookshop didn't count. 'You've done the last two callouts to Whispering Willows, remember?'

'What on earth's that got to do with it?' Clive sounded

impatient. 'You're surely not restricted to only seeing her through work. Has it never occurred to you that people have social lives?' He shook his head. 'Silly me. I forgot who I was talking to. Remind me to explain to you one day what a social life is. Maybe then you'll finally get a girlfriend.'

'Well, you can talk!' Ben swung round to face him, embarrassment making him forget that Clive was his boss. 'When was the last time you had a girlfriend? Maybe you should practice what you preach.'

Realising he might have gone too far he mumbled, 'Sorry.'

'No, no. No apology needed. If that's how you see me...'

Ben risked a sideways glance at his boss, relieved to see he didn't seem annoyed. He was leaning against the worktop, arms folded, looking relaxed. A tall, broad, sandy-haired man, with grey eyes and a rugged complexion, Clive had moved to Tuppenny Bridge from Scotland on a temporary basis after qualifying as a vet and had never left. In his mid-fifties, he was still single, and Ben wasn't even sure he'd ever dated anyone. When he looked at Clive, there was a part of him that couldn't help wondering if he was seeing his future.

'I don't suppose we've got any Penguins?'

Ben grinned. 'I think you've eaten them all.' He poured boiling water into the mugs and added milk and sugar as necessary. After stirring them, he carried two of the mugs out to reception for a grateful Jane and Hannah, then returned to the kitchen.

'You're right. No Penguins. No biscuits at all. It's a disgrace.' Clive was sitting at the table, cradling the mug thoughtfully. 'I really thought you liked her, you know.'

Ben thought about Summer, not even surprised at the sudden fluttering in his stomach. He'd become used to the effect she had on him now. He thought about her glorious shoulder-length chestnut hair, her beautiful green eyes, and that sprinkling of freckles on her nose. But there was more to her than looks. She had a kind, compassionate nature, and seemed to care about animals as much as he did. He supposed that was why he liked her so much.

'Are you even listening?'

Startled and a little embarrassed, he blurted, 'Of course I am. She's okay. Nice girl.'

Clive laughed. 'The look on your face just then makes me think she's more than okay. Who do you think you're kidding, eh? Come on, let me have this moment of joy. I've waited years for you to finally meet a woman who makes your heart beat faster.'

'Don't be daft!'

Aware that his face was burning, Ben turned away and tried desperately to think of another subject.

'How's your mother?'

Clive's tone was offhand, as if he wasn't really interested but had taken pity on him.

Ben shrugged and pulled up a chair. 'You know Mum. She's talking about decorating the study and planting roses in the garden. Can you believe that? It's as if she's oblivious to it all. She was actually hinting that we take on another gardener.'

'I'm sure she knows it's impossible really. Maybe daydreaming is her way of protecting herself,' Clive said softly. 'She's had a lot to cope with, after all.'

Ben stared into his mug of coffee. He didn't need reminding of that fact. It was pretty much all he thought about.

'And Jamie? How's he doing?'

'GCSE year coming up. He's hoping to go to France at the end of the exams. It's a canoeing, windsurfing, and sailing holiday on the Med.' He gave a mirthless laugh. 'Only nine hundred quid.'

'Bloody hell! Didn't he just get back from a school trip?'

'That didn't count apparently since it was in Scotland and not abroad.'

'It cost you enough.'

'Yes, another five hundred. I'm trying to think of a way to break it to him that he probably won't be going to France.'

'Perhaps you should just tell him the truth.'

Clive's voice was gentle, but they'd had this conversation enough times for Ben to know he was deadly serious. Clive was of the firm opinion that Jamie should be made aware of the true state of their finances, and of how much Ben had sacrificed to keep things going.

'You don't have to tell me, but you know what Mum's like. "He's got his exams to think about. He doesn't need that sort of worry."'

'And you do?'

Ben shrugged. 'I've got broad shoulders.'

'If you ask me, it might be the making of him.'

Ben laughed. 'Try telling Mum that. Oh, I don't know. Maybe she's got a point. Why would I put that amount of pressure on him this year of all years?' He sipped his coffee, feeling tired suddenly. 'Maybe when he's done his A levels. When he's settled at university...'

'Oxford or Cambridge, I suppose. You don't even know he'll be accepted.'

'They wouldn't dare refuse him. Mum would stage a sit-in.' Anyway, it wouldn't come to that. Jamie went to an excellent school, his work was exceptional, and his tutors gave glowing reports and had high hopes for him. After everything Ben had done to keep Jamie's education running smoothly, the idea that he wouldn't get into a top university was unthinkable. His younger brother had a glowing future ahead of him; his mum was right about that at least.

'So if he does, what then? Jennifer will insist you both keep quiet because his studies mustn't be disrupted? He gets a job and what? You can't tell him then either, because after all, he's got enough to deal with now he's got a career? She's never going to let him grow up, Ben. You're going to have to force the issue at some point or other. Do it now, before you have a nervous breakdown.'

Ben stared into his coffee cup, wishing it was that easy.

He heard Clive sigh and glanced up at him, seeing the sympathy in his boss's eyes.

'I'm not having a go at you, lad,' Clive said kindly. 'I worry about you, that's all. I don't see how you can keep this going much longer. Why don't you just put that bloody pointless house up for sale and move on with your life? Think how much easier it would be if you didn't have to worry about the upkeep of it.'

Ben didn't have to think. He already knew. He'd daydreamed about it enough times over the years, but always came to the same conclusion.

He couldn't do it. It would break his mum's heart. Monk's Folly had been his dad's pride and joy, and it had meant the world to him, and to Leon. Now they were both gone it was all she had left of them. She clung to that house like a security blanket. How could he take it away from her?

'She'd be devastated,' he said simply. 'It's not an option.'

Clive shook his head and drained his cup. 'Right, I'd best get off to Blake's Farm. One of Jim's calves isn't looking too well.' A quick look through the window at the heavy rain made him wrinkle his nose. 'Lovely day for it—if you're a duck.'

He got to his feet and placed his hand on Ben's shoulder,

giving it a gentle squeeze. 'Give it some thought, eh? All of it. About Monk's Folly, about making your mum face up to the state of everything—and about asking Summer Fletcher out. She's a good-looking girl. Won't be single for long, and if you don't make a move on her there are plenty who will.' He rolled his eyes. 'I'm surprised Ross Lavender hasn't taken her out yet, to be honest.'

Ben's stomach contracted. 'She's not his type! But yes, fine, I'll think about it. Now, get off to the farm because I've got my next appointment in ten minutes.'

Chapter Four

'Are you absolutely sure you want to do this, love?'

Joseph sounded highly doubtful as he frowned down at Summer, who was sitting at the table with a pile of paperwork in front of her. 'It's a really boring job, and I can't pay you any extra for doing it.'

'Joseph, it's just a bit of filing, that's all.' Summer gave him a reassuring smile. 'The accountant will be doing all the hard work. All I have to do is put things in order for him. It's hardly rocket science.' She reached out and stroked Viva, Joseph's little Bichon Frisé, who was nestled in his arms. 'Stop worrying.'

'Huh! Easy to say when I know what a mess it is. My fault. I should have kept on top of things—filed it all away properly instead of shoving everything into that drawer. I say so every year, but I never change.'

'Well, it's just the job for me since it's raining outside. I'll be nice and dry in here, so why would I complain?' She glanced at the kitchen clock. 'You're going to be late if you don't hurry up. You'd better get off.'

'You're right.' Joseph put Viva on the floor and fondled her ears. 'You be a good girl for Summer, okay?' He straightened and gave Summer a rueful smile. 'Those nurses get very shirty if you're late for an appointment. Thanks, love. I appreciate it. I'll see you when I get back.'

'You will. Good luck.'

Joseph hadn't told her why he had an appointment at the hospital, and Summer hadn't asked. It was none of her business, after all, and if he wanted her to know he'd tell her. He'd reassured her that it was nothing serious, and clearly didn't want to say anything else, but she couldn't help worrying, given how tired and run-down he'd seemed lately. The least she could do was help him with his admin. Anything to take some of the pressure off him.

She waited until he'd left the house before she turned back to the paperwork. There were bills and receipts everywhere, and she had a long afternoon ahead of her by the look of it. She heard Joseph's battered old van drive off and crossed her fingers that whatever the reason for his hospital trip, it really was nothing serious.

'Are you going to help me?' she asked Viva, who tilted her head to the side and watched her for a moment, before trotting into the living room.

'Guess not.' Summer picked up the first bill. 'Right, let's get on with this.'

After half an hour or so she made herself a cup of tea, wishing Frankie had stayed on after all. She'd been at Whispering Willows that morning but had decided to leave when she found out Summer would be doing paperwork during the afternoon.

'I'll get my PlayStation set up since it's raining,' she'd told Summer. 'I'm a bit addicted to the *Spider-Man* games at the moment, and Dad and Sally are working so I might as well.'

'Sure, go for it. I'll see you when I get home,' Summer had said. Now, she thought Frankie would have come in useful, supplying her with drinks as she worked.

She sipped her tea then got back to sorting out the receipts and bills. They were in no sort of order at all. Joseph really had just thrown them into a drawer as they arrived, and Summer thought they'd have to get a system in place to make it easier in future.

It was an eye-opener, seeing how much money Joseph spent each month on the sanctuary. Keeping horses certainly didn't come cheap, and it was no wonder the house itself was so neglected. Joseph never seemed to go anywhere or do anything, and she suspected his entire life revolved around caring for his animals.

It was, she thought, a good job he had Ben's boss, Clive, as a friend. If not for him, Joseph probably wouldn't leave Whispering Willows at all, other than to keep his hospital appointments. At least Clive invited him round to his spacious flat above the surgery at Stepping Stones for meals, and they'd spent Christmas Day together.

She totted up how much money had gone on hay alone during the financial year and shook her head. How was Joseph paying for this? He'd retired a few years ago, so no longer had any income from employment, although she assumed he'd get a decent pension or he wouldn't have retired early. Even so, she suspected that wasn't enough to sustain a house and all those horses. He must still have some of his inheritance. His parents must have been loaded.

Finally, having sorted bills from receipts, arranged in chronological order, Summer collected them up and headed into the sitting room to put them away in the dresser drawer.

'What are you up to, mischief?' she asked, noting Viva was over in a corner, nose down as if she was playing with something on the floor. Summer pulled a face, hoping it wasn't a mouse.

She realised Frankie had left her handbag behind, and this was what Viva was playing with. It was tipped on its side, most of the contents spilled on the floor. She hoped Viva hadn't chewed anything because Frankie wouldn't be impressed if she had.

Her heart almost stopped as she reached the pretty Bichon Frisé and picked her up. On the floor was a chewed chocolate wrapper, and there was nothing in it but a few crumbs of chocolate.

Feeling sick with fear, Summer remembered the evening before when Frankie had been munching on chocolate while they watched television at home. She'd wrapped up what remained of it and put it in her bag before announcing she was going to bed. There'd definitely been chocolate in there, but Viva had clearly polished the lot off.

Summer scooped her up with shaking hands, studying her intently. The little dog seemed okay, but she knew that it was only a matter of time before she started to feel the ill effects.

'Oh, Viva, what have you done?' she gasped, her voice coming out in a half sob as she looked around her, panic-stricken. If she didn't get her medical help immediately, Joseph's sweet little dog could die.

* * *

Ben ruffled the Border collie's ears and told him what a brave lad he'd been.

'All done then, Ben?'

'All done. Well, until his booster next year, obviously. He's in good shape.'

Ted Brooks lifted the dog off the table and placed him carefully on the floor. 'He should be. Our Jack and Lucy are devoted to him. They'd be here now if they weren't at the dentist's. Holding his paw, so to speak.'

He grinned, and Ben nodded, understanding the children's devotion to the family dog. He'd been just the same with the Callaghans' cocker spaniels, Bean and Cocoa. They were long gone, and he still missed having a dog around the place.

He handed Ted the dog's vaccination card. 'There you go. Hopefully, I won't see you in here again for another year.'

'Ta very much, Ben. Much appreciated.'

Ted opened the door of the consulting room and ushered the dog out. Before the door swung shut again, Ben heard an anguished voice in the waiting room, and his heart thudded as he thought he glimpsed someone familiar.

He was just about to go into the reception to find out what was going on when the door flew open again and Summer stood there, her hair damp, her face flushed, her eyes full of panic. Jane was just behind her.

'I'm sorry, Ben. She's a bit—'

'It's okay, Jane, I'll deal with this.' Ignoring his churning stomach, he asked, 'What's wrong, Summer?'

There was obviously a problem with Viva, who was in Summer's arms. He hurriedly took the little dog from her and laid her on the table.

'Okay, calm down and tell me what's wrong.'

Jane closed the door on them, and Summer gasped, 'She's eaten chocolate!'

'Chocolate?' Ben reached for his stethoscope.

'It's all Frankie's fault,' Summer continued, her voice choked with tears. 'Fancy leaving her bag at Whispering Willows! What's she playing at?' She

41

rubbed her eyes impatiently. 'No, it's not her fault, not really. It's mine. I should have kept an eye on Viva, but I was so busy with the paperwork for Joseph, and he was out so Viva was left on her own. The bag was on the floor and it must have been open, and of course Viva would eat chocolate if she came across it. Why wouldn't she?'

Ben's heart sank. 'How much chocolate? What sort of chocolate?'

'I can't remember. My mind's gone blank.' The tears were rolling down Summer's face now. Ben hated seeing her so distressed. He'd dealt with upset owners before, many times, but seeing Summer cry was affecting him more than he'd have thought possible.

'Look, it's okay. Don't worry, we'll sort this. Do you know how long ago she ate it?'

'Some time during the last hour. This is my fault! I should have kept her in the kitchen with me, but I got distracted and—'

'Has she been sick, or had diarrhoea?'

Summer shook her head, and Ben listened intently to Viva's heartbeat.

'Well, that seems normal,' he said. He knew, though, that ruled nothing out. If Viva had only recently eaten the chocolate she might not be showing symptoms yet.

'I need you to think about how much chocolate she ate. Can you remember what size bar it was? How much of the bar was left? It's really important, Summer.'

Summer wiped the tears from her face and straightened, making a huge effort to pull herself together. 'It—it was a hundred grams! Yes, definitely a hundred grams.'

Ben raised an eyebrow. 'She's eaten a hundred grams of milk chocolate?'

Viva must weigh less than 5kg. This was a serious emergency.

'No, no. Frankie had already eaten a good half of it before bed,' Summer said. She gazed at Ben, a plea in her eyes. 'Will that make a difference? And it was white chocolate, not milk. Frankie loves the stuff for some reason.'

'White chocolate?' Ben slumped in relief. 'You're sure?'

'Of course I'm sure. It was definitely white chocolate. I always tease her for eating it because it's baby chocolate, isn't it? Why? What does that mean? Is it good or bad?'

Ben could have kissed her, but instead he kissed Viva's nose.

'Good,' he said. 'Very good. I think she'll be fine.'

Summer put her arms around the Bichon Frisé and stared at Ben through tear-filled eyes. 'Are you sure?'

'Yes. I mean, don't get me wrong, white chocolate's not good for dogs. It's full of fat and sugar, and you should keep an eye on her. She may well get a tummy upset. But it's theobromine that's toxic to dogs, and the amount of that in fifty grams of white chocolate is so small the risk of serious illness is negligible.'

'Really? Oh my God!' Summer buried her face in Viva's fur and stifled a sob. Ben considered putting his arms around her but, realising that would be wildly inappropriate, he awkwardly clutched his stethoscope instead.

After a moment or two, Summer raised her face to his and said, 'I'm so sorry to waste your time.'

'You didn't waste my time.' What was wrong with his voice? He cleared his throat, embarrassed. 'It's fine. I'm just glad it was a false alarm.'

'I don't know what I'd have done if anything had happened to her. It would have broken Joseph's heart.'

'You'd better make sure Frankie keeps her bag with her at

all times in the future,' he said, smiling.

Summer straightened, but she continued to stroke Viva, who looked remarkably unfazed by the whole thing.

'I'll never make fun of her for eating baby chocolate again.'

Ben laughed. 'Well, I can't blame you for that. It's awful stuff. I don't know how anyone over two years old can stand it. Give me dark chocolate every time.'

Summer wrinkled her nose. 'That's just as bad. Way too bitter for me.'

'No way! The more cocoa solids the better,' he said. 'Though I'm really glad Frankie doesn't share my taste in chocolate, or we wouldn't be standing here so relaxed, I'll tell you that much for nothing.'

Relaxed? His heart was pounding as if he'd been the one who'd overdosed on some toxic chemical. He just hoped he was fooling Summer into thinking he was feeling perfectly normal.

'Anyway,' he said briskly, 'Viva. She should be fine but ask Joseph to monitor her over the next twenty-four hours. If she has any vomiting or diarrhoea, or shows any other symptoms, such as rapid breathing or tremors, or if she appears unsteady or restless, call me straight away. Day or night, it doesn't matter.' He hesitated. 'You have my number already, don't you?'

'Joseph does,' she said. 'But maybe you should give me it anyway. I mean, you never know, do you? And Joseph might be out, like he is now, so...'

'Well, exactly,' he said, handing her his business card. 'All my contact details are on there. Maybe—maybe I should take your number, too. Er, just in case. You know.'

They eyed each other uncertainly, and Ben wondered if she was as nervous as he was.

'Oh, okay,' she said, after what seemed to him like an interminable pause. 'I'll send you a text now, so you've got it.'

Quickly she tapped out a message and sent it to him.

From Unknown:

My number. Thank you, Ben. Summer x

Ben wondered if the kiss had been deliberate, or if she'd done it automatically without thinking. Best not to dwell on it or he'd drive himself mad.

'Thanks,' he said, putting his phone back in his pocket.

Looking a little embarrassed as she scooped the dog into her arms, she said, 'No, thank *you*, Ben. I'm so grateful, and I'm sorry I pushed in ahead of your other patients.'

'No problem. Just make sure Frankie keeps her chocolate under lock and key or this little one will be in and out of here nonstop.'

'We'll have to call her Hokey Cokey Viva.' Summer giggled. 'Sorry, I think hysteria's setting in. I was so worried.'

Ben smiled. 'I know,' he said softly. 'I know.' Then he blinked, realising Jane was addressing him. She was standing in the doorway, a knowing look on her face.

'What is it?'

'Mrs Kensington's here with her cat. Her appointment was ten minutes ago, and you know how anxious she gets.'

'My fault,' Summer said immediately. 'I'd better be going. I've taken up enough of your time.'

'It was no trouble, honestly.'

He meant it. He wished she could stay longer. As that fact sank in, he reached over and patted Viva. 'Behave yourself, little one. No more snaffling chocolate, okay? Jane, there's no charge for this one.'

Summer opened her mouth to protest but Ben insisted.

'I didn't really do anything. Please, have this one on me.'

'That's so kind of you. Thank you. Again.'

Summer smiled at him, real warmth in her eyes, and he smiled back before realising that Jane was watching him, one eyebrow arched so high it was practically scraping her hairline.

'How are you getting home? It's pouring with rain out there...'

'I'll get a taxi,' Summer said. 'I got one here. I should have made him wait but I didn't know how long I'd be.'

'You might be waiting ages,' he said. 'Maybe I—'

'Mrs Kensington, Ben,' Jane reminded him smoothly. She smiled at Summer. 'Follow me and I'll ring you a taxi from reception. We mustn't hold Mr Callaghan up any longer, must we?'

Summer gave her a rueful look and followed her into reception. Ben stared at the closed door, wondering how he'd found the courage to ask for her number, and if there was any chance at all he'd ever use it. Summer had been in his thoughts more and more lately, and he'd realised the effect she was having on his senses but had tried hard not to think about it.

Well, he couldn't deny it to himself any longer, could he? Even so, there was no point in getting his hopes up, even though he was almost certain now that she was interested in him, too.

The brightness in her eyes, that flush on her cheeks, the way she'd offered him her number and had texted him to make sure he had it... If Viva hadn't eaten that chocolate he would never have had the nerve to give Summer his business card.

As Mrs Kensington hurried in, clutching the cat carrier which contained her precious Abyssinian, Ruby, he could only shake his head at the staggering unpredictability of life and love.

Chapter Five

Ben heard the bedroom door slam and his jaw tightened. He was tempted to storm upstairs after his brother and give Jamie a piece of his mind. He was, after all, behaving like a spoilt brat. And of course, his mother had sided with Jamie. Well, sort of. She'd asked Ben to be considerate of his feelings. As if he was ever anything else!

Shaking with anger, Ben poured himself a glass of orange juice and carried it into the living room. Mum had disappeared into the snug, as she often did when real life threatened to intrude. No doubt she'd be immersed in another cosy, feel-good drama on television. Anything that kept out what she termed 'nastiness'. It was a good job she'd stopped watching the news years ago. She'd have had a meltdown.

He sank onto the sofa and sipped some juice, thinking. Had he been too harsh on Jamie? His brother had, after all, been kept in the dark about the true state of their finances, even though Clive had urged Ben to tell him the truth many times.

How much, he wondered, had Jamie figured out for

himself? They lived in a reasonably large house with two acres of land and spectacular views in a desirable area of the country. Jamie had attended an expensive public school since he was eight, so it was reasonable to assume that he believed they were privileged in their way.

But his fellow pupils came from far wealthier families than his, and none of them had a clue what life was like for other people. Jamie had never understood why he couldn't have the things his school friends took for granted.

Which was why, Ben thought wretchedly, it had all kicked off this morning when Jamie had seen a post on Instagram from one of those so-called friends, posting about a sleepover he'd had with more of their classmates, playing on their expensive games consoles and boasting about owning the latest game that had only been released the day before.

It was natural that Jamie felt left out, but he'd gone on the attack, blaming Ben for it all. He couldn't understand why Ben wouldn't get him the same console, or why he couldn't have the latest games. The fact that this boy's family was clearly much wealthier than his own would no doubt rankle, but Jamie would just have to get used to it.

'It's not like I say no for the fun of it. I just haven't got the money to spare, Jamie.'

'But you've got the money to pay my school fees! Funny that.'

'Nothing bloody funny about it, believe me.'

'Perhaps we could find the money, Ben?' his mother had suggested hopefully. 'Maybe for Christmas...'

'Christmas! I'm back at school in September, and everyone will be talking about their scores on the latest *Call of Duty*. Strike that, they'll have moved on by then. There'll be some other game I'm missing out on.'

'What, like *Call of Duty* 346?' Ben couldn't help the sarcasm slipping into his tone of voice, but how many of those games were there? Was that really all Jamie had to worry about? Lucky him.

'Oh forget it! It's a waste of time talking to you. You're the most boring, middle-aged twenty-nine-year-old ever. I'd pity you if you weren't so bloody annoying.'

Jamie had stormed off then, and his mother had given him a sorrowful look. 'I'm sorry, Ben. Just give him time to cool off. I know he'll come round and will apologise.'

Pinching the bridge of his nose as yet another headache threatened, Ben reminded himself that he needed to make allowances for Jamie. His brother had enough pressure on him this year.

His concern must have showed on his face as his mother frowned at him.

'Don't get so worked up, Ben,' she'd said. 'You'll give yourself an ulcer.'

Was there any wonder? Resentment bubbled up inside him as he thought wretchedly that if she'd only let Jamie go to the local secondary school they wouldn't have all this worry. There'd be money to buy his brother the bloody games console if he wasn't forking out thousands of pounds every year to send him to St Egbert's.

'We need to sit him down and talk to him about money,' he'd said, inwardly flinching as he saw the look of horror on her face. 'He has a right to know, Mum! It's not fair to let him believe we're deliberately depriving him of things.' Not that Jamie would blame their mum. As far as he was concerned it was his brother being mean.

Didn't she realise how hard she was making it for Ben? Or did she just not care? He'd wondered that before, many times, and couldn't shake the fear that that was the case.

After all, he was still here, alive and well, whereas Leon and his dad were long gone.

Remembering that she was still mired in grief, guilt made him back down.

'Sorry.' He rubbed his forehead. 'I'll see what I can do. Maybe in a month or two...'

She'd flapped her hands ineffectually and sighed. 'I just think he's got enough to worry about with his GCSEs coming up. Anyway...'

He wasn't in the least bit surprised by her attitude. She hated arguments and drama—except the TV kind. He wished she'd give him some support. He was tired of playing father to his spoilt younger brother.

He took out his phone and googled the price of a decent games console, his eyes widening as the results appeared on screen. Bloody hell! He couldn't even afford the game, never mind the console to play it on.

Almost without thinking, he opened his contacts list and scrolled down, pausing as he reached Summer's name. It had been three days since she'd brought Viva to the surgery, and he hadn't called her. Then again, she hadn't called him. Oh, why was he even thinking about it? He wasn't in any position to ask her out even if she'd wanted him to, and he wasn't even sure about that any longer. Maybe he'd misread the situation. Maybe she'd just been grateful.

He put his phone down on the desk and stared into his glass of orange juice as he considered his options. He knew Clive was right and it was time he started to treat Jamie as more of a grown-up. Whatever his mum said, he was pretty sure they weren't doing his brother any favours by wrapping him up in cotton wool and keeping the harsh realities from his life. He didn't want Jamie to grow up like her, that was for sure.

He didn't need to tell Jamie everything, but perhaps he should show him another side of life. How other people lived. Let him see the harsh realities and problems that some of their friends and neighbours faced. It would get him out of his bedroom if nothing else.

Maybe he should take Jamie with him on his next callout for a start. He just hoped that wouldn't be to Miss Lavender and her pampered Yorkshire terriers. Goodness knows what impression Jamie would get of 'real life' if his first work experience was at Lavender House.

* * *

As luck would have it, the first callout the very next day was to Whispering Willows, and Ben asked Clive if it was okay for Jamie to attend the visit with him.

Clive grinned. 'Wasn't it my turn to do the first callout today?'

Ben's face burned. 'Well, er, yes, but it just seems like the ideal opportunity for Jamie. I mean, it's not like there's been an accident, or there'll be lots of blood involved. It's a simple check on an old horse with osteoarthritis. A perfect introduction to what we do.'

Clive held up his hands. 'Fine, fine. As long as he doesn't touch anything or get in the way it shouldn't be a problem. Give my regards to Joseph. And to the lovely Summer Fletcher, of course.'

'Who says Summer will be there?'

'I think, since you're volunteering for a callout that should, by rights, have been mine, it's almost certain that she's got a shift today,' Clive said.

Ben couldn't deny it, since he'd heard Summer in the background when Joseph rang the surgery, and even as he drove his ancient Land Rover down the drive towards Whispering Willows, the memory of his boss's knowing wink filled him with embarrassment.

'He's a lovely old fella,' he said, determined to take his mind off that particular subject.

'Who? Joseph Wilkinson?' Jamie sounded doubtful. 'If you say so. Looks like he could do with a bath and a decent haircut if you ask me.'

'Never judge a book by its cover,' Ben said. 'Joseph's just got other priorities, and a haircut isn't high on the list. And he's clean, so don't be rude. Anyway, I wasn't talking about Joseph. I was talking about the horse, Shadow. His owner didn't want him any more because he was too stiff to be ridden, due to the osteoarthritis. He's in a lot of discomfort, but he's always so patient and friendly.'

Jamie rolled his eyes and Ben felt his irritation rising again.

'If you feel like that, why did you agree to come with me?' he asked, unable to bear the stony silence any longer.

Jamie shrugged. 'It's better than being stuck in with Mum all day again. Nothing else to do, is there? My games console is so old I can only play Pong on it. All my friends live miles away, and it's not as if we'll be going on holiday, is it? We never do. I've got to find *something* to do to pass the time or I'll go mad with boredom.'

'Hmm. Just be polite and respectful, okay?'

'*O-kay!* What do you think I'm going to do?'

Ben dreaded to think. Jamie could be a sullen little so-and-so when he chose. He pulled into the stable yard and turned off the engine.

'Right, let's see what we have here,' he said, collecting his bag and beckoning to Jamie to follow him.

Joseph was nowhere to be seen, but Summer appeared at the door of the house and called to him.

Ben stopped and his heart gave that little flutter it always did when he saw her. As usual, he did his best to ignore it and waved to her.

'Summer, hi. This is my brother, Jamie. I hope you don't mind me bringing him, but he's keen to do something to pass the time. You know what bored teenagers are like. He won't get in the way, I promise.'

'Charming,' Jamie muttered.

'Oh, it's fine,' Summer said. 'I've got a bored teenager with me too as it happens. My stepsister, Frankie. Well, she's almost my stepsister. Not long now.'

If he hadn't known better, he'd have sworn she sounded nervous, but there was no reason for Summer to be nervous around him. He must have got it wrong.

'The wedding. Of course.' Ben clutched his bag to him and smiled at her.

Summer smiled back. 'That's right. You *are* coming?'

'Naturally. It's very kind of your mum and Rafferty to invite me. To invite all of us. We'll all be there, won't we, Jamie?'

He glanced at his brother, only to blush as he saw Jamie staring at him disbelievingly.

'Anyway,' he said, after clearing his throat, 'what's the problem with Shadow? Is it the arthritis again, or is there something else?'

'It's the arthritis,' Summer said, her smile fading. 'We're really worried about him, Ben. He's not himself at all.'

'Is he in or out?' Ben asked.

'We've got him in the nearest paddock behind the stables. It's the flattest grazing we have. Joseph and Frankie are with him now. Joseph's ever so upset. We both are. We love Shadow so much. Please help him.'

Ben nodded. 'Let's see what we can do, eh?'

They headed out of the yard towards the paddock, and Ben glanced back at Jamie to check he was following. He was, and Ben realised with some discomfort that he was watching them with a most peculiar look on his face.

Shadow was an old horse in his late twenties. Once a dark dapple grey, his coat had long since turned white, but he was still a beautiful horse, and cherished by Joseph and Summer.

Unfortunately, Shadow's osteoarthritis couldn't be cured. It was becoming increasingly difficult to ease his stiffness and pain, and Ben was deeply worried that Joseph had felt the need to call him out yet again.

'Morning, Ben. Sorry to drag you over,' Joseph said. His brow was creased with worry and Ben's heart went out to him.

'No problem at all,' he assured him, eyeing Shadow carefully.

'He's looking really sad,' said a young girl with blue hair and a nose stud, who Ben supposed must be Frankie. 'Isn't there anything you can do to ease the pain?'

'I take it he's still lame on the trot,' Ben said. 'Has that got any worse?'

Joseph shrugged. 'Fact is, Ben, he doesn't trot any more. Just walks around, proper slow. And—well, he's a bit lame even then.'

'That's not good, is it?' Summer asked.

'No,' Ben said. 'It isn't. Could you walk him out for me, do you think?'

Summer slipped a halter over Shadow's head and began to walk him slowly around the paddock.

'He seems fine to me,' Jamie said.

'Well, he's not fine,' Frankie told him. 'Look at him closely. Even I can see he's lame. We wouldn't have called the vet out if there was nothing wrong with him, would we?'

Jamie hesitated and Ben held his breath, wondering if there'd be a sarcastic comeback. To his relief, his brother merely shrugged.

'No, I suppose not. And you're right, I can see it now.'

Ben held up his hand and called to Summer to bring him back.

'What do you think, Ben?' Joseph asked anxiously. 'Time for another injection?'

'The problem with that,' Ben said, 'is that there are so many sites he'd need injecting. I've seen the X-rays and, believe me...' He broke off, seeing the sadness in Joseph's eyes.

'He's struggling to get up and down,' Joseph said. 'His rear legs shake. I didn't want to admit it, but it's true. I've seen it for myself.'

'There must be something you can do,' Frankie said hopefully. 'Surely you can give him painkillers?'

'More bute?' Joseph suggested.

'What's bute?' Jamie asked.

'It's short for Phenylbutazone. It's an analgesic and anti-inflammatory.'

As Summer and Shadow returned to the gate, Ben reached out and stroked Shadow's muzzle while Summer removed the halter.

'Thing is,' he said, 'he's already on a fairly high dosage as it is. If we're talking about increasing it just to help him get up and down, well.' He shook his head. 'I know you don't want to think about it, Joseph, but the fact is, if he does go down and can't get back up again, well, you know the outcome to that.'

Summer's head jerked up. 'Increase his medication, then! That should help him, shouldn't it?' She looked appealingly at Joseph. 'Won't it?'

'I'd like to say so.' Joseph stroked Shadow's neck sadly. 'I've seen this before though, Summer. One of my father's horses went down and couldn't get back up. Father shot him and I was devastated. I wanted to shoot my father for doing it. But he had no choice because the horse had been suffering for a while and I just didn't want to admit it. Anyway, it was a sad ending for a good horse. I wouldn't want Shadow to suffer in that way.'

'If it hurt him that much, he wouldn't try to lie down,' Jamie said. 'You just said he's still managing it, even if his legs are shaky, so he can't be that bad.'

'It doesn't work like that,' Ben said. 'Horses love to roll, and if he can't do that, where's his quality of life? Apart from anything else, he needs to lie down at some point, even if it's just for thirty minutes, to get a good quality sleep, so he's going to keep trying. If there comes a point when he can't do that...'

'Aye, you're right I suppose.' Joseph wiped his eyes. 'I've seen him standing in the paddock, shifting his weight from one foot to the other. It's not right. I know it.'

'Just give him a bit longer,' Summer pleaded. 'If you increase his meds, just for a while, just to see how he does...' She turned to Ben, her green eyes holding an appeal that he found hard to resist. Even so, he had to put Shadow first.

Joseph shrugged. 'Were his last blood tests still all right? No nasty side effects from the bute?'

'They were okay, and I suppose with Shadow's age and

condition...' Ben ran a hand through his hair, looking doubtful. 'It's your call, Joseph,' he said. 'At least for now.'

'Increase them,' Joseph said slowly. 'But if it doesn't help, I'll not try anything else. I can't put him through any more. If it was closer to winter I'd say put him to sleep now. It'll only get worse as the weather gets colder.'

'Oh, Shadow.' Summer kissed the horse's muzzle, tears in her eyes. 'You poor darling horse.'

Ben swallowed as the urge to put his arm around Summer and comfort her overwhelmed him. Whatever he'd said to Clive, he knew she was more than okay. He couldn't stop thinking about her, and he'd never felt this way about any girl before. Not even close.

Half an hour later, driving back to Stepping Stones, Ben worried about the whole Shadow situation.

'What's up with you?' Jamie asked. 'You're very quiet.'

Ben blinked. 'I was thinking about the horse. I really don't think today's decision was right. It's all right Joseph saying he'll hang on for winter, but Shadow's suffering now. I'm going to have a word with Jonah, see if he's noticed anything when he's done Shadow's feet.'

'What would he know? He's not a vet.'

'No, but he's a registered farrier who's trained for years and knows about horse anatomy. He goes out to trim Shadow's hooves. He'll know if he's having difficulty lifting his feet, how he's standing, if his pain seems to be getting worse. It might be that he can't even manage to have his hooves trimmed before long. Summer mentioned he'd visited last week so I'll speak to him. I might have to have another chat with Joseph.'

He glanced at Jamie and frowned. 'What?' His brother was grinning at him, which baffled him. 'You find all this amusing?'

'No. God, no! What do you think I am? It's horrible, all of it. I'm just smiling because of the way your voice goes all funny when you say her name.'

Ben swallowed. 'Whose name?'

'*Summer.*' Jamie smirked. '*Of course we'll be at the wedding, Summer. We're flattered and honoured to have been invited, Summer. We'll kiss the ground you walk on, Summer.*'

'I have no idea what you're talking about,' Ben said, his hands tightening on the steering wheel.

'Not much. I had no idea you had a crush on Summer Fletcher. Nice one, mate.'

'You and your imagination!'

'It's not my imagination. She fancies you, too, you know. It was obvious. She made those big puppy dog eyes at you.'

Ben's heart skipped but he told himself Jamie was just trying to provoke a reaction.

'Very funny.'

'I'm serious! Mum's going to be thrilled. You know she's counting down the days until she gets grandchildren. I think we'd both given up on you ever getting a girlfriend. Maybe you're more normal than you seem, after all.'

'Thanks very much,' Ben grinned. 'Anyway, what about you and Frankie? I saw you two deep in conversation as we walked back to the yard. What was that about?'

Jamie shrugged. 'Turns out she's a gamer. Her brother got her into it apparently. She's got all the equipment at home, including a VR headset.'

'A what?'

'Oh, Ben, you really should be wearing a cardigan and slippers and sitting in a rocking chair,' Jamie said with a sigh. 'Are you sure you're twenty-nine? Really? I reckon Mum made a mistake and you're at least forty.'

'Don't be cheeky!' Ben started to laugh, but then remembered that Leon would have been thirty-six now and the laughter died immediately.

'Anyway,' Jamie said, 'she's brought her PlayStation with her and some games, so she's said I can go round to The White Hart Inn any time I like, and we can do battle. It's not the same as a gaming PC but it will do. It's better than watching the television with Mum anyway. If I have to watch *All Creatures Great and Small* one more time I'll scream.'

'Never,' Ben whispered deliberately slowly, 'disrespect *All Creatures Great and Small*. James Herriot was a god.'

Jamie sighed. 'All right, all right, I've heard it all before. One day,' he said, 'I'll get you to play a game of *Call of Duty* and you'll never look back.'

That, Ben thought, would never happen. It was as unlikely as Summer Fletcher declaring her undying love for him. Although, come to think of it, he reckoned the Lavender Ladies would give better odds on Ben becoming the world champion *Call of Duty* player than of him and Summer ever ending up together.

If it came to it, he knew which outcome he'd put his money on.

Chapter Six

The flat above The White Hart Inn was packed—or at least, it felt that way to Summer. She and Clemmie were sitting at the kitchen table, watching Mum and Bluebell with some amusement.

Bluebell, the owner of Cutting It Fine, the local hair salon, was trying different hairstyles on the bride-to-be, who was currently issuing intermittent squeals as Rafferty bobbed between the kitchen, the living room, Frankie's bedroom, and back to the kitchen again.

'You're not supposed to see the bride before the wedding day!'

Rafferty looked bewildered. 'Are you joking? We've got three weeks yet. Where am I supposed to go?'

'He's not supposed to see you *in your wedding dress*, Mum,' Summer reminded her. 'That's all. Poor bloke can see you now. It's only your hair, for goodness' sake!'

'But it's my headdress, too.' Mum looked distinctly worried. 'What if we're jinxed, now he's seen that?'

Rafferty held up his hands. 'I've forgotten what it looks like already,' he assured her.

Mum glanced down at the tiara she'd hurriedly shoved on her lap out of his sight. 'Really?' she asked, with evident dismay. 'Is it that forgettable?'

'I can't win.' Rafferty winked at Summer and Clemmie. 'I'm getting out of here, but can you do me a favour? Can you girls keep checking on Frankie and Jamie?' He jerked his thumb in the direction of the hallway. 'They're in her room playing on the PlayStation, and I know they're good kids, and I should be more trusting, but I also know what fifteen-year-old boys are like, so...'

'Oh, do you? And what were *you* like?' Bluebell asked, a wide smile on her face. 'They say the quiet ones are the worst. Are you sure about marrying him, Sal?'

Mum laughed. 'Absolutely one hundred per cent positive. But there's no need to worry about Frankie, love. She's a good girl.'

'Hmm. Hormones,' was Rafferty's telling response. 'I hardly recognise her these days, she's so grown up. I feel as if I've missed a big chunk of her life. Somehow, she's gone from little girl to young woman while I wasn't looking.'

'She's still Frankie,' Summer said, giving him a reassuring smile. 'Trust me. Have you noticed she's ditched the white trainers for more sensible footwear? She's been a great help at Whispering Willows. She's won Joseph over, so that says a lot.'

'We'll keep checking, Mr Kingston,' Clemmie promised.

'Thanks, Clemmie. But please call me Rafferty. I've told you dozens of times. Right, I'm going over to see Zach about the stag night. I'll see you all later. Have fun.'

Once he was gone, Mum whipped the headdress back

out and Bluebell fixed it to her head. 'There, hairstyle number four. What do you think of that?'

Sally peered at herself in the mirror. 'Oh, I don't know. It's a bit formal. What do you think, girls?'

'You look like Princess Anne,' Summer said bluntly. 'It's not you.'

'I see you with a softer, more natural look,' Clemmie said dreamily. 'Maybe you should have some tendrils at either side of your face? Loosen that bun a bit.'

'You should have been a hairdresser,' Mum said, impressed. 'Your hair's lovely, Clemmie. It always looks immaculate, no matter how you style it. It's so thick, too. Not like mine. I'm cursed with fine hair. Is that your natural colour? 'Cos you never have your roots showing.'

'Mm. Thanks. And yes, natural.' Clemmie had gone quite pink, and Summer gave her a sympathetic look. The girl needed to learn how to take a compliment. 'Shall we go in the living room? Leave your mum and Bluebell to it?'

'Sure, why not? I'll just check on Frankie and Jamie first.' Summer winked, finding it amusing that Rafferty was so worried about leaving his daughter and her friend alone.

She popped her head around the bedroom door and, as expected, found the two of them sitting on the bed, controllers in hand, a look of concentration on their faces as they gave their full attention to the television screen and the antics of Spider-Man.

'Checking up on us?' Frankie asked, without looking up.

'Afraid so. We're under orders.'

Jamie tutted. 'Should I be offended?'

'If you ask me, it says more about the oldies than it does about us. They must be sex-obsessed,' Frankie said.

'They are,' Summer told her. 'I have to put a pillow over my head some nights.'

'Oh my God, that's absolutely gross!' Frankie wailed.

Jamie pulled a face. 'That's the most disgusting thing I've ever heard. I'm so glad my mum's single.'

'I'll leave you with that happy thought, then.' Summer smirked and left them to it.

She found Clemmie already in the living room, evidently bored with listening to Sally and Bluebell going on about the wedding. Summer couldn't really blame her. She was pretty fed up with it herself but made allowances because it was so lovely to see her mum happy, and besides, it was thanks to the wedding that she'd soon see her sister, Billie, and her brother-in-law, Arlo, again, when they flew in from Australia. And Gran was coming up here from East Yorkshire, too, which would be an interesting experience.

'I liked your gran when I met her at Christmas,' Clemmie said, when Summer told her about the impending visit. 'She says what she thinks, doesn't she?'

'That's one way of putting it.' Summer's gran had strong opinions and had never been afraid to voice them—something Miss Lavender had learned to her cost when they'd come face to face.

They heard shrieks of laughter coming from the kitchen and Summer rolled her eyes. Clemmie hugged a cushion to her and said, 'So go on then, tell me!'

Summer frowned. 'Tell you what?'

'Tell me what?' Clemmie reared back. 'Are you seriously saying Ben hasn't rung you? Didn't he take your number?'

'Oh, that.' Summer shrugged. 'I wasn't expecting him to ring. It was just about Viva, for emergencies. That's all.'

'But you saw him at Whispering Willows! You never said anything?' She eyed Summer curiously. 'You *do* like him though?'

Summer hesitated, picturing Ben's kind face with those bright blue eyes and wide smile. 'Yes, I like him, but...'

'But what? I really don't see the problem,' Clemmie said. 'The way he nearly had a nervous breakdown when you were eating that vanilla slice it was obvious to me and Dolly that he fancies you. What are you waiting for?'

'Don't be daft! Anyway...' She shrugged. 'Maybe Dolly's got the right idea. Maybe men are better as friends. I mean, how can you know if they're a Rafferty or a Jason?'

'A Jason?'

'My dad.' Summer sighed. 'Don't get me wrong, I love him so much, and he's a great dad. But as a husband he was the absolute pits. How do you know what you're going to end up with?'

'It's never this complicated in books,' Clemmie admitted. 'Book boyfriends are adorable, whereas real men are, as you say, untrustworthy.'

Summer turned to face her, suddenly curious. 'Have you ever been let down by a man, Clem?'

Clemmie, she noted, had gone that familiar shade of pink.

'Not really,' she said. 'It was just kid's stuff.'

Summer eyed her curiously, wondering who the 'kid' was who'd let her down. It would explain why her friend had decided to bury herself in fictional romances, rather than take a chance on a real one again.

'You know what you ought to do?' Clemmie said thoughtfully.

'Huh? About what?'

'About Ben, of course! You ought to show your appreciation for him not charging you for treating Viva.'

'He didn't exactly treat her,' Summer said hastily, feeling queasy with nerves at the thought of acting on Clemmie's suggestion. 'He just listened to her heartbeat and asked me a few questions, that's all.'

'Not long ago he was a lifesaving hero.' Clemmie shook her head. 'How quickly they forget.'

'I still appreciate what he did,' Summer protested. 'I just don't know what you expect me to do about it. Take him a bouquet of flowers?'

'You said he loves dark chocolate,' Clemmie said. 'Why not take him a bar of the best quality stuff from the gift shop? Drop it in tomorrow. Surgery's closed on Saturday afternoons isn't it? That way,' she added, 'you'll get to see inside Monk's Folly, and there aren't many who can say that.'

'Really? Why's that?'

Clemmie shrugged. 'Ben's a bit of a loner. And as for Jennifer, his mum, she rarely goes anywhere.'

'I remember everyone being amazed when she turned up at Kat's baby shower,' Summer said. She remembered back to that evening in December, when her mum's best friend, Katherine Pennyfeather, had held a party at her flat above the Pennyfeathers' wool shop. Jennifer had seemed so quiet and withdrawn, even though everyone had welcomed her with open arms.

'Dolly said something about her still being in mourning for Ben's dad and brother. They died when Ben was a teenager.'

'Did they? What, both of them?' Summer said, horrified.

Clemmie nodded. 'Leon—that's Ben's brother—died in a car accident, and then his dad died of cancer a year later. I think he was already poorly when Leon died. They had an awful time of it, so Dolly says it's no wonder Jennifer fell to pieces.'

Summer's eyes filled with tears. 'Poor Ben. I had no idea. Even so, it's a long time for Jennifer to be grieving.'

'That's what Dolly thinks. Apparently, she hardly ever socialises, and Ben just seems to do his job and then go home. Dolly told me he's never been serious about any girl, and he's not one for pubs or clubs.'

'Doesn't he even have friends?' Summer couldn't imagine Ben wouldn't be popular. He was such a lovely man; how could anyone not want to be friends with him?

'Clive,' Clemmie said. 'I think that's pretty much it.'

'Clive? But he's his boss! That's not the same.'

'They get on really well, though.'

'But Clive's Joseph's friend. They're old men. Ben should be hanging around with people his own age. I remember Kat mentioning that he and Ross used to be friends. It's a shame that ended.'

Clemmie hesitated. 'Oh, that was years ago, and they don't have anything to do with each other now. Haven't for years, apparently. If you ask me,' she added, 'that's a good thing. Ross is vain and shallow and can't keep it in his trousers. You don't want Ben being influenced by someone like him, do you?'

'What's it got to do with me?'

'Yeah, yeah. My mistake. Take my advice and get a bar of chocolate for Ben, then take it round to Monk's Folly. I'm sure he'd love to see you. To be fair, I'm sure he'd love to see anyone.'

'Charming. I feel really special now.'

'Sorry. No offence.'

'None taken. Cup of coffee?'

'Ooh, yes please.'

Summer headed back into the kitchen, deep in thought. Maybe it would be a nice gesture to take Ben some chocolate, and at least it was a small enough present not to cause raised eyebrows. She didn't want him to think she had an ulterior motive, after all. But given what he'd treated Viva for, it would be a light-hearted thank you that no one could read anything more into.

Yes, she'd do that tomorrow. Poor Ben. After everything he'd been through it was the least she could do.

Besides, now she'd heard how reclusive the Callaghans seemed to be—apart from Jamie, by the looks of it—she was dying to have a nosy around Monk's Folly and issue a full report to Clemmie.

* * *

Monk's Folly was a large, solid Yorkshire Dales house, set on a hill on the other side of the River Skimmer. Summer crossed the main bridge that gave the town its name, then followed the rough riverside track that passed for a road until she reached the gate to Monk's Folly, glad that she'd picked a dry, sunny day to visit. She suspected the track would get quite muddy in wet weather.

Viva, Joseph's little dog, pulled on her lead, excited to be out and about. Summer often took her for walks as Joseph admitted that sometimes he was just too tired to do it himself these days. She tried not to dwell on his dwindling energy, nor his recent hospital visit. He'd said nothing about it when he returned and she hadn't liked to ask. If there was something he wanted to tell her he surely would have? Maybe he was just run down, or perhaps he'd had a virus or something?

Anyway, she was glad to have Viva with her for company, as her stomach was churning with nerves, and she was wondering why she'd made such a stupid decision in the first place.

Ben wouldn't want to see her! Why would he? She was just another patient. Well, not even that; she was simply the person who'd brought his patient into the surgery. That was it. How many other 'pet parents' visited him at home and brought him a thank you gift?

Viva seemed to be enjoying the walk anyway. At times she seemed to be dancing on the end of her lead, she was so excited to be in this unfamiliar territory. Maybe Joseph didn't often cross the river. From what Clemmie had said, not many people went near Monk's Folly.

As she grew closer, she noticed that the house had a bit of a bleak look to it. It was built of grey stone and had a slate roof. The garden, such as it was, was overgrown, and there was a general air of neglect about the place.

It was, she thought, pushing open the gate and hoping it didn't swing off its hinges, a bit 'Wuthering Heights'. It wasn't so bad in summer, but she'd bet it would be a different story in the depths of winter. She only hoped it wasn't as grim inside as it looked from out here.

There was a shabby green door set into a porch, and Summer knocked tentatively. The track went past the house and further up the hill to a rather tatty building that she supposed was a garage. It wasn't the most welcoming of places.

Then again, she had to admit the views were spectacular. From up here she could see across the river to the town below, and beyond that to the surrounding fields and hills.

The spire of All Hallows Church pinpointed the location of home for her. The White Hart Inn was just across the road from there, and it gave her a warm, fuzzy feeling inside, realising that this town was where she belonged, and where she was at her happiest. Bemborough seemed a million miles away.

Viva sat down next to her, her head tilted to one side, watching her with some bemusement.

'It's okay,' Summer told her. 'It doesn't look like anyone's in anyway. I'll just post this through the letter box and we'll go.'

As she rummaged in her jacket pocket for the chocolate, the door swung open, making a rather worrying creaking sound, and she came face to face with Jennifer Callaghan.

'I was just—hello.'

Jennifer looked a bit confused. 'Hello?'

'It's—sorry. Hello, Mrs Callaghan. I'm Summer Fletcher, Sally's daughter. You know, from The White Hart Inn?'

The confusion on Jennifer's face cleared and her eyes brightened. 'Oh, of course! You were at Kat's baby shower, weren't you? How lovely to see you again. What can I do for you?'

Summer felt thoroughly stupid as she held out the chocolate, even if it was best quality and had cost her a small fortune from the card and gift shop in Market Place that made most of its profits from gullible tourists.

'I brought this for Ben,' she said. 'It's plain chocolate. He said it was his favourite.'

'It is.' Jennifer gazed at the offering, her brow furrowed. 'It's not his birthday, dear.'

'Oh, I know. It's a thank you. He—he saved Viva's life the other day,' Summer said with a rush, thinking a bit of exaggeration was the only thing that would prevent her from looking like a complete moron in Jennifer's eyes.

Jennifer looked thrilled. 'He did?' She smiled down at the little Bichon Frisé. 'Is this Viva?'

'Yes. She's not my dog, she's Joseph Wilkinson's. But I was the one who took her to the surgery, and Ben was so calm and so kind. I can't thank him enough really, but I thought this would at least show him I appreciated his work.'

'That's so kind of you!' Jennifer's eyes filled with tears,

much to Summer's alarm. 'How lovely. You must come in and give it to him yourself.'

'He's here?' Summer swallowed. Well, she'd been almost certain he would be, hadn't she? That was, after all, why Clemmie had suggested she visit this afternoon. Even so, now that she knew he was actually here she couldn't help wishing he wasn't. He would think she was mad, or worse, some stupid girl with a crush on him. Oh, why on earth had she listened to Clemmie?

'Yes, he's just upstairs. Bless him, he's been at work this morning and he was on call last night. Come in, Summer.'

'Oh no, it's all right,' Summer began, her courage failing her. 'If you can just—'

'Ben! Ben! You have a visitor!' Jennifer beamed at Summer and motioned to her to step inside. 'You're Frankie's stepsister, aren't you? Jamie thinks she's brilliant, and you must thank Sally and Rafferty for me; they've been so kind letting him visit to play games.'

'What about Viva?' Summer asked, half hoping Jennifer would change her mind about letting her in, since she had a dog in tow.

'Oh, bring her in of course. We love dogs. We used to have two, you know. Cocoa and Bean. They were beautiful cocker spaniels. Ben!'

She led Summer down a long, rather dark hallway and pushed open a door on the left. Summer found herself in a large, square room, with a thin carpet and faded wallpaper. She peered round, admitting to herself that it was also more Wuthering Heights on the inside than she cared for, despite the abundance of family photographs and bright orange cushions. It needed a complete makeover. Didn't vets earn good money?

'Take a seat, Summer. I'll go and fetch him. He must be

listening to music or something.' Patting her hair rather distractedly, Jennifer hurried out of the room.

Summer pushed aside a cushion and sank into a shabby old sofa, feeling a pang of compassion for Ben. Vets might earn good money, but after all, he was the only one bringing any into the house. Jennifer didn't work, and Jamie was still at school. Was he responsible for keeping this place going all by himself?

Poor Ben. It must be hard for him to be the sole bread-winner in the family, since his father was long gone. She was surprised he hadn't sold this house and bought something smaller and more manageable. The family must really love it a lot to stay here. She felt disloyal as she wondered what on earth the attraction could be.

It was a couple of minutes later when the door opened again and Jennifer hurried in, followed by a clearly embarrassed Ben. Summer's heart hammered in her chest, and she felt suddenly breathless. How hadn't he been snapped up ages ago by some woman? He was gorgeous!

'Summer. How nice to see you again,' he said, in a tone that suggested it was anything but.

Her heart sank. She knew it had been a mistake. He clearly thought she was some weird stalker with a crush. She would throttle Clemmie when she saw her.

'I'm not stopping,' she told him, hoping that would cheer him up a bit. 'I just brought you this. As a thank you.'

She stood and handed him the bar of Carroll's Premium Dark Chocolate, her face burning with humiliation.

'It's just to say thanks for all you did for Viva,' she said. 'I meant to give it to you when you came to see Shadow, but I forgot.' Mentally she crossed her fingers as she sat down again. 'It's from her, not me. Isn't it, Viva?'

Viva looked at her as if she'd gone mad, and Summer had

a feeling she wasn't the only one, but daren't look up to check.

'Well, er, that's...'

'Lovely! Isn't that lovely, Ben? So kind. It's nice to be appreciated by your patients, isn't it? Summer, would you like a cup of tea or coffee? I'm just about to put the kettle on.'

'Oh no, honestly. I don't—'

'It's no trouble, is it, Ben? It's nice to have visitors for a change. No one ever comes here, do they, Ben?'

Summer risked a glance at Ben and saw his own face was quite flushed, which made her feel a bit better. She stopped worrying about her own feelings and concentrated on his.

'A cup of tea would be lovely, if it's not too much trouble,' she said, smiling at Jennifer, who looked thrilled and hurried off straight away.

Ben ran a hand through his hair and gave her a sheepish grin. 'Thanks,' he said. 'For the chocolate, I mean. Really kind of you, and it's my favourite brand too.'

'Is it? Oh good.' Overcome with relief that he'd actually smiled at her, Summer didn't know what else to say, so she ruffled Viva's ears and fussed over the dog for a few minutes so there was no awkward silence.

Ben sat down on an armchair and hugged a cushion to his chest, as if trying to hide his rather tatty T-shirt. He needn't worry, Summer thought. She didn't care what he was wearing. He could be in a fluffy bunny onesie and she'd still find him attractive.

'You didn't have to bring me a present, you know,' he said. 'It's not as if I did anything.'

'You put my mind at rest, and you didn't even charge me,' Summer said. 'The least you deserve is a bar of chocolate.'

He shrugged. 'Well, if you say so. Would you like some?'

Summer wrinkled her nose. 'Ugh, no thanks. I love

Carroll's chocolate, but not the dark stuff. It's too bitter for me.'

'I'll save it for later,' he said, putting it on the small table at the side of his chair. 'And how are you, Viva? Keeping out of trouble, I hope?'

Summer clutched her knees awkwardly as the dog abandoned her to run to Ben. Now what did she do with her hands? In the end she tucked them under her thighs, only to remove them again when Jennifer returned, carrying a tray of drinks.

'Is Jamie at The White Hart Inn again?' she asked, handing a mug to Summer.

'He is. He and Frankie have really chummed up,' Summer said. 'They've bonded over a mutual passion for Spider-Man.'

'Well,' Ben said, 'as long as he's not wasting his time.'

She caught the edge to his voice and looked at him, surprised.

'It's the summer holidays, Ben.' Jennifer sat down next to Summer. 'It's nice for him to have friends.'

Ben said nothing and Summer sipped her tea, wondering what that was about.

'It's a lovely big house,' she said, looking round and pretending not to notice the state it was in.

'Isn't it?' Jennifer said brightly. 'It's been in our family for many years now. Ever since we bought it back in fact.'

'Bought it back?'

'Summer's not interested in all that, Mum,' Ben said hastily, but Summer corrected him immediately.

'I am, actually. And I was wondering why it was called Monk's Folly too. Was there a monastery on this site or something?'

Jennifer smiled. 'Oh no, not at all. It's a rather sad story.'

She settled herself back in the sofa. 'Do you want to tell it, Ben, or shall I?'

Ben looked gloomy. 'You can,' he said. 'Although,' he added, giving Summer a warning look, 'it's not exactly riveting, so don't get your hopes up.'

'The house is named after Edward Monk, who was an ancestor of Ben's father. Edward was madly in love with a young woman called Arabella Lavender.'

'Lavender? Related to our Miss Lavender by any chance?'

'Absolutely. She was the granddaughter of Josiah Lavender himself, and Edward adored her. The sad thing is, she adored him too.'

'Why is that sad?' Knowing that Josiah had been a famous and wealthy artist, Summer pulled a face. 'Let me guess; her family said he wasn't good enough and she was forbidden to marry him.'

'Oh, not at all,' Jennifer said. 'On the contrary, they were delighted, and eager for the engagement to go ahead. Unfortunately, it was Edward himself who could never quite believe he was good enough for her. Whatever Arabella wanted, Arabella got, and when she decided she wanted him to build a grand house for them to live in after they married, instead of telling her it was an impossible dream, he did everything he could to make it happen. He spent a long time earning enough money to purchase this land, determined that she'd be able to hold her head up in society.'

'She sounds completely spoilt to me,' Summer said. 'If I was Edward Monk I'd have told her to take what I was offering or lump it.'

Ben spluttered with laughter. 'I couldn't agree more!'

'He was just being kind,' Jennifer protested. 'There's nothing wrong with that, is there?'

'Given the way the story ends, there's plenty wrong with it,' Ben said, winking at Summer.

She felt her stomach fizzing in response and tried to concentrate on what Jennifer was saying.

'Well, however you look at it, poor Edward wasted years and got into huge amounts of debt trying to build this dream house of hers.'

'So what happened?' Summer asked. 'Is this the dream house?' Honestly, she wouldn't say it for all the world, but she couldn't believe anyone could consider Monk's Folly a dream house. More like a gothic nightmare.

'No, because Edward never got to finish it. Before he was even halfway through building the house his debts caught up with him and he was forced to sell the land to one Henry Panton, who not only scooped that but Arabella too.'

'Oh no!' Summer realised she'd said that out loud and blushed. 'I mean, what a shame.'

'I know! When it became clear Edward was on the verge of bankruptcy and that the house would never be completed, I suppose she took what she thought was the wisest option. She and Panton were married within three months of becoming engaged.'

'And what happened to Edward?'

'He was heartbroken and left Tuppenny Bridge for good. He never returned.'

'And Arabella?'

'Panton pulled down Edward's house and built this one instead. He called it Monk's Folly—a constant torment of what she'd lost, and the humiliation he'd heaped on her old love. By all accounts he was a vile man, and the marriage was a disaster from Arabella's point of view. She'd inherited her grandfather's talent for art, but Panton forbade her to paint again. She ended up with seven children and died when she was only thirty-nine.'

'Jolly little story, isn't it?' Ben said.

'It's awful.' Summer shivered, thinking she wouldn't like to be in this house at night, with the miserable ghost of Arabella hanging around and the awful Henry Panton's spectre strutting up and down, feeling far too pleased with himself.

'My husband's great-grandfather was a successful businessman, and he returned to Tuppenny Bridge in 1905 and bought the house from Arabella's eldest grandchild. Both Arabella and Henry Panton had long gone by then, and their descendants had married and left the place standing empty. None of them wanted to live in Monk's Folly, which was a bit odd, but their loss was our family's gain.'

'Lucky us,' Ben muttered.

Summer looked at him in surprise and he shook his head and attempted a smile. 'Told you it wasn't exactly riveting,' he said.

'Oh, but it was,' she said. 'Poor Edward Monk. I even feel sorry for Arabella, though she was a spoilt brat to begin with. I guess she paid the price in the end, bless her. Anyway, I'm glad Edward's descendant managed to buy the house and give it back to you all, even if it wasn't the house Edward intended to build.'

'That's why it mattered to my husband so much,' Jennifer said. 'This land should have been his by rights anyway, and Panton ruined things for his ancestor. He always thought Panton would be furious that there were descendants of Edward Monk living in his house now. He felt they'd got justice at last.'

'Bet you're glad you came now,' Ben said, his eyes twinkling. Even so, she detected a trace of anxiety in them—as if he was afraid she would mock them.

'I really am,' Summer said. 'A lovely cup of tea and an interesting tale of local history. What more could anyone ask for?'

Ben looked doubtful, but Jennifer seemed thrilled that Summer was so receptive, and they passed another half hour making general conversation about Tuppenny Bridge, the Lavender Ladies' latest gambling book—they were taking bets on how long it would be before Market Café was sold to yet another new owner, which would make it the fifth in thirteen years apparently—and the blossoming friendship between Jamie and Frankie.

By the time Summer got up to leave—earning resentful looks from Viva who was snuggled up quite comfortably on Ben's knee—she felt far more relaxed, and hoped she'd brightened Jennifer's day a little. Poor woman must be desperate for company. She definitely needed to get out more.

Impulsively, she said, 'I forgot to say that Mum asked me to invite you to her hen night. It's on the Saturday, six days before the wedding. I know it's short notice but it's nothing formal. Just a get-together in the flat above the pub, that's all. She said you'd be very welcome,' she added, mentally crossing her fingers again and hoping her mum wouldn't mind.

'Really?' Jennifer looked stunned. 'Well, er, that's very kind of her, but—'

'It would do you the world of good,' Ben said eagerly. 'You enjoyed Kat's baby shower, didn't you?'

'I suppose I did.' Jennifer swallowed. 'Well, all right. What time should I be there?'

'Er, about seven thirty?'

'Wonderful. Tell her thank you very much.'

'I'll show you out,' Ben said, earning a beaming smile of approval from his mother.

'It was really good of you to make the effort,' he said, moments later, as Summer stood on the doorstep, lead in hand. 'You've cheered Mum up no end.'

'I'm glad,' she said, meaning it. They were both quiet and Summer gazed at him, willing him to ask her out. She couldn't have made it any more obvious if she'd tried, so what was taking him so long?

Ben cleared his throat and her heart leapt in anticipation. 'Did your mum really invite her, or was that a last minute flash of inspiration?'

Summer's cheeks heated. 'Of course she invited her. I'm glad she said yes. She's lovely. Next time I visit I'll bring her some chocolate too.' She smiled, but the smile dropped as she realised what she'd said. 'I mean—'

'It's okay,' Ben said. 'I know what you mean. Like I said, it was nice of you to come, but I'm not expecting you to make it a regular habit.'

Summer wasn't sure whether that was a question, an order, or a simple statement of fact. Either way, it seemed clear he wasn't about to ask her out any time soon, so she shuffled awkwardly and said, 'I'd better go. Joseph will be wondering where this little one's got to.'

She nodded at Viva and Ben straightened.

'Of course. Well, bye, Summer. Bye, Viva.'

With that the door closed and Summer stepped back, not quite sure what to make of it.

'O-kay. Bye, Ben.'

Feeling depressed, she led the little dog back down the track to the gate, trying to make sense of the expression in Ben's eyes as he'd ended the visit. No matter which way she looked at it, she couldn't decide whether he was interested in her or not. Maybe, she thought, he wasn't entirely sure himself. It would explain the way he kept blowing hot and cold with her.

She really couldn't fathom him out, or his mother, come to that. Jamie was so outgoing and lively and had no problem spending most of his time at The White Hart Inn, whereas Ben and Jennifer shut themselves away in that old house, trapped with the ghost of a sad young woman, and surrounded by shabby old furniture that only looked fit for a municipal tip.

Just what, she wondered, were they hiding away from?

Chapter Seven

As if all the excitement about the wedding wasn't enough, Rafferty and Sally were astounded to receive a handwritten invitation for lunch with Miss Lavender and her best friends, the Pennyfeather sisters—collectively known as the Lavender Ladies—and at Lavender House, no less.

'It's like an invitation to a royal garden party.' Sally waved the note at Summer. It was scented with lavender. Naturally.

'More like a summons,' Rafferty replied, grinning. 'What do you think? Are we going or not?'

'Of course we're going,' Sally said. 'She could blacklist us if we snub her.'

Summer and Frankie burst out laughing.

'Blacklist you! Who do you think she is, Mum? The Godmother?'

'She's got a lot of power in Tuppenny Bridge,' Sally said darkly. 'That's why they ask her to turn on the Christmas lights every year.'

'They ask her because she pays for them,' Rafferty said.

'They probably worry she'd withdraw funding if they didn't. Miss Lavender has no real power whatsoever, so don't let her intimidate you, Sally.'

'She's loaded, though.'

'So's Dad,' Frankie pointed out drily.

'And she lives in that big, posh house.'

Rafferty sighed. 'That doesn't make her powerful.'

'And her ancestor was the town's most famous resident, so, you know...'

'Plus, she has her network of spies, working from what masquerades as a harmless wool shop,' Summer added, winking at a grinning Frankie. 'The Pennyfeather Sisters— Secret Agents.'

'I don't know why you two find it so funny,' Rafferty said, a twinkle in his eyes. 'You're invited, too.'

'What?' Frankie gave a cry of dismay. 'No way am I going.'

'Think of the Instagram photos,' Summer said, knowing Frankie's obsession with her social media accounts. 'Lavender House is highly photogenic, and you've snapped Whispering Willows from every available angle by now.'

Frankie considered the matter. 'Suppose it's something different,' she said eventually. 'I've not had as many likes lately, which makes sense. I mean, you've seen one sheep, you've seen them all. Okay, I'll go. If Summer goes, too.'

Of course, it was inevitable that all four of them would accept the invitation, and on Sunday, having arranged cover at the pub, they set off.

'I haven't been down Lavender Lane for ages,' Sally said, gazing out of the car window. 'All these beautiful fields, and the hills, too! It's gorgeous, isn't it? We should visit Lavender House more often, Rafferty. As paying guests, obviously.'

'Isn't this the view you see from the churchyard?' Frankie

asked. 'Me and Jamie were in there the other day, sitting on the bench.'

'Oh?' Rafferty raised an eyebrow as he surveyed her in the rear-view mirror. 'What were you doing in there?'

Frankie pulled a face. 'Sitting on a bench. Didn't I just say that?'

'Hmm.'

'Oh, Dad, give it a rest. How many more times? Jamie and I are just mates, nothing else.' She gave Summer a sly look. 'It's Summer and Ben you ought to be worrying about.'

Huh, Summer thought. *Fat chance.*

Sally turned to look at them. 'Summer and Ben? What's that supposed to mean?'

'Just Frankie being a comedian. Take no notice,' Summer said hastily.

'Hmm. Sounded interesting. If there's anything you want to tell me—'

'Here we are,' Rafferty announced, saving Summer from an interrogation. 'Lavender House.'

Sally gave Summer a knowing look but thankfully turned away from her as the car swept between stone gateposts and up a long drive towards the house. It was a smart Georgian building, very neat and symmetrical, with landscaped gardens you could explore—for a price. According to the signs you had to pay to park too.

'Bit much,' Frankie said, pouting at her phone screen as she snapped a selfie with a view of the house behind her. 'Miss Lavender invited us here, after all.'

'I suppose they've got to earn their money somehow,' Sally said.

In the event, they didn't have to pay. The man at the ticket office informed them they were expected, and that all charges had been waived. They gave each other nervous glances—even, Summer noted, Rafferty—and made their way to the front door of the house.

There was a desk on the right of the large entrance hall. A middle-aged man offered them an audio tour or a guide-book, which they politely declined. They explained they were here to see Miss Lavender, and he looked worried and said she wasn't in the habit of seeing guests. Luckily, at that moment who should wander up but Ross Lavender.

'It's okay,' he told the man. 'Aunt Eugenie's expecting them.' He smiled. 'Follow me.'

Frankie turned to Summer and mouthed, 'Phwoar,' at her. Summer shook her head, noting the gleam in Frankie's eyes as they followed him down a corridor. *Honestly, girls these days!*

'In here,' Ross said, leading them to a door marked 'Private'. He opened the door and ushered them in. They found themselves in a rather chintzy room, with floral sofas, a plush pink carpet, and dusky pink curtains at the windows.

The Pennyfeather sisters waved a welcome, and Miss Lavender beamed at them. 'Thank you, Ross. Come in, come in. Make yourselves at home.'

Boycott and Trueman got to their feet and yapped at the visitors, earning themselves a biscuit for their efforts. It seemed foolish to Summer, rewarding them for yapping, and she wondered what Ben would make of it.

As they entered the room, Ross closed the door behind them and left them to it. They all looked at each other, feeling a little awkward, but Miss Lavender was clearly on a mission to make them feel at home.

'That sofa there.' She indicated a huge, squishy sofa covered in a soft fabric decorated with big pink roses, and frills at the hem. 'That should easily be big enough for all four of you.'

She was right, and they sat down wondering what they'd done to deserve this honour.

'It's very kind of you to invite us,' Sally began, but Miss Lavender held up her hand.

'Not at all. If anything, I feel I should be apologising. You've been here over eighteen months now, and I should have invited you a long time ago. It's nothing formal, of course. Just a little getting-to-know-each-other afternoon tea, that's all. I'm interested to hear about your wedding plans. Not long now, is it?'

Opposite her, the Pennyfeather sisters exchanged mischievous smiles, as if they knew something their guests didn't.

Miss Lavender suddenly seemed to remember they were there and waved a hand in their direction.

'Rita and Birdie insisted on being here. They're incurably nosy, I'm afraid.'

Rita and Birdie, huddled together on a smaller sofa, looked like two tropical birds sitting on their perch. Dressed in lime green dresses, their bright red hair was clipped back with matching purple hair slides, and they had on their usual crocheted waistcoats with multicoloured panels.

'Frankie, this is Rita and Birdie Pennyfeather, Kat's great-aunties,' Rafferty said.

Frankie seemed lost for words as the sisters waved cheerily at her.

'I hope you're hungry. I've bought cream horns from Bridge Bakery especially,' Miss Lavender said. She fixed the Pennyfeather sisters with a beady glare. 'You two, come with me.'

Rita and Birdie sighed.

'No rest for the wicked, Rita.'

'We must have been bloody evil in another life, Birdie.'

Nevertheless, they followed her out of the room. Rafferty, Sally, Frankie, and Summer waited as they listened for their footsteps heading down the hall, then looked at each other, bemused.

Rafferty shrugged. 'Well, they're entertaining if nothing else.'

'I still don't understand why they've invited us,' Sally said. 'Do you think they invite everyone in this town to tea at some point?'

'I shouldn't be at all surprised.' Summer tentatively patted one of the Yorkshire terriers who'd come to investigate her. 'Probably our turn to be pumped for information. Maybe they've got another bet going and we've got inside information we haven't realised. Oh well, I'm quite happy to indulge them. Besides, I love cream horns.'

'Lucky you.' Frankie wrinkled her nose. 'I don't know if I'll be able to eat a thing. They smell of old ladies.'

'They *are* old ladies,' Summer said. 'And it's lavender if I'm not mistaken. Which it would be, obviously.'

'It's very nice of them to invite us,' Sally said firmly. 'Mind you, I hope they're not going to interrogate me about the father of Kat's baby again. I've already told them I don't know who it is.'

'Is that bet still running?' Rafferty asked.

'What bet?' Frankie whooped with laughter. 'You mean Kat doesn't know who Hattie's father is? Way to go, Kat!'

'Kat does,' Sally said. 'She just hasn't told anyone else. No,' she added quickly, 'not even me. Honestly. It's no one's business but hers anyway but try telling the Lavender Ladies that. They won't give up until they know, and they can close the book.'

'They're out of luck if that's what they want,' Summer said.

'Well,' Sally settled back on the sofa and smoothed down her skirt, 'at least we'll have cream horns. That's something.'

They also had dainty little cucumber sandwiches, ham sandwiches, and cheese sandwiches with tomato, all cut into neat triangles, but with the crusts left on. There were macarons, cupcakes so small they were gone in one bite, and mini chocolate eclairs, as well as the cream horns.

They ate their fill, drank several cups of tea, and made polite conversation. Summer noticed Miss Lavender gave the Yorkies several treats from her plate and wondered if Ben had ever discussed their diet with her.

Miss Lavender noticed her watching and beamed at her. 'Aren't they wonderful little characters? They're brothers. They have a first-class pedigree, you know.'

'Joseph's dog, Viva, is a pedigree,' Summer said. 'A Bichon Frisé. He got her from a rescue centre when she was two.'

'How very altruistic of him,' Miss Lavender said. 'I always worry about a rescue dog's character. You can never really be sure, can you? Whereas when you purchase from a reputable breeder...'

One of the Yorkies snatched a ham sandwich from her hand, and she gave him an indulgent smile. Summer thought of sweet, gentle Viva and mentally shook her head.

'Sometimes, you have to take a chance,' she said. 'Imagine if no one gave homes to the dogs in shelters. They'd have to be destroyed. Thank goodness for people like Joseph. All the horses he's rescued, too. He deserves a medal.'

'Hmm.' Miss Lavender shifted in her chair, and Rita and Birdie exchanged glances.

Summer wondered what that was about, but Miss Lavender had already moved on.

'So, to happier subjects. Your wedding. Is everything organised and ready?'

'Just about,' Sally said. 'I had no idea organising a big wedding was so much hassle. My last wedding was a registry office do. A quick in and out really, no fuss or frills. That's why I wanted to do it differently this time. I'm so happy to be getting married at All Hallows.'

'And with our wonderful vicar, Zach Barrington, marrying you, too. And the reception is to be at The White Hart Inn, I understand?'

Summer wondered why she was acting as if she'd only just found out. The invitations had been sent ages ago, so she must have had that information for months.

'That's right,' Rafferty said. 'We're closing the pub to the general public for the day, and we've hired in a catering company so most of our staff can be at the wedding.'

Miss Lavender arched an eyebrow. 'Goodness. That's a lot of money to lose, closing the pub for a whole day.'

'Yes, well, we felt it was worth it.' Rafferty smiled at his bride-to-be.

'And you can afford it, can't you, Rafferty?' Birdie said slyly. 'Kat says you're as rich as Croesus.'

'Birdie! Don't be vulgar.' Miss Lavender shook her head. She looked warily at Sally. 'I expect your mother will be there?'

'Oh of course! She's really looking forward to it.'

'Hmm.' Miss Lavender's tone told them all how she felt about that. She turned a gracious smile on Rafferty. 'I look forward to meeting *your* parents at last.'

'I'm afraid you won't get the chance,' Rafferty said. 'My parents have booked a cruise and they're unable to cancel it.'

Summer noticed him reach for her mum's hand and squeeze it reassuringly. They all knew that Rafferty's parents thoroughly disapproved of him running a pub, and when he'd told them of his engagement to Sally Fletcher, of all people, they'd made it quite clear they wanted nothing to do with the wedding. Luckily, after trying and failing for decades to win their approval, Rafferty had given up caring, and had been relieved to learn they wouldn't be at the ceremony to spoil things.

'That's a shame. Family is so important. I believe,' Miss Lavender said slowly, 'that you're related to the Rochesters. Hasn't Ethan Rochester been invited to the wedding?'

Rafferty's mouth fell open in surprise, but he hastily closed it again and nodded. 'Er, yes, he has. He's a cousin of mine.'

Miss Lavender got to her feet and Summer wondered if she was about to throw them all out. Instead, she walked over to the fireplace and pointed at a painting which hung on the wall.

'Do you see this?' she asked, which Summer thought was rather a redundant question as obviously they could. 'This was Monk's Folly, painted in 1817.'

Rafferty leaned forward and stared at the painting, as Mum breathed, 'Oh, what a beautiful house.'

She was right. Summer stared at the lovely building, surrounded by ornate gardens, and found it hard to imagine it was the same house that she'd visited so recently. What a crying shame. She wouldn't have minded visiting if it still looked like that. Ben, she thought wistfully, deserved a home that stunning. He didn't belong in the shabby old house it was today.

'Is it a Josiah Lavender painting?' she asked.

'Can't be. He died in 1804,' Rafferty said.

Miss Lavender beamed at him. 'Quite right. No, this was painted by his granddaughter, Arabella.'

'Who married Henry Panton instead of Edward Monk.'

They all turned to face Summer, who blushed.

'You know the story?' Miss Lavender asked, clearly surprised.

'Sorry,' Sally said, sounding confused. 'Who's Edward Monk?'

Summer explained the story of Arabella's demands and how they'd cost Edward every penny, and how his rival had built Monk's Folly and named it so in spite.

'I'm impressed,' Miss Lavender said. 'Who told you about this?'

'Jennifer mentioned it when I went to Monk's Folly the other day.'

'You visited Monk's Folly?' Rita and Birdie were agog. 'Were you invited?'

'I took Ben some chocolate,' Summer said. As their faces lit up she added hastily, 'It was a thank you. He helped me with Viva when she got ill. Well, she wasn't ill, actually, but I thought she was. Ben was really kind, and he didn't even charge me, so...'

Too late, she realised what she'd done, as Birdie and Rita grinned at each other in delight. As if they needed any help finding gossip! There'd be a book running on hers and Ben's relationship before the day was out, and everyone in that room knew it.

'Anyway,' Rafferty said, clearly sensing the way the conversation was going and kindly heading it off for her, 'you were saying? About the painting.'

'Oh yes, well. Arabella—as Summer explained—was a talented artist, but when she married Henry Panton he stopped her from painting. This particular landscape was done when he was away on business, and she hid it at her father's home, here at Lavender House. We have several of her paintings, and I personally think she was a great talent, although naturally her work would never command the prices Josiah's paintings fetch.'

'She was certainly gifted,' Rafferty said. 'What a shame she married someone so blinkered.'

'He wasn't just blinkered, he was cruel. Of course, if Edward Monk had been firmer with her, instead of indulging her every whim, this would never have happened.'

'Poor Arabella. This Panton bloke sounds absolutely lovely. Not.' Sally turned to Miss Lavender. 'Fancy Edward Monk being Ben's ancestor.'

'Yes, and unfortunately my own ancestor sold the land back to Ben's great-grandfather and we lost the place.'

'Why would you want it?' Summer said with feeling. 'Believe me, the house doesn't look like that any more.'

Miss Lavender's eyes glistened. 'My dear ancestor, Josiah Lavender, painted the views from there many times. Indeed, some of his best works are of those views. Long before Edward Monk purchased the land, he would spend time there, capturing the changing seasons in the dale, the growth of Tuppenny Bridge which, of course, was so much smaller in his day. It didn't really start to expand until much later in the Georgian period. The house may have changed over the years, but the views are still inspiring.'

She sighed then shook her head and sat down again, reaching for her cup of tea. 'I believe Ethan Rochester is a talented artist himself,' she said. 'And very interested in the art world.'

Summer narrowed her eyes. What did that have to do with anything?

'You're right,' Rafferty said, sitting back and folding his arms, as if he were wondering the same thing. 'His paintings are superb, and if he hadn't been left the business to run by his father I think he'd probably have pursued art as a career.'

'Hmm. And do you think,' she said carefully, peering into her cup, 'that he might be interested in, say, sponsoring a prize? Perhaps setting up a scholarship scheme even?'

Rafferty frowned. 'Scholarship scheme?'

Miss Lavender put down her cup. 'As you know, Ross is an extremely talented artist himself. He's also a good teacher. We're seriously considering opening a school of art in Tuppenny Bridge, and perhaps hiring another teacher to work alongside Ross. Of course, our plans are in their infancy at the moment, and there's a lot to work out, but we'd be looking for financial input from outside sources. Someone like Ethan Rochester, whose name carries such weight, would do a great deal to bring the school to wider public attention. And if we could offer a scholarship in his name—perhaps a trophy too—who knows?'

Summer felt her mum and Rafferty relax, as realisation dawned on them all as to exactly why they'd been invited to Lavender House.

'I can't speak for my cousin,' Rafferty said politely, 'but as you know, he will be at the wedding. Perhaps I can introduce you...'

'And Ross, of course?'

'Of course.'

Miss Lavender smiled. 'Thank you, Rafferty. That's all I'm asking. Most kind of you. Please, help yourselves to the cream horns. We wouldn't want the cream to turn, would we?'

* * *

The Corner Cottage Bookshop was busy when Summer visited on Tuesday, and she had to wait a while before Clemmie was finally free to chat.

'What's with all the blue flags?' she asked, leaning on the counter as Clemmie reached for a sandwich from somewhere at the side of her chair and unwrapped it with eager hands. 'They're all over the market place and there's one flapping around outside your shop.'

Clemmie gave her a sorrowful look. 'Oh, Summer. Do you really not know? It's August the first! Yorkshire Day! We always put the county flags up to celebrate that. Dolly heard two tourists complaining earlier that they looked tacky.' She rolled her eyes. 'Needless to say, they weren't from Yorkshire. Dolly was so incensed she's decided she's leaving ours up permanently.'

Summer laughed. 'Fair enough. Happy Yorkshire Day, then. Where is Dolly anyway?'

'Writing. I know! How selfish can you be?' Clemmie grinned. 'Bless her, she's got a looming deadline so I'm pretty much running this place single-handed at the moment. Typical that it's suddenly got customers. So, how are things with you and Ben? Any progress?'

Summer sighed. 'None whatsoever. I couldn't have been clearer when I went to Monk's Folly, but he still didn't take the hint. In fact, he practically shut the door in my face after more or less warning me not to visit there again.'

'He never did!' Clemmie held her sandwich in mid-air, her indignation obvious. 'Fancy him doing that. I thought Ben was one of the good guys.'

'Oh, I'm sure he is,' Summer said hastily. 'I was exaggerating. It's just that he definitely doesn't know how to take a hint. Or he doesn't want to. I don't know which it is. It's like he really wants to ask me out, and I can see in his face that he likes me, and then suddenly these shutters come down and he backs off. It's so frustrating.'

'Have you ever thought,' Clemmie said, picking a bit of her sandwich off, 'that he's just really shy? Maybe he's hoping you'll ask *him* out.'

It had occurred to Summer, but she wasn't sure she had the nerve to make the first move. And anyway, hadn't she done enough? She'd gone to his house with the lamest excuse, for goodness' sake! What more did he need? She took out her phone and found Ben's number, her thumb hovering over it while Clemmie watched, biting her lip with anticipation.

Summer tutted and slammed the phone on the counter. 'I'm not asking him out,' she said. 'If he's really interested, he'll ring me. End of. Would you like me to make us a cup of coffee?'

'Ooh, would you? Lovely.' Clemmie gave her a grateful smile. 'You make the drinks and I'll try to think of a way of making him ask you out.'

When Summer returned a few minutes later, carrying two mugs of coffee, Clemmie had eaten her sandwich but appeared to have drawn a blank on ways to encourage Ben.

'Maybe you're right,' she said, taking the mug from Summer and nodding her thanks. 'Maybe he's not interested after all. Maybe the whole thing was a waste of time and effort.'

'Oh, thanks very much,' Summer said. 'Just what I wanted to hear.'

Clemmie laughed and reached under the counter, producing a packet of biscuits. 'Have a chocolate HobNob,' she said. 'Everything will feel so much better after that.'

Summer rolled her eyes and took a biscuit. 'We were at

Miss Lavender's on Sunday,' she said. 'We were invited for afternoon tea.'

'Who's we?'

'Me, Mum, Rafferty, and Frankie. The Pennyfeather sisters were there, naturally.'

'Naturally. And to what did you owe this honour?'

'She'd found out that Rafferty's cousin, Ethan Rochester, was going to be at the wedding, and she wants Rafferty to introduce them so she can talk him into providing a sponsorship or a prize or something for her art school.'

'Art school?' Clemmie wrinkled her nose. 'What art school?'

'Oh, that's the other thing. Apparently, she's planning to open an art school for Ross. He'll run it, of course, and it seems they've got big plans for it. She was even talking about making it a residential school. They've got high hopes, I'll say that much.'

'And just where do they intend to run it?' Clemmie's voice was suspiciously harsh, and Summer looked at her in surprise.

'No idea. Are you okay?'

'Why shouldn't I be?'

'You sound a bit funny.'

Clemmie shrugged. 'Don't know what you mean. I'm fine.'

'Okay. Anyway,' Summer said, helping herself to another HobNob, 'it might not come to anything yet. It's just an idea, and Rafferty said Miss Lavender's got enough on her plate running the museum.'

'Oh, it will happen,' Clemmie said tightly. 'What Ross wants, Ross gets.'

Summer lowered her biscuit and eyed her friend curiously. 'Why are you so against Ross? You were a bit horrible about him the other day, come to think of it. All that, "Ross is vain and shallow, and can't keep it in his trousers" stuff. What's Ross ever done to you?'

'He's a book villain,' Clemmie said. 'He's a Willoughby. A Wickham. And something else beginning with W that I couldn't possibly say out loud. I just think men like him are a disgrace.' She frowned. 'Well, don't you? Would you like it if Ben behaved the way Ross did? All those women, one after the other. What about their feelings?' She flicked her thick, blonde plait over her shoulder and said, 'Just be glad you've got a decent one. Ooh, your phone's ringing. I think you'll find that's Ben.'

Doubtfully, Summer glanced down at the phone on the counter and saw Ben's name on the screen. Her stomach flipped over. 'How did you know?'

Clemmie gave her a sweet smile. 'Because while you were making the coffees, I sent him a text from your phone, asking him to ring when he had a spare minute. Looks like he's wasted no time. Look,' she added, seeing Summer's horrified expression, 'it's Yorkshire Day! Where's your Yorkshire grit? Are you going to answer it?'

As Summer continued to stare at her, Clemmie sighed and pressed the green button on the phone, then handed it over, mouthing, 'Ask him!'

Summer swallowed hard as Ben said, 'Summer? Summer are you there?'

It seemed she had no choice but to ask Ben out on a date, but if he said no, it was a distinct possibility that she'd never speak to Clemmie again.

Chapter Eight

Ben had tried to make himself call Summer for days, but the memory of how they'd said goodbye at Monk's Folly made him change his mind every time he picked up his phone.

'Just ask the girl out,' Clive said. 'I don't know what more proof you need that she likes you. She bought you Carroll's chocolate. Have you any idea how expensive that is?'

He laughed as Ben shook his head. 'Oh, go on. What's the worst that can happen?'

'But she didn't say anything to correct me,' Ben said. 'I said I understood her visit to Monk's Folly was a one-off and she didn't say it wasn't.'

'Oh well, that's that then. Trial over, jury returns unanimous verdict of guilty.' Clive rolled his eyes. 'Honestly, you want a written invitation? I give up.'

Ben couldn't help wondering, though, how Summer had felt about Monk's Folly. He'd nearly died of embarrassment when he saw her sitting there in that bloody awful living room, on the ancient sofa that belonged in a skip. If she'd had any doubts about going out with him before, surely seeing the state of the house would put her off for good?

Well, if it had, maybe that was the best thing all round. Getting involved with someone would mean talking to them, going over things he didn't want to remember, confiding in them...

So that Tuesday morning it was one heck of a shock when she sent him a text.

From Summer:

Hi Ben. Could you ring me when you get a spare moment? Thanks. xx

Two kisses! What, he wondered, did that mean?

He didn't tell Clive, because he'd never hear the end of it if he did, but in a rare moment of bravery, born out of frustration and desperation, he bit the bullet and rang Summer as soon as he was on his break.

'I gave up waiting for you to ring me,' she told him, with no preamble.

'I'm sorry. I didn't think you really wanted me to,' he said, which was true.

'Really?' There was a pause. 'Well, I did. That's why I gave you my number. Look, Ben, just say if you're not interested, because honestly if you're not it's okay, and—'

'I am interested!' He realised how eager he'd sounded and modified his tone. 'I mean, I'd like to take you out, if that's what you'd like, too.'

'Well, it is as a matter of fact,' she said. 'So, are we going to meet up or what?'

'I'd love that,' he told her. 'It's just—'

'Just what?' she said. 'Oh, is it about the gossip? I know the Pennyfeathers will be over the moon if they hear about this.'

He could hardly tell her that his first thought had been

that he didn't have much money left to take her anywhere. Besides, she had a point about the Pennyfeathers.

'There's a nice pub over in West Colby,' he said. 'It's about half an hour's drive away, but I've got the Land Rover, if you don't mind its basic lack of comfort.'

She laughed. 'Sounds good to me. When and where?'

He considered the matter. 'Friday evening? How about meeting me at the bottom of the track to Monk's Folly. I'll tell my family I'm going round to Clive's for supper.'

'Really? I'm not bothered about the gossip that much, are you?'

There was a part of him that wanted the whole town to know he was going on a date with Summer Fletcher. But what if she didn't like him and decided never to see him again? How would he face everyone after that?

'I just think it would be nice to have one date without them all knowing, don't you?'

'Okay, fair enough. I'll tell my family I'm going for a drink with Clemmie,' she said, sounding hesitant. 'If that's what you really want.'

'It will be our secret,' he said. 'The Lavender Ladies know everything that goes on here. I'd quite like to keep something from them for once.'

'I'll look forward to it,' she told him, sounding more relaxed.

'Me too,' he said. 'Bye, Summer.'

'Bye, Ben.'

Ben ended the call wondering what on earth he'd just done. It had seemed easy enough when he was talking to her, but now the nerves had kicked in. It had been so long since he'd had a proper conversation with anyone but his family, Clive, and his clients. As for romance, he was practically a novice. What if he did something wrong? What if he upset her without even meaning to? What if he bored her to death? Could he really keep someone as amazing as Summer Fletcher interested?

Oh well, he supposed there was only one way to find out.

* * *

Clemmie, naturally, took full credit for Ben and Summer's date.

'I knew he just needed a nudge,' she said as Summer put the phone back on the counter, feeling dazed. 'So, go on, where's he taking you?'

'I can't say,' Summer said with a shrug. 'It's top secret.'

Clemmie laughed. 'Sure it is.' Her eyes narrowed when Summer didn't laugh too. 'Are you serious?'

'Hmm.' Summer frowned. 'He wants to keep it quiet. Says he's worried about the gossip. Do you mind being my alibi if anyone asks?'

'No, not at all. I can't blame him for that,' Clemmie said with feeling. 'You know as well as I do that the Lavender Ladies would be all over this. Good for Ben, I say.'

'Really?' Summer said doubtfully. 'You don't think it's odd?'

'What do you mean, odd? What's up with you? Why aren't you jumping up and down with excitement?'

'I am excited,' Summer protested. 'Really I am. It's just...' She hesitated and Clemmie leaned forward.

'Just what?'

'You don't think he wants to keep it a secret because he's got another girlfriend?'

There was a moment's silence then Clemmie burst out laughing.

'What's so funny?' Summer asked indignantly.

'You are! Ben? Another girlfriend? That'll be the day.' She gazed up at Summer in amazement. 'Have you not heard anything I've told you? Ben doesn't socialise, let alone date. Besides, he's not that type. He wouldn't cheat. He's not a Ross Lavender!'

'How can we be sure?' Summer asked, butterflies fluttering in her stomach. Now that she was actually going on a date with Ben her nerves were kicking in. What if he turned out to be just like her dad? What if he turned out to be just like *Ian*? She pushed the thought away, refusing to give her ex any head space.

'I suppose,' Clemmie said thoughtfully, 'we can't ever be one hundred per cent sure. But honestly, if I had to put money on any bloke being faithful, it would be Ben. He's just too kind and honest. He's hardly a wolf, is he? More like a soppy old spaniel.'

Summer smiled. 'You're right,' she said. 'Besides, it's just one date. I'm overthinking this.'

'I'll be round tomorrow night,' Clemmie promised.

Summer stared at her. 'What for?'

Clemmie rolled her eyes. 'What do you think? You and I are going to ransack your wardrobe. I'm going to help you pick out an outfit that will knock him dead.'

Chapter Nine

Luckily, that Friday evening Jamie was round at The White Hart Inn, playing games with Frankie, so Ben escaped any awkward questions from his endlessly curious brother. His mother, though, would be left alone and he wasn't happy about that. She looked wistful as he combed his hair in front of the mirror.

'You're looking very smart, Ben,' she told him. 'That's your best shirt! Is it a special occasion?'

'No,' he said, managing a smile. 'But you know Clive. He's a bit old fashioned when it comes right down to it. He likes to dress for dinner when he has company, even if it's just me. Look, are you sure you're going to be okay here on your own?'

She looked surprised. 'Why wouldn't I be?'

'It's just...' He looked around helplessly. 'Isn't there anything on the television?'

'No.' She sighed. 'Nothing that holds my attention anyway.'

'What about a book? Did you manage to get to the

library?'

'No. I didn't bother in the end.' She plucked thoughtfully at the cushion on her lap. 'Maybe I'll bake a cake,' she said eventually. Her face brightened. 'Yes, I'll bake a cake, and I'll take it round to the pub. It will be a thank you for letting Jamie spend so much time there, and for inviting me to Sally's hen night.' She shrugged. 'I know it's not much, but...'

'I'm sure they'll love it,' he said, thrilled that she wanted to go out, and aware that cooking and baking were like therapy to his mother. He wasn't so sure about her going to The White Hart Inn, though. He didn't want them all putting two and two together once they'd realised Summer and he were both out at the same time. Even so, he wasn't going to stop her going. He wanted her to have company. She was alone far too often for his liking.

'Do I look all right?' he asked, turning to face her.

She beamed at him. 'You look very handsome. What a pity it's all going to be wasted on Clive, of all people. Have a lovely evening, darling.'

'I will. You too.'

He kissed her lightly on the cheek and left, hoping she'd be okay.

As the Land Rover drove slowly down the track, his stomach swished around uncomfortably. He patted his pocket, making sure he had his wallet with him. Not that there was much in it, but there should just about be enough to cover the cost of a meal. Providing they didn't go too mad, that was.

It was a warm, sunny evening, and the river was calm—a sharp contrast to how anxious he felt.

Summer was waiting at the end of the track as arranged. His heart leapt as he caught sight of her, looking beautiful in a floral dress and strappy sandals. For some reason he'd pictured her in jeans and wellies. He'd never seen her in a dress before and he asked himself, for the umpteenth time, why she'd agreed to go out on a date with him.

He leaned over and opened the Land Rover door for her. 'Hello. Have you been waiting long?'

She smiled at him, and he wondered how she'd managed to sneak up and steal his heart when he wasn't looking.

'About ten minutes,' she said. 'It doesn't matter. It's a warm evening and it was a nice walk.' She settled into the passenger seat and clicked her seat belt shut. 'You look very smart.'

'So do you. That's a lovely dress.'

'Oh, this old thing!' She laughed. 'No, I'm lying. It's only a couple of months old, I got it from the market. Do you really like it? It's a tea dress apparently. Got a bit of a 1940s vibe going on, don't you think?'

'I suppose it has,' Ben said, not knowing much about fashion. 'Let's go then, shall we? West Colby here we come.'

They spoke little on the way there. Summer stared out of the window, remarking now and then on how beautiful the Yorkshire Dales were as they passed meadows that, just six weeks ago, had been a riot of colour from the wildflowers that bloomed before the hay cutting started.

'This is it,' he said at last, as he turned the Land Rover into the car park of The Farmer's Arms.

'Looks lovely,' she said. 'Have you been here before?'

'No, but Clive has. He and Joseph are always banging on about the steak and ale pie.'

'Clemmie's been here,' Summer said. 'She and Dolly live just outside the village.'

'Keep everything crossed they're not in here tonight then,' he said.

'Oh blimey, that would be typical, wouldn't it?' At least

she laughed about it.

He climbed out of the Land Rover and opened the passenger door, then helped Summer down. 'Ready?'

She nodded. 'Ready.'

A waitress greeted them with a warm smile. 'Good evening. Can I take your name?'

'Ben. Ben Callaghan.'

She checked her bookings and nodded. 'Your table's ready for you, Mr Callaghan. If you'd like to follow me.'

She led them to a table in a quiet corner of the dining room and handed them menus.

'Would you like anything to drink before you order?' she enquired politely.

Ben didn't even check the drinks list, as he was driving. 'A large Coke, please. Summer?'

'Just a Diet Coke for me,' Summer said. 'No ice.'

The waitress nodded and left them alone, and Ben sat back in his chair, feeling the weight of expectation heavy on his shoulders.

'It's a nice pub, isn't it?' Summer remarked, glancing around. 'Smart. Discreet.'

She grinned at him, and he laughed.

'I keep expecting the Lavender Ladies to pop up at any minute,' he said. 'Do you know they're running a book on us getting together?'

Summer's mouth dropped open. 'They never are! Already?'

'Oh, they are. One of my clients told me when I went out to treat a sick cow this afternoon.'

'Nice of him to warn you anyway.'

'Oh no, he wasn't warning me. He was asking for inside information. He'd put a fiver on.' Ben grinned.

'I can't believe the cheek of them.' Summer gave him an

apologetic look. 'This is probably my fault. We were invited for afternoon tea to Lavender House on Sunday, and I might have told them about my visit to Monk's Folly to take you that chocolate. I saw their faces after I'd said it and I knew they'd make more of it than they should.'

'It doesn't matter. They don't know anything for sure, and let's hope we can keep it that way.'

Summer stared at him for a moment, and he wondered what she was thinking, then she opened her menu and began reading it, and a relieved Ben did the same. The ice had been broken and they were off to a good start.

'One large Coke and one Diet Coke with no ice.' The waitress placed the drinks on the table and beamed at them. 'Ready to order, or shall I come back in a few minutes?'

They placed their order—scampi and chips for Ben and chicken supreme for Summer—and the waitress hurried back to the bar with the menus. Ben leaned back in his chair and wondered what to talk to Summer about. He was so out of practice, that was the trouble. What did he know about other than treating sick animals?

'Read any good books lately?'

Had he really just asked her that? He supposed it was because he'd been asking his mum about the library, and it had lodged somewhere in his brain.

She looked a bit taken aback, which wasn't surprising. As chat up lines went it was pretty feeble.

'Not really,' she said. 'It's been a bit hectic these past few months. Clemmie's more of a reader than I am. Sorry.'

Ben held up his hands. 'Oh no, don't apologise! I hardly read at all. In fact, the only books I possess are veterinary textbooks and James Herriot books.'

'James Herriot? *All Creatures Great and Small*?' she asked, smiling.

He grinned. 'That's right. They were the reason I wanted to become a vet.'

She leaned forward, resting her elbows on the table. 'Seriously?'

He nodded, and leaned forward too, his posture mirroring hers. He was on safer ground. 'They really were. I was fifteen when I discovered them, and they changed everything. I couldn't read them fast enough. Have you read them?' he asked hopefully.

'I'm afraid I haven't. I love the programme, though. I'll have to give the books a try. So how did you go from reading James Herriot to becoming an actual vet?'

'It was all down to Clive,' he told her. 'One day, Bean—he was one of our dogs—took ill, and I went to Stepping Stones with Mum for the first time, which is where I met him. He was amazing with Bean. As I watched him work it confirmed for me that it was what I wanted more than anything. While we were there, Mum told him all about my love for Herriot, and how I'd dreamed of being a vet, and instead of laughing or saying something patronising, he took me under his wing. Honestly, I don't know where I'd be now if it hadn't been for him.'

He gazed into the middle distance, remembering. 'He sort of became a second father to me. He helped me through my veterinary studies, and the job was ready and waiting for me when I qualified. I've been so lucky, and I owe him everything.'

'He must think you're worth it,' she said. 'He wouldn't have spent so much time and effort on someone he didn't believe could do the job. It's great to have a career you truly love. How's it going at work now? Any exciting cases?'

'Today? Let me see, what were the highlights? Apart from the sick cow I mentioned, I did a tooth extraction on an elderly lurcher,' he said. 'Removed a lipoma from a rabbit. Oh yes, got mauled by an angry cat who objected violently when I swabbed its infected ear.'

He rolled up his sleeve and showed her the evidence.

'Ouch. Does that happen often?'

'I'm usually quicker at avoiding injury, but for an old cat Winnie was remarkably sprightly. In the main, animals are stoic about illness, but pain and fear are a potent combination, and unlike us they don't have to worry about being polite.'

'I suppose not.' Summer smiled. 'Have you ever been seriously injured by an animal?'

'Not seriously. Had my foot stamped on a few times. Got kicked in the shin by a cow. That was fun. Oh, and a pig knocked me flat on my back when I was training and then loomed over me as if it were mentally sprinkling me with seasoning. That was scary. I'm still nervous around pigs,' he admitted. 'Some of them are huge and they'll eat anything. Vets included.'

Summer's eyes were like saucers. 'Thank God I didn't choose gammon,' she said with feeling, and he laughed.

'What about you?' he asked.

They broke off and sat back as the waitress handed them their meals, and for the next couple of minutes they unfolded napkins and seasoned their food before starting to eat.

Eventually Summer remembered the question. 'What about me?'

Ben shrugged. 'Well, we've talked about my job. What about yours? I know you're mostly voluntary at Whispering Willows, and you top up your income by working at the pub. Is that how you intend to continue? Or will you be looking for full-time work with horses? You seem to have an affinity with them.'

'I love them,' she said. 'And I'd love to work with them full time. Even so, I can't walk away from Whispering Willows. I'm so attached to the place, and to Joseph and Viva, and the horses and ponies and donkeys we have there. I can't imagine leaving. So even though I'd really love a full-time job there, I'll probably volunteer as long as Joseph needs me. He really can't afford to increase my paid hours, so I don't see any other option.'

'That's a shame.'

'Not really.' Summer shrugged. 'You know you said it was your dream to be a vet like James Herriot? Well, my dream was always to live in the countryside and work with horses. That's all I ever wanted. Sometimes, that dream seemed a million miles away. When I lived in Bemborough and worked at the cake factory, I couldn't imagine ever getting away from that life. Yet here I am. Okay, I'm not earning a lot of money, and I spend more time serving drinks than I do feeding horses, but it's worth it. I'm happy. And that counts for a lot, doesn't it?'

'It does,' he said, meaning it. 'Happiness in your job is so important.'

He ate a chip, thinking about his mum and how it would perhaps have been better for her if she'd had a job when Leon and Dad died. It would have given her a focus, something else to think about. And company. Maybe grief never ended, but active mourning should.

'What are you thinking?'

He realised Summer was watching him, a look of curiosity on her face. He was going to make a glib comment but thought suddenly that he didn't want to lie to her or make excuses.

'I was thinking about my mum,' he said.

'Oh.'

'Sorry. It's just—Mum's never had a job. Well, not since she got married. I was thinking it might have been good for her. She ought to get out more, see people.'

Summer seemed to be considering her reply. Ben realised it wasn't great that he'd brought her on a date and had started talking about his mother. He searched around for something else to chat about and something she'd mentioned earlier struck a chord.

'Did you say you'd been invited to Lavender House for afternoon tea?'

Summer spooned up some rice and nodded. 'Yes, but there was an ulterior motive.'

'Naturally.' He smiled, all too aware that, when it came to Miss Lavender, there was always an ulterior motive. 'I wonder what information she was trying to gather from you this time.'

Summer told him about Ethan Rochester, and Ben listened thoughtfully.

'So they're opening an art school?' He prodded at his scampi. 'I wonder where? There's no room at Lavender House, surely? Unless they've got planning permission to build in the grounds. Is it a definite?'

Summer hastily swallowed her rice and shook her head. 'It seems to be just an idea at the moment. Mind you, Clemmie reckons it will happen. She says what Ross wants, Ross gets.' She hesitated. 'She really doesn't like him, you know. What do you think of him?'

Ben thought another change of subject was called for but knew she was waiting for an answer.

'Ross? He's—he's all right.'

Summer tilted her head. 'I heard you and Ross used to be good friends.'

'Oh.' He managed a smile. 'That was ages ago. We were

just kids.'

'What happened?'

'I'm sorry?'

'To break you up. You and Ross.'

He took a sip of Coke. 'We didn't exactly fall out. Just drifted apart. You know what it's like at that age. Teenagers are always like that: finding new mates, moving on.'

She nodded, scooping up some chicken supreme. 'I suppose so. Clemmie's not keen on him anyway.' She smiled fondly. 'She thinks he's a Wickham. You know, a romantic villain. He does seem to play the field a lot, doesn't he? Not a nice man by all accounts, although Mum says he's quite nice when you get talking to him.'

'Ross is okay,' he said. 'People shouldn't judge when they know nothing about it.'

'About what?'

He tried to sound casual. 'I just mean no one knows what's in people's hearts, do they? I don't think you can make assumptions about other people's behaviour because you don't know what's behind it.'

'Testosterone by the look of it,' Summer said. 'You're very loyal considering you and he are no longer friends, which is a good thing, I guess. By the way,' she added suddenly, 'the Lavender Ladies seem to have something against Joseph.'

'Really? What?'

'No idea. It was all a bit weird. I said Joseph deserved a medal for all his kindness to animals and they gave each other very strange looks and changed the subject.'

Ben stared at her. 'What could anyone possibly have against Joseph?'

'Exactly! Whatever it is, it must be a misunderstanding. Or it was the Lavender Ladies' fault. It couldn't possibly be anything Joseph's done.'

Ben smiled, hearing the certainty in her voice. Whatever else Summer was, she was definitely loyal to her friends. It gave him a warm feeling as he thought she was someone he could probably trust with anything. Maybe even his innermost worries. One day.

Summer ate her chicken, then said, 'Jamie and Frankie have really struck up a friendship, haven't they?'

'It's more about having someone to play computer games with, isn't it? Jamie hasn't got any friends nearby. He goes to a public school a few miles away. Most of his school friends are boarders, and they come from all parts of the country, so he doesn't see them in the holidays.'

'Wow, public school.'

'He's incredibly bright,' Ben said, feeling as if he should justify the expense somehow, even though he'd argued against it so many times with his mum. 'His teachers say he's got a brilliant future ahead of him. They think he's got potential to go to Oxford or Cambridge. It would be criminal not to give him every opportunity.'

'It must be expensive, though?'

Ben's spirits sank at the thought of it. 'You could say that. It's given me a few sleepless nights; I can tell you that much.'

'Then why do it? Surely if he's that bright he'd shine just as much at a state school?'

'You sound disapproving.'

Summer shrugged. 'I just think it's wrong that kids from poorer backgrounds, whose parents can't afford to send them to public school, get an inferior education and have far fewer advantages.'

'But sometimes it's about priorities,' he said, aware that he was parroting his mother's side of the conversations they'd had all too frequently. 'Not all parents whose children attend those schools are rich. Look at me! It's surely about deciding where you want to spend your money and making sacrifices for your children's sake?'

Summer gave a sarcastic laugh. 'You are kidding, right? A lot of parents can't afford to give their kids three meals a day, never mind put money aside for a private education. You're living in a dream world if you think it's an option for more than the lucky few.'

Ben knew what she meant, but he didn't feel he could admit he was only paying for Jamie's fees because his mother had begged him to. He'd already mentioned her on their date once. Summer would think he was a complete mummy's boy at this rate.

'Well,' he said defensively, 'Jamie lost his brother and his dad when he was little more than a baby. He has barely any recollection of them, and I think the least he deserves is the best education I can afford. He's been robbed of everything else.'

'Oh, Ben.' Summer placed her hand over his, her eyes warm with sympathy, as if their conversation about public schools had never happened. 'It must have been awful for both of you, and for your poor mum. I'm so sorry.'

Ben felt the warmth of her touch and it was as if the chips of ice that had kept his heart frozen all those years were finally melting. They gazed at each other, forgetting their food was going cold.

Then Ben jumped as a hand suddenly grasped his shoulder.

'Evening, Ben, Summer.'

Startled, they looked up to find Bluebell and her daughters, Buttercup and Clover, grinning knowingly at them.

'Fancy seeing you here,' Bluebell said. 'Sadly, we're just leaving, but before we go, I can heartily recommend the strawberry tart. It's to die for.'

Chapter Ten

'You're being very brave,' Summer observed, as Ben steered the Land Rover into the car park at The White Hart Inn later that evening. 'Aren't you worried someone will see us together?'

He switched off the engine and turned to her, a twinkle of amusement in his eyes. 'I think that's what they call locking the stable door after the horse has bolted.'

'You mean, because Bluebell saw us together?'

'Her, and them.' He nodded over to where a man and woman were strolling towards their car, eyeing them with open interest.

Summer recognised them as regular customers at the pub and knew they'd have realised who she was and who she was with immediately.

'Oh, trust me,' Ben said, a note of resignation in his voice, 'it will be all round Tuppenny Bridge before we've even had breakfast tomorrow.'

'It's not that bad!' She laughed, then narrowed her eyes. 'Is it?'

'Wait and see.' He fumbled in his pocket for his phone as a message alert sounded. 'Sorry, won't be a minute.'

From Mum:

Just got home from The White Hart Inn. Jamie is with me. Hope you and Clive are having a nice evening. I'm going to bed so can you make sure Jamie doesn't stay up too late? Thank you. xxx

To Mum:

I won't be long anyway, but I'll keep an eye on Jamie. xxx

'Anything important?' Summer watched him carefully.

'Just Mum. Nothing to worry about.' He put the phone back in his pocket and smiled at her. 'What were we talking about?'

'I was about to say, I'm not bothered about people knowing, are you?'

Ben hesitated. 'That depends.'

'On what?'

He looked adorably embarrassed, and Summer nudged him. 'Go on, on what?'

'On whether or not you want to go out with me again,' he admitted eventually. 'It would be really humiliating if everyone was talking about our so-called relationship, and you'd already told me this was a one-off experience, never to be repeated.' He eyed her nervously. 'Wouldn't it?'

Summer almost gasped as realisation dawned. So that was why Ben had wanted to keep it quiet! Relief made her take his hand and squeeze it.

'I'd love to see you again. I really enjoyed tonight. That's if you want to see *me* again of course.'

'I do. I did. I mean, I absolutely would. Do. You know what I mean.'

She smiled. 'I know what you mean.'

'Although...' Ben's eyes sparkled with sudden mischief.

'Go on.'

'It might be quite fun if the Lavender Ladies were kept in the dark for a bit. We shouldn't make it too easy for them.'

'But you said they'll know by tomorrow, thanks to Bluebell,' she reminded him.

'They'll know we had one date. But there's no reason to confirm or deny anything is there? It would drive them insane if we kept insisting we were just friends. Friends do go out together after all.'

'Hmm.' She couldn't help it. The nagging worry was back, and she shifted uncomfortably in her seat, not sure whether he was speaking the truth. Was that the real reason he didn't want to confirm they were seeing each other?

'What is it? You think I'm being mean to them?' he asked anxiously.

'No, no. It's not that.' Summer paused but couldn't hold back any longer. 'Ben, can I ask you something?'

'Of course,' he said, squeezing her fingers. 'Anything.'

'Are you seeing someone else?' There, she'd said it, and she waited breathlessly for his response while staring intently at his face, searching for any signs that he might be trying to conceal something from her.

His look of astonishment told her he was being honest with her when he said, 'Someone else? Of course not! Why would you think that?'

'Sorry,' she said, feeling a bit ashamed. 'It's just...'

'Because I wanted to keep this quiet? You think I've got a secret girlfriend?'

To her relief he didn't laugh at her or get annoyed.

'I haven't,' he said simply. 'There's only you, I promise. I just thought we could have a bit of fun with the Lavender Ladies, that's all. Everyone deserves a bit of fun now and then, don't they?'

Summer watched him curiously as a shadow passed over his face. There it was again, that wistful look that she'd noticed on a few occasions now. She wondered what caused that sadness to wash over him at the most unexpected times.

'Of course they do,' she said. 'And I'm sorry I had to ask. It's just—well, I have a hard time trusting men.' She held up her hands. 'I know it's not fair, and you don't have to tell me not all men are like that. I think the problem is I don't trust my judgement. Not any more.'

He unclipped his seat belt and twisted round in his seat to look at her better. 'Because of your dad?' he asked gently.

She hesitated, wondering whether to risk telling him about Ian, but decided it was too soon. Besides, she didn't want to sully their evening together by bringing that man into the conversation.

'Yeah. I trusted him,' she said simply. 'All those years and I had no idea that he'd cheated on my mum repeatedly. And when I found out I just thought, how did I not know? How did he fool me all that time? I lived with him! I thought I knew everything about him.' She shook her head. 'If I couldn't spot the signs with him...'

'But he wasn't cheating on *you*,' Ben pointed out. 'It was your mother he was lying to. I'm sure he was one hundred per cent genuine with you. Besides, why would you be looking for signs of cheating in your dad? Don't be so hard on yourself. I promise you, I'm not like that. And I know, all men probably say that, and I can't really prove it. Only time will do that if you're willing to take a chance.'

There was a distinctly hopeful look in his eyes, and Summer found herself relaxing. It felt good to have finally told someone how she felt and not have them judging her. Something told her Ben would never do that, and maybe, if there was any man she could put her trust in, it was him.

'I'm game if you are,' she said.

'Definitely.'

Her heart skipped a beat as he gazed at her, and they moved a little closer to each other. She was sure he was going to kiss her, convinced she saw desire in his eyes that matched her own. His gaze lingered on her lips, and he leaned forward slightly...

A car door slammed next to them, and they both jumped a little.

Awkwardly, Ben dropped a light kiss on her cheek.

'I'd better get back home,' he said, sitting up straight and fastening his seat belt.

'Yes, me too.' Summer opened the car door. 'I'm happy to wind the Lavender Ladies up,' she told him. 'You're right, it would be fun.'

'Keep them guessing?'

'Absolutely.'

'Sounds good to me.' He gave her a warm smile. 'I won't keep *you* guessing, though, Summer. I promise.'

Her heart lifted and she nodded. 'See you soon, Ben.'

'Very soon.'

She hurried towards The White Hart Inn and turned, watching as he manoeuvred the Land Rover out of the car park and headed back to Monk's Folly.

Hugging herself, a smile on her lips, she opened the back door of the pub and went inside.

* * *

Despite Ben's warning, Summer hadn't really believed that news could travel so fast around Tuppenny Bridge. He wasn't wrong, though. Frankie woke her up the next morning by bouncing on the bed and dragging the duvet off her.

'You kept that quiet! You and Ben? Why didn't you tell me?'

Summer stared at her in disbelief. 'What the heck are you on about?'

She smirked. 'Don't deny it. The postman's been. You two are the talk of the town.'

Struggling to sit up, Summer ran a hand through her tangled hair and groaned. 'What time is it?'

'Eight o'clock. You've really slept in. Tiring evening, was it?' Frankie gave her a knowing wink and Summer tutted impatiently.

'Not the way you mean, it wasn't.'

'Why are you still in bed then?' Frankie asked.

Funnily enough, Summer had slept better the previous night than she had for months.

'Well, why are you up early?' she said. 'You're rarely up before nine these days.'

'Jamie's coming round. We're going to York on the train. Dad says it's okay. Breakfast's ready,' she added, hurrying to the bedroom door. 'You'd better eat it all up. You'll need to keep your strength up.'

'Cheeky mare!'

But Frankie wasn't the only one full of beans about Summer's date with Ben. Sally looked fit to burst with excitement, and even Rafferty was beaming.

'What a morning this is! Billie and Arlo just called. They've landed,' Mum said, dropping a kiss on her cheek.

Billie and Arlo were heading straight from the airport to Norfolk to see Arlo's and Frankie's mum, Elizabeth, after which they were driving up to Bemborough to stay a few days with Summer and Billie's dad, then heading to Tuppenny Bridge for the wedding. Sally had been longing to see them for ages, so it was no wonder she was already excited, without Summer's news stirring her blood even more.

'Then I find out you've been having secret assignations with Ben! Why didn't you tell us?' Sally demanded. 'You never said a word when you got home last night. Jennifer came round while you were out, you know. She brought us a cake and she never breathed a word. She ended up staying ages and watching a film with us. I thought it was funny, her coming here. And there was me thinking you'd been out with Clemmie.'

'Jennifer didn't know either,' Summer said. 'We didn't want the Lavender Ladies to get wind of it. We should have known better really.'

'I'm sure Ben will take care of you,' Rafferty said. 'He's one of the best. Everyone speaks very highly of him.'

'I'm so happy for you, love.' Sally placed a plate of bacon and eggs in front of Summer. 'Ben will make you a good boyfriend you know. He's got his own house after all, and he's a vet, of all things. And it's nice that we get on with his mum and brother. One big happy family.'

'Steady on!' Summer said, remembering hers and Ben's pact to have fun at the Lavender Ladies' expense, and knowing her mum would never be able to keep a secret this important. 'This is why we didn't tell you. You and Jennifer will have us married with kids before we know it.'

'Oh, don't be silly, Summer.' Sally handed her a mug of coffee. 'Although would that be such a bad thing?'

'Mum! It was just a date.'

'All right, all right. When are you seeing him again?'

Awkwardly, Summer prodded at her fried egg with her fork. 'We haven't made any definite arrangements.'

'You should have decided something,' Mum told her.

'Don't let it drift. I'd give him a ring if I were you. Fix the next date up as soon as possible.'

'Don't do it, Summer!' Frankie sounded appalled. 'That would be sad! Have some self-respect.'

'I'm not going to, don't worry. We're not joined at the hip. Like I said, it was one date.'

Anyway, if she didn't get in touch with him, it would give him a chance to miss her. Bloody hell, she was thinking like a fourteen-year-old. What on earth had happened to her?

Chapter Eleven

'All I'm saying is, I don't think it's right that you accept all that from Frankie.' Ben ran a hand through his hair, his voice tight with frustration. 'I'm not saying they're not nice clothes. Of course they are. I mean, look at the price tags! But that's the point, isn't it? She's spent hundreds of pounds on you and she's only a teenager. Can't you see it's not right? Not decent?'

He'd hardly been able to believe his eyes when Jamie returned home laden with shopping bags after a day in York with Frankie, who'd apparently been given a credit card by her doting mother to buy whatever she wanted. Clearly, what she wanted was to turn Jamie into some sort of clothes horse.

'Decent?' Jamie glared at him. 'Do you think it's decent that I haven't had any new clothes for a year? My trousers and jeans are way too short for me, but I don't suppose you've noticed that. Not that you care. As far as you're concerned the only clothing that matters is my bloody school uniform. If

I can hold my head up at school, you don't care about the rest of my life.'

'Stop swearing and don't be ridiculous. There's nothing wrong with your clothes.' A tiny element of doubt crept into Ben's mind. Was there? He had to admit he hadn't really noticed, and Jamie had grown an inch or two this past year. Maybe his younger brother was right. Even so.

'If that's true, all you had to do was come to me and ask me. I'd have bought you some new clothes.'

'From the market? Thanks a lot. And why is it okay to ask you for money, but not take it when it's offered by Frankie?'

'Because you're my brother!' Ben said, exasperated. 'We're family. Frankie's just—'

'Frankie's my friend,' Jamie snapped. 'Probably my best friend. We had a great day in York. Absolutely the best. We shopped; I had my hair cut—'

'I can see that,' Ben said grimly. 'At some swanky salon, no doubt.'

'Better than Cutting It Fine!'

'What's wrong with Cutting It Fine?'

'It's full of women! The salon I went to had proper male stylists, who really knew what they were talking about.'

'And charged an extortionate fee for their expert advice, I expect.'

'I don't know what they charged,' Jamie said sulkily. 'Frankie never told me. What does it matter?'

Ben sank onto the sofa. 'It does matter, Jamie. Do you want people to think we need charity?'

'Maybe,' his mum said thoughtfully, 'we should give him a monthly clothing allowance, so he can buy things for himself whenever he needs.'

Ben stared at her incredulously. 'A clothing allowance?'

'Yes!' Jamie's eyes shone with excitement. 'That would

be great. That way I wouldn't have to pester you every time I needed something and—'

'And where are we going to get the money from to give him this allowance?'

Maybe, Ben acknowledged, his voice had been louder than he'd intended, but he was at the end of his tether. Was his mother living in cloud cuckoo land? Where were they supposed to find any spare money from to give to Jamie? Correction, where was *he* supposed to find it?

She looked flustered. 'Maybe we could cut down on something else?'

'Like what?' There was nothing else to cut down on, unless she intended them to see by candlelight and eat cold baked beans out of a tin every mealtime.

Seeing the despair on Jamie's face he softened. 'Look, maybe I could ask Clive if you could help out at the surgery for a bit of money.'

Jamie eyed him suspiciously. 'Doing what, exactly?'

'I don't know. Maybe you could help Jane with the filing or the paperwork. Do some reception work. Clean out the animal cages...'

He broke off as Jamie screwed up his nose in distaste.

'He can't get a job, Ben,' his mother said anxiously. 'He needs to study. His GCSEs are this year.'

'Huh!'

Jamie swung round and glared at Ben.

'What's that supposed to mean?'

'Well,' Ben said, 'I thought you were going to spend the summer holidays getting ahead with your work. I gave you the biggest bedroom so you could fit your desk and laptop in there, and so far I've seen precious little evidence of you using either of them. It would be different if there was a television and a PlayStation in there instead, I suppose. I wouldn't be able to drag you away. It's an important—'

'Don't!' Jamie held up his hands. 'I don't want to hear how important this year is for me. I'm sick of hearing about bloody school and exams and university. I might not even go to university.'

'Oh, Jamie, don't say such things!'

Ben saw the look of horror on his mother's face and tried to reassure her.

'He doesn't mean it. He's just trying to wind us up.'

'I'm not! I've been thinking about it for weeks. Maybe I'll leave school at sixteen and get a job.'

'For God's sake, I haven't got time for this. I've got to get to work.'

'Lucky you. Hey, you never know, I could be saying the same thing this time next year.' Jamie's tone was taunting, and Ben glared at him.

'You think it's as easy as that? That you'd walk into a job as soon as you left school?'

Jamie shrugged. 'Then I'll do an apprenticeship. Or go to college and get some vocational qualifications.'

'In what?'

'Anything. Who cares? Oh forget it. I'm going to Frankie's for breakfast. We'll go online. Start looking at courses.'

He slammed the door and Ben stared at it for a moment, wondering if he'd been like that at Jamie's age. Well, no, of course not. By Jamie's age he'd had the weight of the world on his shoulders. But at thirteen, fourteen... He had to admit, he'd been worse than Jamie. He'd had a hell of a bad attitude, no interest in school at all, and a fierce dislike of being told what to do.

It was odd how things turned out. If they hadn't lost Leon...

But they had. And everything had changed from that moment.

'You won't let him leave school will you, Ben? It would break your father's heart. He wanted the best for both of you, and after all, you went to university. It's only fair that Jamie gets his chance, too.'

'I know that, Mum. Don't worry.'

She nodded uncertainly and left the room.

Sickened, he rested his head on the back of the sofa and closed his eyes, wishing he could forget, but knowing he never would. And knowing peace of mind was something he'd long since given up on.

* * *

The following day, Ben drove steadily down the drive to Whispering Willows, his heart heavy with sadness. This wasn't going to be an easy callout by any means. Even so, he was glad Joseph had come to his senses and decided enough was enough.

Jonah had only confirmed what Ben had suspected. Chatting on the phone after the previous visit to Whispering Willows, the farrier had told Ben that Shadow was clearly having difficulty lifting his feet and seemed to be in great discomfort.

It was time. Jonah knew it, Ben knew it, and it seemed at last that Joseph knew it, too. Whether Summer had come round to that way of thinking was another matter.

Despite the sadness of his visit, he was undeniably excited to be seeing her again, although he wished it could have been in happier circumstances.

Clive had been thrilled to bits when a client informed him Ben had been on a date with her, although a little put out that Ben hadn't told him the news himself.

'It was just a meal with a friend,' Ben said, remembering the Lavender Ladies and determined Clive wasn't going to let the cat out of the bag.

'Rubbish! You've started the engine now, lad. Got to keep enough pressure on the accelerator or it'll stall. Do you need any money to take her out? I can give you an advance on your wages if you like.'

Ben had refused, knowing an advance might be a short-term solution, but it wouldn't help him on payday at the end of the month when his bank account looked even emptier than usual.

He'd put aside his last few pounds for Sunday when, he'd promised himself, he would spend the day with Jamie. He couldn't really afford it but the relationship between him and his brother was currently so dire that he had to do something about it. Maybe getting away from Monk's Folly and doing something different would make Jamie realise that Ben wasn't his enemy. He could only hope so, though seeing how reluctantly Jamie had agreed to their day together he wasn't convinced.

So with no money to spend on Summer, he'd thought they could go for a walk. Somewhere romantic. That was all they needed. A stroll by the river would be lovely at this time of year...

Joseph's call to the surgery that morning, however, had changed things. He wasn't sure Summer would be in any mood for a romantic walk after what was about to happen.

He chewed his lip as he wondered what her reaction would be. He only hoped she wouldn't cause a scene. He understood how emotional it was, saying goodbye to any animal, but it wouldn't do Shadow any favours, and right now, he was the priority. His comfort and security were paramount.

As Ben parked the Land Rover in the stable yard, Joseph came out from a loosebox, his face lined with sadness.

'Morning, Ben. Sad day.'

'It is indeed. I'm very sorry, Joseph.'

Joseph looked up at the clear blue skies. 'Seems all wrong on a day like this. Should be raining. Feels bad to let him go on such a sunny day.' He sighed. 'Still, I've put it off long enough. I knew it was coming. I should have done something about it sooner, but I didn't want to believe it. I wanted to give him until the weather turned, but this morning—well, he only just managed to get up. It was a real panic situation, and I saw the fear in his eyes, and I thought, no, that's it. Sorry, lad, but there's no point in dragging this out any further. It's not fair to him is it, Ben? I'm right, aren't I?'

'You're absolutely right,' Ben reassured him. 'If it helps, Clive and Jonah agree with you. At some point soon he's going to lie down, or fall, and be unable to get up. Best to act now before it's too late. He's in pain and suffering, and any delay would only be cruel.'

'He's in here. I brought him in, away from the other horses. They're all turned out, bless them.' Joseph looked pale.

'I'm sorry to ask, but I'll need to see his papers and you'll need to sign a consent form.'

'That's all right. I know all about it. Not my first, is he?'

'No,' Ben said sadly. 'He's not. But what you do here, Joseph, is amazing, and so worthwhile. You give second chances and happy lives to horses that wouldn't otherwise have had one. You should be proud of yourself.'

He stared into the loosebox, a sigh escaping his lips as he saw Shadow standing there, his eyes dull with misery.

'No Summer?' he asked, seeing no one was with the old horse.

Joseph gave him a guilty look. 'Thought it best she wasn't here. She's not ready to say goodbye to him.'

Ben looked at him in alarm. 'But she does know?'

Joseph rubbed his chin. 'I'll deal with that when I next see her. She can't do anything about it, so why put her through it? Best to tell her when it's over and done with.'

'But she might want to say goodbye!' Ben thought Joseph was making a mistake, although he understood his reasoning. Even so, Summer would be heartbroken when she arrived at Whispering Willows and found Shadow already gone. 'Honestly, Joseph, I think you should reconsider. It's not fair on her. She'll be devastated.'

'She'll be devastated either way. Sometimes you have to make tough decisions,' Joseph said simply. 'This is mine.'

Ben could hardly argue with that. Joseph was the owner, and Ben had to abide by his wishes, however much he'd like to refuse.

Paperwork done, they faced up to the task ahead. Joseph had asked that Shadow be euthanised by injection.

'I don't want the other horses to hear the gun,' he said. 'And they will, and they'll know. Bad enough as it is. Besides, guns always remind me of my father. Injection's calmer, kinder somehow. I know it's more expensive but...'

'And you've arranged for disposal afterwards?'

'Yes. A chap from the equine crematorium up at Ravensbridge is coming for him. It'll be a group cremation. Cheaper, and what do I need his ashes for? I've got his last horseshoe and I'll add that to the collection. Besides, he'll always be in here.' He tapped his chest, roughly where his heart was. 'They all are.'

Ben nodded. 'I'm sure they are. Did you want to stay with him, or—'

'I'll stay. Least I can do.'

'Just be careful. We don't know which way he'll fall, and you'll need to get out of the way in time.'

'Like I said, Ben. He's not the first.'

If Shadow knew what was about to happen, he gave no sign of it. Or maybe, Ben thought, he was in such pain that he no longer cared. He gently rubbed the horse's muzzle and told him what a good lad he was, while Joseph murmured a goodbye into Shadow's ear and thanked him for being such a wonderful friend and companion.

The sedative was administered, and then the lethal injection was given. Shadow gradually collapsed and lay there, issuing a couple of gasps. Ben reassured Joseph that this was simply a reaction to the anaesthetic drugs, and he wasn't suffering, even though he realised Joseph had probably heard it all before.

Joseph sat beside Shadow, stroking his face as Ben monitored the horse's pulse. Eventually it was over, and Shadow was gone.

Ben helped Joseph to his feet and they both looked down at the beautiful, white horse.

'Looks peaceful, doesn't he?' Joseph murmured. 'No more pain or suffering now, lad. Gallop free.'

He patted Ben's arm. 'Thanks for that, Ben. I know it never gets any easier. Would you like a cup of tea?'

Ben hesitated but realised Joseph could probably do with some company. 'I'll follow you in,' he said. 'I'll just sort everything out in here.'

Joseph nodded, gave Shadow one last, sad glance, and

headed into the house. By the time Ben joined him he was sitting at the table, cradling a mug of tea, and Ben sat beside him.

They sipped tea in silence, each lost in their own thoughts. Ben thought he'd never get used to this part of the job, though at least Shadow's death had been peaceful. He'd had to euthanise a horse after a terrible accident once, and that had been far from peaceful. He was glad Shadow had slipped away with his owner by his side, at the home he'd loved.

'I'd better be going,' he said at last, getting to his feet. 'Are you sure you don't want me to wait for the collection with you?'

'No, it's all right, Ben. I know you've got plenty to be getting on with.'

'And you'll not forget to send his passport in?'

'I'll not forget.' Joseph smiled. 'Thanks for your help, but you can stop worrying now. It's up to me from here on in.'

Ben nodded and they headed out of the back door. Ben stopped in his tracks and his heart thumped with alarm.

'Oh no,' Joseph muttered behind him. 'That's all we need.'

Summer was staring at them, and judging by the tears streaming down her face, she'd already seen for herself what they'd done.

'You didn't tell me?' She shook her head, as if unable to believe they could be so cruel.

Ben glanced round at Joseph who held up his hands in a defensive gesture. 'I'm sorry, Summer, I really am. But I thought you'd be better off not knowing, lass. It's not something anyone should have to see, and me and Ben, we dealt with it.'

'But I never got to say goodbye!' Summer's voice came

out in sobs. She turned to Ben, and the pain in her eyes nearly broke him. 'How could you do that to me? You know how much I loved him. Why couldn't you have waited for the winter? I thought we agreed!'

'It wasn't fair on him,' Ben said. 'I know it's hard to accept, Summer, but he was suffering, and—'

'You should have given him injections! Or more of that bute stuff. There was no need to kill him! You could have given him more time if you'd just tried.'

Ben sighed. 'And whose benefit would that have been for? Not Shadow's. He was in pain. Every day was a struggle. You don't believe me? Ask Clive. Ask Jonah. They'll tell you the same thing.'

'It couldn't have waited until the end of summer?'

'No, Summer, it couldn't.' Ben straightened and faced her squarely. 'Please believe me. It's my job to do all I can to make sure animals don't suffer. Shadow *was* suffering, but he isn't any more. Surely, that's what matters? I know it's hard to accept, but when you take responsibility for any animal, you have to be prepared to make harsh decisions. I'm sorry you feel I let him down, but I promise you, both Joseph and I acted out of compassion, and in his best interests.'

'You should have told me! I should have been here!'

He couldn't argue with that. She was right. She should have been.

He moved towards her, but she stepped back, and he realised she was in no mood for any conciliatory gestures right now, and that if he stayed he would only make things worse. She needed time to come to terms with it all, and he understood that.

'I'll get off. You're sure you can manage?' he asked Joseph quietly.

'Oh yes,' Joseph said, nodding calmly. 'There'll be a few

tears and maybe a tantrum or two, but I can handle it. She's going to have to get used to this sort of thing if she wants to work with horses. Simple as.'

They shook hands and Ben walked over to the Land Rover, giving Summer a sympathetic look as he passed her. She didn't even look at him, too caught up in her grief, he thought sadly.

He started the engine and turned the car. As he drove slowly down the driveway, he glanced in his rear-view mirror and saw Summer, clearly sobbing, in the stable yard. Joseph put his arms round her, and, to Ben's relief, she didn't pull away but allowed herself to be held and comforted.

Ben wished he could have been the one to hold and comfort her, but he supposed as long as she was getting hugs from someone it really didn't matter who. He just hoped she wouldn't see him as the bad guy in all this for long.

Chapter Twelve

The noise in the flat above The White Hart Inn on Thursday was so loud that Summer thought the customers in the pub downstairs would be complaining.

Even so, she couldn't blame anyone in the room for that. She'd done a fair bit of shrieking herself when the door opened, and Rafferty led Billie and Arlo in.

As for her mother...

Summer watched, smiling, as her mum hugged Billie as if she'd never let her go. Had it really only been eighteen months or so since they'd said goodbye? In some ways it seemed like a lifetime ago, so much had changed.

'Summer!'

Billie finally managed to untangle herself from their mother's grasp and hurried over to hug her sister.

'Look at you! You're looking fabulous,' Summer told her, meaning it. 'Have you had work done? You look younger!'

Billie grinned. 'How cheeky are you? Are you saying I looked old before?'

'You looked permanently knackered,' Summer teased. 'Working in Australia obviously suits you.'

'It does,' Billie nodded. 'We're better looked after there, and there's nowhere near as much pressure. We definitely made the right decision.'

'Finally,' Arlo said, giving his wife a knowing look. 'Took you long enough to make it.'

'Oh, give over,' Billie said, laughing.

Billie couldn't deny she'd had a wobble, though, because they'd all witnessed it. Right at the last minute, just days before they'd been due to fly to Australia, Billie had had a meltdown, deciding she wanted to stay in the UK after all.

Arlo had been very patient and understanding about it all, even though he was devastated, and had promised to support his wife no matter what she chose to do.

Luckily for him she'd come through the crisis of confidence and their plans had gone ahead. Looking at them now, Summer had to agree that it had been the best thing for them. Nursing in Australia was obviously a lot less stressful.

'You do look well, Billie,' Mum said. 'And you, Arlo, obviously.'

'Obviously.' Arlo ruffled Frankie's hair, causing her to pull a face and pat her head, making sure her space buns were still intact. 'What the heck's happened to you? I barely recognise you.'

'It's called growing up,' Frankie said. 'You should try it.'

Even so, there was affection in her voice and a sparkle in her eyes. She adored her big brother and had no doubt missed him a lot. She'd admitted to Summer that she wished it had been Ellis who emigrated, rather than Arlo.

Billie caught Summer's eye but quickly reassured Frankie that she looked amazing.

'I don't know. We go away for a year and a half and when we come back you're a young woman.'

'Have you eaten? Are you hungry?'

There was Sally in full maternal mode again. It was as if they'd never been away.

Billie and Arlo agreed they were starving, so Rafferty announced he'd make something to eat for everyone while Sally showed them to their room. Actually, it was Summer's room, but she'd generously given it up while they were staying.

The White Hart Inn had four bedrooms: two doubles and two singles. When Sally and Rafferty first moved in, they'd had a double room each. Since getting together, they shared Rafferty's old room, and Summer had taken Sally's room when she moved in last January.

For now, she was in one of the single rooms that overlooked the village green, next to the other single room occupied by Frankie.

'Oh, it was no trouble at all,' she told Billie, when her sister thanked her for giving up the room. She grinned cheekily. 'How long are you staying again?'

Billie and Arlo were, in fact, staying until a couple of days after the wedding before flying home to Australia. They approved of their room, and after Arlo left them to it, Billie, Summer, and their mum hugged again, delighted to be together after such a long time apart.

'Hey,' Billie said at last, 'what's happened to Frankie? What's with the blue hair and the nose stud? I feel quite sad looking at her. They grow up so quickly, don't they?'

'Listen to you, sounding like an old woman!' Summer said, laughing. 'Can't you remember what it feels like to be fourteen?'

'Not really,' Billie admitted. 'A lot of water's gone under the bridge since then.'

'She's not really different underneath the new look,' Sally said. 'And she's promised to lose the space buns for the wedding, so that's something.'

'I can't wait for the big day. I'm so happy for you, Mum, I really am,' Billie said. 'Rafferty's a lovely man, and you deserve someone like him. Mind you, he's lucky to have you, too.'

'And are you sure Arlo doesn't mind?' Mum asked.

Billie laughed. 'What, about you two getting married? Are you kidding? He's over the moon. He thinks you'll make his dad really happy, and he's not wrong, if you ask me.' She raised an eyebrow at Summer. 'What about you? Any boyfriend on the horizon yet?'

'Ooh, hasn't she told you?' Sally clapped her hands, thrilled to be able to share the news. 'She's going out with someone!'

Billie's eyes widened. 'Seriously? Who's this then? Tell me more.'

'His name's Ben,' Sally said, as Summer inwardly groaned. 'He's a—'

'Good friend,' Summer said. 'We had one meal at a restaurant and that's all there is to it.'

'Hmm. Where have I heard that before?' Billie jerked her thumb in their mother's direction, clearly remembering how she and Rafferty had insisted they were just good friends for what felt like forever. 'Must run in the family.'

Summer rolled her eyes and headed into the hallway, but not before she heard her mother say, 'Take no notice of her, love. She's smitten with him; you mark my words. He's ever so nice, if a bit shy. He's a vet, you know...'

* * *

Summer spent a few hours that afternoon giving Billie and Arlo a brief tour of Tuppenny Bridge. They were both impressed, agreeing with her that the little market town was like something off a jigsaw puzzle or a chocolate box. Summer couldn't help but feel proud of the place and thought Australia surely couldn't hold a candle to it.

Billie had shown the most excitement when she spotted Millican's Fish and Chip Shop, so their mum had decided that tonight's tea would be fish and chips for everyone, and Summer headed out at six o'clock to get it.

As she headed back towards The White Hart Inn, parcel of food in her arms, her heart did a jig and her face began to burn as she spotted Ben walking towards her. She thought maybe he hadn't noticed her, and for a moment she considered ducking into a nearby shop to avoid him and save them both the embarrassment but realised all the shops had closed for the evening.

To her surprise and discomfort he headed straight for her. At least he was smiling.

'I went to the pub, but your mum told me you'd gone to Millican's,' he said.

Summer tried to sound casual. 'Yep, fish and chips all round. Billie and Arlo are here, all the way from good old Oz, so you can imagine they're craving these. I don't know if they have fish and chip shops in Australia, but even if they do I shouldn't think they can hold a candle to Millican's, and anyway, I don't imagine they have haddock there, although I'm not really sure...' She shut up, realising she was babbling, and that Ben was eyeing her steadily.

She sighed. 'Ben, I'm sorry. I really am. I meant to call you, but with Billie and Arlo arriving it's been one thing after the other. I need to apologise for the way I spoke to you when we were at Whispering Willows...'

He raised an eyebrow. 'That doesn't matter.'

'Of course it matters! Joseph told me what really happened. How it was you who wanted to call me and how he wouldn't let you. I'm sorry. I should never have had a go at you.'

'You were upset,' he said gently. 'Honestly, it doesn't matter. Think no more about it.'

She looked up at him, hardly able to believe how well he was taking it. 'Really?'

'Of course. And just to show you there are no hard feelings I have a present for you.' He dug into his jacket pocket and grinned as he handed her a bar of chocolate.

'Carroll's Premium Milk Chocolate!' Summer laughed, partly, it had to be said, out of relief that he wasn't holding a grudge. 'My favourite!'

'So I heard,' he said. 'Are we good?'

'Oh, Ben, of course we are! And not,' she added hastily, 'because of the chocolate.' She hesitated, wondering if she had the nerve to ask him, but ploughed on deciding nothing ventured nothing gained, and he could say no if he wanted to.

'It's Rafferty's stag night tomorrow,' she said. 'I was wondering—'

'No,' he said. 'I'm not going. I was invited, but it's not really my thing.'

'That never occurred to me,' she admitted sheepishly. 'What I was going to say was, Jonah's asked me if I wouldn't mind babysitting Tommy for him. I thought maybe you'd like to come round? He'll be in bed,' she added quickly, in case he shied away from spending an evening with a six-year-old boy.

'He won't be any trouble. Well, Jonah says he won't be, anyway.'

Ben hesitated and her heart sank.

'I've got some webinars to watch for my CPD,' he said. 'Various health issues in the horse. I should have watched them ages ago, but I've been putting it off. I swore I'd get them done this week and I'm spending the day with Jamie on Sunday. I'm on call tonight so that would only leave Saturday if I helped you babysit.'

'Oh, right. What's CPD?'

'Continuous Professional Development. We're obliged by law to put in thirty-five hours a year. We do online courses and take webinars, usually in term time, but I purchased these webinars to watch at any time and I really need...' He rolled his eyes, then laughed. 'What am I saying? Honestly, what an idiot! I'd love to.'

'Really?' She beamed. 'Seven thirty at Forge Cottage, even if you can only stay a couple of hours it's better than nothing, isn't it? You can meet me there if you like.' She gave him a knowing look. 'We can sneak you in after Jonah's gone. That will fool the Lavender Ladies.'

'That wouldn't be fair on Jonah. He needs to know I'm there. But don't worry,' he added. 'I know Jonah, and he's definitely not one for gossip. If I tell him not to mention it to anyone he won't, believe me.' He laughed. 'We'll still have to be a bit sneaky though, what with the Pennyfeathers living down Forge Lane. Those net curtains will be twitching like crazy.'

She tapped the side of her nose. 'Top secret mission. So... It's a date then?'

'It's a date.'

She smiled. 'I'd better get back,' she said, nodding at the parcel of fish and chips in her arms. 'They'll be cold.'

'Nothing worse than cold fish and chips is there? See you tomorrow, Summer,' he said with a wink. 'Enjoy the chocolate!'

As she headed back towards The White Hart Inn, she couldn't imagine managing even a mouthful of the chocolate, let alone the fish and chips. She was so happy she could burst. Who could possibly eat at a time like this?

Chapter Thirteen

Jonah Brewster lived in the beautiful Forge Cottage down Forge Lane, which lay between the church and All Hallows' Vicarage. Like many farriers these days, he mainly worked from a van rather than the old forge attached to his cottage, and travelled around quite a bit as the catchment area for his services was large. Forge Cottage had once been two cottages, but they had been knocked through many years ago, making his home larger and more comfortable than most of the other properties down Forge Lane.

Just over a year ago his ex-wife had died unexpectedly, and Jonah had found himself with guardianship of her little boy, Tommy, who he'd adopted while the couple had been married.

Summer admitted that she didn't know Jonah very well, although she'd talked to him a little when he visited Whispering Willows. Apparently, it had been Kat who'd recommended her to him as a capable babysitter. Ben knew him quite well, though, and Jonah raised no objections when he arrived at Forge Cottage on foot and explained that he'd be babysitting with Summer, if that was all right.

'I'm only staying a couple of hours,' he said. 'But we'd really appreciate it if you didn't mention this to anyone. You know what it's like around here and we don't want the Lavender Ladies making more of it than it is.'

Jonah, a tall, muscular man with dark hair and blue-grey eyes, grinned. 'Say no more. I won't breathe a word. I wondered why you hadn't turned up in the Land Rover. Thanks so much, both of you, for looking after Tommy for me. I won't be late, and he should sleep through. He's pretty good once I've tucked him in and read him a story. I never hear a peep from him until the morning.'

He gave them his phone number for emergencies, despite Ben's reminder that he already had it, and was clearly anxious about leaving the little boy.

'If he does wake up—'

'If he does we'll deal with it,' Ben said firmly. 'Go on. Stop worrying and enjoy yourself.'

Jonah nodded. 'Thanks. See you about ten thirty.'

When he'd finally gone Ben and Summer looked at each other and laughed.

'I take it he's not used to leaving Tommy at home,' Summer said.

'Full-time parenthood kind of got foisted on him,' Ben said ruefully. 'He takes his responsibilities very seriously.'

He had every sympathy for Jonah. Sometimes he felt as if fatherhood had been foisted on him, too. He'd only been sixteen when his dad died, and it seemed as if he'd been taking care of Jamie ever since. Not to mention his mother.

'Coffee?' Summer asked. 'And I think Jonah said there were biscuits if you're hungry.'

'Coffee would be great. I'll leave the biscuits for now.'

He went into the living room, and within a few minutes Summer joined him, carrying two mugs of coffee.

They settled themselves on the sofa and looked at each other, suddenly awkward.

'Would you like to watch something on the television?' Ben asked.

Summer shrugged. 'I'm not sure what's on, but okay. As long as we keep the volume low.'

He looked around for the remote control then pressed a button, wincing as the television blared out loud enough to wake the residents of the churchyard at the end of the lane, never mind Tommy.

'Why are adverts always so much louder than the programmes?' he wondered aloud as he jabbed at the volume button. Nervously he sipped his coffee, wishing he hadn't because it was far too hot. He put the mug on the floor and leaned back, wondering what they were going to talk about.

'How's your mum?' Summer asked politely.

Ben blew out his cheeks. *Stubborn, blind, cruel...*

He wondered where that thought had come from. Yes, she was stubborn, and totally oblivious to how low he was feeling, but cruel?

Surely, he thought desperately, she must see how soul-destroying it was for him to work so hard just to keep Jamie in school and stop Monk's Folly from falling down around their ears? No one could be that blind. And if she did see it, how could she be anything but cruel? If her happiness and Jamie's future mattered more to her than Ben's...

And there it was again. The dark shadow that haunted him. How could he blame her for putting herself and Jamie before him? Everything that had happened to them was down to him. It was, after all, his fault that Leon had died.

'Ben?'

He blinked, realising he hadn't replied to her question. 'She's fine,' he said briefly. 'Same as always.'

'Is she definitely going to Mum's hen night tomorrow night?' Summer asked eagerly. 'Mum's looking forward to seeing her.'

'I hope so. She hasn't said anything about changing her mind.'

Conversation died and they looked at each other.

Ben pulled a face. 'Sorry. Now that we're alone together I haven't the faintest idea what to say.'

'Well...' Summer blushed, looking prettier than ever. 'Maybe talking's overrated anyway.'

The look in her eyes told him she wasn't suggesting they played Scrabble. Ben's stomach contracted with sudden longing, and he leaned towards her, closing his eyes as he moved in for their first kiss.

She gave a squeal, and he leapt back in horror, wondering if he'd misread the signals. He was so out of practice, that was the trouble, and if he'd offended her...

Summer was staring at her jeans in dismay. 'I forgot about the mug of coffee!'

He realised that she'd moved towards him, too, oblivious to the fact that she'd had a mug balancing on her knee at the time. The liquid had soaked into her jeans and, more worrying, had also dripped onto Jonah's cream carpet.

'I'll get a cloth,' he said and hurried into the kitchen.

'You'll need more than that,' Summer called after him. 'Gran told me how to clean up coffee once. You need to blot it until hardly any coffee comes off on the cloth then make a mixture with a little bit of washing up liquid and white vinegar in warm water.'

'I'll see if Jonah's got white vinegar,' Ben said.

With Summer's help he sorted the mixture and under

her direction he applied it a bit of a time, making sure he blotted it frequently with a dry cloth until the stain had thankfully gone.

As he finished off by sponging it with cold water and blotted it dry for the final time, Summer sponged down her jeans. Ben gave her a sideways glance and resisted the urge to tell her to take them off to dry.

'Is it okay? Do you think it will stain?' Summer asked anxiously as she gazed down at the carpet.

'It should be okay,' he reassured her. 'Thank goodness for your gran.'

'Hmm. Not many people say those words,' she said laughing. Then she wrinkled her nose. 'That's taken us fifteen minutes. I'm so sorry. Trust me.'

Her face was scarlet with embarrassment as he shook his head. 'It doesn't matter. No harm done.'

'Except—well, it couldn't have happened at a worse time, could it?'

Ben couldn't help but agree, although he naturally didn't say so out loud.

'Still,' she said hopefully. 'It's sorted now, right?'

'Right,' he said softly, and stepped towards her, stroking away a strand of hair that had fallen in front of her face. His stomach was doing the most peculiar things, and his throat tightened with longing as he gazed into her green eyes.

'Daddy!'

Ben couldn't believe it as Tommy's voice, which, at that moment, seemed louder than an air raid siren, wailed down the stairs pulling them apart yet again.

'He's awake?' Summer's incredulous tone told him she couldn't believe it either. 'I thought Jonah said he never woke up!'

'He did say that,' Ben agreed. 'We don't seem to be having much luck tonight, do we?'

'Daddy!'

'Oh, poor little mite sounds scared,' Summer said. 'I'd better go and see to him.'

She ran upstairs and Ben shook his head, wondering if fate was having a laugh at his expense. He collected the empty mugs, the bowl of water, and the cloths and carried them into the kitchen, pouring the water away and rinsing the cloths out in the sink. He briefly considered making them another coffee, but then decided that would be a distraction. As soon as Summer came back downstairs he didn't want bloody beverages getting in the way of their kiss. Because he *was* going to kiss her. He'd made up his mind about that.

Heading back into the living room he dropped onto the sofa and waited. After a few minutes he increased the volume on the television a little and gazed at the screen, watching the antics of the residents of *Coronation Street* without having the first idea what they were talking about or what was going on.

After a few minutes he wondered if he should go upstairs and see if everything was okay. Summer seemed to be taking a long time settling Tommy down.

It crossed his mind that maybe she was staying up there deliberately. Was she avoiding his kiss? Maybe she'd changed her mind. Maybe he'd got it all wrong. Maybe he ought to make another coffee after all.

The door opened and she walked in, and Ben sat up straight as he saw she was carrying Tommy in her arms.

'He had a nightmare,' she said softly. 'He was quite upset, bless him.'

Ben gazed at the little boy in red and white pyjamas, his

face tear streaked as he clung to Summer with one arm, a teddy bear clutched tightly in the other. His heart melted.

'Oh, poor little thing. Come on, Tommy. Come and sit here next to me.'

Summer put him down on the sofa and sat on the other side of him.

'Where's Daddy?' Tommy asked, wiping his face, and staring up at Ben with large brown eyes.

'He's just gone out to see his friends,' Ben explained. 'But it's okay because I'm looking after you with Summer. You know me, right?'

'You're the horse doctor,' Tommy said.

Ben smiled. 'That's right. I'm Ben, the horse doctor. And this is my friend, Summer. She works with horses, too. Do you like horses, Tommy?'

'I like donkeys better,' Tommy admitted. 'I had a ride on a donkey at the seaside. She was called Josie and she was grey.' He grinned suddenly. 'She pinched my ice cream.'

Ben and Summer laughed.

'That's donkeys for you,' Summer said. 'We've got donkeys at Whispering Willows. You'll have to ask your daddy to bring you one day, and I'll introduce you to them. Best not bring an ice cream, though.'

Tommy shook his head, eyes wide. 'No way! They're not having my ice cream! Donkeys are naughty. I still like them, though.' He hesitated. 'Can I have a biscuit?'

'Well...' Summer looked at Ben who raised an eyebrow.

Jonah hadn't said anything about giving Tommy snacks if he woke up. Then again, he hadn't specifically said not to, and surely one biscuit wouldn't hurt?

One cup of hot chocolate, three biscuits, and a whole string of episodes of *Paddington* on Netflix later, Tommy was finally asleep. Ben carried him upstairs and laid him carefully in bed, hardly daring to breathe as he tiptoed out of the bedroom and closed the door as quietly as he could manage behind him.

'I can't believe he's finally gone to sleep!' Summer sounded worn out. 'Shame in a way. I was just starting to enjoy *Paddington*.'

Ben laughed. 'I loved the films. Don't tell anyone, though. It would ruin my street cred.'

'You were really good with Tommy,' she said, a note of admiration in her voice. 'So patient and kind. It was lovely to see you with him.'

Ben shrugged, embarrassed. 'I was just trying to make him feel safe,' he said. 'He doesn't know me that well, and he doesn't know you at all, so it must have been scary for him.'

'It was a stroke of genius, finding *Paddington* on Netflix,' Summer told him. 'I wouldn't have had a clue. I suppose it's because you kind of act like a parent to Jamie, don't you? You must be the best big brother ever.'

Ben hardly knew where to start with that. She couldn't be more wrong if she'd tried.

'I mess up with Jamie all the time,' he admitted. 'We used to be closer, but—I don't know. Lately we seem to be growing apart. I try to make conversation with him, try to spend time with him when I can. He doesn't want to know. He's changed a lot over the last few months. It's all about wanting things we can't afford, and he's become obsessed with social media for some reason. Honestly, sometimes I think he hates me.'

'I'm sure he doesn't,' she added reassuringly, 'I'll bet he appreciates everything you do for him really.'

'I think Leon would have done it so much better,' Ben said wistfully. He started, aware that he'd brought his older brother up without prompting, something he never did.

148

He really wished he hadn't when Summer made herself more comfortable on the sofa and said eagerly, 'Tell me about him. I'd love to hear what he was like.'

Ben swallowed. 'He—he was a good man. Everyone loved him.'

His brother's image flashed before his eyes. Responsible, kind, thoughtful Leon. He'd turned down the opportunity to go to university, deciding instead to go straight into the world of work. Their father had been a technical brewer at the Lusty Tup brewery a few miles away, and the company—a successful independent brewery with an excellent reputation—had taken Leon on as a production assistant.

Leon was bright, hardworking, and capable, and had every intention of working his way up to a senior position at Lusty Tup. Their father had been delighted when he chose to make brewing his profession too and looked forward to many years of working alongside his son.

Ben had drunk Lusty Tup ale a few times, but to him it tasted bitter. He knew that had nothing to do with the brewery, or the quality of the beer. It was the memories attached to it that made the famous local ale, for him, undrinkable.

'Did he look like you? Or Jamie?'

Ben considered. 'More like Jamie. They both took after Dad in appearance. Darker hair and eyes. I'm more like Mum, I guess.'

Summer's eyes crinkled with sympathy. 'It must have been awful when you lost him. How old was he when he died?'

His heart thudded. 'Twenty-two. He had everything going for him. Friends, a promising career at the Lusty Tup Brewery, a girlfriend...' He shrugged. 'He was going out with Kat. You know, Katherine Pennyfeather?'

'He was?' Summer shook her head. 'I had no idea. Poor Kat.'

'It should never have happened,' he said bitterly. 'It was a clear, mild night. There was no reason for him to crash the car. There were no other vehicles involved. It was so unfair.'

Summer took his hand. 'I'm sorry. I never meant to upset you.'

'It's not your fault.' Far from it. The only person to blame for this whole mess was himself. He knew it, his mother knew it, maybe even Jamie knew it. It terrified him that, maybe one day, Summer would have to know it too.

How would she feel about him then? Would she still think he was a wonderful brother? Somehow he doubted it, and he couldn't imagine she'd think he was boyfriend material either.

'Well,' she said softly, 'at least your mum and Jamie had you to rely on. You've had so much to carry over the years, Ben. I think you're amazing, I really do.'

'Oh, Summer...' Ben shook his head, wishing he could tell her how wrong she really was, but as she gazed at him with those stunning green eyes that were brimming with compassion, he found himself wanting to believe her.

He had to remind himself to breathe as she moved closer to him and put her hand to the side of his face. His own hand covered hers and he leaned in, closing his eyes.

The front door opened, and they heard voices in the hall. Ben's eyes flew open, and Summer hurriedly dropped her hand and settled herself on the sofa as if she'd been watching television.

Jonah walked into the room, followed by Rafferty.

'What are you doing here?' Summer asked, clearly surprised to see her future stepfather.

'I came to walk you home,' he explained. 'Sorry, I didn't realise you had Ben here...'

'You're early,' she said, glancing at the clock on the mantelpiece. 'It's only just ten.'

Rafferty and Jonah exchanged amused looks.

'We weren't exactly out on the town,' Rafferty pointed out. 'It was just a drink at The Black Swan and a quiet meal at the Indian restaurant in Torsbeck.' He nodded at Ben, the hint of a smile on his face. 'I can highly recommend it, if you're ever looking for a decent place to eat.'

Summer gave Ben an apologetic look. 'I'd better...'

'It's okay,' he said. 'You get off home with Rafferty. I'll fill Jonah in on tonight.'

She looked reluctant. 'Are you sure?'

'Absolutely.' He gave her a bright smile. 'I'll see you soon, okay?'

She nodded and got to her feet. Rafferty gave Ben a sheepish smile as they headed to the door, followed by Jonah. Ben heard Summer insisting she didn't want paying, and Jonah insisting she take the money, then the door opened and closed, and Jonah headed back into the living room.

'Sorry, mate,' he said. 'Rafferty wanted to walk her home and you asked me not to mention that you were here. Besides, you told me you were only staying a couple of hours, so I thought you'd be gone by now.'

'It didn't quite go according to plan,' Ben admitted.

Briefly, he explained about Tommy's nightmare, apologising for the biscuits and the hot chocolate.

Jonah sighed. 'Typical. He never wakes up usually. Don't worry about the snacks. It won't hurt him this once.' He glanced at the television. 'I see he had you wrapped around his little finger. How many episodes did you have to sit through?'

'Of *Paddington*?' Ben grinned. 'Too many. Although to be honest, they got quite addictive in the end.'

'I know! I won't tell if you don't.' Jonah raised an eyebrow. 'Not the evening you had planned, I guess.'

'Not really.' Ben shrugged.

'Never mind. There's always the next time.' Jonah patted him on the shoulder. 'Let's have a nightcap, eh, and you can tell me all about this secret relationship with the lovely Summer Fletcher.'

* * *

'Are you sure this is all you wanted from a hen night, Sal?' Kat's forehead creased with worry as she wandered into the kitchen at The White Hart Inn. 'It doesn't seem like a great way to celebrate, being stuck in your own home. Honestly, you and Rafferty make a right pair, what with his stag night being nothing more than a meal at The Spirit of India.'

'It's no use, Kat,' Billie said. 'I told her we should be going on a mega pub crawl, but she's just not interested. This is the best we're going to get so you may as well give it up.'

'Oh, well, fair enough.' Kat poured herself a glass of fruit juice and tilted it in Sally's direction in a silent toast. 'It doesn't bother me anyway. I've only hired the babysitter until ten and I can't drink alcohol thanks to breastfeeding, which is—'

She broke off at a knock on the door, and within ten minutes the flat was a hive of activity as Dolly, Clemmie, Bluebell, and Ava, the vicar's wife, arrived. Frankie took one look at the heaving mass of chattering women and escaped to her bedroom, taking a bottle of Coke and a plate of food with her.

'Bloody hell. No one told me Miss Marple was coming,'

Dolly said to Summer in dismay as Miss Lavender arrived with Isobel, the wife of her great-nephew and Ross's older brother, Noah. 'We'll have to be on our best behaviour now. She'll be on the prowl all evening, listening out for the gossip. Just watch what you say if there's anything you'd rather she didn't know. Thank God the Pennyfeathers aren't here too.'

Famous last words. Just five minutes later, there they were, resplendent in matching yellow dresses and their trademark gaudy crocheted waistcoats. Birdie had a green butterfly hair slide in her hair, while Rita wore a bright pink hairband. They certainly stood out from the crowd, and Summer saw the stunned expression on Billie's face as she was introduced to them.

'We're so excited to be here,' Birdie told Mum. 'Thanks so much for inviting us. It was a real surprise.'

'You're not kidding,' Dolly said, rolling her eyes. She turned to Sally. 'So what's on the agenda tonight, love?'

'The usual hen night antics.' Kat caught her Aunt Birdie's eye and said sheepishly, 'Having a nice chat with friends. Lovely food.'

'I don't know what hen nights you've been to,' Dolly told her. 'Personally, I don't think you can call it a success until the bride's been given a lap dance by some hunky bit of stuff in a fireman's outfit.'

'Well, honestly,' Isobel said. 'You certainly weren't at my hen night.'

'As I recall, I wasn't invited,' Dolly pointed out.

'No.' Isobel gave her a prim smile. 'You weren't.'

'There's plenty to eat in the kitchen,' Sally said, clearly alarmed that hostilities were about to break out. 'Feel free to help yourselves. Now, who wants their glass topping up?'

A couple of hours later and everyone was a lot more

friendly, but Summer realised Jennifer hadn't turned up after all.

Even as the thought crossed her mind Kat said sadly, 'What a shame Jennifer didn't come.'

'She doesn't know what she's missing,' Bluebell remarked, waving one of Rafferty's home-made savoury sausage rolls as she spoke. 'Smashing spread, Sal.' She narrowed her eyes at Isobel, who was warily prodding a mini quiche. 'Don't you think?'

'Hmm.' Isobel sounded far from convinced. 'You can't go wrong with the old standbys can you?'

'Did your Noah go on the stag night?' Dolly asked Isobel in a tone that suggested she highly doubted it.

Isobel gave her a cool look. 'Hardly. He had work to do at home. He can't spare the time for...'

They all waited to see how she was going to finish that sentence, but she didn't bother. Instead she shrugged and nibbled tentatively on the quiche.

'He's such a hard worker,' Miss Lavender said fondly. 'Of course, what else could you expect? He became a headmaster at such a young age, and that only goes to show how diligent he truly is. He's devoted to his work.'

'Not like Ross, then,' Bluebell said with a sly grin. 'He has, er, other priorities.'

'Ross is a creative talent,' Miss Lavender said firmly. 'Such people have different mindsets. Ross must fill the creative well on a regular basis. It's all part of his genius.'

'Fill the creative well?' Dolly sniggered. 'Is that what he calls it?'

'He's a really talented artist,' Sally said in a conciliatory tone. She nodded at the painting that hung on the wall of Frankie and her brothers, Ellis, and Arlo. 'He did that for me for Rafferty's Christmas present, and we both think it's amazing.'

'It's a wonderful painting,' Miss Lavender said proudly. 'Ross has natural talent. It can't be taught.'

'Then why does he give art lessons?' Bluebell asked. 'Seems a bit of a con in that case.'

'Ross can teach technique,' Miss Lavender said patiently. 'He just can't give someone without that gift the ability to paint the way he does.' She gave Bluebell a pitying look. 'You wouldn't understand, dear.'

'Well, if Ross ever wants to give me lessons in technique,' Bluebell said, winking at the others, 'I'd definitely be up for it.'

'I'd love to paint again,' Ava said dreamily, as if she hadn't noticed the laughter that Bluebell's comment had caused. 'I haven't picked up a brush in years.'

'Can you paint, love?' Sally asked, awestruck. 'I didn't know that.'

'Oh, I'm not very good,' Ava said hastily. 'But I did used to enjoy it.' She sighed. 'Until life and children and other stuff got in the way.'

'Well, I think if you want to paint you should,' Bluebell said firmly. 'Maybe *you* should ask Ross for lessons. What do you say, Miss Lavender?'

Miss Lavender nodded. 'He's very busy right now,' she said. 'He has enough one-to-one students, but he and I have been talking about this very thing recently...'

'Huh!'

Isobel seemed to realise she'd said that out loud and blushed. 'Sorry, Aunt Eugenie,' she said, rather flustered. 'Noah told me how Ross is haranguing you to set up his so-called art school. It's not right. He's had more than enough money from you already.'

'I'll bet Noah's had his fair share, too,' Summer whispered to Clemmie, but to her surprise, Clemmie didn't smile.

'It's like I said,' she whispered back, sounding annoyed, 'what Ross wants, Ross gets.'

Summer raised an eyebrow as a sudden thought occurred to her. Was it possible that it was Ross who'd hurt her? Ross Lavender, of all people? But surely not. He was so far from being Clemmie's type it was laughable. No, she must be wrong there.

'Ross has had no more than Noah,' Miss Lavender said, in a tone that suggested she was rather annoyed with Isobel but was doing her best not to show it. 'I don't have favourites.'

Summer noticed the delighted looks on Rita's and Birdie's faces as they waited for Isobel to argue her point. To their obvious disappointment the conversation was headed off by Bluebell, who regretfully announced she'd have to take her leave.

'I need to check my house is still standing. The girls have invited a few of their mates over, and we all know that never ends well,' she said cheerfully. 'Thanks ever so much for inviting me, Sally. I shall see you on Friday morning to do your wedding hair!'

Sally swallowed. 'Oh heck, don't say it like that. It makes it seem so close.'

'It *is* close,' Birdie said eagerly. 'We can't wait, can we, Rita? We've got our best frocks all pressed and ready.'

'Lord help us,' Miss Lavender said, rolling her eyes. 'I must do something about that.'

Dolly and Clemmie were also ready to go and had booked a taxi to take them back to their pretty cottage just outside West Colby. It was quite isolated, so there wasn't even the option of a bus at this time of night.

As the party fizzled out, Frankie evidently decided it was

safe to come out of hiding. She wandered into the living room and reached for the television remote.

'I hear you've been spending a lot of time with Jamie Callaghan,' Miss Lavender said, eating cake as she watched Frankie over her lemonade glass with narrowed eyes.

Frankie was busy staring at the television screen, where some woman was running for her life through a forest, pursued by a weird looking creature that did a lot of grunting.

'Hmm,' was all she managed.

Summer gave her a wry grin and collected some empty glasses from the coffee table. She stacked the dishwasher and headed back into the living room, in time to hear Birdie say, 'It's lovely to see Jamie with a girlfriend at last. It will do him the world of good. He needs a bit of fun in his life.'

Frankie dropped the remote and turned to them, a look of horror on her face. 'I'm not his girlfriend,' she said, in a tone that suggested she never would be either. 'We're just pals, that's all.'

'Oh.' Rita and Birdie exchanged disappointed looks. 'Are you sure?'

'Absolutely positive,' Frankie said. 'He—' She shrugged and turned back to the television. 'Well, anyway. We're not.'

'Such a shame,' Rita said. 'It would have been smashing if the two brothers were dating two sisters. Well, stepsisters at any rate.'

'At least Ben's sorted now, thanks to you,' Miss Lavender said, beaming at Summer. 'He'll make you an excellent boyfriend, I'm sure. He's a good man.'

Summer's face burned, and Birdie narrowed her eyes. 'You *are* going out with Ben, aren't you?'

She gave Summer an innocent smile that didn't fool her for an instant.

'Sorry,' she said, mindful of the bets on their relationship, 'but it was just one meal out. That's all.'

'Are you sure?' Rita sighed. 'That's a bit of a bugger all round if you don't mind me saying so. That family needs some good news if you ask me, after everything they've been through.'

'All right, Rita,' Miss Lavender said, raising her eyebrows in warning.

'She's right, though,' Birdie said. 'It's been tough for them, especially Jennifer, after what happened to poor Julian and Leon.'

Frankie lowered the volume of the television, having finally found something interesting enough in the conversation to make her forget about the low-budget horror film.

'Who's Leon?' she asked.

Summer sat down. 'Ben and Jamie's older brother,' she said quietly. She glanced over at Kat who'd been in the process of shrugging on her coat. She'd gone a bit pale.

'He was a nice young man.' Miss Lavender sounded wistful. 'Polite, intelligent, well-mannered.'

'Beautiful manners,' Rita said. 'Always kind to us, wasn't he, Birdie?'

'Always,' Birdie said, nodding emphatically. 'Crying shame what happened to him.'

'What *did* happen to him?' Frankie couldn't hide her impatience.

'Car accident.' Miss Lavender brushed cake crumbs from her skirt, and then looked around in embarrassment, as if she'd only just realised her Yorkshire terriers weren't around to pounce on them. 'Mercifully, he was killed instantly, so he didn't suffer. Twenty-two he was. Little more than a child really.'

'Poor Jennifer.' Her mum dropped into a chair. 'I can't imagine anything worse. I really can't.'

'Jamie had another brother! I can't believe he never told me,' Frankie said.

'I don't think Jamie will have any memory of him,' Miss Lavender said sadly. 'It's nearly fourteen years ago, so Jamie was just a baby.'

'Was it really as long ago as that?' Birdie tilted her head to one side and considered. 'How old's Ben now? Twenty-nine, is he? And he was fifteen at the time, so yes, fourteen years ago or thereabouts. Shocking. I remember it as if it were yesterday, don't you, Rita?'

'I do. Tragic. Well, it broke Kat's heart didn't it, dear?'

Sally frowned. 'Kat's heart?'

'She was going out with Leon at the time, weren't you?' Birdie smiled sympathetically at Kat who finished buttoning her coat.

'I really have to go now. The babysitter...'

'Of course. Are you all right, love?' Sally frowned in concern as Kat hurried to the door.

'Me? Of course.' Kat shrugged. 'It was a long time ago. I'll see you tomorrow, Sal. Thanks for a lovely evening.'

'And then of course, just a year later, Jennifer lost her husband to cancer, and those boys lost their father,' Miss Lavender continued, not seeming to notice that Kat had left the flat. 'Jamie probably can't remember *him* either. Such a shame.'

'He doesn't talk about his dad,' Frankie said quietly. 'About either of them. At least, not to me.'

'And Ben became the man of the house at sixteen,' Birdie said. 'Lot of responsibility that. He grew up fast.'

'Had to,' Rita said.

'Bit of a wild child before that, do you remember?'

Ben? Summer couldn't imagine it for a second and couldn't resist checking they were talking about the same person. 'Are you sure? *Ben Callaghan?*' She almost said *My Ben* but caught herself in time.

'Oh yes. He was a proper scamp,' Rita assured her. 'Always up to mischief.'

'That was one word for it,' Miss Lavender said. 'I seem to recall he was more than a scamp. He was a rude, bad-mannered, spoilt brat.'

'*Ben?*' They had to be joking. No way could Ben ever have behaved like that.

'Losing his brother had a huge effect on him, dear,' Miss Lavender said quietly. 'And when his father died—well, he had to grow up overnight, take responsibility for his family.'

'And for Monk's Folly,' Birdie said. 'Lot to take on that, especially at sixteen.'

'Quite.'

'So, Jennifer lost her son, followed a year later by her husband, and Ben inherited Monk's Folly? Her husband didn't leave it to her?' Mum asked.

'Evidently not,' Miss Lavender said. 'He was quite an old-fashioned chap, and he really wanted Monk's Folly to stay in the family, so I suppose it was natural he'd leave it to his male heir.'

'In case Jennifer married again and her new husband got his mitts on the place,' Rita said wisely.

'Not that there's any chance of that. Jennifer's barely spoken to a soul since they passed,' Birdie added. 'Well, tonight's a case in point. She was invited, wasn't she, but has she turned up?'

'Of course not,' Rita said. 'She's wasting away in that house of theirs.'

'It was an awful time,' Ava said, gazing into the middle

distance as if seeing it all playing out in front of her eyes. 'I was expecting Beatrix, and Zach was thrown in at the deep end. It was his first job as vicar,' she said. 'Before that he'd been a curate over in Wensleydale. We'd only been here a couple of months when the accident happened, and everyone was in shock. Of course, they were looking to Zach for comfort and help, and I know he felt that burden deeply.' She sighed. 'I don't suppose I was much use to him really.'

Summer wiped her eyes. She'd known about Leon and about Ben's dad, obviously, but hearing it from other people made it seem more real somehow. Ben always seemed to underplay what he'd gone through. She'd had no real idea of how much had landed on his shoulders.

Frankie rubbed her eyes. 'This is awful!'

Ava hiccupped. 'It certainly is. My bloody glass is empty again. Sally, be a darling and pass me the bottle.'

* * *

Kirkby Skimmer was hardly on a par with Leeds or York, but as far as Skimmerdale went it was probably the closest thing to a vibrant city there was. Like Tuppenny Bridge it was a market town, but it was much larger. Dominated by the ruins of Skimmerdale Abbey which looked down over the town and the river, it was blessed with far more facilities than any other place in the dale.

One of its main draws, for the residents of Skimmerdale at least, was its cinema, and it was there that Jamie and Ben spent a few hours that Sunday afternoon, watching an action-packed superhero film that Jamie had begged to see.

Ben had dreaded it, but to his surprise he found he enjoyed it, and at several points during the course of the film his hand, on its way to filling his mouth with popcorn, had paused mid-air, because he was so riveted by some event onscreen.

When they finally stumbled out of the cinema, blinking in the light of day, Jamie gave him a sly look.

'You loved that, didn't you?'

'It wasn't bad,' Ben said, then grinned. 'Okay, it was really good. Miles better than I expected. Popcorn wasn't bad either.'

Jamie pulled a face. 'Don't know how you can eat that stuff. I'm starving.'

'Burger?'

Jamie's face lit up. 'Seriously?'

'Yep. Let's push the boat out. Let's have fries too.'

Jamie laughed. 'Wow, and it's not even my birthday! Come on then.'

There was no McDonald's or Burger King or any other fast food chain store in Kirkby Skimmer, but there was a cute little café that did the most delicious cheeseburgers that locals raved about.

Settling at the table after placing their order, Ben said, 'It's great, being here with you. I'm really enjoying myself.'

'Are you?' Jamie sounded surprised. 'Wouldn't you rather I was at home studying for my GCSEs?'

Ben sighed. 'I want you to have a social life, Jamie. The only reason I worry about your grades is because I don't want you to waste the opportunity you've been given. You're so bright. Everyone says so. Mum's so proud of you, you know. It would make her day if you got into a good university.'

'Yeah, yeah, I know.' Jamie rolled his eyes. 'Did you want to go to university? Or were you emotionally blackmailed into it too?'

'Is that how you see it?' Ben raised an eyebrow. 'Are you really saying you don't want to go to university? I thought you were just kicking off. All that stuff about leaving school and getting a job —you weren't serious?'

'Who says I wasn't?' Jamie leaned forward. 'So go on. Whose idea was it that you go to uni? Yours or Mum's?'

At least Ben could answer that honestly. 'It was mine,' he said. 'Oh, she wanted me to go, don't misunderstand me, but as soon as I made up my mind I wanted to be a vet there was no swaying me.'

Jamie shrugged. 'Maybe that's the difference. You had a clear idea about what you wanted to do. I don't.'

'But if you get a good degree you can do anything! And by the time you leave school you might have a clearer idea anyway.'

'I wish I was like you,' Jamie admitted, surprising Ben who'd thought his brother would rather die than be anything like him. 'You knew what you wanted so clearly. You didn't let anything stop you, and it fitted in with Mum's plans for you beautifully. You were lucky.'

'I was. Clive helped. He was amazing.' Ben honestly didn't know where he'd be without him. 'He was so patient with me. Looking back, I have no idea why he took me under his wing the way he did, but I'm so glad he did. He gave me so much encouragement and support, and then, at the end of my studies he gave me a job. I mean, it all fell into my lap.'

Lucky, he thought, didn't begin to cover it. He could never thank Clive enough for all his help, nor pay him back for the opportunity he'd given him. Clive was far more than a boss to him.

He supposed, when he considered it, he really was like a second father, always ready to listen and advise, not just about his professional problems but about his personal life, too. He only hoped Jamie would one day be lucky enough to find a mentor like Clive.

The waitress brought their burgers, fries, and milkshakes over and, after a few appreciative comments about how appetising it all looked, they ate hungrily, conversation temporarily on hold.

Ben watched his younger brother fondly. It was good to see Jamie looking so happy and relaxed. It had, he realised, been some time since he'd been anything but sullen or angry. What had happened to him? What had happened to their relationship? He knew, of course, probably better than most in fact, how difficult the teenage years could be for a boy, but he couldn't help worrying that something was preying on Jamie's mind. This change in attitude had only really happened since the summer holidays started.

More specifically since Frankie had arrived. He couldn't be a hundred per cent certain of course, but he was almost sure of it.

He dabbed his mouth with a paper napkin and eyed Jamie a little nervously.

'Is there—is there anything you want to tell me?'

Jamie gulped down a mouthful of fries and stared at him. 'About what?'

'Well, that's the point. I don't know.' Ben shrugged. 'I just think you seem to have something on your mind, and... well, I'm here for you if you need to talk.'

Jamie sucked banana milkshake through a straw, watching him suspiciously.

'You don't have to look at me like that,' Ben said. 'It wasn't a trick question. I was just wondering, that's all.'

'There's nothing wrong,' Jamie said eventually. 'I don't know what you mean.'

'Okay, fair enough.' He didn't believe him, but he didn't want to push him either. 'These fries are delicious, aren't they? And the cheeseburger... I can't remember the last time

I had fast food. You forget how tasty it is, don't you? Even if it's not that great for your health.'

'Yeah, well, we can't be sensible all the time.'

Ben bit down his irritation as Jamie took his phone from his jacket pocket and began tapping the screen.

'What are you looking for?' he asked, trying to keep his voice light.

'Just checking out the socials.' Jamie shrugged and began scrolling.

'Looking to see what Frankie's up to?' Ben suggested, hoping his annoyance didn't show in his voice.

Jamie stopped scrolling and looked at him. 'What's that supposed to mean? Why would I be checking out Frankie's socials?'

'I don't know.' Ben shrugged. 'It was just a question.'

'You don't like Frankie, do you?'

The question took him by surprise. 'Why on earth would you say that? I've got nothing against Frankie.'

'Sure you haven't. I saw you looking at her at Whispering Willows. I could see the cogs turning in your brain. *Teenage girl. Danger, danger! Potential threat to Jamie's academic career. Blue hair. Nose stud. Possible delinquent. Alert, alert!*'

Ben tutted impatiently. 'Don't be stupid. I'm sure she's a nice enough girl. And anyway, she helps out at Whispering Willows. I hardly think a delinquent would bother to do that.'

'Hmm. Tell your face that.'

Ben pushed his food away. 'You know, you've got me down as some boring, staid middle-aged man,' he said. 'I'm not even thirty yet and—'

'You don't have to tell me that! I can't believe how old you act for your age. Lighten up, Ben.'

'You think I wasn't a teenager once?'

'Hard to believe,' Jamie mumbled, tapping on his phone screen.

His brother had no idea, Ben thought. Jamie was an angel compared to Ben at that age. He could tell him some things that would shock him, change his opinion of him forever.

'Can you put the phone away please?'

Jamie scowled. 'Why? I'm not hurting you.'

'We're supposed to be spending the day together. That was the whole point of today wasn't it? To have fun. To spend time together, just you and me.'

'Is it? I thought it was to make sure I'd dropped the idea of leaving school and getting a job.' Jamie smirked. 'Didn't Mum put you up to this?'

'No she didn't!' Ben was stung that Jamie had so little trust in him. 'I felt that you and I were growing apart, and it upset me. I think we should try to communicate a little better, that's all. That's why, if something's bothering you, I really hope you'll feel able to tell me. I'd hate to think you were struggling with something you couldn't tell anyone.'

Jamie shrugged. 'It's okay, Ben. You don't have to worry about that. I've got Frankie to confide in if I need someone. Not,' he added hastily, 'that I do. Everything's fine. Eat the rest of your cheeseburger and stop worrying.'

He frowned at the screen and began tapping something out. A message of some sort perhaps, to goodness knows who. Frankie?

Ben realised he wasn't hungry any more. He watched Jamie typing, feeling a mixture of resentment and sadness. He'd really hoped today would be a breakthrough in their relationship, but it seemed his brother had no interest in building bridges.

Maybe, he thought, it was too late. Maybe they'd grown

too far apart to ever be close again. Maybe trying to play the responsible guardian had cost him his brother. He should have taken him out more often, had fun with him, spent quality time with him in the present instead of constantly thinking about his future.

Jamie clearly had no time for him. Ben prodded the straw in his milkshake, which was growing more watery by the minute, and pondered how it was that the more he tried to put things right for his family, the worse things seemed to get. Sometimes, life seemed very unfair.

Chapter Fourteen

'Monday morning.' Sally gulped. 'Rafferty, it's our wedding week.'

'It is." Rafferty beamed. 'I can't believe the day is almost here at last, and I'll finally get to make you my wife.'

Summer and Frankie gave mock groans as Rafferty stooped to kiss his fiancée before taking his seat at the breakfast table.

'Dad, that's gross. We're eating,' Frankie said, waving her toast and marmalade at him in disapproval.

'Give over,' Sally said. 'You saw a lot worse than that on that film you were watching yesterday afternoon.'

Rafferty laughed. 'Sorry, Frankie, no concessions for anyone this week, not even children. We're going to be sickeningly loved up until the minute we say I do.'

'And then it all stops, and you'll hate each other?' Summer asked, picking up her mug of coffee and giving him an innocent look.

'That's not what he meant, and you know it.' Mum

leaned over and put her arm around Rafferty's neck, dropping a kiss on his cheek. 'I do love you.'

'That's quite a relief,' he said, his eyes twinkling. 'We've got a whole bunch of guests coming to this wedding and it would be a lot of hassle if you'd changed your mind.'

'I'll not change my mind, have no fear of that,' she said.

'Oh, pur-lease.' Summer winked at Frankie. 'There should be some sort of law about people having to listen to this soppy stuff from their parents.'

'You can have too much of a good thing, Dad,' Frankie said as she chewed her toast. 'No wonder Billie and Arlo went out so early. Avoiding you two, no doubt.'

'Not at all,' Rafferty said. 'They're picking Mona up from Bemborough, remember?'

Sally gave Frankie a worried look. 'Are you sure you're going to be all right on the sofa, love? It's just, I can't expect my mother to sleep on there at her age, and with Summer working so much it wouldn't be fair.'

'It's no problem, Sally,' Frankie said. 'Summer's letting me put my stuff in her room, and as long as I've got the use of a mirror, and a socket for my hairdryer, I'll be fine.' She turned to Summer. 'Are you at Whispering Willows today?'

'No. I've got a shift in the pub later this afternoon but I'm at the stables tomorrow morning.' She couldn't help feeling a bit worried about it. 'Hopefully Joseph will manage.'

'Well,' Frankie said, 'me and Jamie were going to ask him if he needed any help from us. I've picked up enough from you to be of some use, and Jamie can help with mucking out and grooming and stuff. I'll show him what to do.'

Summer thought it sounded amazing, but she was doubtful Jamie was really up for it.

'You do know Joseph can't afford to pay you? You might

not mind but won't Jamie? Besides, he doesn't strike me as the mucking out type. Isn't he more of a games fanatic?'

'To be honest, we're fed up being stuck in so much. It was his idea to give me a hand, anyway. I didn't ask him.'

'In that case, great. Joseph will be delighted.' And it was a weight off her mind, too. She also thought it would please Ben that his brother was finally doing something more productive than sitting in front of a screen all day.

Summer risked a glance at her mother, relieved to see she and Rafferty had stopped slopping over each other and were focused on something more sensible. Breakfast. 'How about you, Mum?'

'I'm not working until the evening shift, so I thought I'd check everything is in order with the flowers and the cake.'

'Billie and Arlo are taking Mona to Skimmerdale Abbey later this morning,' Rafferty said, helping himself to corn-flakes. 'They thought they'd best have a look around the Dales a bit since they won't be here long.'

'Oh, don't remind me!' Mum exclaimed. 'I can't believe they'll all be leaving on Sunday. They've only just got here!'

'Well, you'll be leaving, too,' Summer pointed out. 'Off to Paris. How fabulous will that be?'

'And when you get back from there, I'll be going home to Norfolk,' Frankie said. 'I'm going to miss Tuppenny Bridge, though.'

'Are you going to Skimmerdale Abbey with Gran and Billie and Arlo?' Summer asked her mum.

'Aw no, not without Rafferty. He's working in the pub this afternoon too and it wouldn't be fair.'

'Tell you what, why don't we both go?' Rafferty asked. 'Nice day out. Do us good. I can swap a shift with someone this afternoon and work the evening shift with you. What about you, Summer? Do you want me to get cover?'

'No.' Summer sighed. 'It wouldn't be fair on the other staff if they were having to cover two of us. I'll do the afternoon shift as planned, but I can check the flowers and cake for you this morning, Mum. Put your mind at rest.'

'Aw thanks, love. You're a star.' Mum's eyes sparkled with happiness. 'I can't wait. A lovely sightseeing trip with our Billie, Arlo, and Mam.'

'And me,' Rafferty said, with mock indignation.

'That goes without saying,' she said, smiling back at him.

* * *

As Summer had suspected, the woman behind the counter at Bridge Bakery was reassuring. 'The cake will be delivered to The White Hart Inn first thing on Friday morning. Tell Mrs Fletcher not to worry about a thing. It's looking smashing, love.'

As Summer wandered towards Green Lane she thought about Jennifer and why she'd decided not to attend the hen night after all. What had changed her mind? It seemed a real shame to her.

She hadn't been able to stop thinking about the conversation they'd had with the Lavender Ladies and Ava about Leon's and Julian's deaths. It all seemed so tragic, and she couldn't imagine how much pain Jennifer and Ben must have been in. At least Ben seemed to have moved on, built a career for himself, whereas Jennifer...

Isobel Lavender was out when Summer entered Petalicious, Isobel's flower shop overlooking the village green, but her trainee, Kelly, was all smiles behind the counter.

'Everything's in hand,' she said, in answer to Summer's query about the wedding flowers. 'Just what your mum ordered. Isobel's done loads of weddings so tell her not to worry.'

Summer thanked her and turned to leave, but a bucket by the door caught her eye, and as a thought crossed her mind she reached down and picked up a bunch of flowers, which she placed on the counter.

Half an hour later, she knocked on the door of Monk's Folly, flowers in her arms.

After a few moments, Jennifer opened the door, a knife in one hand.

'Oh goodness! I wasn't expecting visitors.' She glanced down and blushed deeply. 'Oops! I forgot I had this apron on. How embarrassing.'

'Sorry, I didn't mean to interrupt you. If you're cooking...'

'Oh, it's just a casserole for dinner tonight,' Jennifer said, waving the knife around a bit too casually for Summer's liking. 'Ben's usually starving when he gets home from work, and casseroles are so easy, aren't they? It's lovely to see you, Summer. Were you here for something specific?'

Summer thrust the flowers into Jennifer's arms. 'I bought these for you while I was in town. Just a little present from me to you.'

Jennifer stared down at the beautiful blooms in her arms, then gave her a puzzled look.

'For me? I don't understand. It's not my birthday.'

'Doesn't have to be a reason does there?' Summer asked. 'I just thought you'd like them.'

'I do. I do like them.' Jennifer sounded dazed. She shook her head. 'I'm so sorry. Where are my manners? Come in, come in. I'll put these in water and make us some tea. You would like some tea?'

'Well,' Summer said brightly, 'I wouldn't say no. I'm always ready for a cuppa.'

Jennifer was already heading down the hall and Summer followed her.

'What a massive kitchen,' she said with genuine surprise. 'You could fit our whole flat in here!'

Jennifer laughed as she lay the flowers on the draining board.

'I'm not so sure about that,' she said as she filled the kettle. 'Although, I suppose one takes for granted how large this house is. I'm sure it's not as smart as the one in your flat, though. These units have been here for decades. The whole place needs a good refurbish to be honest.'

'Do you do a lot of cooking?' Summer asked.

'Oh yes, every day. I find it quite therapeutic. Cooking takes your mind off things. That's what I've always found anyway.'

'Shall I make the tea, while you put those flowers in water?' Summer suggested.

'That's kind of you. The mugs are in the cupboard above the kettle, and the tea and sugar canisters are next to the microwave.'

Summer got to work while Jennifer expertly arranged the flowers in a vase.

'You've made a good job of that,' she told her when Jennifer had finally finished.

'Well, how could I not with such beautiful flowers?' Jennifer stepped back and tilted her head as she surveyed the arrangement. 'Thank you so much. I'm really touched by the gesture.'

'Oh, think nothing of it.' She squeezed the teabags then took a carton of milk from the fridge.

Jennifer stood the vase on the kitchen windowsill. 'I'll put them in the sitting room later.'

She picked up an onion and reached for the vegetable knife.

'Am I in your way?' Summer asked, aware that she'd been in the middle of making a casserole.

'Why don't you take your tea through to the sitting room?' Jennifer said. 'I'll finish in here and join you in a jiffy. You know the way.'

Summer picked up her mug of tea and did as she suggested, wrinkling her nose as she entered the room. A second visit had done nothing to change her mind about how drab this house was. She really didn't understand why they didn't just put the place on the market and find somewhere more manageable. She wouldn't live here for anything. It gave her the creeps.

She settled herself on the shabby sofa, pushing aside the orange cushions that were valiantly trying to add some vibrancy to the place, and sipped her tea, trying not to be too nosy but failing dismally. There were photographs dotted around the room and she couldn't help but peer at them, curiosity getting the better of her.

Summer had been too overwhelmed on her last visit to take much notice, but today she saw a large, framed photograph of a couple on their wedding day. The beautiful bride had to be Jennifer. There was no mistaking the light brown hair, so like Ben's, the twinkling eyes, and wide smile. Her groom was a handsome man in a morning suit. She thought he looked kind.

She spotted a school photograph of Ben. There was no doubt in her mind that it was him. Those blue eyes—she'd know them anywhere. But he had a look about him that was unfamiliar. A defiance she didn't recognise. She remembered what Miss Lavender had said about him being a brat when he was a child. As she stared at the photo she could, for the first time, believe it.

Beside him was a photo of Jamie, looking not much different from the way he looked now. Beside that picture, though, was another one that made her sit up straight and peer closer.

She gazed at the image of a teenage boy. He had his father's dark brown hair, but his mother's and Ben's smile. Just looking at him, Summer could see a kindness there. He had none of young Ben's defiance. He looked open and likeable, and she swallowed down the grief for the family who must have loved him so much and felt his loss so keenly.

'Oh my God,' she murmured. 'It's just awful.'

'What's awful?'

Summer jumped guiltily as Jennifer entered the sitting room, carrying her own mug of tea. She smiled at her, but her smile faded as she saw the look on Summer's face.

'What is it? What's wrong?'

'I'm really sorry,' Summer said. 'I was just wondering. Is that young boy Leon?'

Jennifer gazed over at the photo, her smile dying. 'Yes,' she said quietly. 'That's Leon. Did Ben tell you about him?'

As she sat down in the armchair by the fireplace, Summer shifted nervously.

'I'm so sorry, Jennifer. He sounds like a lovely man.'

Jennifer swallowed. 'He was. Good as gold. I was very proud of him.' She sipped her tea, composing herself. 'I expect Ben told you about his accident?'

'He did. It must have been terrible.' Summer wished she knew what else to say. Somehow, she doubted 'terrible' was an adequate description of the impact Leon's death must have had on the family. She tried to imagine what they'd feel like if something happened to Billie, but the thought was so painful she pushed it away.

Jennifer gave a faint smile. 'You could say that. It was a horrible time. Honestly, it almost broke us. Jamie was only one and didn't understand. He kept saying Leon's name—it was one of his first words, you know—and every time he did it tore us apart. And Ben...' She paused, her eyes shimmering with tears. 'Well, Ben was never the same again.'

Summer realised her own eyes were blurry, and there was a lump in her throat, imagining Ben at that age. Just fifteen and coping with all that grief.

'My husband, Julian, was devastated. He was ill, you see. He'd been diagnosed with cancer and was already weakened from chemotherapy. For him to suffer such loss when he was already going through so much...'

'You were all going through so much,' Summer murmured. 'Too much. Life's so unfair sometimes.'

'Yes,' Jennifer said. 'It is. Julian was extremely close to Leon. They'd even worked together you know, so it was hard for him to stay positive. I don't know. Maybe if the accident hadn't happened, if Leon had still been around, maybe Julian would have lived a little longer. Who knows? As it was, he passed away just a year after Leon. I like to think they're together now. It's my only comfort in all this really.'

Summer felt sick. 'I can't imagine what you went through. I don't know how you got through it. How any of you did.'

'What's that saying?' Jennifer said, wiping her eyes. 'People are like teabags. You never know how strong they can be until they're in hot water.' She gave a short laugh. 'Well, this has turned into a bit of a gloomy conversation, hasn't it? I'm not complaining, you know. Life is what it is, and I'm sure I've had it easier than many. I still have Ben and Jamie, for a start. I'm very lucky.'

They were quiet for a moment or two, sipping their tea.

'Why did you really come here, Summer?' Jennifer asked suddenly. 'Don't get me wrong, the flowers are gorgeous, and I really appreciate them, but there must be a reason you'd visit here when Ben's at work.'

Summer blushed. 'I was a bit worried about you,' she admitted. 'You didn't turn up for the hen night and we were expecting you, and I just thought...'

Jennifer's eyes widened. 'I'm so sorry! I meant to ring your mother and send my apologies, but it went out of my head. I had a bit of a migraine I'm afraid. Such a shame.'

She didn't sound very convincing, but Summer let it pass.

'Oh well,' she said. 'As long as you're okay now.'

'You're a very thoughtful girl, Summer,' Jennifer said. 'I'm very glad you and Ben are friends, and if Frankie's anything like you I'm glad she's chummed up with Jamie. Your mother's very kind, letting him spend so much time at the pub. I did tell him they could play their games here, but Jamie didn't seem keen. I suppose it does him good to get out of the house now and then.'

Summer thought Jamie probably couldn't wait to escape from this gloomy old pile but kept her thoughts to herself. She wondered what Jennifer meant when she'd said she and Ben were friends. Was she being polite, or was that what Ben had told her? Was that all they were? It wasn't as if they'd kissed, although they'd definitely come close on Friday evening. If only fate hadn't conspired against them who knows what might have happened? She felt quite hot at the thought and took another sip of tea to cover her embarrassment.

'I suppose,' Jennifer said, 'that it's a bit too quiet for him here.' She glanced around, a sad look on her face. 'You know, when we were all together it was a different place. We had Leon and Ben, and Jamie was toddling around getting into all sorts of mischief. And Julian and I were very happy. Very happy. Then he got ill, and it all changed.' She shook her head, her eyes bright with tears. 'I hope one day Ben and Jamie will fill this house with children again. It deserves that. This house wasn't built to stand empty.'

She leaned forward as if confiding a great secret to Summer. 'Leon used to go out with Katherine you know.'

Summer nodded. 'So I heard.'

'I thought the two of them might get married one day. When I found out she was expecting Hattie I was thrilled for her, of course, but there was a part of me that felt heartbroken for Leon. It should have been his baby. That's why I had to go to the baby shower. For his sake. Does that sound stupid?'

'No, not at all,' Summer reassured her. *Well, a bit weird maybe, but who am I to judge?*

'And then, when she wouldn't reveal who the father was...' Jennifer's face flushed with embarrassment. 'Please, don't ever tell Ben this, but I half hoped it was his.'

'Ben's?' Summer frowned as a memory stirred. Kat's baby shower. Jennifer had admitted that it had crossed her mind she remembered. Kat had been quite clear that it wasn't his baby and no wonder. She probably saw Ben as a younger brother, given she'd gone out with Leon.

'Wishful thinking,' Jennifer said. 'I knew it wasn't his deep down, of course. But it would be nice to have a grandchild. And I do worry about Ben. That's why I'm so glad he's got you. He should be around people of his own age. It's time he had some fun in his life. I think you're just what he needs, Summer.'

'Er, thank you.' Summer wasn't sure how to respond to that, so she drained her tea instead.

'I want my boys to have everything they can out of life,' Jennifer said. 'Leon lost it all you see. He was robbed of his chance to get married, to have a child of his own, to have fun. He was robbed of everything. It was so unfair. He didn't deserve it, he really didn't. And that's why Ben should—'

She broke off and stared at the door. 'Ben!' Her voice was a little too high-pitched, revealing her embarrassment.

Summer spun round and saw the man himself lurking by the door. Her delight at seeing him quickly turned to concern as she saw how pale he looked. He was holding on to the door handle for grim death, and his blue eyes were wide with what looked like shock.

Blimey, is he that surprised to see me here?

'What are you doing home?' Jennifer asked, her voice far too cheerful.

'I—I forgot my lunch,' he said.

'So you did,' Jennifer said. 'I remembered earlier but it clean went out of my mind again. It's in the fridge. I'll get it for you.' She got to her feet. 'Would you like another cup of tea?' she asked Summer. 'I'll be making one for Ben.'

Ben looked appalled and Summer wasn't sure what to make of it all. He'd been absolutely fine with her on Friday evening. Why was he looking at her now as if he couldn't wait for her to leave?

'Sorry,' she said, getting to her feet. 'I really ought to get back. I'm working at the pub this afternoon, so I need to get ready.'

'I'll, er, just go upstairs and wash my hands,' Ben said.

He practically shot out of the room, and Jennifer gave

Summer an awkward look, which made it obvious that even she thought he was behaving oddly.

'Do give your mother my apologies about the hen night,' Jennifer said, as she showed Summer to the door.

'I will. And you'll be at the wedding? Two o'clock at All Hallows Church, and afterwards at The White Hart Inn.'

'Of course. We'll be there. It will be lovely to see inside the church again. I haven't been in there for...' Jennifer smiled softly. 'Well, a long time. We'll see you on Friday, Summer. And thank you again for the beautiful flowers. They've absolutely made my day.'

Summer was relieved to leave Monk's Folly, making her way along the rough, uneven track that led to the bridge without once looking back.

Ben had clearly overheard his mother talking about grandchildren. What if he thought it was Summer who'd brought the subject up? He'd be worried she was going to start looking at bridal magazines and hinting about engagement rings next. Oh heck, and when they were babysitting she'd praised him for being so good with Tommy!

He'd definitely think she was getting ideas. How embarrassing! She wasn't sure she could ever look him in the eye again.

Chapter Fifteen

There were raised voices in the flat above The White Hart Inn that evening when Summer walked in after her shift in the pub.

She grinned to herself as she remembered why. Gran!

Sure enough, as she walked into the kitchen Gran was sitting at the table, haranguing Summer's mum and Rafferty about the fact that smoking wasn't allowed anywhere in the flat.

'All I'm saying,' she said, waving an unlit cigarette around, 'is that it's a bloody long trek down them stairs at my age just to have a quick cig. And look, I'm not asking to smoke in my bedroom, am I? Or even in the living room. It's just the kitchen, that's all. And if you're worried about a fire hazard, well, there's nothing to catch fire here. It's all hard surfaces and tiles. And look, the sink's right there. Right there!' She jabbed the cigarette in the direction of the sink unit as if they didn't believe her. 'If by some miracle I did start a fire I'd soon put the bugger out, wouldn't I?'

Rafferty shook his head in amusement, but Mum folded

her arms and surveyed Gran with a determined look in her eyes.

'Give it up, Mam. It's not going to happen. We've told you a dozen times or more, this is a no-smoking building, and if you want a cig you'll have to go outside and smoke it, and that's that.'

'And me, a pensioner,' Gran said with a sigh. 'Some might call that an abuse of my human rights.' She looked round and her eyes lit up as she saw Summer. 'Here she is! Now you'll stick up for me won't you, love? Tell them to let me have a cig in the kitchen, there's a good lass.'

'Sorry, Gran. I'm on their side in this,' Summer told her.

Gran tutted impatiently. 'Bloody hell, even you!' She narrowed her eyes. 'You've lost weight. Aren't you eating properly?'

'I'm eating normally,' Summer assured her, pulling out a chair and sitting at the table opposite her. 'And I haven't lost any weight. My clothes aren't loose anyway.'

'I can tell,' Gran said firmly. 'You still messing around with them horses?'

'Yes,' Summer said. 'Still working at Whispering Willows. Still love it there.'

'It's not proper work for a bit of a lass if you ask me. No wonder you're fading away to nowt. You need a few good Yorkshire puddings inside you.'

'Is that a euphemism?' Billie asked, giggling.

'It's a fact.' Gran pushed her cigarette back in its box and stuffed it inside her handbag. 'You, on the other hand, have put a few pounds on. Suppose it's all them barbecues they have down under.'

Billie rolled her eyes as a grinning Arlo nudged her.

'Cheers, Gran.'

'It's smashing to see you again,' Summer said, meaning it.

She bent down to give her gran a kiss and was rewarded with a fond smile.

'Aw, it's smashing to see you, too. All of you. I've missed you, though I'm buggered if I know why, given you won't even let me have a cig in comfort. I'll have to have a cup of tea. Steady meself for the long trek downstairs.'

Summer saw her mum give Rafferty a weary look as Billie filled the kettle. She wondered if Gran had been on such fine form all day and was quite glad she hadn't gone sightseeing with them all if that was the case.

Frankie strolled into the kitchen and Gran immediately reared back in mock horror.

'And have you seen this one?' she asked Summer. 'Couldn't believe my eyes when I saw her. Blue hair if you please! She was such a bonny little lass last time I saw her too, and now look at her. She looks like one of them punk rockers. She wouldn't come to the abbey with us, you know. Oh no. Like you, she is. Off to mess about with them horses. I'll bet she frightened the poor buggers to death. It'll be pierced nipples next, you wait and see.'

'Gran!' Summer said, horrified on Frankie's behalf.

'Good idea,' Frankie said with a shrug. 'As soon as I'm old enough.'

'There you go! What did I tell you?' Gran said triumphantly, as Sally shot a clearly aghast Rafferty a reassuring look. 'I hope you're not having blue hair for the wedding, young lady. That's all we need, isn't it? Bloody Marg Simpson walking down the aisle behind our Sally.'

'Take no notice of her, Frankie,' Billie advised. 'She only says these things to provoke a reaction.'

'Yeah, I figured that out ages ago,' Frankie said with a shrug. 'She loves me really, don't you, Mrs Baker?'

Gran's eyes widened. 'Well, of all the cheek!' She shook

her head in disbelief. 'Why would I want to provoke a reaction, eh? Me? Anyway, love,' she added, nodding at Frankie, 'call me Mona.'

Billie poured the tea and there was sweet silence for a few minutes as they all sat at the table and drank it.

Gran closed her eyes blissfully. 'Just what I needed after today,' she said. 'What a day it's been an' all. I've been dragged from pillar to post, I really have. Haven't had chance to draw breath all day.'

'It doesn't seem to be affecting your speech,' Sally said drily.

'Did you enjoy your trip to Skimmerdale Abbey?' Summer asked them all.

There was an exchange of looks and she hid a grin, imagining all too well that it hadn't exactly been the restful day they'd hoped for. She wondered why they'd expected any different with Gran in tow. She supposed it was the triumph of hope over experience.

'Personally,' Gran said, 'I wouldn't pay all that money to go in and look around a bunch of ruins. If I wanted to look at derelict buildings all day I could go into town and look at that shopping centre the council's been promising to do up since Moses were a lad.'

'Right,' Rafferty said briskly, 'what do you all fancy for tea? It will have to be something quick because Sally and I are working soon. How about my quick and easy teriyaki chicken? Or would you prefer fajitas?'

'You know me, love,' Gran said. 'I'm very easy going. Just don't do me anything too spicy. And no garlic. And none of them funny vegetables.' She got to her feet. 'Anyway, I'm off out for a cig now, so just give me a shout when it's done, and providing I haven't frozen to death I'll come back up for it.'

'It's a warm evening, Gran,' Summer said, laughing.

'You'll be fine.' She stood too. 'Does anyone mind if I get a quick shower before we eat?'

'Go for it,' Billie said. 'I'll get one later before bed.'

Summer headed towards the bathroom. Realising she needed a clean bath towel she unlocked the door again to get one from the cupboard and was surprised to see her gran waiting for her on the landing.

'I thought you were going outside,' she said.

'I am, but I wanted to tell you something first.' Gran winked at her and bundled her into her bedroom. 'This'll make your day, love. Couldn't say anything in front of that lot, for obvious reasons. It's about Ian.'

Summer's heart stilled at the mention of his name, and all the feelings of shame and embarrassment flooded through her again.

'I heard it from Becky Walker at the Co-op, 'cos her daughter, Emma, works at The Four Feathers and she saw it all with her own eyes. Made my day!'

She gave a snort of laughter and Summer tensed, waiting for her to tell the story.

'Sitting there in The Four Feathers he was, bold as brass, with a bit of stuff hanging on to his every word, the way they do.'

Gran sniffed, apparently forgetting that Summer had once been Ian's 'bit of stuff' too.

'Any road, the door opens, and this woman bursts in, face like thunder, and she has a right go at this lass who's sitting with him. Proper fireworks there was. Emma told Becky she thought they were going to have a proper punch-up over him, and there he was, sitting there, not saying a word or trying to calm them down.'

'Sounds about right,' Summer murmured. He'd probably

enjoyed it. Two women fighting over him? He'd be in his element.

'Ah, but he got his comeuppance,' Gran said darkly. 'Emma said all of a sudden they just stopped arguing and looked at him. Then the lass who'd come storming in, she picked up his pint of lager and poured the whole lot over his head, right there and then in front of everyone. And she told him exactly what she thought of him an' all. And then—' She chuckled to herself, clearly enjoying the scene she was imagining in her mind, '—and then the other lass, she grabs a pint from someone else's table and pours that over his head, too. And she tells him what she thinks of him an' all! Then, believe it or not, the two of them marched out of the pub arm in arm.'

She leaned back, closing her eyes as she laughed. 'And to cap it all, the bloke on the next table threatened to punch his lights out if he didn't pay him for the pint of bitter the lass had pinched off the table! Oh, I wish I'd been there! Serves the bugger right. Becky told me Emma said he was mortified. Couldn't crawl out of there fast enough. That'll teach him. And his new shirt dripping wet with beer an' all. Couldn't happen to a better bloke.'

She mopped her eyes and patted Summer's arm. 'Any road, I'll go downstairs for my smoke now and let you have that shower. Just thought you'd enjoy hearing all about it.'

She planted a kiss on Summer's cheek and hurried out of the bedroom, and Summer dropped onto the bed feeling dazed.

The humiliation she'd felt when she'd found out he was cheating on her had come flooding back. She'd been wary of men ever since she discovered her dad's double life, but Ian had chipped away at the wall she'd built around herself and won her over. Finding out he was exactly the sort of man she'd feared becoming involved with had broken her heart and knocked her confidence all over again.

Once more she'd questioned her judgement, beating herself up about how she'd managed to get it so wrong. But how, she'd asked herself, could you possibly know? It seemed to her that there was no way to be sure, and she'd vowed to keep her distance from men in future, and stay well clear of relationships which, it seemed to her, only brought heartache.

But then she'd met Ben, and somehow he'd broken through her defences, and she'd begun to believe he was one of the good ones. What if she was wrong about him? What if she was making a fool of herself yet again? The way he'd looked at her this morning... Okay, so she and Jennifer had been talking about grandkids and stuff, but honestly, the look on his face! If she had to put a name to it she'd have said it was panic.

Did that conversation really merit such a strong reaction? And what was the real reason for keeping their relationship a secret?

She couldn't help worrying that, yet again, she was making a complete fool of herself.

* * *

As Summer entered The Corner Cottage Bookshop the following day, there was a clanging on the stairs as Dolly made her way down, her hand trailing along the wrought iron banister, her heels making a ringing sound on each step.

'Morning, Summer,' Clemmie called, glancing up from the novel that lay open on the counter in front of her.

'Morning. Good book?'

'Brilliant.'

'Must be.' Dolly winked at Summer. 'It's the third time she's read *Persuasion* to my knowledge. Haven't you got a home to go to, by the way? You can't keep away from this place!'

Summer smiled.

'I'm about to make a coffee,' Dolly continued. 'Do you want one?'

'I wouldn't say no,' Summer said, leaning on the counter. 'Gran got here yesterday and she's already taken over the flat. I thought I'd come here instead for a bit of peace.'

Dolly nodded. 'Say no more. Coming right up.'

Clemmie put her book away, with some reluctance, and folded her arms. 'Is she that bad already? I wasn't expecting to see you this morning.'

'It's not the morning, however much you keep insisting it is!' Summer laughed. 'Are you half asleep or something? It's twelve-fifteen. I've just finished my stint at Whispering Willows, so I thought I'd pop in and see how you were before I start my shift at the pub at two. It's all go, you know. Well, for some of us, at any rate.'

Clemmie gave her a knowing look. 'Hmm. And why are you really here? Spill the beans.'

'I don't know what you're talking about.'

'Right, okay. I'll play the long game.' She picked up *Persuasion* and flicked to the page with the bookmark.

Summer took the book from her hands, slapped it on the counter, and leaned on it, causing Clemmie to cry out, 'Don't damage it!'

'Damage it?' Summer rolled her eyes. 'How can leaning on a book damage it? Here, put it back in its safe place if it makes you feel better.'

'Thanks.' Clemmie tucked it back under the counter. 'So, are you ready to talk?'

'Ooh, sounds promising.' Dolly carried in a tray of three mugs and a plate of biscuits from the little kitchen at the side of the shop and set it down on the counter. 'Am I about to hear some juicy gossip? Or am I about to be banished to the back room so you can gossip in peace?'

'It's not gossip,' Summer said reluctantly. 'It's just embarrassing.'

'Aw, we promise not to laugh.' Dolly patted her shoulder. 'Come on, tell your Auntie Dolly all about it. I'm a good listener. Ask our Clemmie.'

Clemmie didn't look convinced. 'Yeah, she's great, as long as you don't expect to get a word in edgeways while she's busy dishing out her advice afterwards.'

'I don't care about that,' Summer said. 'I don't think you can help anyway. I'll never be able to face Ben again.'

She told them what had happened at Monk's Folly and the look on his face when he'd walked in on hers and Jennifer's conversation.

'Sorry,' Dolly said when she'd finished, not looking as if she were sorry at all, 'but I think it's funny. I'd love to have seen Ben's face. Bet it frightened the life out of him.'

'Dolly! Don't be awful.' Clemmie looked deeply wounded on her friend's behalf. 'It's not funny.'

Dolly tutted. 'Oh, come on, it is. Ben heard them mentioning kids and did what all normal single men do. He freaked out. What you've got to understand is that the weaker sex—that's men if you hadn't realised by now, however much they like to tell you otherwise— are delicate little flowers when it comes to settling down. It has to be approached carefully, gently. They need time to get used to going out with someone, and they practically need therapy to discuss marriage. With Jennifer banging on about babies, it's a wonder he didn't run for the hills.'

'I think there was more to it than that.' Summer sipped her coffee and leaned against the counter. In the cold light of day her concerns about his reaction hadn't lessened, and Gran bringing it all back about Ian hadn't helped calm her nerves. 'We seem to get really close and then... I don't know. It's like he backs off, scared.'

'Which is what I've just explained,' Dolly said. 'If it's any consolation, in my experience they only get this panicky over women who actually matter to them. If he didn't care he wouldn't give a monkey's who you spoke to or what about. Take comfort from that.'

'I'm not into playing games,' Summer said fiercely. 'I deserve better than that.'

'You do,' Clemmie said. 'I'd be just as upset as you, Summer. In fact, I'd hide away and never be seen again if it had happened to me.'

'Thanks for that.' Summer nudged her, almost making her spill her coffee.

'Don't be daft. The pair of you are too soft,' Dolly said.

Honestly, how Dolly dredged up romantic feelings to write in her books Summer couldn't imagine.

'Ben's a sensible sort of bloke. He knows what Jen's like. We all do. Head in the clouds most of the time, and as soppy as this one here,' Dolly added, nodding towards Clemmie. 'Besides, everyone knows what mothers are like for wittering on about grandkids. Bet your mum's just the same, Summer. Ben will have forgotten all about it by now.'

'Will he?' Summer asked doubtfully.

'Of course he will. Trust your Auntie Dolly.' She glanced at her watch. 'Bloody hell, I didn't realise the time,' she said anxiously. She slurped the rest of her coffee and banged the mug on the counter. 'I'm going to have to go home, Clemmie.

I've got a Zoom call with my editor, remember? Will you be okay on your own?'

'I suppose I'll find a way, although you're very selfish. If it had been tomorrow, it wouldn't have mattered. You know it's always quieter on market days,' Clemmie joked.

'Isn't it just? Too many people flocking round the second-hand book stall instead of coming in here,' Dolly said. 'Tight beggars. Oh well, can't complain.'

'Yet you do,' Clemmie said. 'Frequently.'

'Cheeky sod.' Dolly laughed and fished her handbag from behind the counter. 'I'm sure you'll manage somehow. I'll love you and leave you, ladies. Don't do anything I wouldn't do.'

As she headed towards the door, she turned to Summer. 'If I were you, I'd have a chat with Ben. Clear the air. Especially if he's going to be at the wedding on Friday. Ooh, not long now! I'll see you then if not before.' She wagged her finger sternly. 'Get it sorted, girl. Stop being a wimp.'

She opened the shop door and the bell jingled as she left.

'She's right, you know,' Clemmie said thoughtfully. 'Look, why don't you go over to Stepping Stones and see him now? I'm sure you'd both feel better if you got things sorted.'

'I can't go over there,' Summer said. 'I'm embarrassed enough, thank you very much.' She rolled her eyes. 'Anyway, I'm sure there'll be enough people at the wedding for him to avoid me completely if he feels the need.'

Clemmie's face took on a more hesitant look. 'Are there a lot of people invited then?'

'Half the town I think. Mum's certainly making up for the quiet registry office do she had with Dad. And you know how Rafferty likes to think of himself as the genial pub landlord, centre of the community. Of course, with it being a Friday, not everyone will make it to the service, but the reception in the pub afterwards is practically open season, and it's set to go on through the evening, so I think most people will turn up at some point during the celebrations.'

'Is—is Ross coming, do you know?'

Summer frowned as the theory she'd dreamed up at the hen night resurfaced. 'Possibly. He's invited. Does it matter?'

Clemmie shrugged. 'Why should it matter?'

'Then why did you mention him specifically?'

Clemmie opened and closed her mouth without speaking. Her cheeks were pink again, which surely meant only one thing. Summer could hardly believe she was thinking it, but the idea wouldn't go away.

'Clemmie,' she said cautiously, 'is Ross the man who hurt you?'

Clemmie's already pink cheeks deepened in colour, and she backed away, clearly flustered.

'I told you; it was just kid's stuff.'

'But it *was* Ross?'

She didn't answer at first, her eyes darting along the counter as if she were desperately looking for something to distract them both. Eventually admitting defeat, she sighed and said, 'Well, maybe it was. But it was ages ago.'

'Clemmie!'

Clemmie's head shot up at Summer's exclamation, and she met her friend's incredulous stare with defiance.

'What? You don't think I'm good enough for Ross Lavender?'

'Why would I think that? I'm surprised, that's all. Ross just doesn't seem your type. Not at all. And you've always seemed so scathing about him, I just assumed...' Summer put her hand on Clemmie's. 'I'm sorry. I'm guessing he cheated on you.'

Clemmie pulled her hand away and picked up her mug. 'I really don't want to talk about it.'

'Okay, we won't. If that's what you want.' Summer felt a pang of disappointment. She'd thought she and Clemmie were good friends and had hoped they would share confidences. After all, she'd admitted her feelings for Ben. It hurt a little that Clemmie clearly didn't trust her enough to reciprocate.

As if reading her thoughts, Clemmie said, 'It's nothing personal. It's just—it still hurts.'

'How long ago was this?' Summer asked. 'I promise I won't ask anything else. I'd just like to understand how raw this is for you.'

Clemmie bit her lip, clearly undecided whether to tell her or not.

'You said it was kid's stuff,' Summer said. 'Did you mean that literally?'

'I was twenty and he was twenty-three,' Clemmie said.

'Hardly kid's stuff then! And—and you went out together how long?'

'Does it matter?' Clemmie's eyes flashed a warning and Summer held up her hands.

'Okay, I won't ask anything else. Sorry, Clem.'

They stood in silence for a few moments, sipping now and then at their mugs of coffee.

'Eighteen months.'

Summer blinked. 'Sorry?'

Clemmie sighed and put down her mug. 'We were together eighteen months. Then we weren't. Now, can we talk about something else, please? Like you and Ben.'

Realising Clemmie really had said as much as she wanted to about her relationship with Ross Lavender,

Summer let the subject drop. Not that she thought Clemmie's suggested alternative was any better.

'Can't we talk about the weather? Or cats? Or the state of the economy?'

Clemmie laughed, much to her relief. 'No thanks. Really though, Summer, joking aside, are you going to put things right with him?'

'How would I do that? Come to think of it, *why* would I do that? He's the one who couldn't wait to get rid of me.'

Clemmie frowned. 'He's a nice man, and thoughtful. I mean, he ordered that book for his mother as a surprise, didn't he? And you can't go wrong with a man who buys books as presents if you ask me.' Her eyes lit up. 'Oh wow! It came in this morning! He's supposed to be picking it up when he's got time. Why don't you take it over to Stepping Stones? That would be the perfect excuse. Tell him I asked you to deliver it as a favour!'

'Don't be daft.' Summer was surprised at how nervous she felt. 'I'm sure he can pick it up himself when he's good and ready.'

'But it would save him a trip,' Clemmie said. 'Coming here takes him out of his way. He can drive home straight down River Road, so it's a bit mean making him take a detour to Market Place, don't you think?'

She gave her a sly look and Summer shook her head, all too aware of the game she was playing.

Even so, she had a point, as did Dolly.

'Okay,' she said with a defeated sigh. 'Get me the damn book!'

Chapter Sixteen

The door of the consulting room had barely closed on Ben's patient when it was pushed open again and Clive strolled in, carrying two mugs of coffee.

'Don't tell me you made those?' Ben said, raising an eyebrow.

Clive frowned. 'Of course I didn't. Why on earth would I, and what difference does it make? Anyway, that's your last patient for the morning, so you've got plenty of time to chew the fat with me before I go on my callouts.'

'Have I? Am I not allowed a lunch break then?'

'You're not seeing your next patient until two.' He nodded at the clock on the wall which showed it was now twelve thirty-eight. 'You've got loads of time, so stop complaining.'

Clive settled himself on a stool and stared at Ben expectantly.

Ben sipped his coffee, not sure what was going on.

'Well?'

'Well what?' Ben asked, puzzled.

'Oh, come on, lad! Don't keep me in suspenders! You've had a face like a wet week all day. What's wrong?'

'I don't know what you mean,' Ben replied.

Clive pulled a face. 'Oh, okay. Like that, is it? *Mind your own business, Clive.* I get it.'

'There's nothing to tell,' Ben said, laughing in spite of himself. 'Stop fishing.'

'I don't believe you,' Clive said. 'You were perfectly happy when you left here to go home for your lunch yesterday, but you came back looking like your mother had given you sardine sandwiches. And we all know,' he added, 'how much you hate sardine sandwiches.'

Ben couldn't deny that. Just the thought of them made him feel queasy.

'You know, I'd like to think you and I are more than just boss and employee,' Clive said slowly. 'I hoped we were friends. Good friends. Maybe,' he said thoughtfully, 'even best friends. Almost. Though don't tell Joseph that. I must say I'm quite hurt you can't confide in me.'

'I can't confide in you because there's nothing to tell.'

'Oh. Okay. So boss and employee then.' Clive nodded and took a Penguin biscuit from his pocket. 'I've got another one here for you,' he told Ben. 'But since you're just my employee I think I'll hang on to it. Give it to my friend. Joseph.'

'You wouldn't!'

'Oh, I would, lad. I would.' Clive waved the Penguin in front of Ben, grinning widely. 'Are you weakening? Do you give in?'

'It's nothing really. I'm probably making more of it than it was.'

He couldn't tell Clive the truth. He just couldn't.

Clive's eyes narrowed. 'Why don't you tell me, and I'll tell you if you're making too much of it. Fair enough?'

'Must I?'

'Here, have a Penguin to sweeten the deal.'

Ben unwrapped the Penguin and nibbled it thoughtfully.

'Bloody hell, Ben! Eat it properly. You're making me nervous. So go on, tell me.'

Tell you? Tell you that I walked in on my mother about to reveal the awful truth to Summer about what I'd done? How I'd ruined her life, Jamie's life, and that I should pay for it for the rest of mine? He mentally shuddered at the thought. *Never in a million years.*

'It's just... Well, I babysat for Jonah's little boy the other night. At least, I helped Summer babysit to be more accurate.'

Clive's Penguin hovered in mid-air as he eyed Ben with excitement.

'You and Summer babysat together? This is huge. This is real progress! So, why the long face?'

Briefly, Ben told him all about his failed attempts to kiss her.

'Oh,' Clive said dismissively. 'Is that all? I mean, it's a shame and everything, but it's not as if she rejected you, is it? This was all outside forces, nothing to do with you or anything you'd done wrong. I don't know why you're giving it a second thought. There'll be plenty of other chances.'

'Maybe I'm cursed.'

Clive threw back his head and laughed, causing some of his coffee to splash out of the mug and land on his lap. 'Talk about being dramatic! Look, next time you see her just lock those lips in position before anyone else can get in the way. Once that first kiss is over you'll feel so much better.'

He crunched his Penguin for a moment, considering.

'She's really got to you, hasn't she?' he said at last. 'Summer Fletcher. According to Jane you waived the consulting fees for her when she brought Joseph's Bichon Frisé in the other week. Very telling. Not that I blame you. I wouldn't have charged Joseph for that anyway.'

'Fancy Jane telling you that!'

Clive shrugged. 'She didn't. She told Hannah, who told me. The girl's beside herself with excitement, bless her. Jane did tell us both that you looked all moony-eyed about her and couldn't stop staring at the poor girl though.'

'I wasn't!'

'Tell Hannah and Jane that. They've practically got you married off. And they're not the only ones.'

'I didn't do anything for the Bichon,' Ben explained. 'It was a false alarm so why would I charge her? Honestly, you three are as bad as each other. The Lavender Ladies have got nothing on you.'

'Funny you should say that,' Clive said. 'Did you know they've got a bet on about you and Summer? I bumped into Birdie at the post office. She wanted to know if I'd any inside information, because the winner stands to pocket a few quid depending on when you two get together.'

'That's old news,' Ben said. 'I'm surprised you've only just heard. Bit of a cheek, though not surprising. They'll bet on anything, however unlikely.' He shuffled awkwardly. 'Who's betting against us getting together?' he asked, trying to sound as if it didn't matter.

'Oh, no one. Everyone's agreed it will happen. The betting is on when. Eugenie's got you down for Christmas. Birdie and Rita don't think you'll be able to wait that long. They're convinced you'll hook up officially at the wedding.'

He laughed as Ben's mouth dropped open. 'Don't look so shocked! You know the Lavender Ladies. They know everything that goes on in this town. They probably knew you'd fallen for her before you did.' He leaned forward and lowered his voice. 'You *have* fallen for her, haven't you?'

'Based on gossip from the Lavender Ladies?'

'And Jane.'

'Okay, and Jane.'

'And Hannah, obviously.'

'Obviously.'

'And Bluebell.'

'Oh of course! Bluebell.' Ben rolled his eyes. 'Case closed then.'

'Well,' Clive said, 'you can't deny the evidence is mounting up. Chocolate hand-delivered to Monk's Folly, a romantic meal at The Farmer's Arms. And now I know you've been babysitting with her...' He cocked his head to the side, giving the matter some thought. 'I wonder how much the Lavender Ladies would pay me for that little nugget of information?'

Ben shook his head. 'You're incorrigible.'

'All's fair in love and making a few quid. Look, all I want to know is, who's likely to win the money, eh? When are you and Summer going to go public? Might have a bet on myself unless they forbid it. They're canny old birds, and after all you and I are best friends. I mean, I gave you my Penguin. What more can I say?'

Ben couldn't help laughing. 'If I knew I'd tell you, but the way things stand right now...'

His heart sank and his laughter died. How could he risk getting closer to Summer? If their relationship developed he'd have to confide in her. He'd have to tell her the truth about Leon before his mother did. He couldn't bear the thought of seeing the same look on Summer's face that he'd seen on his mother's the night of the accident.

He could remember it as if it were yesterday. That awful look in her eyes. He'd seen it so clearly—how ashamed she was of him. How much she loathed him.

He'd known then that she would never forgive him, not really, but it hadn't stopped him doing everything he could since to try to win her forgiveness.

'Rubbish!' Clive broke into his thoughts, which was probably a good thing. 'Pretty girl like that. She obviously likes you so just get on with it.'

'What have I got to offer someone like Summer?'

'What are you talking about? You're a personable enough young man. Not bad looking, if you like that sort of thing. Good, respectable job. Own home.' He grinned. 'No worries about getting a mortgage there. You're a professional, Ben. Most women would bite your hand off.'

'I really don't think they would.'

Clive eyed him thoughtfully for a moment. He put his mug on the counter and carefully folded his Penguin wrapper.

At last he said, 'Is this about the money?'

'Of course it's about the money!' Ben said, seizing on the excuse which was, after all, partly true. 'What else would it be about?'

'But what difference does money make?'

'Oh, come on! You do know who Rafferty Kingston is? His ex-wife created Lightweights—you know, the slimming club? He had shares in it, and then she sold it to Pounddroppers for millions. He's loaded.'

'Ooh, someone's been googling. But what's that got to do with you and Summer? Look, I think you're doing her a grave disservice,' Clive said firmly. 'She works at the pub; she's got a roof over her head. What does she need your money for? And she doesn't strike me as someone who's overly fussed about it anyway. Her stepfather might be rich, but she wasn't born to it, that much is obvious.

'Rumour has it her real dad's a taxi driver and she grew up in an ex-council house. Have you heard that one? Rita got it from Mrs Millican at the chippy, who swears it was told to her in confidence by Jim Barrow, the ticket man at Lavender House, who claims his wife heard it from Buttercup at Cutting It Fine. How can it possibly be untrue?'

His eyes twinkled with amusement and Ben wished he could find it as funny as Clive did.

When he didn't respond Clive sighed.

'If you ask me, you're overthinking this. Looking way too far ahead. You might not even like the girl once you really get to know her, but you won't find that out until you-know-what happens, will you? You know what they say in that old song. It's all in the kiss.'

Ben forced a smile. 'I suppose you've got a point.'

'Of course I have. You should know, Ben, I'm usually right.' Clive eased himself off the stool. 'Stop being a wuss. Tell her how you feel, then give her a big smacker and everyone can collect their winnings, or not as the case may be, and live happily ever after. I can't cope with all this drama; it's giving me indigestion. I'll give you until the end of the wedding. If you haven't plucked up the courage by then, I'll do it for you. Tell her I mean, not kiss her. And don't,' he added sternly as he headed towards the door, 'think I won't! I might just put a little flutter on this myself so it's in my interests to interfere.'

Ben had a horrible feeling he would, too. What was he supposed to do? He wanted to kiss Summer so badly it hurt but seeing her with his mother had reminded him that if he allowed himself to get too close to her it was inevitable that, at some point, he'd have to tell her what he'd done. And then...

The door swung open, and Jane stood there, her eyes wide with excitement.

'Ben, you have a visitor,' she said, or rather squeaked. She gave Clive a knowing look. 'It's Summer Fletcher,' she added, barely able to contain her glee before she rushed back into the reception.

Ben and Clive exchanged stunned glances.

'This is excellent,' Clive said. 'I'll send her in straight away, and I'll expect a full report when you're done. Don't let me down.'

* * *

Summer's face was flushed when she walked into the consulting room.

Ben half smiled; his stomach was too knotted to manage the full deal. He realised his hands were trembling and stuck them in his pockets so she wouldn't notice.

To his eyes, she looked more beautiful than ever, despite being dressed for the stables. It was just his luck. It would have been so much easier if she'd looked terrible.

'This is unexpected. What can I do for you?' He wondered how he'd managed to sound so normal but was highly relieved he had.

To his surprise, she suddenly thrust a carrier bag into his hands.

'What's this?'

'Clemmie asked me to deliver it,' she said hurriedly. 'It's that book you ordered for your mum. It arrived at the shop today. She said you can pay next time you're in the market place.'

'Oh.' He glanced at the bag, noting the Corner Cottage Bookshop logo. 'I'd forgotten all about it,' he said, putting it on the consulting table. 'It's nice of you to bring it but there was really no need. It's not her birthday for a few weeks so there's no hurry.'

'That's what *I* said. Look, Ben,' she said suddenly, 'I think we need to get a few things straight.'

He hadn't expected that, and it threw him. 'Oh? Like what?'

'What you heard yesterday—me and your mum.'

She cleared her throat, obviously anxious, and he wasn't sure whether that helped or if it made him feel worse. His heart thudded and he waited for the inevitable questions about Leon.

'I'd hate for you to think that I was encouraging her.'

He wasn't sure what she meant by that, and his confusion must have shown on his face because she said quickly, 'About the baby talk, I mean.'

'Baby talk?'

'All that stuff about wanting to fill the house with grandchildren and about me being just what you need.'

Her face was bright pink now. He wanted to kiss her so badly it hurt. That's what they'd been talking about? That's what Summer was worried about? He felt a weight lifting and almost hugged her there and then.

'Honestly, Summer, don't worry about that. It really doesn't matter. Not at all.'

He smiled at her, hoping she'd return the favour, but she still looked worried.

'The thing is,' she said hesitantly. 'I saw your face.'

His stomach plummeted as he eyed her uncertainly. 'What do you mean?'

'Oh come on, Ben! You looked appalled; you really did.

203

And I don't know whether that's because you didn't want me to get any ideas about settling down with you, or because you didn't like me going to Monk's Folly and chatting with your mum full stop.'

'It's—no, it's—'

'The thing is, I told you right at the beginning, after our date at The Farmer's Arms, that I didn't want to be messed about again, after everything my dad had done to Mum.'

'I know. I remember.'

'But it wasn't just about Dad,' she said.

There was a long pause and he waited, sensing whatever she had to say was difficult for her.

'When I worked at the cake factory, there was this man who worked in packing. Ian. We started seeing each other and I honestly thought... Well, anyway, it turned out I wasn't the only girl he was seeing. I wasn't even the only girl from the factory he was seeing. All his mates knew about it, which made it even worse. I felt like such an idiot, like everyone was laughing at me behind my back.'

'I'm sorry, Summer,' Ben said softly. 'That must have been horrible.'

'It was. It brought it all back. Everything Mum had been through. I couldn't get out of that cake factory fast enough. I grabbed the first job that came along at a supermarket, even though it didn't pay any better. I just wanted to get away from the gossip and seeing that creep every day.' She closed her eyes, remembering. 'In the end it didn't matter because I moved here to Tuppenny Bridge before I even started the new job.'

'Is that why your mum asked you to move here?' he asked.

She shook her head. 'She doesn't know about him. No

one knows except Gran. Apart from her you're the first person I've ever confessed to.'

'Confessed? It's not a guilty secret. None of that was your fault.'

'I'd never understood before, you see,' she burst out. 'How Mum hadn't realised what Dad was up to, I mean. But Ian made me see how easy it is to be fooled by someone you love. Or at least, someone you think you love. I didn't have a clue.' She shook her head. 'Why do people do such cruel things? And how can you ever really know what's in someone's head?'

'I suppose...'

'What I'm saying is, it was hard enough for me to trust you. I was so scared you were another man keeping secrets, and I really can't cope with that. So I need you to be sure, Ben. I need you to be absolutely one hundred per cent certain that you want to be with me or there's no way I can do this. I can't go through it all again. I just needed you to be clear on that.'

'Well,' he said, feeling sick to his stomach, 'I'm very clear on it now.'

She waited, watching him closely as he struggled with what she'd just told him. She didn't want a man who was keeping secrets from her. It couldn't be any clearer, could it?

Summer dropped her gaze and shuffled awkwardly. 'Right, well I'd better get off. I've got a shift at the pub soon.'

She headed towards the door and turned back to him, her eyes shimmering with tears.

'Hope your mum enjoys the book. Bye, Ben.'

The door swung shut and she was gone.

Ben puffed out his cheeks, staring at the floor as he replayed everything that had just been said.

'Well! Of all the feeble...!'

He looked up to see Clive standing in the doorway looking disgusted.

'You were listening?'

'Of course I was bloody listening! I think I deserve a medal for not barging in and translating for you. Bloody hell, Ben. What's wrong with you, lad? Are you completely oblivious to the workings of the opposite sex?'

'What do you mean?'

'What do I mean?' Clive rolled his eyes. 'I give up. The girl was begging you to tell her you wouldn't let her down, that you were reliable, that she could trust you.' He snorted. 'Do I even know you?'

Ben narrowed his eyes. 'It's not that easy!'

'Of course it's easy. She likes you. A lot. You like her. A lot. Are you sure it was the Andersons' collie you castrated the other week?'

Ben gasped. 'Wow! You're brutal.'

Clive shrugged. 'I'm going out. Call just came through from Carson's Farm. Sick pig. Probably not as sick as I feel right now, but there you go.'

He marched out of the consulting room, letting the door swing shut behind him. Ben stared after him for a moment then drained his coffee with shaking hands, feeling more depressed than ever.

The door opened again, and Clive popped his head round, holding out his hand.

'Sorry I was a bit harsh on you,' he said, sounding sheepish. 'It's only because I care, honestly. Here, have my last Penguin.'

Ben stared at the chocolate biscuit in Clive's hand for a moment, then he barged out of the consulting room, almost knocking into his startled boss.

'Ben?'

Ben didn't stop. He hurried through the reception area and out into the car park, looking everywhere for a glimpse of that chestnut hair.

She was just heading through the gates, and he called her name as he sped up, desperate to make her stop.

She turned, clearly surprised as he ran up to her. 'What is it?'

What was it? He didn't even know what he wanted to say to her. Where were they supposed to go from here? Because the truth was, he *was* keeping a secret from her. A terrible secret. But even as he looked at her, he knew it wasn't the sort of secret she feared. She'd been begging him to tell her he wouldn't play games with her, that he wouldn't cheat on her. Well, he could promise her that at least.

Summer was frowning at him, a puzzled look in her eyes, but also... Ben's heart skipped. There was something else in her expression. Was it hope?

Taking his courage in both hands he said, 'I'm sorry. I really messed up there, but it was only because you surprised me, that's all.'

'It's okay.' She shook her head, laughing nervously. 'I suppose it was a bit intense. But the thing is, Ben. I like you. I really like you. But I have to be sure you're not playing games. Do you want to go out with me or not?'

He cupped her face in his hands and kissed her gently. The softness of her lips against his made him tremble, and as her hands cradled his own face and she returned his kiss, it became more urgent, as if everything he'd kept pent up for so long inside him was finally breaking free.

At last—too soon—they broke apart, and Summer stared up at him.

'Bloody hell.'

He gave her a wary look. 'Bloody hell good or bloody hell bad?'

She kissed him again, a quicker kiss this time, but long enough to stir his blood all over again.

'Bloody hell, *amazing*,' she murmured. 'What took you so long?'

It was a sentiment echoed by Clive, who was—rather embarrassingly—standing at the door, arms folded, when Ben finally returned to the surgery, having arranged to pick Summer up after work the following day.

'That,' Clive said with obvious pride, 'was brilliant. Well done, lad. I knew you had it in you. What took you so long?'

Ben grinned at him, suddenly sheepish, and Clive ruffled his hair.

'Here you go,' he said, handing Ben the Penguin. 'Looks like you're going to need all your energy. Besides, you deserve it.'

Chapter Seventeen

His mother was so excited about Ben dating Summer that she'd offered to cook for them both.

'Just invite her round here,' she said. 'I'll set the table and make everything look lovely. I'll cook you a wonderful dinner and then Jamie and I will make ourselves scarce, won't we, Jamie?'

Jamie glanced up from his mobile phone. 'Yeah, no problem. Go on, Romeo. Ask her round.'

There was a distracted look about his brother that worried Ben.

'Are you okay?' he asked. 'You haven't been off that phone all evening.'

'Just browsing,' Jamie said. 'So, yeah, bring Summer round. Nice to see you acting like a normal bloke for a change, isn't it, Mum?'

'Oh, Jamie, don't be so unkind,' she replied.

Jamie shrugged and tapped his phone again. Ben rolled his eyes.

He followed his mother into the kitchen as she began to prepare a light supper for them all.

'The truth is, I don't have the money to take Summer anywhere, but I don't think bringing her back here is a great idea for a first date.'

'It's not your first date though, is it?' she said. 'It's your second.'

'Even so. It's a bit sad, don't you think? Taking your girlfriend back to your house for a date so soon in a relationship. Especially if your mum cooks the dinner.'

His mother beamed at him as she cracked eggs into a bowl. 'So it *is* a relationship? I'm so happy for you, Ben. Summer's a lovely girl, and you so deserve this.'

With a huge effort, Ben pushed away the clamour of voices in his head that immediately assured him he far from deserved it. He looked at her, unable to hide his surprise.

'Really?'

'Well of course.' She laughed. 'It's about time you had some fun.'

'I was thinking I could take her for a walk by the river,' he said hesitantly.

She pulled a face. 'You can't call that a date,' she said. 'Do you want her to think she's not worth the effort? After all, that's just not true, is it?'

'Of course it isn't, but I don't know what to do about it.'

She finished beating the eggs and added seasoning, then melted butter in a pan. 'Why don't you just tell her you're a bit low on funds then?'

'That's what Clive said.'

'Wise man.'

'He said she might offer to pay for our date herself.'

His mother looked horrified at the suggestion. 'Ben! You can't possibly ask a lady out and expect her to pay.'

He couldn't help smiling. 'I thought you said Clive was a wise man.'

'Well, he is, but nobody's perfect,' she said, pouring the eggs into the pan and tipping it to make sure they covered the entire surface.

'Don't worry. There's no way I'd ask Summer out if I couldn't afford to pay. But that does mean I'm stuck for somewhere to take her—at least until next payday.'

She chewed her lip, thinking, as she drew a line through the egg mixture then tilted the pan to ensure it filled up again. Suddenly her eyes lit up and she said, 'Got it! I can't think why it never occurred to us before. A picnic, Ben. I'll prepare the food and you take her for a picnic on the riverbank. It will be lovely. We've had such beautiful sunny weather, I'm sure she'll love it.'

Ben considered it. 'I suppose a picnic could work.'

'Of course it will work. What could be more romantic than a picnic on a riverbank on the perfect summer's evening? It'll transform an ordinary walk to something magical. Leave the food to me. Just call Summer and ask her not to eat before you pick her up.'

'You really think she'll go for it?'

She beamed at him. 'Trust me on this. So are you going to call her?'

'Yes, I'll call her. But, Mum, leave the food to me, okay?'

'Oh, but, Ben, I'd love to do it.'

'I know, and I appreciate that, but this is my date, and I want to do something nice for Summer, all right?'

She smiled. 'Of course. I understand. Just give me a yell if you get stuck.'

They heard the living room door slam and footsteps on the stairs as Jamie ran upstairs. Then the bedroom door above their heads banged shut.

Ben sighed. 'What's up with him now?'

'I have no idea. It must be something he saw on social media. I don't know why he keeps looking. It seems to put him in a terrible mood. Shout up to him will you, Ben. Tell him this omelette will be ready in a minute or two. Ham, cheese, and mushroom okay?'

Ben nodded, distracted.

'And you'll ask Summer on the picnic?'

'Yes, Mum,' he said, shaking his head. 'I won't get any peace until I do, will I?'

'Not really. Now go and tell Jamie about the omelette.'

Ben hurried through the to the living room and opened the door.

'Jamie! Supper's nearly ready.'

'I'm not hungry.'

Ben sighed. 'Well, if you don't eat now I can guarantee you'll announce you're starving ten minutes after we've finished eating ours.'

There was silence for a moment, then Jamie yelled, 'Oh for God's sake! All right. Give me five minutes.'

Frowning, Ben wondered what had rattled his younger brother this time. Was he just being the moody teenager that he seemed to have turned into these past few months, or was there more to it than that? His eyes fell on Jamie's phone lying on the coffee table.

'Is he coming down?'

Mum was standing at the door, and as he looked at her, he saw her gaze slide to the coffee table.

'What is it?' she asked. 'Why were you looking at his phone?'

'I was wondering what's going on with him,' Ben admitted. 'He's not himself and I can't help thinking there's something we don't know.'

'Well...' She hesitated. 'I mean, we can always check his phone. Although really, I don't think we'll find anything to worry about. You installed that app on it before we gave it to him, remember? The one that monitors his online behaviour.'

'I know, and I'm careful to check what he's doing on there,' Ben said. 'Jamie knows that, so I can't imagine he'd risk looking at anything he shouldn't. But he's so obsessed with social media these days I can't shake the feeling we're missing something.'

'Well, there's only one way to find out.'

After all, he'd informed his brother that was the deal. Jamie was allowed a mobile phone as long as he agreed that Ben would monitor his activity on there. Of course, Jamie hadn't liked it, but Ben was adamant.

'It's not about invading your privacy,' he'd explained. 'It's about your safety. It's that or you don't get a phone. Take it or leave it.'

Of course Jamie had agreed, however reluctantly, and Ben hadn't really worried about him being on the device at all. Not until this summer anyway.

He picked up Jamie's phone and tapped the screen, punching in the pin number his brother had told him.

'It's the wrong one!' He stared at his mother. 'He's changed the pin number!'

'He never has! Well, the little monkey.'

'Okay, if he wants to play it that way.' Ben put Jamie's phone down and took out his own. 'I'll check in on the app, see what he's been up to. I usually look most evenings anyway but I've been a bit—distracted—this week. More fool me.'

He quickly found the monitoring app on his phone and sat down, scrolling through Jamie's online activity while his mum anxiously peered over his shoulder.

'Anything unusual?'

Ben frowned. 'Nothing that I can see. He's spending a lot of time on Instagram but there's nothing dodgy on there as far as I can tell.'

'No dangerous websites?'

'He wouldn't be able to access them. I put a block on them.' He shook his head. 'No text messages to worry about either. Honestly, I can't see a problem.'

'Well, that's good, isn't it?' Mum said hopefully.

Ben returned to Instagram, wondering if Jamie had sent messages from there or received any. His main worry was that his brother was being cyberbullied or trolled. He'd definitely set Jamie's account to private, though, and there was nothing that caused him any concern when he checked.

Looking at the photographs he'd posted there was nothing particularly interesting except...

'What is it?' Mum asked as Ben stared at the photograph in surprise. He held up his phone to show her. 'Well,' she said, 'I would never have thought...'

She gazed at the photo of Jamie and Frankie, looking very close as they snuggled together, all smiles for the camera.

'It doesn't mean anything,' he said doubtfully. 'Does it?'

'I'm sure it doesn't,' she said. 'Although... he's got his arm around her, and she's pouting for the camera like those silly models you see on the television. Oh, Ben, I hope he's behaving himself. They're both under sixteen after all, and he swore to me they were just friends.'

'Of course they're just friends,' he reassured her, although he was beginning to wonder. Jamie and Frankie were spending a lot of time together lately, and it was only since Frankie had arrived on the scene that his brother seemed to have become obsessed with social media.

She was something different, he supposed. Interesting. With that blue hair and the nose stud and all that money to flash around, how could Jamie not fall under her spell? And he was naïve in so many ways.

But Frankie would be going home soon, and then what? He didn't want Jamie to waste his precious GCSE year pining away for a girl who lived miles away. This was the worst possible time for him to become distracted by a relationship. If his brother wasted this opportunity Ben wasn't sure his mother would cope.

Chapter Eighteen

Wednesday evening was bright with glorious August sunshine. Ben and Summer strolled past the bridge, Ben carrying a picnic basket in one hand and holding Summer's hand in the other.

'This is such a lovely idea, Ben,' she told him. 'I can't remember the last time I had a picnic. Oh, yes I can. It was on the beach at Burlington-on-Sea with all my family and Rafferty's family. Seems like years ago now. Anyway, that was nothing like this. This is so romantic.' She smiled up at him. 'Let's hope there are no spies around. News sure got around fast last time we went out together.'

'I told you it would,' he said. 'This town's a hotbed of gossip. I've been stopped more times in the street this last couple of weeks than I've been stopped in all the years I've lived here. Everyone wants to know what's going on with me and *that lass at t'pub.*'

She laughed. 'Is that what they call me? And have you told them what's going on with us?'

'I said we'd gone out for one meal, and they should mind their own business,' he said.

'Clemmie practically shone a light in my eyes when I called in at the bookshop this morning,' she told him. 'She wanted to know everything. And Mum said Bluebell told her they were sitting there that night in The Farmer's Arms watching our every move and analysing our body language. How embarrassing.'

They reached a good spot on the riverbank and Ben spread the picnic blanket on the ground. He'd sensibly decided to stay on the Monk's Folly side of the river, knowing the other side was far busier and they'd be more likely to be seen.

'At least Miss Lavender's given us her seal of approval,' Summer said as they settled on the blanket and opened the basket. 'Not that she knows about today but in general.'

'I'm in her good books ever since Clive put me in sole charge of looking after her Yorkies. She's got to keep on the right side of me, hasn't she?'

'She's clearly revised her opinion of you since you were little.' Summer stared at the food Ben had set out on the blanket. 'This looks lovely.'

Ben gave her a quizzical smile. 'You're being very polite. I know it's not exactly classy. I'll be honest, I don't have much to do with cooking and stuff. I mean, I can do the basics, but Mum loves it so much there's never been any real need. So, well...' He waved a hand at the picnic. 'As you can see, it's nothing to write home about.'

'It looks good to me.'

They each took plates and filled them up with some of the sandwiches Ben had made, and the bacon, cheese and tomato slices that he'd bought from Bridge Bakery.

'What did you mean,' Ben asked suddenly, 'about Miss Lavender revising her opinion of me?'

'Oh!' Summer waved a hand dismissively. 'Just something she said at Mum's hen night.'

'What did she say?'

'She said—well, she just said you were a bit of a brat when you were little. The Pennyfeathers said you were a little wild, that's all. But they all agreed you're not like that any more. That you changed after—after what happened.'

'Oh,' he said, not wanting to go down that particular rabbit hole. 'Anyway,' he added brightly, 'are you enjoying that?'

'Mm. Delicious.' She gave him a knowing smile. 'I do love these slices from Bridge Bakery.'

'You've got me,' he told her. 'But the sandwiches were all made with my own fair hands. Mum wasn't impressed but then she's a perfectionist in the kitchen. How about your mum?'

'My mum?' Summer burst out laughing. 'My mum's idea of cooking is pricking a film lid with a fork and sticking a dish in a microwave for a few minutes. Mind you, I can't really blame her. Dad would never eat anything unless it came with chips so there wasn't much point in expanding her repertoire. Anyway, she hardly cooks at all since she got together with Rafferty, since he's so good at it and loves it. He even made the food for her hen night.'

'I wish Mum had gone to that,' Ben said. 'It would have done her the world of good.'

'Why didn't she? She told me she'd had a migraine and forgot to cancel but I'm not convinced. What do you think changed her mind?'

He sighed. 'Last-minute nerves I suppose. She's so out of

the loop I think every venture into the wider world fills her with dread.'

'Doesn't she go shopping, though? She must step outside Monk's Folly sometimes.'

Ben thought about it. Mostly, he realised, the shopping was done by him or—on rare occasions—by Jamie. She would tell Ben what she needed, and he'd nip to Maister's after work. The small supermarket was just off Station Road near Market Place, so it was no hardship, and of course he had the Land Rover, so it seemed to make sense.

Now he wondered if he should have coaxed her to do the shopping herself. Even if he'd taken her in the car at the weekend it would have got her out of the house. Maybe he'd suggest that to her for next week.

'Sometimes. Did the hen night go all right?' he asked. 'I couldn't believe how early Jonah and Rafferty got home from the stag party, could you? Hardly a wild night out obviously.'

She giggled and his heart leapt at the sound. 'What do you expect with a vicar organising it?'

'Zach?'

'Well, he is Rafferty's best friend. Arlo's giving Mum away, and his younger brother is acting as best man, but won't be here until the day of the wedding, so Zach stepped in to plan the stag night. Although,' she added, her eyes glittering with amusement, 'how much planning it took to book a table at an Indian restaurant is anyone's guess.'

'I'm sure Rafferty enjoyed it though.'

'He did. He's hardly one for wild nights out. Neither is Mum. She was quite happy with a few friends coming round to the flat. Poor Frankie hid in her bedroom all evening.'

'Oh? Why's that?'

'You know what teenagers are like. They find everything ultra-embarrassing and anyone over thirty too ancient to bother with. She was hoping Mum would get professional caterers in so she could photograph the food for Instagram, and she refused point blank to share pictures of her dad's offerings.' She giggled. 'Why anyone wants to look at pictures of other people's food is beyond me anyway, but Frankie reckons it's a sure-fire way to get likes. People are very strange.'

'Hmm. I know what you mean about teenagers. Jamie's just the same, and he gets in quite a strop sometimes when he's been on social media. I don't think it's very good for them at all but try keeping them off it. He never used to care about it until this summer. I think it must be Frankie's influence,' he said, trying to sound light-hearted. 'Jamie thinks I'm boring and old-fashioned because I don't bother with it, but who even has the time? And what's the point of it anyway?'

'I suppose back in your day,' Summer teased, 'teenagers went out and talked to each other, instead of sitting in their bedrooms all night playing computer games and forming virtual friendships. I do take his point. You are only twenty-nine after all. Mind you, I can't be bothered with social media either, so I'm on your side really.'

Ben thought about his own teenage years, and the friends he'd hung out with back then. What they'd got up to. He'd been about to pick up a sandwich, but his appetite appeared to have deserted him suddenly.

Summer's eyes were full of curiosity. 'Does it bother you? Jamie and Frankie, I mean.'

Anxious to reassure her, he shook his head. 'Not really. I'm glad he's got a friend close by.'

'But...?'

Was it that obvious?

'I just wish he'd study a bit harder,' he confessed. 'This holiday was a great opportunity for him to get ahead. He's got his GCSEs this year and it's important that he works hard if he's going to go to a good university.'

'You've really set your heart on him going to uni, haven't you?'

Ben nodded. 'It would mean the world to Mum. She's so keen for him to do well. To be fair he's really bright. His teachers are confident he can achieve top grades, and it would be a crime for him to throw that away. Trouble is, he seems to be having doubts about his future.'

'You mean, about going to university?'

Ben wasn't sure if he should say what was on his mind but realised he couldn't keep quiet about it. It was too important.

'It's this friendship he's got with Frankie,' he said reluctantly. 'He seems to be changing before my eyes, and I'm worried about him.'

'But I thought you were okay with them hanging out together?' Summer said, looking puzzled.

'I was. I am. I mean, Frankie's a nice girl—different, but nice. It's been good for him to have someone to hang out with. It's this Instagram thing. He's obsessed. I'm tempted to take his phone away, or even limit his hours on it, but I don't think it would go down well if I did.'

'You're not kidding,' Summer said. 'It would be like disconnecting him from his air supply.'

'I know, I know.' Ben sighed. 'But he's changing and it's not for the better. Do you know Frankie spent a small fortune on new clothes for him in York?'

'Yeah. Her mother gave her a credit card, and she wanted to treat him. She didn't mean any harm. Frankie loves shopping, and she probably had great fun treating him. Anyway, she's somehow managed to persuade him to put in some hours at Whispering Willows, so it's not all bad. Joseph's over the moon with them both, and it's a weight off my mind, knowing he's got help when I can't be there.'

'You're kidding?'

'You didn't know?'

'Nope, not a clue. That's great. I'm so relieved he's getting outside and doing something other than playing on games. I don't know how she managed to talk him into doing it, though.' He hesitated. 'Are you sure she and Jamie are just friends? You haven't noticed anything that suggests they're going out together?'

'No, nothing. Frankie's very clear they're not boyfriend and girlfriend. Where is this coming from?'

He shook his head and smiled at her. 'Just me being an overprotective big brother. Jamie will be fine, I'm sure.'

'I'm sure he will,' she agreed. 'Like you say he's bright. Anyway, would it matter if they *were* seeing each other?'

'Only that Frankie will be going back home soon, and the last thing I need is Jamie moping around after her. Broken hearts and GCSEs aren't a good combination.'

She laughed. 'Teenagers have a way of finding their way through the messiness of life and coming out the other side. Look at us!'

He reached for her hand. 'You're absolutely right. Have a chocolate chip cookie. Bridge Bakery's finest.'

She laughed. 'I'd rather have something else, if it's all the same to you.'

His heart thudded and he leaned in for a kiss.

Summer sighed with pleasure. 'You're very good at kissing, you know. If there'd been A levels in that subject you'd have got top grades.'

'Well, thank you for that. However,' he added, 'I'm actually aiming for a degree.'

'Maybe we should do some more revision then,' she said,

pushing the picnic basket to one side and moving closer to him.

After that they lost all interest in eating, and the remains of the picnic lay untouched and forgotten.

'We could do this again tomorrow,' Ben murmured as they sat, some time later, with their arms around each other, gazing contentedly at the river, and smiling at the ducks that swam up to investigate them. A man in a kayak went by and they waved to him as he nodded and called good evening to them.

'I wish we could,' Summer said regretfully. 'I promised Mum I'd spend tomorrow evening at home. We're having a girly night to calm her down before the wedding. I'd love to be here with you again.'

'There'll be other evenings,' he promised. 'Other picnics.'

'And lots more kissing,' she said, making him laugh.

He tapped her nose. 'Definitely lots more of that,' he said. 'It's compulsory.'

She snuggled against him and said, 'Are you coming to the wedding, or will you be at work?'

'I'm working, but Clive's said we can close early, so hopefully I'll be at the reception at some point. Are your mum and Rafferty all set to get married?'

'You'd think so, considering how much planning and detail has gone into this wedding.' Summer rolled her eyes. 'Somehow, Mum's still finding things to worry about. It will all go okay in the end, I'm sure.'

She wrinkled her nose. 'Ellis will be here on Friday morning.'

'Ellis?'

'Rafferty's youngest son. You know, I told you, he's the best man. Although if he's the best man, Lord help the rest of them. He's an artist who lives in Devon. I haven't seen him for over a year and a half, but he's coming to the wedding.'

'You don't sound too keen.'

'I'm not. I'm just glad we've no room for him in the flat and he's staying at The Lady Dorothy instead,' she said, referring to another pub in Tuppenny Bridge that stood at the other end of the market place from The White Hart Inn.

She sipped some fruit juice that Ben had thoughtfully packed. 'Ellis had a bit of a crush on me,' she admitted. 'As in, he truly believed his feelings were reciprocated, and that it was just a matter of time before I fell into his arms.'

Ben's stomach lurched. 'Really? But they weren't? Reciprocated, I mean.'

'Definitely not!'

The certainty in her tone gave him reassurance. 'Not your type then?'

'Definitely not,' she repeated, giving him a playful grin. 'I seem to fall for brown-haired, blue-eyed vets, so you've been very lucky.'

'Rather than Devonshire artists?'

'Rather than anyone. Besides...' She lay down beside him, and he stroked her hair, feeling a surge of happiness as she twisted around and rested her head on his lap, 'he reminded me too much of my dad.'

'Your dad? In what way?'

She didn't reply at first, as if she was thinking it through.

'I suppose,' she said, 'because of the way he convinced himself he was madly in love with me, the way Dad always said he was mad about Mum, even though he was always chasing other women. And Ellis was already seeing someone when he first started flirting with me. She dumped him, apparently, and good for her.'

'Your dad's behaviour's really affected you, hasn't it?' he said sympathetically.

'I love my dad,' she said. 'Don't think I don't. And he's changed a lot since him and Mum divorced. He's had therapy, and he's really trying to be a better person. But he made her very miserable for a long time, and really, it feels as if their whole life together was based on lies.

'And that was the thing with Ellis. I couldn't really believe a word he said, because he lied, as much to himself as anyone else. I couldn't live like that. You know, Mum, Billie and Gran, they all knew what Dad was like, but they didn't tell me. They thought they were protecting me, but all that did was make it more of a shock when I found out the truth. I really thought he was one of the good guys.'

'I'm so sorry you went through all that,' he told her, seeing the pain in her eyes. 'I never meant to hurt you, you know, or make you feel as if I was playing games with your feelings.'

She smiled at him. 'I know that now. We've both made mistakes, but that was then.'

'And this is now,' he said softly.

'It certainly is.' Summer gazed up at him. 'So, my very own James Herriot, have you been bitten or kicked by any ungrateful patients this week?'

'Not a patient. Thought I was going to get thumped by an owner though.'

Ben began to tell her about the case of an overweight bull terrier and his overprotective owner, who insisted the dog didn't need to be put on a diet and took exception to Ben's diagnosis of obesity.

In the back of his mind, though, he kept thinking about what she'd said. It must have taken Summer a huge leap of faith to take a chance on going out with him. She clearly had trust issues, and who could blame her?

The knot of tension in his stomach tightened. He was falling in love with her, there was no hiding from that now, but that meant only one thing. The time was coming for him to tell her the truth. If they were to make a go of this relationship there had to full disclosure.

And the one thing Ben was sure about now was that, more than anything, he wanted this relationship to work.

Chapter Nineteen

With the wedding due to take place at two o'clock the following day, Rafferty and Arlo had been banished to The Lady Dorothy on Thursday evening, while Summer and her mum, together with Gran, Billie, and Frankie had a cosy evening, settling down to watch soppy films on television, chat about the forthcoming nuptials, and reminisce about Billie and Arlo's wedding.

'So much has happened since then,' Sally said. 'It's amazing to think it's only been two and a half years. Look where we were then to where we are now.' She put her arms around Billie and Summer, who were sitting either side of her on the sofa. 'I'm so glad your dad's doing okay, and that he's not upset about the wedding.'

'Honestly, Mum,' Billie said, 'he was really pleased for you both. You don't have to worry about him.'

'I've told her that 'til I'm blue in the face,' Gran said. 'She'll never change. Still,' she added, a smile on her face, 'that's what makes her Sally, and that's why we love her so much.'

Summer, Billie, and Sally all stared at her in shock.

'Wow, it really is a special occasion,' Billie said. 'I don't think you've ever said anything so nice about any of us.'

'I'm happy and mellow and all's right with the world,' Gran said, nodding contentedly. 'I've finally found a pair of shoes that I like for the wedding, Rafferty's bloody awful parents won't be there which means I won't have to look at their sour faces all day, and most importantly, my girl's finally getting the happy ending she deserves. Nothing can spoil that for me.'

The mellow mood didn't last long for any of them.

When the wedding day dawned, the flat above the pub became a whirlwind of panic, missing make-up bags, laddered tights, and frequent, fevered glances at the kitchen clock, followed by gasps of horror at how quickly time was passing.

Ellis was due to arrive at around ten o'clock, and would be going straight to The Lady Dorothy, where he had a room booked, to meet his dad and Arlo. Summer was glad to have Billie, Frankie, and Gran on hand to help keep her mum as calm as possible.

Gran had insisted on doing her own hair, but Sally, Billie, Frankie, and Summer spent ages at Cutting It Fine, along with Kat who'd joined them to get her own hair done, having left baby Hattie with the Pennyfeathers.

'They're so excited,' she told them. 'The aunties, I mean. Although Eugenie has rather thrown a spanner in the works.'

'Oh?' Sally raised an eyebrow, unable to turn her head as she was sitting underneath a hair dryer. 'What's happened?'

'Eugenie didn't want them to show you up—for that, read *her* up—at the wedding, so she forked out on some dresses for them that are similar to the one she's going to be wearing. Honestly, they're beautiful, but of course they're not to the aunties' taste, and they're grumbling like mad. I don't think they'll dare not wear them, though, so be prepared for a big surprise at the church. They might actually turn up looking normal for a change.'

'Bless them,' Sally said, laughing. 'They can turn up wearing ponchos and sombreros over leather chaps and cowboy boots for all I care. As long as they're happy.'

Arlo popped his head round the door, causing shrieks of protest from both the customers and hairdressers.

'Rafferty's not with you, is he?' Sally said.

Arlo laughed. 'He wouldn't dare. He's holed up in The Lady Dorothy, don't worry. Your chef—Chris, is it?—just asked me to tell you that the caterers are here and the cake's arrived safely. Everything's going to schedule and you're not to worry.'

'Aw, that's so thoughtful of him. I was going to ring and ask but I didn't like to pester him. Thanks, love.'

'You're very welcome. I'll see you later, Sally. Not long now!'

He gave her the thumbs up and closed the door again.

Sally leaned back and fanned her face with her hand. 'I'm having palpitations.'

'Get your laughing gear around this then,' Bluebell said, handing her a glass of sparkling wine. 'That'll sort you out and calm you down. You heard the man. Everything's going to plan, so there's no need to worry. It'll be fine, Sal.'

'It was good of Chris to offer to oversee everything at the pub,' Sally said. 'It's his day off, you know. All the staff are coming to the wedding, bless them.'

They had to force a late breakfast down themselves when they got back to the flat, although Sally barely ate a thing. Gran, on the other hand, tucked into bacon sandwiches as if she hadn't a care in the world, ventured outside to smoke one of her beloved cigarettes, then finished the cycle with a hot, strong cup of tea.

She was made up, hair done, and dressed up by one o'clock, and couldn't understand all the fuss. She sat on the sofa watching *Escape to the Country* on iPlayer while all around her chaos ensued.

She only glanced up when Summer and Billie turned off the television and said, 'Well, what do you think?'

Gran looked them up and down with suspiciously misty eyes. 'You look smashing,' she told them. 'That colour really suits you both. You look like floating clouds.'

'Not us, Gran,' Summer said. 'Mum!'

Gran turned her head, and she gasped as Sally smiled at her from the living room door. She was wearing a floor-length ivory satin gown with a Bardot neckline and full skirt, and she looked the picture of elegance. Her hair was swept up in a casual updo, with tendrils of hair at either side of her face, and a sparkly crystal halo nestled into the top of the bun.

'Well, by hell.' For once, Gran seemed to have nothing else to say.

Sally walked into the room, Frankie at her side.

'What do you think, Mam?'

'Sally, love.' Gran shook her head. 'You're beautiful. Absolutely beautiful. By, Rafferty's a lucky fella. I hope he knows it.'

'He does,' Frankie said. 'He's going to be ecstatic when he sees you walking down the aisle, Sally. You really do look lovely.'

'Not mutton dressed as lamb?' Sally asked anxiously. 'I saw an article on the internet the other day, and it said tiaras should never be worn by brides over thirty, but I'd already bought it by then.'

'Bugger the internet,' Gran said. 'And bugger anyone

who tells women what they should and shouldn't wear. You look stunning, Sally, and that's all I'm saying, cos there's nothing else to say.'

'You look lovely too, Gran,' Billie said, and Summer had to agree. Gran was wearing a powder blue dress with a matching jacket, and even though she'd refused to go to the salon with them, her hair was neatly styled, and her make-up was understated but surprisingly glamorous.

'Well, we're all bloody gorgeous, let's face it,' Gran said.

Summer's stomach fluttered. Would Ben agree? She glanced down at her long, smoke blue dress and mentally crossed her fingers. He was more used to seeing her in jeans and wellies, so this would be quite a shock to him.

Rafferty had offered to pay for a car to take them to church, but Sally didn't see the point. After all, All Hallows was only across the road from The White Hart Inn, and she said she'd rather walk.

They set off at five to two, Gran grumbling about having to walk in her new shoes, even though she'd had the option to be taken in a car but had turned it down.

Arlo was waiting for them outside the church door, looking smart in a dark suit, white shirt, and smoke blue cravat.

His eyes widened when he saw them, then he gave a low whistle as he put his arms around Billie.

'Wow, you all look amazing. Sally, you're a stunner! Dad's going to be over the moon.'

'Give over.' Sally blushed. 'Is he okay? No problems?'

'Everything's fine. He's waiting at the front with Ellis, and he's already looking like the cat that got the cream.'

'So he should,' Gran said. 'Right, I'll go in first and get seated. Are you sure you're going to be all right?'

'She'll be absolutely fine,' Summer said. 'Go on in, Gran,

so they know we're here and waiting.'

Gran kissed Sally on the cheek and smiled at her, her eyes shining with unshed tears even before the ceremony had begun.

'I'm that proud of you, Sally,' she said softly. 'And I know your dad would have been too.'

Her mum, Summer thought, was in danger of bursting into tears, and Billie evidently felt the same as she chivvied Gran into the church and then began joking that she'd probably got nothing but cigarettes in that little clutch bag of hers. Anything, clearly, to take their mum's mind off what lay ahead.

They heard the organ strike up Wagner's Wedding Chorus and Frankie said, 'Oh crikey, this is really it, isn't it?'

'You look like a princess, love,' Sally assured her. 'We can do this. Ready?'

Frankie nodded and Sally lifted her chin. Arlo slipped his arm through hers and smiled at her. 'You really do look amazing. I'm so pleased for you both. I know you're going to make each other very happy.'

'I'm going to be a sobbing mess at this rate,' Sally said. 'Come on, before I ruin my mascara.'

All Hallows Church was a surprisingly large and rather grand building, with magnificent stained-glass windows, stone columns and carvings, and polished wooden pews. Summer couldn't deny she felt a bit grand herself, walking behind her mum and Arlo, with Frankie in front of her and Billie at her side. It was like being part of a coronation procession, and so far removed from her normal, everyday life that it hardly seemed real.

She was too busy concentrating on her mum to pay attention to who was in the congregation, so had no idea if Ben had miraculously wangled his way out of work and made it to the service or not. She was determined not to let that distract her right now.

She saw a beaming Zach nod at Rafferty, who turned to face them; she saw the look of wonder and delight on his face when he saw his bride-to be, and the expression of pure love in his eyes when she reached his side.

Summer swallowed down a lump in her throat. That was what she wanted, more than anything. Someone who loved her the way Rafferty loved her mum, who didn't chop and change his mind, always wondering if there was someone better out there the way her dad had. She thought about Ben and butterflies danced in her stomach. She was sure her faith in him was justified and it was a good feeling.

Billie took Sally's bouquet from her, then the three bridesmaids sat next to Gran on the front pew as the service began.

Despite their nerves, neither Sally or Rafferty made any mistakes. Guided by Zach, who was clearly quite emotional himself, they said their vows clearly and with feeling, and apart from the occasional gurgle and one or two sneezes from baby Hattie, who was perched on Kat's knee a couple of pews behind Summer, there was a hush in the church as everyone listened to the service.

Three hymns, a couple of readings, and a few prayers later, and Sally and Rafferty were man and wife at last.

A barrage of petals was thrown at the happy couple, led by Kat, in place of the traditional confetti which was banned at All Hallows. Summer thought it made a much more sensible, as well as attractive, alternative, and happily joined in with scattering petals over her mum and Rafferty, who laughed in delight.

'Summer!'

Ellis looked and sounded thrilled to see her and he kissed

her lightly on both cheeks. 'You look fantastic! Oh my God, your hair! What happened to your hair? You used to be blonde!'

He caught sight of Frankie and pulled her over. 'And what happened to *your* hair? You used to be ginger!'

'I was never ginger,' Frankie said crossly. 'I see you haven't changed much.'

'Oh, don't be like that. You look great, sis, blue hair, piercing and all. I can't believe how much you've grown up.' He smiled at her, then his gaze returned to Summer. 'And that dark hair suits you, you know. Brings out the green in your eyes. It's lovely to see you again—both of you.'

Summer eyed him suspiciously, but he seemed genuine, so she nodded and smiled back. 'And you, Ellis. Come on, I think we're wanted for the photos.'

Once the formalities were over and people could relax, Summer was able to look around and take note of who else was there. There was no sign of Ben, and she tried not to feel disappointed. After all, he'd told her that he'd have to work. At least Jennifer was present, along with Jamie, and Summer was delighted she'd made the effort to socialise, knowing how much it cost her to do so.

Miss Lavender was looking elegant in an ankle-length lavender dress. Her white hair was neatly styled, and she wore a soft rose lipstick.

'You look absolutely beautiful, Sally,' she said. 'And you look most handsome, Rafferty.'

'You look beautiful, too, Miss Lavender,' Sally told her.

Miss Lavender clutched her arm. 'My dear, I'm so very sorry. I did my best, but as you can see, they simply won't be told.'

Summer frowned, wondering what she meant.

'Bloody hell,' Gran said. 'I've seen it all now. Would you

look at them two!'

They all turned to see the Pennyfeather sisters heading arm-in-arm towards them, wide smiles on their faces. As Kat had said, Miss Lavender had clearly bought them new dresses—soft, chiffon, silver-grey gowns that fell to their ankles and would have looked amazing in other circumstances.

Unfortunately, the Pennyfeathers had teamed them with lime green Crocs, and were wearing their usual crocheted waistcoats rather than smart jackets or elegant cardigans. With glittery tiaras adorning their dyed red hair, they looked even more outlandish than usual, and Summer could only stare at them, wondering how on earth someone like Kat could possibly be related to them.

Kat pulled a face. 'I know what you're thinking,' she said. 'You'll never change them, though, so why even bother to try?'

Rafferty, however, clearly couldn't care less. 'You look incredible,' he told the beaming sisters. 'Thank you for coming to our wedding, and for being—well—you.'

'Oh, you old charmer,' Rita said, tapping him playfully on the arm.

'What a silver fox.' Birdie batted her eyelashes at him. 'You're a lucky woman, Sally.'

Sally laughed. 'Don't I know it.'

'I'm embarrassed for them,' Miss Lavender said, and Gran nodded in agreement.

'They look bloody awful.'

They stared at each other awkwardly as it dawned on them that after their less-than-friendly encounter last Christmas they'd finally agreed on something.

After the photos were taken, the guests drifted across the road to The White Hart Inn, where the room was tastefully decorated in smoke blue and taupe. The guests drank wine and mingled while Bing Crosby, Dean Martin, and Frank Sinatra crooned softly in the background, courtesy of a surround sound system.

Summer was less than thrilled to discover she had to stand at the entrance to greet the guests, along with Sally, Rafferty, Gran, Arlo, Billie, Ellis, and Frankie.

'It's tradition,' Billie whispered. 'Just go along with it, for Mum's sake.'

Summer, who had no idea what she was supposed to say to people and found herself muttering, 'Have a lovely time,' to everyone who shook her hand, was relieved when Clemmie walked in, looking lovely in a bright pink dress that showed off her fair colouring beautifully. Her thick, blonde hair was as immaculate as always, styled in soft waves that fell to her shoulders.

Clemmie ignored the offered handshake and gave Summer a big hug. 'You look fabulous! Wasn't it a lovely wedding? Your mum looks gorgeous. Dolly was actually crying; can you believe it? Have you seen the Pennyfeathers? Miss Lavender's face was like thunder.' She stopped to draw breath. 'No sign of Ben?' she asked, peering around as if he might be hiding somewhere.

'No,' Summer said. 'Although he did say he wouldn't make it to the service.'

'But this is the reception!'

Summer shrugged. 'He said he'd be here at some point.'

Clemmie whispered, 'Still keeping it quiet from the Lavender Ladies?'

Summer nodded. She'd confided in Clemmie about the breakthrough in their relationship and had told her about the picnic.

'It's just for now,' she said, seeing the look of disappointment on her friend's face. 'We're just winding them up for now. We'll go public when the time's right.'

She was sure of it, although she couldn't shake the nagging thought that she'd rather like to be able to tell everyone that she and Ben were a couple, even if it meant the Lavender Ladies getting what they wanted and cashing in. It had been different when they hadn't been sure of their feelings but, speaking for herself, she'd never been more certain of anything. She was falling for Ben and would have happily shouted it from the rooftops.

Maybe, she thought, he wasn't quite there yet, but that was okay. She'd wait.

'Have you met Ellis?' she asked to distract Clemmie, and nodded her head in his direction.

Clemmie grinned. 'I have. He shook my hand very politely. I've got to say, he's much more handsome than I expected. Did he try anything on with you?'

'No, funnily enough he was perfectly reasonable.' Summer lifted her eyebrows hopefully. 'Maybe I'm yesterday's news.'

'Talking of yesterday's news...' Clemmie curled her lip as Ross walked through the door, a gorgeous redhead on his arm. 'I'll go and find a seat.'

Summer gave her a sympathetic hug then turned to see Ross kissing Sally on both cheeks. He shook Rafferty's hand, then thanked them both for the invitation. Frankie looked fit to burst when he dropped a kiss on first Billie's, then Summer's cheek, before moving on to her.

'You all look beautiful,' he said.

Oh, Summer thought, he was a charmer all right. She could see why anyone who didn't know what he was like would be attracted to him. He was dark-haired and dark-eyed, with a neat beard that gave him a rather dashing look.

Although she didn't know for certain what he'd done to Clemmie, she could make an educated guess. His reputation spoke for itself. Summer had no time for him and didn't even reply to his compliments. He merely introduced the redhead as 'Felicity', so she guessed the poor woman was just another in a long line of dates.

Bluebell, Buttercup, and Clover swept in on a wave of hairspray and perfume, followed by Zach and Ava and their children, Dion, and Beatrix. Zach had changed into regular clothes, and Ava looked as effortlessly perfect as always.

'Isn't she marvellous? We're so lucky to have her as our vicar's wife. Her father was Giles Wilson-Davis you know,' someone whispered to Summer. She glanced around, but whoever had imparted the information had drifted off, so she had no way of asking who the heck Giles Wilson-Davis was.

She smiled warmly as Jennifer and Jamie arrived. Jennifer shook hands with everyone in the line-up. 'Thank you for the invitation. It's kind of you to invite us.'

'I'm over the moon you're here, love,' Sally told her. 'It wouldn't have been the same without you. Nice to see you too, Jamie. You scrub up well!'

'Very smart,' a smirking Frankie told him.

'I feel stupid,' he said, glancing down at his trousers and shirt, which were the most formal Summer had ever seen him wear. 'You look great, though.'

Jennifer leaned towards Summer. 'Ben will be overcome when he sees you looking so lovely. He'll be here soon, but don't worry, I won't breathe a word.'

Summer nodded and smiled as the thought of Ben's arrival made her insides melt. Just how, she wondered, was she going to conceal from all these people just how much he mattered to her? This was going to be tougher than she'd ever imagined.

Chapter Twenty

The meal, everyone agreed, had been delicious. The speeches had gone down well, and the obvious emotion in Rafferty's voice had provoked a storm of clapping from everyone in the room, who were clearly moved by his obvious devotion to his new bride.

Then the music started, and Mum and Rafferty had their first dance, quickly joined by several other couples, including a very loved-up looking Billie and Arlo.

Summer couldn't help but glance repeatedly at the door, hoping that Ben would walk in. She really hoped he hadn't been called out to an emergency.

Clive and Joseph wandered over and handed Summer a glass of wine.

'Cheer up,' Clive said. 'He should be here any minute now.'

Summer blushed. 'That obvious?'

'You're not very good at hiding your feelings,' Joseph told her, giving her an affectionate smile. 'Oh, come on! Think I don't know? You were practically floating around the stables yesterday, so even if Clive hadn't tipped me off you were on a date with Ben the night before I'd have had a pretty good idea.'

He nodded over to where the Lavender Ladies were sitting, watching Summer with interest. 'See they're keeping their beady eyes out. They'll be hoping for some action today and a flurry of new bets no doubt.'

'To be honest,' Summer said, 'I couldn't care less about their bets. I'm not bothered who knows about us. I never really was.'

'Isn't this exciting?' Jennifer hurried past them, glass of champagne in her hand.

Clive smiled fondly. 'It's good to see her mixing with people again, isn't it? It's been far too long.'

Summer couldn't agree more. She watched as Miss Lavender put her arm on Jennifer's and the two of them began chatting, quite animatedly. Whatever they were on about it was good to see Ben's mum making the effort to socialise, and she knew he'd be over the moon to see her having fun. If he ever got here.

'I can't believe how gorgeous this room looks.' She turned at the sound of Zach's voice at her side. 'They've done a cracking job, haven't they?'

'Yes, I suppose they have.'

In fact, it looked a picture, with fairy lights strung across the ceiling, chairs with swags in taupe or smoke blue, and tables covered in crisp white cloths, with tea lights in glass bowls at their centre.

Ava was at Zach's side. 'Nice idea, isn't it? Inviting practically the whole town.' She gasped as Buttercup barged into her, causing wine to slop over the side of her glass, narrowly missing her dress.

Buttercup hadn't even noticed. 'Have you heard the

gossip? That bloke over there, chatting to Ross, is Ethan Rochester! *The* Ethan Rochester of Rochester's Department Stores. Who's the woman, do you know? And why would someone like him be talking to Ross, of all people?'

Summer guessed it was probably about the art scholarship Ross and Miss Lavender were hoping Ethan would fund.

'The lady next to him is his wife, Cara, I think,' she said, remembering seeing the couple at Billie and Arlo's wedding.

'Interesting,' Ava said.

'Well, Ross seems to think so.' Buttercup nodded over to where Ross, Ethan, and Cara Rochester were standing, deep in conversation.

'I wonder what they're talking about,' she said. 'You wouldn't think they'd have anything in common, would you?'

'Art,' she said. 'Ethan's an artist like Ross.'

'Ooh look! Jennifer Callaghan and Miss Lavender are joining them,' Buttercup said, her eyes wide with curiosity as the two women approached Ross and the Rochesters. 'Hmm, they seem quite serious, don't they? I'm dying to know what she's saying to him, aren't you?'

'Not particularly,' Clive said bluntly.

Evidently disgusted at their lack of interest, Buttercup flounced off to tell someone more receptive of her great discovery.

'Summer! Come and dance!'

Summer forced herself not to roll her eyes as Ellis took the glass of wine from her hand and placed it on a nearby table.

'Oh no, it's okay,' she began, but Ellis wasn't taking no for an answer.

He put his arm around her waist and whirled her away onto the dance floor.

'Do you mind?' she said testily. 'I said no.'

He looked sheepish. 'Sorry. I didn't mean anything by it. I thought I was rescuing you from those old men.'

He glanced over at Clive and Joseph, who were watching them curiously.

'Joseph's my employer, and Clive's the local vet,' Summer said. 'They're lovely people actually. We were having an interesting conversation.'

Ellis sighed. 'Do you want to go back to them?'

She hesitated. 'No, it's all right. Just don't do that again, okay?'

'Promise.'

'How are things going with the art business then?' she asked, determined to keep the conversation light.

'Really good. I've been producing cards; did Dad tell you?'

'Cards?'

'Christmas cards, birthday cards, that sort of thing. I found an excellent local printer and I'm stocking them on my website now. I'm doing mugs and calendars and all sorts, as well as selling the prints. It's going brilliantly, actually. I'm looking at Christmas decorations next.'

'That's fabulous, Ellis,' Summer said, meaning it. 'I told you you were talented, didn't I? I'm so glad you went for it and stopped wasting your time.'

'It was all thanks to you, you know,' he told her. 'When you bought me those colouring pencils as a gift it made me think you really believed in me, and that was the first time I'd honestly thought I could do it. Thanks, Summer.'

Summer didn't quite know what to say to that. 'It's all right,' she said awkwardly.

There was always that balance to strike with Ellis. She didn't want to hurt him and was glad he'd made something of his life at last, but she didn't want to get too enthusiastic because he might just start all that lovey-dovey rubbish again, and she really didn't want that.

'Are you seeing anyone?' he asked suddenly, and she inwardly groaned as alarm bells rang in her head.

'None of your business.'

'Ouch!' He pulled away from her slightly, and she saw amusement in his eyes. 'That's a bit evasive.'

She decided the only way to deal with Ellis was to fight fire with fire.

'What about you?'

To her surprise, he smiled. 'Actually, yes, I am.'

It was her turn to pull away. 'You are?' Of all the things she'd expected him to tell her, that wasn't one of them. 'Seriously?'

'Don't sound so surprised. Not everyone finds me loathsome and unlovable.'

'I didn't find you...' She didn't finish the sentence, worried even now where it would lead.

'We've been seeing each other for six months,' he told her. 'She's lovely, Summer. I'm sure you'd like her. She keeps me in line, pipes me down when I'm getting above myself.'

'Which is just what you need,' she said.

'Exactly!'

Summer saw the light in his eyes and realised he was genuine. Feeling more relaxed around Ellis than she ever had before, she leaned into him as they resumed dancing. 'So tell me about her then. Don't keep me in suspense.'

'Her name's Laura, and she's a year younger than me.'

'And what does she do for a living? Is she an artist too?'

'She's a nursery teacher.'

'A nursery teacher!'

Ellis laughed. 'I know. Who'd have thought it?'

'How on earth did you meet her?'

'At a party. Her sister's going out with Beau's boyfriend's brother.'

Summer's mind did some gymnastics as she tried to follow that. 'Got it. Well, well. I'm happy for you, Ellis. Why didn't you bring her to the wedding?'

'She's a bit shy, and I thought all these people would overwhelm her. We're going up to Norfolk in a few weeks, and I'm going to introduce her to the family there. I'll give Dad a few months to settle into married life again before I bring her up here to meet him. I think they'll love her as much as I do though.'

'Whoa! Love her?'

He looked a bit embarrassed. 'I know what you're thinking. Too soon. You're wondering if I'm racing ahead of myself, the way I did with you. You needn't worry. She's as smitten with me as I am with her. Ask Beau if you don't believe me.'

'I believe you.' She did, too. Something in his expression told her this was the real deal. She felt weak with relief. 'I'm pleased for you. I hope it works out.'

'Thanks, Summer. I really am sorry, you know. When I look back at the way I behaved... Well, I was an idiot.'

'You were,' she said bluntly. 'But I guess everyone's entitled to a second chance.'

'We all grow up eventually,' he said. 'Even us stupid men, once we find the right woman.'

'May I cut in?'

Summer's insides dissolved as she turned her head and saw Ben standing there, looking and sounding all confident and masterful. He was wearing a navy-blue suit and white shirt, and he'd never looked more handsome.

Ellis glanced at him then at Summer.

'Ah,' he said and smiled. 'Be my guest, mate.'

He let go of Summer and Ben immediately took hold of her.

'I warn you now,' he said, his eyes twinkling, 'I'm a terrible dancer.'

'It doesn't matter,' she told him, laughing. 'You do realise the Lavender Ladies are watching us?'

He held her tighter and whispered in her ear. 'I really don't care.'

* * *

Ben hadn't meant to make such a very obvious announcement to the town when he'd entered The White Hart Inn after finally finishing work, but when he saw Summer looking so utterly stunning he hadn't been able to stop himself from heading straight for her.

He wasn't sure who she was dancing with, but it didn't really matter. All that mattered was making sure she knew, without any shadow of a doubt, that she meant the world to him, and that he couldn't believe his luck that someone like her would look twice at someone like him.

When the music ended they remained in hold, and then danced to the next song, unable to take their eyes off each other.

'You're so beautiful,' he told her, meaning it. He'd always thought she was pretty, but today she looked amazing, her chestnut hair falling in waves to her creamy shoulders, that beautiful smoke blue dress showing off all her curves and doing things to him he'd never experienced so intensely before.

She blushed. 'Thank you. You look fantastic in a suit. I

mean, you look fantastic all the time, but... Oh, well, you know what I mean.'

'I'm sorry I'm so late,' he said. 'I tried to get away earlier, but you know how it is. The best laid plans and all that.'

'It doesn't matter,' she said. 'I'm sorry you missed the food, though.'

'I don't think I could eat a thing,' he admitted. 'My stomach's in knots.'

'Nervous about dancing?'

'No,' he said smiling. 'Because I'm with you.' She laughed and he groaned. 'That sounded so corny didn't it?'

'It did a bit, but it's okay. I like corny. Corny's good.'

'You're in luck. There's plenty more where that came from. You're talking to the king of the chat-up lines here, as you've no doubt noticed.'

'It hadn't escaped my attention. You know, you're wrong. You're not a bad dancer at all.'

'You're too kind. Who was that man you were dancing with when I so rudely interrupted?' he asked.

'That,' she said, 'was Ellis.'

'The famous Ellis. Did he behave himself?'

She looked amused. 'He did actually. Would you believe it, he's met someone. He even said he was in love with her. He's a different man, thank goodness. Seems like he's grown up.'

'Ah well,' he said, 'it happens to the best of us.'

'I think you've always been a grown up,' she told him. 'You haven't had much choice. But now, Ben Callaghan, you're going to have some fun, because I'm going to make sure of it.'

He laughed, thinking he liked the sound of that, but his laughter died when he saw the look in her eyes. Overwhelmed with desire, he pulled her to a halt and kissed her right there and then, in front of everyone.

Dimly he was aware of clapping and cheering, and as they broke apart he looked round, his face burning as he realised they were the centre of attention.

'You little beauty,' Clive called. 'You've just won me fifty quid!'

'I knew I should have put a bet on,' Joseph groaned.

'I was too cautious,' Dolly said with a sigh. 'I'd given them another month to come clean.'

'Don't tell me them bloody Lavender Ladies have been betting on our Summer and this lad getting together?' Gran shook her head in amazement. 'Is there nothing they won't open a book on?'

'Very little,' Ava assured her. 'In fact, I can't think of anything to be honest. They're strangers to shame.'

'Well,' Gran said, 'it seems everyone knew about these two but me.' She collared a surprised Bluebell. 'You can tell me all about him. I've heard you're a proper gossip.'

'We seem to have caused a bit of a scene,' Ben said.

'We do. I hope Mum and Rafferty don't mind. It's their big day after all.'

Sally and Rafferty, however, couldn't have looked happier as they rushed up to hug Summer and Ben.

'I knew it!' Sally said. 'I knew you two were smitten with each other. I'm so glad you've finally realised it.'

'Smile, please,' Frankie called, holding up her phone. 'This is going right on my socials.' She whispered something to Jamie who nodded, as the pair of them moved to stand directly in front of him and Summer. Frankie held up her phone again.

'Selfie!'

Jamie hooked his arm over her shoulders and put his face

close to hers. Frankie tapped the screen, then showed him the picture.

He nodded approvingly and Frankie showed it to Ben and Summer.

'Doesn't it look great? One for Instagram, I think.'

'Oh, Ben, I'm so happy for you.'

His mum put her arms around him and hugged him tightly, and he swallowed down the emotion as she whispered, 'And your dad and Leon would be too.' She stepped back and smiled at him, tears in her eyes, then turned to Summer. 'I'm so glad you two are together. You're such a lovely girl. Ben couldn't have picked anyone nicer.'

She genuinely looked pleased for him, and he realised his vision was blurry and that he was in danger of making a total fool of himself.

'Thanks, Jennifer,' Summer said gratefully. 'We're really glad you approve.'

'You must come for your tea one night,' Jennifer said, taking her hand. 'I'll cook. I insist upon it. And any time you want to stay over you don't have to ask. I'm very open minded.'

Ben hardly knew where to look, but at least the embarrassment helped him push back the tears that had threatened just moments before.

'Thanks for that, Mum,' he muttered, wondering how Summer had reacted to her comment. His heart thudded and he smiled as he saw her watching him, a distinct gleam in her eyes.

'That's really kind of you,' she said. 'I'll bear that in mind.'

'You missed the food,' Sally said, giving him a look of dismay. 'Are you hungry, love? If you go into the kitchen and tell the staff what happened I'm sure they could rustle something up for you.'

Ben realised that, actually, he was hungry. He'd been at work all day, grabbing half a sandwich in his lunch break, and then he'd gone straight from the surgery to the pub, having brought his suit with him to change into. He'd had nothing to eat, and it was now almost seven o'clock.

'I'll do that,' he said. 'Thanks, Sally.'

Summer took his hand. 'Come on then, let's see what we can find.'

As they headed towards the kitchen, Miss Lavender and the Pennyfeathers hurried towards them.

'Ben Callaghan, I could throttle you!' Miss Lavender said.

Ben's eyes widened. 'I'm sorry?'

'It's her own fault,' Birdie cried, clapping her hands in delight. 'We said you'd get together at the wedding, didn't we, Rita?'

Rita nodded. 'We told everyone that was our best guess, but did they listen? Eugenie,' she added, rolling her eyes, 'said Christmas.'

'Christmas!' Birdie gave Miss Lavender a look of pity. 'We warned you, Eugenie. You can't say we didn't.'

She beamed at Ben and Summer. 'We stand to make a killing on this. People should have had faith in you. *We* did. It was quite obvious you were destined to be together.'

'Ah well,' Miss Lavender said, shaking her head. 'You can't win them all.' Her eyes twinkled. 'Anyway, I'm happy to lose this bet, given the outcome. I couldn't be more pleased for you both. You certainly deserve this.' She hesitated. 'Ross is very happy for you, too.'

Ben straightened. 'Ross is here?'

'He was. He's just left. Taken...' She frowned, obviously trying to remember the girl's name.

'Felicity,' Birdie supplied helpfully.

'That's right. He's taken her out somewhere. I'm not sure what they're doing.'

Ben could imagine what Summer was thinking but said nothing. 'Well, if you don't mind,' he said, 'I was just going to get something to eat. I haven't had anything much all day and I'm hungry.'

'Of course. We won't keep you any longer.'

The three of them scuttled off and Ben and Summer grinned at each other.

'Food?' she asked.

'Food.'

The kitchen was a whirlwind of activity and the minute they set foot in it they felt in the way.

'Tell you what,' Summer said, 'why don't we go upstairs, and I'll fix you something to eat in our kitchen.'

'Are you sure?'

'Of course. I'm not the world's best cook but I'm sure I can do something to stave off the hunger pangs.'

He followed her up the stairs and she showed him into the flat. He'd never been up here before and was pleasantly surprised and not a little envious.

It was large enough to be comfortable but not so large it would be a hassle to keep warm. And it was modern and bright and had a kitchen that didn't look as if it had been fitted when the pub was built, and carpets that weren't worn away almost to threads in places.

Summer made him sit at the table while she looked for something quick and easy to make him, even though he offered to do it himself.

'Beans on toast?' she suggested doubtfully. 'I know it's

not exactly Masterchef standards, but it's filling, and we can't be away from the reception too long.'

Ben was quite happy with that, so she quickly made them for him and sat down opposite him to watch him eat.

He felt a bit self-conscious and took extra care not to spill anything on his suit.

'Ben,' Summer said hesitantly, 'can I ask you something?'

'Uh-huh.' He hastily swallowed some toast and said, 'Sorry. Of course. Anything.'

'What made you decide to go public today? I mean, after everything you said about keeping it quiet and making the Lavender Ladies wait.'

'Did you mind?' he asked worriedly. 'I should have checked with you, shouldn't I? But—the truth is, what I said about not telling anyone because of those bets, that's not really the main reason I wanted to keep it quiet.'

'Oh?' She eyed him thoughtfully. 'You said, right at the beginning of all this, that you didn't want anyone to know because I might decide I didn't want to be with you after all, and it would be too embarrassing if everyone knew I'd dropped you. But that's still not what all the secrecy was about, is it? It can't be.'

Ben sighed and pushed the almost-empty plate away.

'Honestly? I think it was. I was scared to tempt fate. I couldn't believe you'd really stick with me once you got to know me. I still can't believe it to be honest.'

'You're too hard on yourself,' she said, tilting her head to the side and eyeing him with compassion. 'Why wouldn't I want to be with you? You're amazing. Kind, caring, decent.' Her mouth curved upwards as she added, 'And very, very sexy.'

He shook his head, laughing gently, then reached over and took her hand. Their fingers entwined and he said, very seriously, 'I know how hard a step this was for you, Summer. I know how much it cost you to put your trust in me. Look, I'm not perfect and I make mistakes. I've made mistakes in the past. Big ones. But I promise you that I'll never let you down the way your dad and Ian did. I'm not that person. Whatever else I am, I'm no cheat.'

'You don't have to tell me that, Ben,' she said quietly. 'I already know. That's—' She swallowed. 'That's one of the reasons why I really think we can be happy. Build a life together.'

His heart skipped as he stared at her, seeing the pink flush on her cheeks and the awkward look in her green eyes.

'If that's what you want too,' she said nervously.

He thought about Leon, and about the news he would have to break to Summer very soon. Because now they'd come this far there was no turning back. He'd fought against getting close to anyone for years, all too aware that intimacy meant honesty, and that any kind of loving relationship would come with a price. The price of revealing the truth about that night and what it had cost his brother.

He hadn't thought he'd ever be able to get past that but looking at her now he knew he had to. She mattered far too much for him to let her go. That meant taking a risk. A big risk. But he had to do it and soon. She deserved that at least.

If she couldn't deal with it—well, at least he'd know he'd done the right thing. But right now she was waiting, and he couldn't put off telling her what was in his heart any longer.

His fingers squeezed hers reassuringly.

'I'd like that,' he told her gently. 'It's exactly what I want, too.'

Chapter Twenty-One

After all the excitement of the wedding, it was a quiet weekend at The White Hart Inn. Sally and Rafferty had spent their wedding night at a hotel in Kirkby Skimmer, returning by Saturday lunchtime to spend a final day with Billie, Arlo, and Ellis, who were all returning home on Sunday.

'It seems like only five minutes since we got here,' Billie said, looking a bit tearful. 'I'll miss you all, I really will.'

'But not for long,' Rafferty said. He winked at her, and she smiled.

'True enough.'

'Not for long? What's that supposed to mean?' Sally asked.

Rafferty and Billie grinned at each other.

'Are you going to tell her?' Billie clearly couldn't wait another moment.

'Sally,' Rafferty said, putting his arms around her waist. 'You and I are going to be spending Christmas in Melbourne with Billie and Arlo. What do you think of that?'

Sally's face was a picture. 'You're kidding!'

'Not at all. It's all booked. Three weeks in Australia: a week in Melbourne, and two weeks in Sydney.'

'And before you start complaining that a week with me and Arlo isn't long enough,' Billie added, knowing her mother all too well, 'we're coming to Sydney with you. It's going to be a fun summer break, although I warn you, you'll find Christmas a bit odd. No chance of snow, I'm afraid.'

'Oh my goodness!'

Summer couldn't help smiling. It had been planned for ages, and she'd been dying for the moment when Rafferty sprang the surprise on her mum.

'Oh, but what about Mam and Summer? We can't leave them alone for Christmas!'

'I asked them if they wanted to come with us,' Rafferty said. 'Didn't I, ladies?'

Gran nodded. 'He did. Quite persistent, in fact. But honestly, I can't be doing with flying all that way, and then trekking round sightseeing, day in, day out. Besides, I like Christmas to be wintery. How can I wear my Christmas jumper and listen to Michael Bublé when it's sunny outside? It would spoil the whole thing. No, I'm staying put in England this year, thanks all the same.'

'And I'm staying right here, to oversee the pub and help at Whispering Willows. I've got no time to be flying off to Australia at such a busy time of year,' Summer said. 'Anyway, I'll be going there myself in the spring with Dad. I don't need two trips.'

'And you don't have to worry about us being lonely,' Gran said, 'because I'm coming here to stay with her, so we'll have each other and it will be smashing, won't it, Summer? Might even let that Ben fella come round for a bit of dinner, if he behaves himself.'

Summer smiled, though the thought of poor Ben being interrogated by her gran was a bit unnerving. She remembered, all too well, what Arlo had gone through. Arlo probably still had nightmares.

She thought it best not to mention that she'd checked with her dad about his plans for the festive season, not wanting him to be alone either. He'd told her he planned to work through it all. Lots of taxi drivers wanted time off to be with their families, so there'd be plenty of work for him, and he was happy to do it. He assured Summer that they'd make up for it in Australia in April, and that she had no need to worry about him, which had put her mind at rest.

On Sunday it was time for all the tearful goodbyes. Ellis hugged Summer and told her he hoped she'd get to meet Laura very soon.

'And maybe I'll get the chance to meet this vet properly,' he added. 'I'd like to know what he's got that I haven't.' Seeing her face he burst out laughing. 'Joke! Honestly, I couldn't be happier for you.'

He and Arlo hugged Frankie and told her to stop growing up so fast because it was unnerving seeing their kid sister turning into a woman before their eyes.

Sally and Rafferty were taking Gran home on the Sunday afternoon, and Billie and Arlo were going with them. They were all staying at her house overnight before catching flights to Paris and Melbourne from Leeds/Bradford Airport the following morning.

By late Sunday afternoon, the flat above The White Hart Inn seemed empty. At least Summer could move back into her old bedroom. She put fresh bedding on her bed, did the laundry, and cleaned up, not wanting her mum to come home to any mess.

Frankie had been invited to spend the night at Monk's

Folly, which Summer thought would do Jennifer some good. It would surely make a change for her to have some female company overnight. She just hoped Frankie wouldn't spend the whole evening playing computer games with Jamie but would spend some time talking to his mum.

Her heart leapt as her phone pinged and she saw Ben's name on the screen.

From Ben

I hope everyone got off all right. I miss you! Frankie got here safely, and Mum's prepared a feast for her. I wish you could have come over, too. Or I could have come to you. Anyway, have a good shift at work and I'll see you tomorrow evening. xxx

She couldn't help smiling. Only Ben would punctuate a text message so carefully. One day, she thought mischievously, she'd send him a message in text speak. It would baffle him.

From Summer

It's very quiet here. Everyone's gone now and the flat's very empty. I wish you were here. I miss you, too. Just about to go downstairs so will speak to you tomorrow. Looking forward to seeing you. xxx

Time to go to work. With a five-hour shift ahead of her this evening and an eight-hour shift at Whispering Willows the next day, she decided an early night would be called for. She needed all the sleep she could get, especially since she and Ben were going to meet up tomorrow evening.

Sleep came easily that night. She wasn't nervous about being alone in the flat, and her eyes closed the minute her head touched the pillow.

It seemed to her, however, that only minutes had passed before they flew open again at a loud bang on the door. She glanced at her bedside clock, realising it was six forty-five and her alarm would be going off in fifteen minutes anyway. Who the hell would be banging on the door at this time of the morning?

Dragging on her dressing gown she padded through to the hallway and checked the chain was on the door before unlocking it. Before she could turn the handle, Ben tried to push it open.

'Summer, let me in!'

She closed the door, slid back the chain, and did as he asked, shocked to see how stricken he looked.

'What is it? What's happened?'

'Is she here?'

Summer's heart thudded. 'Is who here?'

'Frankie! Who else?'

'Frankie? She spent the night at Monk's Folly, didn't she?'

Ben sank onto the sofa and put his head in his hands. 'That's what we thought, but they're both missing, and Jamie's backpack's gone. We have no idea what time they sneaked out.' He lifted his head and she saw a maelstrom of emotions in his eyes. 'They could have been gone all night. I can hardly believe I'm saying this, but I think they've run away together.'

'Don't be daft!'

Summer couldn't believe he was even suggesting such a ridiculous thing. Why would Frankie and Jamie run away together? They weren't even a couple. And run away from what? Frankie was perfectly happy staying here, and she was looking forward to going back to Norfolk to catch up with her best friend again.

'Have you and Jamie had a row or something?' she asked, confused. 'Because this makes no sense. Why would they run away?'

'I don't know. I have no idea what's going on with him lately. He's been different this summer holiday. Edgy. Irritable. Always complaining about something or other, as if nothing's good enough for him any more.'

'But that doesn't explain why he'd run away. And it certainly doesn't explain why Frankie's gone with him.'

'You don't think…' He hesitated. 'You don't think she'd encourage him to go somewhere with her without telling us?'

'Frankie? Of course not! She's a good girl. Sensible. She wouldn't encourage Jamie to do anything so irresponsible. Anyway, where would they go?'

'I don't know. Maybe someone's organised a party or a rave or something.'

'A rave? Is it 1990?'

'You know what I mean.'

'What on earth makes you think she'd drag Jamie off to some party without telling us?'

'Well…' He shrugged helplessly. 'She's always on that phone of hers, isn't she? That's how these things are organised, isn't it?'

'And Jamie isn't?'

'He is now! He didn't used to be, but since she arrived…' He shook his head, exasperated. 'This is getting us nowhere. If you don't know anything I'll have to get off. I'll ring the police or something.'

'Ring the police? How long have they been missing?'

'I told you; we don't know. They sneaked out. It's so bloody irresponsible! Poor Mum's in a terrible state. As if she hasn't been through enough.'

'Ben, Frankie and Jamie are good kids, and they're sensible,' she said, her tone softening as she realised this might be affecting him in ways she couldn't begin to understand.

'They wouldn't run away. They must have decided to go somewhere for the day. It's the only explanation.'

'If that's true why did they leave the house before we were up? Why didn't they tell us last night that they were going somewhere?'

'It just doesn't add up,' she said, baffled. 'Have you tried ringing them?'

He rummaged in his jacket pocket and held up two mobile phones.

'Is that...?'

'We found them in Frankie's bedroom after we'd tried calling Jamie's phone and heard it ringing from there. They've left both phones behind so we couldn't track them. Talk about devious. And doesn't that just confirm that they're doing something they shouldn't be!'

'I can't believe it,' Summer murmured, her anxiety growing as she realised the teenagers had no way of getting in touch with anyone if they needed help. 'Why would they do that?'

'Who knows what's in their heads?' he said. 'I knew he was spending too much time with Frankie when he should have been studying, getting ahead for his exams. He needs to get into the habit of revising early, but instead he's been wasting his time with some kid whose only ambition is to get Instagram likes.'

Summer stared at him. 'Are you putting all the blame on my little sister?' she asked testily. 'Because I'm telling you now, you've got her all wrong, and I'm not going to stand here and listen to you insulting her.'

He got to his feet. 'I'm wasting time here. I only came to see if they'd come back to the pub. I'll let you know if I hear anything.'

'Whoa!' Summer grabbed his arm. 'Where do you think you're going?'

'To find them!'

'Not without me you're not,' she said. 'Give me five minutes.'

She'd have to ring Joseph, she realised, as she hurriedly dragged on her jeans in her bedroom a few moments later, as she might well be late going into Whispering Willows today. She felt bad about that, but there was no way she was leaving Ben to search for Frankie and Jamie alone. The mood he was in he might do something reckless.

'Right,' she said, fastening her hair back into a ponytail as she hurried through to the living room, 'I'm ready. Let's go.'

* * *

'Where do we even start?'

Standing outside The White Hart Inn a few minutes later, Summer and Ben gazed around Market Place, suddenly horribly aware that they had no clue where to begin their search.

'What about the churchyard?' Summer said. 'Everyone goes there to think and talk. Maybe they're sitting on one of the benches, making plans as we speak.'

Ben looked doubtful but agreed it was worth a shot. However, the churchyard was empty, apart from a cat, which gave them a disgusted look as they approached, as if annoyed that they'd disturbed its early morning peace and quiet.

'This is pointless,' Ben said. 'They could be anywhere by now.' He clutched Summer's arm suddenly. 'The train station! Why didn't we think of it before? Come on, they might be waiting to catch a train.'

'A train to where, though?' Summer shrugged. 'Where would they be going at this time on a Monday morning?'

'We can ask them that when we finally catch up with them,' he said. 'Come on, let's take the Land Rover.'

As they hurried back towards The White Hart Inn, where Ben had parked his car, they heard someone calling their names. Looking across Market Place they both groaned as they saw Miss Lavender strolling towards them, Boycott and Trueman trotting beside her.

'My goodness, you two are up and about early,' she said, giving them judgemental looks, as if she'd already decided that Ben had spent the night at the pub with Summer. Summer could almost hear her thinking, *while the cat's away...*

'I'm sorry, Miss Lavender,' Ben said, opening the Land Rover door. 'We haven't got time to chat this morning, I'm afraid.'

She nodded. 'Always in a hurry, you young people. That's the trouble with today's generation. It must run in the family. Jamie was just as abrupt with me last night.'

Summer had been distracted by one of Miss Lavender's Yorkshire terriers as it cocked its leg and relieved itself against one of Ben's tyres, but her head shot up as Ben gasped. 'Jamie? You saw Jamie last night?'

'Was he with Frankie?'

Miss Lavender gazed from one to the other of them. 'He was, yes. I called over to them, but he simply nodded at me, rather curtly I have to say, and then looked away.'

'Where did you see them?' Ben asked urgently. 'How long ago was this?'

'Really, Ben, give me a chance to think.' Miss Lavender eyed them with some concern. 'I get the impression you're worried about something. Is everything all right?'

Summer could see the impatience in Ben's eyes and decided she should smooth things over before he said something he'd regret.

'I'm afraid Jamie and Frankie have gone somewhere without telling us, and we're a bit worried. With Mum and Rafferty being away, Frankie's my responsibility for the next few days, so obviously I'm concerned. I really need to find them, just to make sure they're okay, but we have no idea where they've gone.'

'I see.' Summer could see the cogs turning in the old lady's mind. 'Well, they were standing outside Millican's at about—' she tilted her head, thinking, '—eleven o'clock last night, I should say. Frankie was on her mobile phone, of course. Really, children are never without them these days, are they? Jamie was standing right next to her—'

Ben interrupted her. 'I'm sorry, Miss Lavender, did you say Frankie was on her phone?'

'Yes, that's right. Ross and I were walking the dogs through Market Place, you see. I don't usually go so far from home at night, but we had things to discuss and before we realised it, there we were. Of course, if we'd known they were planning to run away we'd have stopped them, or at least called you, but we just assumed Jamie was walking Frankie back to The White Hart Inn.'

'Where would she get another phone?' Summer asked, puzzled.

'And what would they be doing outside Millican's?' Ben questioned. 'It's not even open on Sundays. It doesn't make sense.' He turned to Summer. 'They wouldn't have been going to the station then. Not at that time. The last train would have gone, and the waiting room would be locked. They wouldn't wait overnight on the platform.'

'I wonder if Birdie and Rita know anything?' Miss Lavender said thoughtfully.

Ben gave her a puzzled look. 'Why should they? They live down Forge Lane.'

'Oh yes, but they have their ways and means, and one never knows. Here, can you hold the leads a moment, Ben?'

Ben looked anguished as the dog leads were pushed into his hands. Summer gave him a sympathetic smile and a shrug. Right now, it seemed to her the Pennyfeather sisters were their only shot. If Jamie and Frankie *had* been heading to the station last night, as unlikely as that seemed, they would already have caught the first train this morning.

She watched, open-mouthed, as Miss Lavender rummaged in her handbag and drew out a walkie-talkie.

Ben gasped. 'You're kidding!'

Summer wondered why he sounded so shocked. That the Lavender Ladies possessed such a method of communication didn't surprise her in the least.

'Painted Lady to Red Admiral and Holly Blue. Are you receiving me?'

The walkie-talkie crackled, and Ben and Summer exchanged bemused glances.

'Painted Lady to Red Admiral and Holly Blue. Are you receiving me, over?'

'Holly Blue here. Is that you, Eugenie?'

Miss Lavender rolled her eyes. 'This is Painted Lady. How many more times? And don't forget over.'

'Over what?'

'Give it here, Birdie. You're as much use as a marshmallow hammer. Eugenie? I mean, Painted Lady, is that you? Over.'

Ben groaned. 'We really haven't got time for this, Miss Lavender. We need to start looking.'

Miss Lavender held up a hand to silence him, and despite her worries Summer couldn't help feeling amused as Ben shut up immediately.

'This is Painted Lady. Red Admiral, we have an emergency here, over.'

'Ooh!' Two voices echoed through the walkie-talkie, clearly thrilled. 'What's happened?'

'Over,' Miss Lavender reminded them sharply.

'Over? You haven't told us anything yet.'

Ben clearly couldn't restrain himself any longer. He grabbed the walkie-talkie from a startled Miss Lavender's hand and spoke into it with some desperation.

'Rita, Birdie, this is Ben Callaghan. I need your help. Have you seen my brother, Jamie, this morning? Or Frankie Kingston even?'

Miss Lavender gave him a thoroughly disapproving look and took the device from him. 'Thank you very much,' she said coldly. 'There are ways and means, young man. Ways and means.'

'We haven't seen them, Ben,' one of the Pennyfeathers said. 'Not this morning.'

'Over,' the other one supplied helpfully.

Ben slumped. 'It was worth a shot,' he said. 'Thanks anyway.'

'But Edie Cathcart saw them last night if that's any use. Over.'

Ben gaped at the walkie-talkie and Summer said, 'Who's Edie Cathcart?'

'She lives at the last cottage on Station Road, in that little row before you turn off for the station,' Miss Lavender explained.

'How on earth would they know she'd seen them?'

Summer asked. Really, the Lavender Ladies were almost supernatural.

'Can you expand on that, Holly Blue? Over.'

'Well,' came the reply, 'Dave's just dropped us off a pint of pasteurised, and we asked him if he had two cherry yoghurts, because we just fancied a cherry yoghurt this morning, didn't we, Rita? And he said he was very sorry, but he'd just given the last cherry yoghurt away.'

'Is this at all relevant?' Ben asked desperately. Summer, meanwhile, was still trying to process the fact that Tuppenny Bridge had an actual milkman. She couldn't remember the last time she'd seen one in Bemborough.

'Yes, it is, young man, so be patient,' came the rather annoyed reply. 'Anyway, as I was saying, we had to make do with strawberry, and Dave said it was unusual really, because normally he'd have at least one cherry yoghurt left at this time of the morning, but that Miss Cathcart had opened the door to him when he dropped off her milk, and she asked him if he had a cherry yoghurt, because she daren't risk her usual toast and marmalade, due to a dodgy tooth. It had been giving her gip all night, hadn't it, Rita?'

'Over,' added Rita. 'Yes, it had. And it turned out that Miss Cathcart had been woken up by toothache last night at about ten past eleven, and she heard a taxi running its engine for a few minutes right outside her cottage, and of course, with it being so warm at night right now she had her window open, so she could hear it perfectly clearly.'

'Over,' Birdie said, rather smugly. 'Well, that was all she needed, what with the tooth throbbing and everything, so she got up to close the window—after giving the driver a piece of her mind naturally—and who should she see but young Jamie Callaghan and that girl of Rafferty's from the pub getting into the taxi. And she shouted at them that some people should have more consideration for others, and the driver just laughed, can you believe it, and she was that upset about it that when Dave arrived with the milk this morning she was still annoyed, and poor Dave got the whole story, even though he still had twelve deliveries to make in Tuppenny Bridge, including ours.'

'Mind you, she's not normally such a crosspatch. It'll be because of her tooth. Nothing worse than toothache, is there?' Rita finished. 'Over.'

'And did she happen to hear where the taxi was heading?' Miss Lavender asked, before Ben had chance.

There was a slight hesitation, then Birdie said, 'Shouldn't you say over?'

'Did she hear where they were going?' Ben said loudly, since Miss Lavender seemed too stunned by Birdie's remark to answer. He added—with some force—'Over.'

'Now, I don't want you thinking Edie's a nosy parker, because she isn't,' Rita replied.

'Definitely not,' Birdie added. 'But with the window open and everything, and it being a quiet, calm night, well...'

'Over,' Rita said. 'So yes, as it happens she did hear. They were going to— now, where did she say again, Birdie?'

There was a mumbling sound and Ben waited impatiently. Miss Lavender frowned, seeing the look on his face, and he tried to stand still, though he was clearly about to burst with frustration.

'It sounded like Beaumont Tower,' Birdie said. 'Leastways, that's what Edie Cathcart told Dave, and he's got a very good memory has Dave. Has to have, really. Being a milkman. Over.'

Summer wasn't entirely sure what that had to do with anything, but she was grateful for Dave's exceptional memory anyway. She glanced at Ben, who was already on his mobile phone, probably googling Beaumont Tower. The Yorkies strained on their leads, annoyed at having to stand still so long, and Miss Lavender gave them a sympathetic look.

'Thank you for that, Holly Blue, Red Admiral. We'll meet in the usual place at six p.m. for a debrief. Over.' She switched off the walkie-talkie and put it back in her handbag before the Pennyfeathers could protest at the abrupt termination of their involvement in this thrilling episode, then took the leads from Ben.

'The only thing I can find is a Beauman Towers,' he said, looking up. 'It's about an hour and a half's drive away from here though. That would be expensive in a taxi!'

'But Frankie's got a credit card,' Summer pointed out. 'What is Beauman Towers anyway?'

Ben looked deeply worried. 'It's a hotel. A very grand hotel by the look of it.'

'Dear me,' Miss Lavender said. 'One doesn't like to think the worst of people, naturally, but why are they going to a hotel at their age?'

'There's probably some sort of conference or event on,' Summer said quickly. 'Come on, Ben, let's go. Thanks so much for all your help, Miss Lavender, and tell the Pennyfeathers we really appreciate what they did.'

'You'll let me know everything's all right?' Miss Lavender asked, with some alarm.

'Don't worry,' Ben said grimly. 'The Lavender Ladies will have their information and their pound of flesh as soon as possible.'

Miss Lavender shook her head. 'I'm asking as a friend, Ben, that's all. I wouldn't want anything to happen to them.'

He hung his head. 'I'm sorry, Miss Lavender. That was uncalled for. I'm just so worried.'

'Of course you are, dear. Ben...' She patted him on the arm and smiled kindly at him. 'Drive carefully, won't you? It looks like rain.'

They looked at each other and Ben swallowed, then nodded. He and Summer climbed into the Land Rover, and they drove away, leaving the old lady standing by the pub, the Yorkshire terriers pacing restlessly beside her.

Summer watched her in the wing mirror. She was staring after them, a look of concern on her face. *Drive carefully...*

She shivered and glanced at the speedometer, all too aware of how distracted Ben was. After what had happened to Leon, she'd be keeping an eye on that.

Chapter Twenty-Two

'So this Beauman Towers,' Summer said, after they'd driven in silence for ten minutes or so. 'Where exactly is it?'

'The Lake District.'

'The Lake District?' Summer let out a low whistle. 'Well, I suppose if they're going to stay in a hotel, the Lakes are a decent enough place to be.'

Ben gave her a sideways glance that told her he wasn't finding this at all funny.

'They won't be doing what you think they're doing,' Summer said. 'You can stop worrying.'

'Oh?' Ben gripped the steering wheel. 'And what exactly do I think they're doing?'

'Well...' Summer's voice trailed off. 'Whatever it is, clearly it's not playing chess.'

'He's fifteen,' Ben said.

'And she's fourteen!' Summer hit back. 'What do you think they're up to?'

He didn't reply, focusing on the road ahead which, to be fair, was a relief.

'She's got some sort of hold over him,' he said at last. 'I don't know what it is, I really don't. All I know is, he's a different boy these past few weeks.'

'So you've said.' Summer folded her arms. 'But put it this way, if they *are* up to something they shouldn't be, he's older than her.'

'And she's the one who booked the hotel. It's her credit card,' Ben replied. 'There's no way on earth that Jamie could afford it, I'll tell you that much.'

'You're thinking the worst of them here,' Summer said. 'Look, Frankie's a good kid and she wouldn't... Well, she wouldn't.'

'If they think they're in love, who knows what they'll do? You know what teenagers are like. All those hormones sloshing around all over the place. Given the means, it's hardly beyond doubt that they'd do something they shouldn't.'

'Not all teenagers think with their genitals,' she said crossly.

'Really?'

She raised an eyebrow. 'Did you?'

Ben bit his lip but didn't reply.

'Well,' she said, slightly thrown by his silence, 'I didn't. To be honest, I was always more interested in horses than boys. My mates at school used to think there was something wrong with me. I could reel off all nine British pony breeds but ask me who was in One Direction and I'd go blank.'

She laughed. 'I had posters of Highlands and Shetlands and New Forests and Dartmoors on my wall. My friends' bedrooms were plastered in pictures of Harry Styles and Olly Murs.'

She wasn't sure if he was listening or not and sighed. 'Anyway, not all girls are sex-obsessed as teenagers, that's all.'

'Sometimes it's not about what *you* want though, is it?' he said, in a voice so low she had to strain to hear him.

'I'm sorry?'

His jaw clenched and she thought he was going to ignore her. They drove in silence for a few minutes, then he said, 'Sometimes it's about peer pressure. About wanting to fit in and be accepted.'

'I don't think many teenagers would go as far as having sex just to please their mates!'

He turned slowly to look at her and she saw the embarrassment in his eyes and gasped.

'You didn't!'

Turning back to the road he said, 'No. As it happens I didn't, but if circumstances hadn't prevented it, who knows? I don't think I'm the only teenager who made that mistake, so forgive me if I don't share your faith in the logic and reasoning of Jamie and Frankie. We must get to this hotel and stop them before they do something they'll both regret.'

Summer hardly knew what to say to that. 'Who was she? Did you know her well?'

He nervously tapped his fingers on the steering wheel and seemed to be considering his answer. 'The truth? It was the first and only time I ever met her. I don't even know her name.'

'Oh, right.'

'I know. I was stupid, pathetic. I was at a party, desperate to impress a bunch of morons who were so drunk they'd probably have forgotten all about it the next day anyway.'

She stared at him. 'I just can't imagine you being like that. You're always so responsible.'

He didn't answer but his expression confused her.

'Ben, is there something I don't know? I just don't understand why you're behaving like this. It's so out of character. I

271

mean, I know Jamie and Frankie shouldn't have gone off without telling us, but they're decent kids and I'm sure they're okay. Why are you being so weird?'

Grimly he stared ahead at the road. 'I don't want Jamie to go off the rails. I don't want him to ruin his life like...'

'Like what?' she asked confused.

'Like I did.'

She reared back, baffled by his remark. 'How did you ruin your life? From where I'm sitting you've made a pretty good life. You went to university, you qualified as a vet, you've taken care of your mum and Jamie. I mean, you should be really proud of yourself.'

'Proud of myself?' He gave a bitter laugh and shook his head. 'Oh, Summer, if you only knew.'

Worried, she said, 'Well, why don't you tell me then?'

Miss Lavender had been right, she realised. It was starting to rain. Drops of water pattered onto the windscreen and Ben's expression darkened.

'If I tell you,' he said, 'you'll never look at me in the same way again.'

She gave a short laugh, more from nerves than anything. 'Don't be daft! Nothing you could tell me would make me change how I look at you.'

'Oh, don't say that. You have no idea.'

She gazed out of the window, aware of the grey sky and swollen clouds, and noticing suddenly how bleak the landscape looked right now. She wondered what Monk's Folly looked like at this moment. It would be more Wuthering Heights than ever.

Ben flicked the windscreen wipers on to clear the glass.

'Just tell me, Ben,' she said quietly. 'You might as well. You've come this far, and you know I'll always be wondering if you don't.'

'The fact is, Summer, I wasn't always a good person.'

She thought back to what Eugenie Lavender had told her and remembered the photo of schoolboy Ben. That defiant expression on his face, so unlike the open friendliness of his older brother.

'You mean when you were a teenager?'

He nodded. 'I was obnoxious, spoilt. I thought I could do whatever I liked. I hung out with a group of lads from the school, and they used to take the mickey out of me for living in Monk's Folly. They assumed I was rich and posh, and they were merciless. So I used to do whatever they wanted to prove to them I was just like them.' He shook his head. 'Why I'd want to be like them I have no idea, but at the time it seemed important.'

'Peer pressure,' she said. 'Most teenagers are desperate to fit in with their peers.'

'Which is why I don't want Jamie to make the same mistake.'

'But it's normal! It's part of growing up. I was no different.'

'But I doubt very much that you were as badly-behaved as I was. I was rude and cheeky to people, I shoplifted from local shops, I even set off fireworks to frighten the Pennyfeather sisters.' He gave her a rueful smile. 'Not that it did. They threatened to shove a rocket up my arse and light it and I ran a mile.'

Summer couldn't help smiling. Birdie and Rita struck her as just the types to carry out that threat. Nothing and no one could intimidate them.

'I was always in detention or being excluded,' he said. 'I was even threatened with permanent expulsion. Mum and Dad were at their wits' end, and Leon—' he swallowed hard. 'Leon was always telling me how unfair I was being to them, and that I was throwing away my future trying to impress idiots who didn't even care about me. I didn't listen, and when I found out Dad was ill, I got worse if anything.'

She saw his jaw clench.

'It's okay, Ben.'

The rain was coming down faster now and he flicked the windscreen wipers to permanent.

'It's really not okay,' he said. 'I was grounded—again— when my friends came over and told me there was a party going on. One of them had a brother who lived in Pellston, just outside York, and we were all invited to his house-warming bash. Of course, my parents said no but I didn't listen. I sneaked out of the window and down the drainpipe and we all piled onto the train to York.'

He was silent for a moment, remembering, and she waited, a knot of anxiety tightening in her stomach.

'It was the worst mistake of my life, and one I'll regret till my dying day.'

'What happened?' Summer asked, almost afraid to know.

'We were drunk,' he said briefly. 'Things got very out of hand and someone reported us to the police. They arrived, saw a bunch of underage lads drinking and carted us off to the station to calm us down and let us cool off in cells for a while. They called my parents to collect us, but Mum was out, and Dad was too ill to come. He'd not long had a bout of chemotherapy and he just wasn't up to it. Leon volunteered.'

Summer felt sick with dread. 'Was that the night...?'

He nodded. 'He never made it. No one knows what happened, why his car came off the road. It was a clear evening, and no other vehicles were involved. Something caused the accident, but no one can give me any answers, and all I keep coming up with is that he was so angry with me, and so worried about the effect my behaviour was having on our sick father, that he didn't concentrate on the road. It was my fault, Summer. My brother died because of me.'

'Ben,' she said, feeling devastated for him, 'you can't possibly know that.'

'I know he wouldn't have been driving if I hadn't gone to that party,' he said bitterly. 'No matter what anyone says there's no denying that fact.'

She supposed he was right, but even so, he couldn't blame himself for an accident.

'The only thing I can be thankful for—and it's not much I'll admit—is that I didn't go ahead with sleeping with that girl, because if that *had* been my first time and it had happened that night... You want to know something else?' He hesitated, then shook his head. 'No, forget it. You probably despise me enough as it is.'

Summer eyed him nervously. 'You didn't...'

He turned to face her. 'Didn't what?'

'I'm sorry. It's just the way you talk about yourself, with such hate, as if you can never forgive yourself for what you did. I just wondered...'

'If I'd tried to force myself on a girl?' He gave an abrupt laugh with no humour in it. 'Your opinion of me's crashed already, I see. I would never do that! Bloody hell. She was the one who—well, anyway, she was eighteen, and let's just say it wasn't my idea.'

Summer leaned back in her seat, not wanting to think about it. But if not that, what had he been about to tell her that would make her despise him?

A few minutes later she got her answer.

'It turned out she had a boyfriend, and he caught us. I expected he'd thump me, but he didn't, and I foolishly believed I'd got away with it. It turns out he was already on probation, and he couldn't afford to get into a fight, so he did something else. He rang the police and reported us. Had the whole lot of us carted off for underage drinking.'

'Pretty tame of him really,' Summer said. 'How do you know it was him, though? Did he admit it?'

'I never saw him again, but I don't see who else it could have been. There were no close neighbours to get wound up about the noise. The house was in the middle of a field. No, it could only have been him, and who can blame him? But you see, if I hadn't got close to that girl that night, just to shut my so-called friends up, he wouldn't have called the police, and I wouldn't have been taken to the police station, and they wouldn't have called home, and...'

He didn't have to finish the sentence. Ben had paid a heavy price for his teenage drunkenness. But Leon had paid an even higher one.

'After that, everything changed. Dad never got over it and it felt as if he gave up, so in a way I also felt responsible when he died of cancer a year later. Maybe, if Leon had lived, Dad would have lived longer, too. Because of me, Mum and Jamie lost two people they loved dearly. It seemed to me that I could never make up for that, but at least I could support them financially and do the best I could for them both, and that meant putting Jamie through school and giving him the chance of a decent future, and hanging on to the family home, no matter what it cost.'

'So that's why you've scrimped and saved to keep Monk's Folly, and send Jamie to public school,' she said. 'Oh, Ben.'

'Dad had been putting money aside to get me through university, although I doubt he ever expected me to go. I wasn't going to take it, but then I realised becoming a vet could enable me to help Jamie in the future. There was no money left for him, you see, so he had to be my responsibility. I became focused on school work and passing my exams. Did extra revision classes, some GCSE resits alongside my A levels. Anything to put it all right.' He lifted his chin. 'I can understand if you feel differently about me now. Honestly, I can barely look at myself in the mirror most days so I wouldn't blame you if you despised me.'

'Of course I don't despise you!' She realised tears were rolling down her cheeks and wiped them away. 'What you did back then—no one can blame you for that. You were just a teenager, a child really, and you have to forgive yourself. You were under pressure from those boys at school, as well as dealing with all the emotional upset of having a sick father. You must forgive yourself, Ben, you really must.'

'Mum hasn't,' he said.

Summer's head jerked up in shock. 'What do you mean, your mum hasn't? Of course she has! I'll bet she never blamed you in the first place.'

'You didn't see her face that night,' he said, increasing the speed on the wipers. 'The look she gave me, Summer! I'll never forget it as long as I live, and I know, I absolutely know that she blames me and always will.'

Summer didn't know what to say. She couldn't believe that was true. Jennifer adored Ben and wanted him to be happy more than anything.

'You know,' Ben continued, 'Ross tried to stop me. He went to the school Jamie goes to now. He hated the gang I hung around with and tried to make me see sense, but I wouldn't listen. If I'd just *listened* to him!'

Summer blinked in surprise. Ross had been the sensible one? She hadn't expected that. Maybe that was why they'd drifted apart then. Maybe Ross had been so appalled at what happened he couldn't forgive Ben.

It was odd, seeing Ross as the voice of reason and Ben as the wild child. How things had changed.

'You have to move forward,' she told him. 'You can't keep wallowing in all this misery and guilt, or how will you ever have a future?'

'I didn't think I did,' he said flatly. 'Until I met you.' Before she could answer he hurried on. 'So you see, peer pressure isn't some harmless teenage thing. Jamie's not the kid he was a few months ago, and I'm worried someone's exerting influence on him. If it's not Frankie then I'm sorry, but I can't imagine who else it is because those two seem thick as thieves. Parties can be so easily organised online, and if they've sneaked out to attend one at this hotel, anything could have happened. They could be drunk, they could be in trouble, they could be doing something right now that they'll regret forever. And if they are I'll never forgive myself for that, either.'

Summer leaned back in her seat, hardly able to take it all in. That Ben had been carrying such a burden all these years broke her heart. She just hoped Frankie and Jamie weren't going to add to his troubles.

* * *

Beauman Towers was clearly a luxury hotel, set in acres of grounds, not far from the beautiful and popular tourist town of Keswick.

'Wow,' Summer said, as they stepped out of the car onto the drive and gazed up at the large, white painted building with its grey, slate roof. 'I wonder how much this set her back? Elizabeth's going to be ecstatic when she gets the credit card bill. Not.'

She wondered briefly how Rafferty was going to explain their daughter's hotel stay to his ex-wife, and didn't envy him the task. She was dreading trying to explain how she'd let

Frankie escape to the Lakes without her even knowing, but at least Rafferty was a reasonable human being. Elizabeth would flip.

'It doesn't look the sort of place that would allow teenagers to have a party and get drunk,' she said hopefully.

Ben didn't look reassured. 'I suppose we'd better go in and see if we can find them then.' He looked up at the sky, now almost colourless as it hung low over the fells. 'At least it's stopped raining. It will make the drive back easier.'

There was an awkwardness between them that she longed to take away, but she didn't have the first idea how to. What could she say to him right now? Besides, he was so focused on saving Jamie from himself that he probably wouldn't be interested in anything else. They needed to find the runaways as quickly as possible and get at least one problem sorted out. Everything else could wait. There was way too much to unpack right now.

'What do we do if the receptionist won't tell us which room they're in?' she asked. 'They might not be able to. You know, guest confidentiality and all that.'

'Then we point out that their *guests* are underage teenagers and we'll be calling the police if they don't help us find them.'

They pushed open the doors and found themselves in a beautifully decorated lobby, with plush carpets and an immaculate reception area.

'How do you think they've booked in, being underage?' Summer whispered.

'I suppose it's hard to tell with teenagers these days. Maybe they can pass for eighteen, and with Frankie having a credit card...' Ben shrugged. 'I guess we'll find out.'

The man behind the desk couldn't have smiled any wider as he greeted them.

'Welcome to Beauman Towers. Are you here to check in? I'm afraid you'll have to wait until twelve o'clock, but you're welcome to make use of our facilities until then if you'd like to give me your names.'

'We're not here to check in,' Ben said. 'We're here to see my brother and his girlfriend. We believe they've taken a room here.'

The man looked distinctly uncomfortable.

'Oh, really? Well, I'm afraid I'm unable to give out any personal information about our guests. We pride ourselves highly on our confidentiality.'

'I imagine you do,' Ben said, returning the man's smile with considerably less warmth. 'But you see, my brother and his girlfriend happen to be under the age of eighteen. In fact, they're both under sixteen, so if you've given them a room today I'm afraid it will be a police matter. Do you understand?'

The man eyed him nervously and Summer said quickly, 'It's not your fault, but we really do need to find them as soon as possible.'

'I'm sorry, I can't help you.' The man gulped. 'After all, I only have your word that these people are under sixteen, or that you're who you say you are. Maybe I should call the manager?'

'I think you'd better,' Ben said.

'Ben?'

At the sound of Jamie's voice, Ben and Summer swung round, and Summer leaned against the reception desk, weak with relief to see Jamie standing there looking perfectly all right, except for the baffled expression on his face. Her relief vanished almost immediately, though, as she realised Frankie wasn't with him.

'Jamie! Thank God!' Ben pulled his brother into his arms

and hugged him tightly. 'What the hell are you playing at?' he said roughly. 'Have you any idea how worried we've been?'

'Jamie, where's Frankie?' Summer asked.

Jamie, who'd extricated himself from Ben's grasp with some difficulty, gestured casually to the door. 'She's out there, exploring the gardens. I was just going to fetch her.'

'Is this your brother?' the man behind the desk asked indignantly. 'Well, I'm very sorry, but for one thing there's no way I'd have believed he was eighteen, not for a single second. And for another, he definitely hasn't got a room here. I'd have remembered *him* if he'd been to the reception desk, and I can tell you now he most certainly hasn't.'

Ben and Summer looked at Jamie.

'What the hell's going on?' Ben asked. 'What are you doing here? And why did you sneak out last night without telling us? Have you any idea how worried we've been? Mum's beside herself. Mum!'

He turned to Summer. 'I need to call her, let her know everything's okay,' he said. 'Keep an eye on this one please.'

Jamie rolled his eyes. 'Bloody hell, Ben. Chill.'

'Never mind, chill. And stop swearing.'

Ben called his mother and Summer could hear him reassuring her that her son was safe and well, as she took a seat beside Jamie in the lobby.

'Right,' Ben said grimly, shoving the phone back in his pocket. 'You've got some explaining to do. And you'd better make it good, for your sake.'

'Let's get Frankie first,' Summer pleaded. 'I need to make sure she's okay.'

Ben nodded. 'Fair enough. Maybe it's best she's here, too. We need to hear what they've got to say for themselves. Both of them.'

Chapter Twenty-Three

Sitting in a pagoda in the hotel gardens ten minutes later, Ben eyed a clearly sheepish Frankie and a sullen Jamie and said, 'Well, go on then. I'm waiting.'

'There you go again,' Jamie said. 'Talking to me like I'm a kid!'

'You are a kid,' Ben said. 'You're fifteen years old. Frankie,' he added meaningfully, 'is only fourteen. What do you think you're playing at coming to a hotel? You do know there are laws about these things?'

'Laws?' Jamie frowned. 'What laws?'

'Ben,' Summer said hastily, 'I think you've got the wrong idea, I really do.'

Frankie and Jamie exchanged puzzled glances, then Frankie said, 'You think we're together? Me and Jamie? You think we've come here to...' She wrinkled her nose. 'Ugh! No offence but Jamie's a mate, nothing more. That would be weird.'

'Very weird,' Jamie agreed. 'But thanks for thinking I'd drag Frankie here to have sex with her. Bit of a waste of time really, considering she was supposed to be spending the night at Monk's Folly and we could have done what we wanted while you and Mum were fast asleep.'

Ben had to admit he had a point.

'So you're not boyfriend and girlfriend?'

'I don't know how many times we have to say it,' Frankie said with a sigh. 'No, we're not.' She gave Jamie a pleading look. 'Why don't you tell him?'

'Tell me what?' Ben asked suspiciously. 'What's going on with you two? Why are you here?'

Jamie gave a heavy sigh. 'It's because of Eloise.'

'Eloise?' Ben frowned. 'Who the hell's Eloise?'

'Eloise Beauman,' Frankie said helpfully. 'Her parents own Beauman Towers and the family live here. That's who we came to see.'

Summer smiled. 'Ah! I see.'

'Do you?' Ben asked, perplexed. 'I don't.'

Jamie rolled his eyes. 'Okay, so Eloise is a weekly boarder at St Egbert's. And—' he gave Ben a look of defiance, '—and she's my girlfriend.'

'Your girlfriend?' Ben couldn't believe Jamie had a girlfriend he'd never even heard of. 'How long has this been going on?'

'A whole term,' he said grudgingly. 'She's ace, Ben. You'd love her, honest you would, if you'd just give her a chance. She's really smart, and so funny. She makes me laugh all the time. She's top of her class in three subjects and she wants to be a doctor. A surgeon, actually. I reckon she could be, too. She's clever enough.'

Ben stared in amazement at his younger brother, whose demeanour had thoroughly transformed, his face taking on a distinct radiance when he talked about this wondrous creature, Eloise. He was obviously smitten with her. How had Ben missed that?

'It doesn't explain though,' he said, 'why you ran away last night and came here. What was so important that you took a taxi all the way from Tuppenny Bridge to the Lakes?'

Jamie bit his lip, saying nothing.

Frankie shrugged. 'It's because they'd had a falling out. Eloise has been winding him up all through the summer holidays by posting pictures of herself hanging out with some of their school mates.' She nudged Jamie. 'Got a bit jealous, didn't you, mate? Thought she'd finish with you to go out with one of them.'

'She sounds charming,' Ben said drily.

'It's not her fault,' Jamie said. 'It was me overreacting.'

'I wonder where he gets that from,' Summer murmured.

'If she's messing you about already...' Ben said with a sigh.

'She's not! I mean, she always said she was just having some fun because I wasn't around and they live closer to her.' His face flushed a little as he admitted, 'She wanted to stay with us at Monk's Folly for a week or two. Her mum and dad are always so busy with the hotel, and she gets left on her own a lot to entertain herself.'

'In a five-star hotel with all these facilities?' Ben raised an eyebrow. 'I'm sure she's got plenty to do.'

'But she said she'd rather be with me any day of the week,' Jamie said, sounding rather proud of the fact.

'Well, you never said anything,' Ben said defensively. 'If you'd asked, maybe she could have stayed.'

'That's what I said,' Frankie agreed. 'But he wouldn't ask you, so she's been having gaming evenings for their friends, and going round to the homes of those who lived nearest to her. They've had *Call of Duty* tournaments and posted the pics on Instagram, and it was driving Jamie mad. So...' She looked at Jamie, waiting for him to continue.

'I know it's a bit daft. When I think about it now it was a stupid idea,' Jamie mumbled. 'I just wanted to make her jealous. I thought if I posted photos of me hanging out with Frankie, Eloise would realise how horrible it felt. I put a couple on my own account, but we thought it would look more realistic if Frankie posted most of the pictures on her account, tagging me in them so Eloise would see them.'

'Nice plan,' Summer said. Whether she was being sarcastic or not Ben wasn't sure. 'I take it it worked.'

'Not at first,' Frankie said. 'She didn't reply at all, so we upped the stakes, posing cosier photos of us together, including at the wedding.'

'Then,' Jamie said, clearly embarrassed, 'on Saturday night she rang me up going mad at me. She'd seen the photos and she was proper furious! She told me I'd made an idiot of her, and she dumped me, there and then.'

'Jamie was in a right state,' Frankie said, 'so we decided the best thing to do would be to travel here and see her face to face to explain everything to her. He needed me with him because he didn't think she'd believe him if he was on his own. We got here well past midnight, and I rang Eloise to tell her Jamie was outside and would she come and talk to him?'

'Hang on,' Summer said. 'That's another thing. You left your phone at Monk's Folly, but Miss Lavender saw you on one last night. Whose phone is that?'

Frankie and Jamie exchanged glances.

'Burner phone,' Frankie said.

'A what?' Ben stared at her.

'You know, a cheap phone that you throw away after you've used it. We knew you'd be able to track us on ours, so I bought one from Maister's yesterday. Jamie put Eloise's number in it before we set off.'

'Well!' Ben shook his head feeling dazed. 'You had it all planned out, didn't you?'

'I can't believe how sneaky you two are,' Summer said. 'It was really irresponsible of you, though. Anything could have happened to you, and we wouldn't have been able to track you down. Never *ever* do something like that again.'

Ben couldn't agree with her more, but he said nothing. He didn't even look at her, too afraid of what he'd see in her eyes if he did.

'Well, anyway,' Frankie said, 'Eloise came down and they had a proper row in the gardens, but I managed to explain, and I convinced Eloise that there was nothing between me and Jamie, and that he'd just been trying to get her attention.' She smirked at Jamie. 'Kissed and made up didn't you, mate?'

Jamie gave Ben an awkward look. Under other circumstances Ben would have laughed.

'Why didn't her parents ring Mum and tell her you were safe?' he demanded.

'They didn't know we were here, honestly! Eloise smuggled us up into her room and we spent the night there.' Jamie held up his hands quickly. 'It's okay, don't get the wrong idea. Frankie shared Eloise's bed, and I was on the sofa.' He puffed out his cheeks. 'You should see her bedroom, Ben. It's proper luxurious. Got a massive television on the wall and she's got her own en suite bathroom. It's fantastic.'

'That's all very well and good,' Ben said, 'but why didn't you just tell me about Eloise in the first place? This could all have been sorted out if you'd just told me what was going on.'

'You wouldn't have listened.'

'Of course I'd have listened! All you had to do was—'

'Oh, who are you kidding?' Jamie's expression darkened and his aggressive tone stunned Ben. 'All you ever care about is work. Your work—which is the be all and end all of your life —and my work. School. Lessons. Grades. Revision. GCSEs. Prospects. University. That's all I ever hear from you and from Mum. You never once ask me about my friends, or my personal life. You never question that I'm stuck at Monk's Folly alone every weekend and holiday while all my school mates go on holidays and hang out together. You don't ask because you don't care. All you want from me is to pass my exams and go to university. You're obsessed, and I'm sick of it.'

Ben stared at him, staggered by the level of resentment in Jamie's tone. 'That's not true! Why do you think I took you out for the day? I wanted us to spend time together, have a laugh. You could have told me about Eloise then, but you didn't. I care about your welfare, of course I do. I just want you to be happy, that's all. I want the best for you. It's my duty as—'

'As what? My father? You're not my father, Ben!'

Ben felt sick at the fury on Jamie's face. 'I know I'm not your father, but I'm all you've got and—'

'No, you're not all I've got! I've got a mother and she's even worse than you.'

'Don't say that about her!'

'Why? Because we can't upset her? Because she's been through a hard time? Haven't we all? Why can't you see that you've created a monster?'

'I have no idea what you're talking about! Mum lost her son, then she lost her husband. She's grieving. The least I can do is try to make her life easier in any way I can.'

'And by doing so you condemned us all to a life of misery!'

Ben was thoroughly confused. 'I don't understand what you're saying.'

'No, you don't. Do you honestly think I don't know, Ben? Do you think I'm so blind that I can't see that every penny you have is going on sending me to that bloody school? You're so blinkered. All you think about is pleasing her and getting me through my education, and maybe you really do believe that's the best you can do for me too. But what about the rest of my life, Ben? What about *your* life?'

Summer got to her feet. 'I think this is between the two of you. We'll be in the hotel reception when you're ready to leave.'

Gently she led Frankie out of the garden, leaving them to it. He supposed he should be grateful to her for that because he was reeling by then, and further humiliation would have been unbearable.

'What do you mean, the rest of your life?'

Jamie sighed, exasperated. 'I mean what about having fun? What about family time? What about holidays? You work hard, you do extra hours, and what have you got to show for it? You want to know why I didn't tell you about Eloise? Partly it was because I knew you'd disapprove. Anything that distracts me from my studies is a waste of time as far as you're concerned. And then there's Mum, who insists she just wants us to be happy, but is so stuck in the past that she's ruining our future.'

'That's not fair!'

'Yes it is. You know, we did *Great Expectations* last year at school. I thought, that's Mum. Miss Havisham. Except instead of the eternal jilted bride, she's the eternal grieving widow. I'm surprised she's not permanently dressed in black, with cobwebs all over the dining room and the remains of Dad's wake moulding away.'

Ben didn't know how to answer. Did Jamie have a point?

'But the other reason was because of Monk's Folly.'

'Monk's Folly?' Ben was confused. 'What's that got to do with anything?'

Jamie gave him an incredulous look. 'It's got everything to do with everything! It dominates our bloody life. Every penny you don't spend on my education goes to keeping that place running. And for what? It's a bloody eyesore. If I'd told you about Eloise, if I'd told Mum about her, you might have suggested she visit so you could vet her. Can you imagine if I'd brought her to Monk's Folly, when she lives in Beauman Towers?' He gave a cry of despair. 'Bloody hell, now I've actually seen where she lives it's even worse. Monk's Folly is an ugly old pile that should have been pulled down years ago if you ask me.'

Ben wondered how to answer without making it very obvious that he agreed.

'Mum loves that house. All right, it needs a bit of care and attention—'

'Care and attention? Ben, every room needs decorating. Every carpet needs replacing. The windows rattle. It's freezing cold. The heating system is archaic. It's an embarrassment, nothing more, nothing less.'

'It meant the world to our father,' Ben said. 'You know the story.'

'So what?' Jamie shrugged in despair. 'Dad's gone, Ben. Whatever the house meant to him, it really doesn't matter any more. This isn't about Dad. It's about you and me and Mum. It's about what's best for our family. Monk's Folly is a drain on you financially, as is my stupid school.

'I kept trying to make you see that. I pushed you and pushed you, making you pay for me to go on that boring school trip that I knew you couldn't afford, just hoping you'd see sense and throw in the towel. But no. You clung on, getting into even more debt, no doubt. And for what? I'd have been just as happy at the local comp. Happier even because we wouldn't all be paying such a high price for me to go there. And I don't just mean financially.'

'You're not leaving school! You have your GCSEs coming up.'

'I know that.' Jamie bit his lip. 'Even so, I'm leaving after I've done them.' He held up his hand. 'You can argue all you like. I'm not staying on in the sixth form. It's a waste of money and I know you can't afford it. I can go to college to do my A levels. There's no reason for me not to.'

Ben eyed him hopefully. 'So you *are* going to do your A levels? You're not going to go looking for a job or an apprenticeship?'

'I was going to, more to spite you and wake you up than anything else,' Jamie admitted. 'But no. I'm going to do my A levels, and I want to go to university. You're right about that. But not at your expense, Ben, and not at the expense of our family. I'll stay on to do my GCSEs but after that, I'll take it from there. Okay?'

Ben nodded. 'Okay.'

Jamie stared at him for a long moment. 'I know you blame yourself, Ben.'

Ben's head jerked up and he felt the colour drain from his face. 'What—what do you mean?'

'You know what I mean. For Leon's death. I know you torture yourself about going out that night, blaming yourself for his accident. I see it in your face every day. I want you to know that I don't blame you. I've never blamed you. But you know what I do blame you for?'

Ben shook his head, unable to speak.

'I blame you for enabling our mother to hide away from the world and sit there in that dump wasting her life away. I blame you for not standing up for me. I blame you for not standing up for yourself. I get that you feel guilty, and you want to make it up to her, but as far as I can see all you've done is ruin things for her. She should have pulled herself together years ago. That's what you should feel guilty about, if anything.'

He stood, looking at Ben with a trace of shame in his eyes. 'I'm sorry. I know you did what you thought was best. And I'm sorry that I worried you today. We'd better go and find Frankie and Summer.'

Ben got to his feet feeling shell-shocked. When he'd woke up this morning he'd had no idea what lay in store for him today. Everything Jamie had just told him had knocked him for six and he wasn't sure how he was going to process it all.

And then there was Summer. He'd finally revealed his secret and hadn't a clue how she was taking it. Would she ever look at him in the same way again or had he ruined things between them for good?

He should be at work right now, and he supposed he'd have to go in once they got back from the Lakes, but all he wanted to do at that moment was crawl under a rock and hide away from the rest of the world.

He had no idea what to do next.

* * *

The journey home to Tuppenny Bridge was a grim one. Ben drove in silence, his brow furrowed as he concentrated on the road ahead. At least, that's what he appeared to be doing, though Summer couldn't imagine that he wasn't churning over the things he'd just heard from Jamie. How could he not be?

Jamie sat beside him, lost in his own thoughts, saying nothing after his earlier outburst. She supposed he had nothing left to say.

Summer and Frankie sat in the back. Frankie had attempted conversation, but Summer's warning glance told her that now wasn't the best time to chat. She could see Ben was in shock, and it was clear he had a lot of thinking to do.

She couldn't help feeling sorry for him and wondered how much more guilt he could cope with, even though a part of her couldn't help but feel vindicated that her faith in Frankie had been justified.

Of course, Frankie shouldn't have helped Jamie get to the Lakes, and she shouldn't have sneaked out of Monk's Folly at that time of night without telling anyone, but she'd acted out of kindness, and she'd meant well. Even Ben had admitted that when he'd finally managed to speak.

She saw his reflection in the rear-view mirror and her heart went out to him. He looked so bleak and broken. She longed to hold him and comfort him, tell him he wasn't a bad man and didn't deserve to beat himself up like this, and that nothing that had happened to him was his fault. People had done far worse and had got away with it all scot-free. It seemed to her that fate had punished him most unjustly for being nothing more than a gullible teenager and an overprotective brother.

Somehow he had to forgive himself for what happened to Leon and move forward. She wondered if that was part of the reason he'd not wanted the Lavender Ladies to find out about their relationship. Did he think people would judge him for enjoying himself? Did he judge himself?

Although it had been years since the accident, she

thought that, it probably seemed like yesterday to Ben. But if he couldn't let the past go, how could they have a future? He would be working against them the whole time.

She'd come to realise over the last few months, thanks to conversations with both her parents, how much damage self-loathing could do to a person, and to a relationship. Her dad had hated himself, and it had eaten away at his marriage to her mum, destroying something that could have been so good from within. He had almost destroyed her mum in the process.

Summer couldn't put herself through that, and she couldn't stand by and watch while Ben continued to press the self-destruct button over and over again. She knew where that led. She'd seen her dad do it so many times.

'Would you do me a favour?'

She realised he was watching her in the mirror and blushed, as if he'd been reading her thoughts.

'Sure, if I can.'

She glanced out of the window, amazed to see they were nearing Tuppenny Bridge already. It seemed to have taken them no time at all to get home, even though the journey to Beauman Towers had appeared endless.

'If I drop you all at Monk's Folly, would you go inside with Jamie? Explain to Mum what happened and make sure she's okay. I know she was terrified when we realised he was missing, and even though I called her I know she'll be in a bit of a state when she sees him.'

'Of course, but aren't you coming in?' Summer checked the time on her phone. 'Are you going straight to work? Surely Clive would understand.'

'I have things to do,' he said briefly. 'Please, Summer? I'd appreciate it.'

She nodded, realising it was important to him, even

though she was sure he was going to stroll into Stepping Stones and get on with work as if nothing had happened.

It wasn't good for him, she thought. He needed time to mull things over, get over the shock of the events of the morning. Somehow, though, she thought he would do what he always did. Focus on work and do the best he could at whatever job he was doing. That was Ben all over.

Her heart sank as she realised that, until he learned to deal with his pain in other ways, there was no way forward for him. For them. There was nothing she could do about it.

As agreed, Ben drove them to the end of the track that led to Monk's Folly. They got out of the car and Summer leaned in the driver's side window as Frankie and Jamie trudged through the gate and up the drive to the house.

'Are you sure you won't come in?' she asked. 'I seriously think you should, Ben. You can't just—'

'I'd better go,' he said brusquely. 'I'll see you later. Thanks for this, Summer. I really appreciate it, and I'm sorry. Really sorry. For all of it.'

She jumped back as he began to reverse back down the track.

'Okay,' she muttered to herself as she turned to Monk's Folly. 'Guess I'm on my own, then.'

She glanced back over her shoulder at the retreating Land Rover and blinked away tears.

'I guess we both are.'

Chapter Twenty-Four

Ben drove along the track, his eyes fixed on the way ahead as he muttered to himself, 'Don't look back, don't look back.'

If he looked back and saw Summer standing there he might just stop the car and run to her, but what would be the point of that? There was a part of him that was desperate to talk to her, to plead with her if necessary. The bigger part of him, though, knew that right now he had to get his head straight.

Everything had changed and he had to find a way to deal with it. Not just for the sake of his and Summer's relationship, but for his mum and Jamie, too.

He crossed the bridge and drove up River Road. As he drew near to Daisyfield Cottage he slowed, then found himself pulling up. He wound down the window and gazed at the home of Mr and Mrs Eckington, where he'd spent many a day in his childhood.

It was as pretty as ever. Roses climbed the honey stone walls, sheep grazed on the hill behind it, and oxeye daisies flourished in the grass verges. He couldn't bear to see such a beautiful place standing empty.

Daisyfield Cottage couldn't be more different from Monk's Folly, he thought wistfully, remembering all the happy times he'd spent there as a child.

Mrs Eckington had always had something delicious baking in the oven, and Mr Eckington had happily shown him things to do in the garden, or had sat with him in their cosy kitchen, having long and interesting chats about school and books and television programmes and goodness knows what else—listening intently and taking the thoughts of a small boy perfectly seriously—while his wife buttered scones for them and watched on fondly.

Their daughter had already left home by then, so they'd welcomed visits from Ben and, occasionally, from Leon too. It had always felt like such a warm and comforting place.

Now it was cold and empty. Mrs Eckington dead and gone. Mr Eckington at his daughter's house in a city. It was as his mother had said. Nothing stayed the same. Everything had its season.

Winding the window up a little he drove on, making his way into town. He parked the Land Rover in Market Place, dropped a pound coin in the honesty box, and headed purposefully towards All Hallows.

The churchyard was huge, with mature trees and ancient tombs to the left of the church, and younger trees, neat gravel paths and newer gravestones to the right.

It was also quite long, and there was a paddock at the far end with sheep grazing in it. A neatly trimmed hedge on the far right of the churchyard separated it from the gardens of a row of cottages, and beyond those there seemed to be nothing but lush, green, rolling hills. Strategically placed benches ensured that visitors could sit and contemplate the view in peace.

He made straight for his favourite bench, under a tree and facing the Garden of Ashes. He ignored the fact that it was still damp from the rain and sat down under what was now a blue sky, admiring the glorious scenery. Occasionally, a gentle breeze caused the trees to lightly rustle, and there was the odd buzz of an insect, but generally, all was quiet. It was hard to believe the market place with its shops and pubs was just outside the gates.

He'd known where he needed to be before he was even halfway home, and had made up his mind to go there, rather than facing his mother or having to listen to Jamie repeating the explanation for his behaviour.

It wasn't that he was being cowardly, or uncaring. Well, maybe it was in a way. But the truth was, if he didn't get away by himself, give himself a chance to be alone, to think, he might well explode.

He wasn't even sure how he'd got home, and it filled him with dread when he realised he'd apparently driven all the way back from the Lakes on automatic pilot, his head so full of other thoughts that he hadn't even registered the journey home.

Was that, he wondered, what had happened to Leon that night? He gazed across at his brother's memorial. Had Leon been so angry with Ben for sneaking out of Monk's Folly, for getting into such a state at that house in Pellston and forcing him to drive all that way to collect him, that he'd switched to automatic pilot, too? Is that why his car had gone off the road that night? Is that what had killed him?

He stared at the vase of roses on the stone that lay above his brother's ashes, almost willing Leon's spirit to appear and explain exactly what had happened. He was sick of going over and over it in his mind, trying to work out what had caused a fatal accident on a clear night, with no other vehicles involved.

It had never made sense to him, unless Leon had been so preoccupied with Ben's behaviour that he'd been distracted. Now that he'd driven home thinking of little but Jamie's own behaviour today, he could understand how it had happened more easily. Ben had been lucky today, but another time...

He shivered and put his head in his hands, weary to the bone. Only two o'clock and he'd been to the Lake District and back already and had been informed—as if he needed telling—just how badly he'd let Jamie down.

But how, he asked himself, as if pleading with some unseen jury, could he possibly have known what was going on in his brother's mind? Jamie had given no sign that he'd been going through something like this, and he wasn't a mind reader, was he?

And what he'd said about their mother. Hell, he'd really messed up. How could he have got things so badly wrong?

Why couldn't he be the big brother that Leon had been to him?

He wasn't sure how long he'd been sitting there before he became vaguely aware of someone standing close by.

'Mind if I join you?'

Ben's heart thumped at the sound of Summer's voice.

'What are you doing here?'

She sat down next to him on the bench and folded her arms, gazing straight ahead of her.

'Miss Lavender and Zach spotted you as they left the church earlier, so they rang Monk's Folly to check that Jamie and Frankie had got home safely and told us where you were. I came straight away. To be honest, I thought I'd have missed you by now, but you're still here.'

'Still here,' he said. 'How's Mum?'

'Absolutely fine. Jamie's fine. Frankie's fine. More to the point, how are you, Ben?'

Ben didn't know where to begin so he nodded at the garden of ashes in front of them.

'He's right there.'

'Sorry?'

'Leon. He's right there; his ashes are buried under one of those stones, next to Dad's. See that one with the white vase and the roses? That's Leon. That's my brother.'

'I'm so sorry, Ben.' She reached for his hand and held it tightly. 'I had no idea you'd been grappling with all this guilt. It must have been eating you up every day. I'm really glad you finally told me about it all. I just wish you'd told me sooner.'

He frowned. 'Do you? It hasn't...'

'What? Made me hate you?' Her eyes were full of sadness. 'Of course not. The only person who hates you is yourself.'

'Maybe that's true,' he said, 'but Jamie made it very clear I'm hardly his favourite person. Not that I blame him. You know, I honestly thought I was doing the best for him and for Mum, but he's made me question everything today.'

He twisted round on the bench and stared at her intently.

'I'd understand, you know. If you wanted to end things...'

Summer gave an impatient sigh. 'Ben, I don't want to end things. As far as I'm concerned what happened with Leon was a terrible accident, and you're not to blame. You're a good man who's just tried to make up to your family for something that wasn't your fault. It doesn't change how I feel about you.'

'Really?' he asked hopefully. 'You think we've still got a future?'

She eyed him steadily. 'Well,' she said at last, 'that's up to you. I've got to be honest with you. I want us to have a future together, of course I do. But I've seen what happens when someone hates themselves so much that they're eaten up with it. How it affects not just their life, but the lives of people who love them. You have to put the past behind you and move on or how can we ever make it work?'

'I know that,' he admitted. 'I just don't know where to start.'

'Start at the beginning,' she suggested. 'Where did it all go wrong?'

He rubbed his forehead, remembering. 'The night the police took me home. Dad was so sick they'd made him go to bed, and Mr Eckington had gone to the hospital to identify Leon because Mum was in no fit state. When they told me what had happened...' He swallowed down the tears. 'You should have seen Mum's face, Summer. I'll never forget the expression in her eyes as long as I live. I knew, right there and then, that I had to do everything I could to make her forgive me. Even if it took me the rest of my life.'

'So you indulged her.' Summer shuffled closer to him, putting her arm around his shoulders as he shivered. 'Whatever Jennifer wanted or needed, you made sure she got it?'

'All she wanted,' he said quietly, 'was to turn Monk's Folly into a shrine. Dad adored that house. God knows why. You know, the funny thing is, she hated it for years. She was always complaining about how big and cold it was. But after Dad died she became obsessed with it. The solicitor suggested selling it, you know, but she wouldn't hear of it.'

'Wasn't the house left to you, though?' Summer asked, puzzled. 'Wasn't it your decision?'

'Yes, although she had control until I turned eighteen. But even then, how could I go against her like that? By that time things had settled into a pattern. She'd stopped going out. Everything was about fulfilling Dad's wishes. Do you know, she hasn't changed a thing in their room since he passed? Or Leon's. They're literally shrines. And Dad had wanted me and Jamie to go to university because Leon didn't, so she insisted that had to happen. Then it was private education for Jamie and—well, you know the rest.'

Summer puffed out her cheeks, thinking. 'It seems to me,' she said, 'that you've been a bit of an Edward Monk.'

He raised an eyebrow. 'Sorry?'

'That story your mum told me about how Monk's Folly got its name. Edward Monk could have had a happy life with Arabella Lavender, but he was too daft with her. He wanted her to be happy, so he gave in to her. He threw away their future to give her what she thought she wanted. In the end they were both miserable. If he'd just done what he thought was right in the first place they could have married and lived happily ever after.'

Ben leaned back on the bench and stared up at the sky.

'What are you thinking?' she asked gently.

'I'm thinking... I'm thinking I've a lot of thinking to do.'

She squeezed his hand and got to her feet. 'I need to go to Whispering Willows,' she said. 'Poor Joseph was expecting me this morning. He said it's okay, but I feel bad so I'm going in for a few hours anyway.'

'Will I see you later?' he asked hopefully.

She hesitated then, to his disappointment, she shook her head. 'I don't think so, Ben.'

His stomach plummeted and he stared up at her. 'Okay.'

'It's like you said, you've got a lot of thinking to do. Right now, I'd only get in the way of that. You need to figure things out for yourself, because until you do, we won't be able to move forward.'

'Yes,' he said quietly. 'I get it. You're right.'

She planted a kiss on his forehead. 'When you're ready I'll be here,' she promised.

He watched her walk away and his eyes narrowed.

She was right, about so many things. He thought about Edward Monk and what she'd said about going back to the beginning.

He stared at his brother's memorial.

'I wish you were here, Leon,' he said quietly. 'I don't know what to do. I don't know how to put this right. How do I give Jamie a better quality of life? How do I fix things so me and Summer can make things work? And how do I do all that without breaking Mum's heart?'

That was the question. His gaze moved to his dad's memorial next to his brother's. 'I wish you were here too,' he said, his voice breaking with emotion. 'You'd know how to handle Mum. You'd know what to do for the best. I need you both to help me. It's too much!' He rubbed his face. 'What would *you* do?' he asked them.

There was no answer of course. They couldn't help him any longer. This was down to him. It was all down to him. He supposed it always had been.

He got to his feet. 'One thing at a time, I guess. Wish me luck.'

Chapter Twenty-Five

The staff at Lavender House knew Ben quite well. As a vet, he visited the place often—far more regularly than he needed to thanks to Miss Lavender's demanding nature—so the ones on duty today raised no objection to him making his own way to her apartment at the back of the house and hadn't rung through to ask if it was okay for him to do so. She was therefore clearly surprised to see him, but pleased too, judging by the smile on her face when she opened the door.

'Ben! How lovely to see you. I noticed you at the church earlier but didn't like to interrupt. You seemed to be deep in meditation.'

That was one word for it he thought wryly.

'May I come in?'

'Of course, of course.'

She ushered him into her pink living room, where he was immediately investigated by Boycott and Trueman who had been, he noticed ruefully, tucking into cake from little dishes on the floor.

'It's Josiah Lavender's birthday,' she told him, clearly

noticing his disapproving glance. 'A special occasion, which we always celebrate with cake.'

He knew he should remind her, yet again, that so many treats weren't good for the dogs, but he didn't have the energy. It wasn't as if she listened anyway.

'How are things, Ben?' she asked, motioning to him to take a seat. 'I hear the errant runaways made it home safely.'

'They did. No harm done.'

'I hope they had a good explanation for causing you so much worry,' she said. 'Fancy running off like that in the middle of the night! I can't imagine what they were thinking.'

'Well,' he said heavily, 'that's teenagers for you. You know what it's like when your hormones are all over the place. We were all that age once.'

'Goodness, Ben! As if I can remember that far back.' Miss Lavender laughed. 'You know, when I was a teenager, we didn't even *have* teenagers. Or if we did the term wasn't in common usage. Things were very different then.' She shook her head, remembering. 'My mother was appalled by the youth of my day. She blamed Elvis Presley for their dreadful behaviour. Said his gyrating hips had brought about the end of civilised life as we knew it.'

She offered him cake which he politely refused.

'I suspect,' she said sitting down, the plate of cake on her lap, 'that you're here for a more important reason than to discuss Elvis Presley or the terrible behaviour of teenagers. What can I do for you?'

Ben didn't know where to begin, so he decided to plunge straight in with the question before he changed his mind.

'Would you be interested in buying Monk's Folly?'

She didn't reply and he rushed on, feeling an urgent need to explain. 'For your art school, I mean. I was thinking about it, and I know you're looking for premises. You always said that Josiah Lavender loved the views from up there, and often painted them from the land that Monk's Folly was built on. The art students would love to paint them, too, I'm sure. There's plenty of room for accommodation and classrooms. I know it needs a bit of work but...' His voice trailed off and he rubbed the back of his neck, feeling stupid. 'Too much work probably,' he admitted.

Miss Lavender pursed her lips, her eyes narrowed. 'Have you discussed this with your mother?'

It wasn't the response he'd hoped for, or expected. He gave her an indignant look.

'You do know the house belongs to me? My father left it to me, not Mum, and—'

She held up her hand. 'Ben dear, I'm perfectly well aware of that. It's just...' She broke off and watched him for a moment, her eyes full of compassion. 'I gather your mother never mentioned our conversation at Rafferty and Sally's wedding.'

'What conversation?'

'Ah, I thought as much.' Miss Lavender nibbled on some cake and Trueman and Boycott got to their feet and gathered round her, clearly hoping for more themselves.

'At the wedding reception Ross and I had an interesting chat with Ethan Rochester about the art school. He seems quite keen to help, which is good news. Of course, it all hinges on us finding suitable premises, and they're in short supply around here. Monk's Folly has always been my preferred choice, and although Ross wasn't so keen at first, the lack of alternatives made him see things in a different light.

'So, well, we approached Jennifer with the suggestion at the wedding. Not,' she added quickly, 'because her opinion overrode yours. As I said, we're well aware who actually owns Monk's Folly. But you see, Ben, we knew, as does just about everyone in this town, how much the house means to her since your father and Leon passed, and we felt it only fair that we find out how she would feel about leaving.'

Ben felt a sudden nausea. 'How did she take it?'

Miss Lavender broke off some cake and threw it to the dogs.

'She said no. A flat *no*. Not a *maybe*, or a *give me some time to think about it*. It was definitely out of the question.'

Ben had feared as much. 'I see.'

'I don't know if that changes things for you,' she said gently, 'but I thought I should put you in the picture before we continue this conversation.'

He leaned back on the sofa and closed his eyes a moment, thinking. It wasn't as if it had come as any surprise to him. He'd known it was going to be tricky the moment the idea had come to him. Even so, hearing it in such stark terms stung. How was he going to do this? Did he have the right to hurt his own mother all over again, after everything he'd already put her through?

'Why do you want to sell the house?' Miss Lavender asked. 'Don't get me wrong, I'm very keen to buy it, but I want to know your reasons. You've hung on to it for so long I never expected you to let it go. Why now?'

Ben exhaled slowly. 'Initially it occurred to me that I could rent part of it to you instead,' he admitted. 'I thought I could use the money from the rental to do up our part of the house and make decent living quarters for us.'

She shook her head. 'That wouldn't work, dear. We have big plans. There are going to be studios and galleries, a dining room, and residential accommodation. We would need the whole house.'

'I understand that,' he said. 'Besides, I quickly realised it wasn't a solution. We need to make a clean break. I think it's time we all started living again. And quite frankly, Miss Lavender, that house is suffocating us.'

'She won't like it,' Miss Lavender warned. 'You know what she's like.'

'She's turned it into a shrine to Leon and Dad,' Ben said simply. 'I let her do it. I stood back and watched her withdraw from the world and I did nothing to stop it. I let her dictate what I should and shouldn't be doing, and what was best for Jamie. I allowed her to wallow in grief and misery, and drag me and my brother down with her. It has to stop.'

'Sometimes,' she said, 'you can love someone too much. I understand why you've been so patient with her, Ben, but sometimes loving someone means saying no to them. You know who you remind me of?'

'Yes,' he said in a resigned voice. 'Edward Monk. Summer already told me the same thing.'

She smiled. 'A wise girl that one,' she said. 'She's good for you, Ben. You've lost that haunted look you had for years. That sadness behind the eyes that I've seen in you for so long. Summer has taken it away. It's as if she's chased away the ghosts.'

He bit his lip. 'Some of them maybe,' he said at last. 'Others will haunt me forever.'

'It wasn't your fault, Ben,' she said. 'You do know that, deep down, don't you?'

He stared at her, amazed.

'You think I didn't realise? The way you changed after Leon died—I knew it was more than grief. Only guilt can make someone age so much overnight, and you did. You took on far too much responsibility, and the way you let your mother take over your life, and Jamie's, well... But, as you said, it has to stop some time, doesn't it?'

'I owe her so much,' he murmured, feeling guilty for just being at Lavender House now, discussing the subject.

'But you know you're right to be here,' she said, 'or you wouldn't have come, would you? You wouldn't have asked me if I'd like to buy Monk's Folly. Which I would, by the way. If you're absolutely sure you want to sell it to me.'

'And Ross definitely wants it?'

She eyed him steadily. 'I've always been very sad that you two stopped being friends,' she said. 'I think he was, too.'

Ben flushed, wondering how much Miss Lavender knew about that night. Did she know Ross had tried to warn him? Did she realise that her great-nephew had barely so much as glanced at him since, unable to meet his eyes, so disgusted with him for what his behaviour had led to?

If she did she didn't seem to share Ross's disgust. Even so, he was sure she'd got it wrong. It was quite clear to him that his former friend had washed his hands of him since Leon's death, and he'd never blamed him for that. He'd have walked away from himself if it had been possible, after all.

'He thinks it will make a good art school?' was all he said, not wishing to go any deeper into the subject of Ross.

She nodded. 'He remembers it from when he used to visit you, of course. He thinks it will be very suitable.'

'I wasn't joking,' Ben said hesitantly, 'when I said it needs a lot of work doing to it. It's in a bit of a state. It will probably need rewiring, a new heating system and boiler, the windows will need replacing.' Now that he thought about it he realised he could go on for ages, listing all the jobs that would need doing to make Monk's Folly anywhere near good enough for a residential art school.

Luckily she stopped him at that point.

'Naturally. We're all aware that nothing's been done to

the house since your father died. Or indeed, since some time before that.'

'And it hasn't put you off?'

'On the contrary. We'll have to remodel it anyway, so we might as well do the lot. Make it the way we want it from scratch.' She beamed at him. 'I think we're both rather looking forward to it.'

'Then...' Ben hesitated. 'Have we got a deal?'

'And what about your mother?' she asked.

Ben thought about her, sitting in that living room at Monk's Folly, surrounded by the photographs of happier times. He thought about his dad and Leon, who'd loved the house so much. It had been his dad's pride and joy, and he remembered he'd often spoken about passing it on to future generations.

But would Dad really want them all to struggle on through life, not able to afford to do anything? Would he be happy that his wife was a recluse, rotting away within its walls?

Ben couldn't believe it. Yes, his dad had loved Monk's Folly, but he'd loved his family far, far more. He wouldn't want the house to cost them their happiness.

He thought about Jamie, and his increasing misery and frustration. His dad would have hated to see that.

And he thought about Summer, and how badly he wanted to be with her. She'd said she wanted to be with him, too, but only if he sorted himself out. She'd seen what her mother had suffered as her dad sabotaged every chance of happiness they had. He couldn't put her through the same ordeal. He wanted to make her happy. He wanted to give them the best chance of making a good life together that he could.

He took a deep breath. 'I'll deal with Mum. Monk's Folly is mine to sell, and that's my decision.'

She smiled at him. 'I'm proud of you. In that case, Ben, let's talk about money. And do please have some cake. This is definitely a day of celebration.'

* * *

Eugenie Lavender might think that today was a day worth celebrating but his mother, when he broke the news to her, clearly didn't share her opinion.

When he returned to Monk's Folly, he found her and Jamie sitting in the kitchen. Frankie had apparently gone home with Summer before Summer came to find him, and Jamie was now showing his mother photographs of Eloise on Instagram.

'Oh, isn't she pretty?' Mum said, patting his shoulder as she peered at the screen. 'And you say she wants to be a surgeon? How amazing! I'm so happy for you, Jamie.'

Jamie lifted his gaze and, seeing Ben there, stiffened as if expecting another argument.

'I need to talk to you, Mum,' Ben said firmly. Somehow he knew that this was no time to sound hesitant or apologetic. She had to know he was serious, that there was no talking him round.

'I suppose it's about me,' Jamie said glumly. 'And you want me to make myself scarce, right?'

'No actually, on both counts. This affects you as much as it affects Mum, or me for that matter. You should stay.'

They both looked at each other, then at him.

'Are you okay?' Mum asked nervously. 'You sound a bit...'

'A bit what?'

She didn't reply but watched him, a hint of uncertainty in her eyes.

He pulled out a chair and sat down, facing them across the kitchen table.

'There's no easy way to say this,' he said, trying to sound as kind as he could. 'I want you to know that this has been done with your best interests at heart. In the best interests of all of us.'

'Ben, you're scaring me,' she said. 'Just tell us what's happened.'

He steadied himself, bracing himself for her outrage. 'I've agreed to sell Monk's Folly to Eugenie Lavender.'

There was a stunned silence.

Jamie said, 'Are you joking?'

Ben didn't miss the excited tone in his voice, nor the hopeful gleam in his brother's eyes.

'I'm absolutely serious. She and Ross are going to turn it into an art school. It's perfect for them, just what they've been looking for. Of course, they're going to have to do a lot of work to it, and that was reflected in the price we agreed, but she certainly hasn't robbed us. It's a really good price. Far more than I expected. We'll be able to buy somewhere smaller and easier to manage and have plenty left over to make life so much easier for ourselves. Jamie's school fees will be covered, and we won't have to worry about paying the fuel bills and...'

His voice trailed off as his mother stared at him, her face pale.

'That's brilliant!' Jamie sounded ecstatic. 'Oh, Ben, that's fantastic!' His enthusiasm dampened a little as he turned to his mother. 'Isn't it?' he asked hesitantly.

'How could you do this to me, Ben?'

She shook her head as if denying it could possibly be true.

'Mum, you've got to understand—'

'I do understand!' Her voice rose as she glared at him, fury suddenly replacing shock. 'I understand that your father and Leon meant nothing to you! I understand that everything they loved and cared for doesn't matter to you. This house was their home! All we have left of them! And you want to sell it to the Lavenders to become an *art school*?'

The last two words were so dripping in scorn and contempt that Ben winced.

'That's not fair!' Jamie turned desperate eyes on Ben. 'Don't listen to her! You're doing the right thing; you know you are. Mum, you know Ben loved Dad and Leon. It's horrible to say they don't matter to him. If they didn't matter to him, do you honestly think he'd have stuck it out here as long as he has?'

Ben had an awful feeling his mother wasn't even aware that Jamie had spoken.

'I won't let you do it,' she said. 'There must be something I can do to stop you. I'll see a solicitor, get legal advice. This is my *home*!'

Something snapped in Ben. She was actually threatening to contest the sale of Monk's Folly? There was no way he was going to sit back and let her do any such thing.

'Your home?' he cried. 'Wake up, Mum! This isn't your home. It's your bloody tomb!'

There was a shocked silence. Even Jamie looked stunned at his outburst. Ben felt a momentary pang of guilt but pushed it away. He couldn't let her gain any ground. He had to make her see the truth.

'This is your tomb,' he repeated, as calmly as he could manage. 'And you've buried Jamie and me in here with you.

It has to stop. Can't you see what it's doing to us? To all of us?'

Her eyes filled with tears. 'I don't know what you mean.'

'Yes, you do.' Wearily, he rubbed his forehead. 'I know how much you love and miss Dad and Leon, but you can't carry on like this. The truth is, we can't afford to hang on to this house, and Dad would understand that. It needs far too much work doing to it, work that I can't undertake because every spare penny I have is going on Jamie's school fees. You know that, deep down.' He held up his hand to silence her as she started to protest. 'Yes, you do. And I also know...'

He paused, pain twisting inside him as if someone had taken a knife and plunged it through his stomach, turning it round and round to prolong the agony. 'I also know that you think it's a fitting punishment for me to spend the rest of my days buried alive in this place, and that you believe the least I can do—the very least—is give everything I earn to ensure Jamie gets the kind of life he deserves.

'Maybe I've let you get away with punishing me for so long because I felt I deserved it too. But things have changed now, Mum, because I can see that it's not just me who's being punished but Jamie, too. And surely, even you wouldn't want that?'

Jamie closed his eyes for a moment and when he opened them Ben was sad to see tears spilling out.

'I'm sorry,' he said. 'I never meant for you to go without for my sake, Ben. You have to believe that. I never wanted this.' He waved his arms around as if encompassing the entire house, his entire life. 'Any of this.'

'I know that,' Ben said gently. 'It's not your fault. I've never blamed you for it.' He eyed his mother sadly. 'I've never blamed you, either. I understand that what I did to you was unforgivable. I totally get that you want to punish me.

But enough's enough, Mum. How long do I have to go on suffering? How long does Jamie?'

She seemed unable to speak. Her eyes were fixed on his, and he couldn't read the expression that was in them. She opened and closed her mouth several times as if she had no words to reply.

Ben sighed. 'And then there's Summer. I really like her, and by some miracle she really likes me—even now after I told her what I did, all those years ago. I think, if I can finally break free of this place and start to move on with my life, that she and I could have a future together. But if I stay here, it will never happen. Apart from anything else, I refuse to entomb her here with me. She's done nothing wrong. I won't let her share my punishment.'

'Ben...' Jamie shook his head and turned to his mother. 'Mum, please, say something!'

Jennifer promptly burst into tears.

Jamie put his arm around her, and, after a moment's hesitation, Ben went to sit at the other side of her, taking her hand in his.

He didn't urge her to stop crying, but let her sob, realising that it would probably do her good. Maybe, he thought, he should have cried more. It might have helped release the grief, the pressure.

He'd thought he was being brave, holding all that inside, refusing to let it go. Now he thought it had probably been a sign of cowardice, not bravery. It took courage to face up to those feelings, and he'd spent years running away from his. Let his mother cry for as long as she needed.

After a couple of minutes he got up and made them all cups of tea. That was, after all, the cure-all. No matter what was going on in life, the answer was always to make a cup of tea.

He handed an ashen-faced Jamie his, then put a cup in front of his mother.

'I've put extra sugar in,' he said gently. 'For shock.' Even though he knew an additional spoonful of sugar in a cup of tea wouldn't make any difference whatsoever, it had seemed the right thing to do. 'I'm sorry, Mum. I know I've hurt you all over again, and I wish I could find a way to make it up to you, but—'

'Stop it!'

Her voice cut through him, and he sat down, cradling his own tea in hands that suddenly felt as cold as ice.

She wiped her face, swiping away the tears that had dampened her cheeks.

'You've got it so wrong,' she said, so quietly he could hardly hear her. 'How could you think that of me? How could you believe I'd be so—so *cruel?*'

He swallowed, but now was no time to back down or avoid confrontation. They'd come this far. It was time to be honest.

'I saw your face,' he said, not looking at her because he couldn't bear to. 'That night when the police brought me home, and you told me what had happened to Leon. I saw it right there and then. The hatred. The anger. The pain. I knew you blamed me, and that you'd never forgive me. I don't blame you,' he added quickly. 'What I did that night was so stupid, so irresponsible, so—'

'You were a teenager.'

It was a simple statement of fact, but she had a puzzled look on her face as if she couldn't understand what he was talking about.

'I'm sorry?'

She shook her head. 'Ben, you were a teenager. You did what so many teenagers do. You sneaked out of the house to go to a party; you drank alcohol when you were underage; you rebelled a bit against your parents. Do you honestly think I blamed you for that?'

'But—but look what it led to,' he whispered.

'It was an accident! It wasn't your fault!'

'If I hadn't gone to that party Leon wouldn't have had to come and fetch me—'

'And if I hadn't gone out that night I would have been the one to collect you from the police station, and he'd be safe at home!' She gave an anguished moan. 'Oh, if you only knew! If you only knew how many times I've gone over and over that in my mind. Why did I go out that night? Why couldn't I have been in when Leon took that call? I've tortured myself about that for so many years.'

She ran a hand through her hair. 'You think I looked at you that night with hatred? Well, if I did it was hatred for myself. I was ashamed, Ben! I was ashamed that my actions had led to Leon dying in that accident. I could barely look at you because I felt I'd robbed you of your brother. I still carry the shame and the guilt of that with me.'

Ben could hardly take it in.

'You—you blame yourself?'

'I'm a mother!' she cried. 'It was my job to keep you both safe. But where was I when you sneaked off to that party? Where was I when that call came through? Where was I when poor Leon got into that car?' The tears were falling again now. 'Out enjoying myself,' she said bitterly. 'I told myself I deserved a night out because life was so relentlessly hard, with your poor dad being so ill. I just wanted one night. One night when I didn't have to think about what lay ahead for him. One night when I didn't have to watch him suffering. It was just one night,' she whispered. 'But you all paid the price for my mistake.'

'But you can't possibly blame yourself!' Ben could hardly believe what he was hearing. 'You and Dad were going through hell. Of course you deserved a night out with friends. And even if you'd been at home, the chances are Leon would have offered to collect me anyway. You know he would.'

'We'll never know, will we?' she said sadly. 'That's my burden to bear.'

'Would you have blamed me?'

Jamie's question made them both turn to stare at him, baffled.

'Blame you? For what?' Ben asked.

'I sneaked out of here last night to go to the Lake District, and you had to drive there to pick me up. If something had happened to you, would you have blamed me?' He turned to his mother. 'Would *you*?'

They were both silent, and Ben thought about what his brother was saying.

'When I got back,' he said slowly, 'I realised I'd driven all the way home on automatic pilot. I couldn't even remember the journey. I don't think I was paying attention at all, because my mind was so full of other things. I thought, when I looked back at it, how lucky I was that nothing happened.'

'And if it had,' Jamie repeated, 'would you have blamed me? Would it have been my fault?'

'Of course not,' Ben said. 'It would have been mine, if anything, for not concentrating.'

Jamie turned to his mother. 'Would *you* have blamed me?'

'No! Jamie, of course I wouldn't. Or Ben. It would just have been...' She broke off and swallowed down her tears.

'An accident?'

Ben and his mother looked at each other.

'That's what it was,' Jamie said. 'You can blame your-selves for ever and a day, but the fact is, Leon was driving that car and whatever happened on the road it had nothing to do with either of you. If Ben had been killed today it wouldn't have been my fault. I wasn't driving. And it wouldn't have been Mum's fault for not going instead of Ben. She couldn't change what happened in that car.'

He took a sip of tea. 'I don't remember Dad or Leon,' he admitted regretfully. 'I wish I did. But from what I know about them, neither of them would want this. They wouldn't want to see us punishing ourselves.

'Mum, Dad would have hated you to become such a recluse. I get it, okay? You were out having fun the night Leon died, so now you stay in and don't go anywhere. But what good does that do? And Ben, he wouldn't want you working your fingers to the bone and going without even basic pleasures to keep this roof over our heads. Not when you could be free of it all and have a decent life at last.

'I know, I know. I'm only a kid. I don't understand.' He shrugged. 'Maybe I understand more than either of you, because unlike you two, I don't have that guilt weighing me down, colouring my vision. I see it clearer. Maybe,' he added, the trace of a smile on his lips, 'you two should start taking advice from me for a change.'

For a long moment no one spoke, and the only sound was the ticking of the kitchen clock.

'Ben,' Mum said at last, 'I'm so, so sorry. I love you so much. None of this—*none of it*—was your fault. Please believe me when I tell you, I have never blamed you. Not for a single second.'

Ben put his head in his arms and, for the first time in many years, he let the tears fall.

Chapter Twenty-Six

Summer leaned over the bottom half of the loosebox door and watched, smiling, as Joseph patted the donkeys and told them to tuck in. He'd filled their hay nets and, as he opened the door to join Summer, the donkeys finally began to eat.

'They'll be all right, I reckon,' he said, nodding approvingly at them. 'They seem to be in good health, and at least they have each other. Always a good thing when they arrive with a friend.'

'Thank goodness the man's nephew knew about them,' Summer said. 'Can you imagine how long they'd have been left alone if he hadn't?'

The donkeys—Diamond and Sapphire—were getting on in years, and had once belonged to an elderly man who'd kept them in a paddock, a couple of miles from his home. Unfortunately, the man had recently died, and the donkeys had been left with no one to visit them, check up on them, or refill their water buckets. There had been enough grass in the paddock to stop them from going hungry, but they could have been seriously dehydrated if the man's nephew hadn't learned of his uncle's death and remembered the donkeys.

As he lived miles away and didn't want the responsibility of caring for them, someone had suggested he contact Whispering Willows, and now here they both were, settling into their new home.

'They can stay in here overnight,' Joseph said. 'The vet's coming in the morning to give them the once over, and when they get the all-clear they can go out into the fresh air with the other donkeys.'

Summer's stomach tightened. 'So Ben's coming here in the morning?'

Joseph gave her a wry look. 'It'll be Clive. We've already arranged it.'

'Right.'

They turned and began walking towards the house.

'Clive tells me you and Ben haven't seen each other since you got back from your jaunt to the Lakes,' Joseph said hesitantly. 'Is that right?'

Summer gave him a sideways look. 'Do you and Clive often discuss our private lives?'

'Well...' He rubbed his chin. 'Truth is, there's nothing much else to talk about. Even me and Clive get fed up with discussing horses sometimes. Not often, I'll grant you, but sometimes. Who else are we going to talk about, eh? You two are the only people we have anything to do with, really. Anyway, we care about you.'

'And it has nothing to do with a certain bet that's running about us, I suppose?' Summer said. 'Is Clive worried he'll have to pay the winnings back because it was a false start?'

Joseph looked appalled. 'As if! Any road, it wasn't a false start, was it? Clive would be a bit peeved if it was.'

'I wouldn't be that chuffed about it myself.'

Joseph opened the back door of the house and gestured for her to go in first. Summer did so, and as was the tradition, she headed straight to the kitchen to wash her hands and put the kettle on.

'I don't tend to get involved in other people's business,' Joseph said, washing his own hands as she rummaged in the cupboards for mugs and teabags, 'but I will admit to being a bit surprised that you and Ben seem to have come to a halt. Thought it was going great guns the way you two carried on at the wedding.'

'It was,' she said sadly.

'Ah.' Joseph nodded sagely. 'Right. That's a shame. You know that lad couldn't take his eyes off you all afternoon. Me and Clive were taking the mickey out of him, I'm afraid, but it was irresistible. If he'd been a cartoon he'd have had red love hearts pouring out of him and popping over his head like bubbles. Honestly, it was almost laughable. That's why we were so convinced you two would stay together, because let's face it, you've been mooning about after him long enough, too.'

'I have not,' Summer said indignantly.

Joseph arched one of his bushy eyebrows, and she relented.

'Okay, maybe that's true.' She sighed. 'I do like him, Joseph. I like him a lot. But sometimes that's not enough, is it? Ben has issues, and until he deals with them I don't see a way forward for us. The truth is, I told him to sort them out and that I'd be waiting for him when he had. Well, I'm still waiting, so what that means is anyone's guess.'

'No, well, I take your point.' Joseph reached for the tin of biscuits and placed it on the table. 'I'm not one to give anyone advice about love and all that stuff, but I will say that Ben's a good man. Clive thinks the world of him, and Clive doesn't give out praise lightly. For what it's worth, I think Ben's had a rotten time of it, and a fair amount of bad luck, and I believe he's so decent that he takes the weight of the world on his shoulders when he really shouldn't. Time he had a bit of fun, if you ask me, and you seemed to put the smile on his face for a while. I'm sorry there's no getting around that.'

Summer handed him a mug of tea, frowning. 'I didn't say there was *no* getting around it,' she said.

'No, no.' Joseph held up his hands. 'But it seems to me that you've accepted there's no future with him, so maybe that's for the best. If he can't make you happy, then what's the point? You have to think about yourself first, fair's fair.'

Summer sat opposite him and reached for a biscuit. 'Of course he *could* make me happy,' she said defensively. 'It's not like he's a bad person or anything.'

'But he obviously hurt you.'

She snapped the biscuit in half. 'He didn't hurt me. It's himself he's hurting. That's the trouble. He's trapped in this mire of guilt and self-hatred, and he can't seem to move past that. I had to walk away until he fixed things or we'd both have ended up unhappy, wouldn't we?'

'Absolutely,' Joseph agreed. He took a sip of tea. 'To be honest, I think you've done the right thing. Nice lass like you needs a bit of fun in her life. You don't want someone as miserable as Ben Callaghan dragging you down, making you miserable alongside him.'

'Ben's not miserable!' Summer said urgently, desperate to convince him. 'He can be very funny at times. You make it sound as if he's always gloomy and depressed when that's just not true.'

'Is it not?' Joseph looked surprised. 'I thought he was a proper misery guts, but if you say he's not...'

'Of course he's not. He's just got a lot of responsibility, that's all. There's so much more to Ben than all that.'

'Huh!' Joseph rolled his eyes. 'If you say so.'

'I do say so! You know yourself what a good vet he is. You know how kind and compassionate and dedicated he is to taking care of animals and doing his very best for them.'

'Yes, Summer,' Joseph said patiently, 'but that's animals, isn't it? What use is that to you? It's people he fails so badly with.'

'How can you say that? He's worked so hard and taken care of his mum and Jamie, having no life himself. Ben hasn't got a selfish bone in his body. He's the most generous, loving, kind-hearted man I've ever met, and...'

'And?'

Summer was staring at the wall as if she'd seen a ghost. 'Oh, bloody hell,' she murmured. 'I've been an absolute moron, haven't I?'

'Well,' Joseph said, cradling his mug of tea, 'far be it from me to pass comment on other folks' private lives, but if what you're telling me is the truth then, frankly, I'm baffled as to why you let him slip through your fingers. Man like that? Sounds like the perfect boyfriend if you ask me. I can't think what you're playing at.'

Summer eyed him suspiciously. 'You set me up, didn't you?'

'Would I?'

'Yes,' she said gloomily. 'I think you would. But you're right. I should have been there for him when he needed me, not left him to sink or swim on his own. Oh, Joseph, I've really screwed this up. What should I do?'

Joseph gave her a gentle smile. 'Why don't you go and find him and tell him what you've told me? I reckon no man would be able to resist any woman who thought so highly of him. And I also reckon, after the rotten time he's had of it lately, that it would do the lad the world of good to hear what you really think of him. He needs someone on his side. Don't you think?'

Summer pushed her mug of tea away and got to her feet. 'He'll be at Stepping Stones, won't he? Surgery?'

Joseph glanced at the clock on the wall and nodded. 'Reckon so.'

'I'm going to find him,' she said. 'Wish me luck.'

He raised his mug of tea to her. 'Somehow,' he said, smiling, 'I don't think you're going to need it.'

* * *

Ben handed the medication to Mrs McCoy and patted her German shepherd's head with affection and sympathy.

'There you go. He'll need to finish this course of antibiotics to make sure the infection clears up properly, and you'll have to bath him every three days with this special shampoo. We'll see how he gets on, but I'll need to see him again when the antibiotics are finished to check the infection's gone, and that his skin condition is clearing up. Okay?'

Mrs McCoy nodded. 'Thanks ever so much, Mr Callaghan. How much do I owe you?'

'If you speak to Jane at the reception desk she'll sort that out for you.'

He waited until she'd left the consulting room then washed his hands and moved over to his computer.

Four o'clock. He had half an hour to grab a drink after typing up his notes before his next round of appointments at four thirty. Only two hours to go until the end of the working day, and then he could leave here and go to The White Hart Inn.

His stomach did a somersault, which was most uncomfortable, as he thought about what he was going to say to Summer—always supposing she let him in, of course. She might not even allow him to set foot in the flat, which would make things very difficult. He could call her, but she might not answer the phone, and anyway, what he had to say to her should be said in person.

Maybe, he thought, he could ask Frankie for help. She might step in and secure him access to the flat. She'd seemed a forgiving sort of person when he'd apologised to her for assuming she'd led Jamie astray.

She'd simply shrugged and said, 'Oh, no worries. As long as it's all sorted now it doesn't matter, does it?'

He'd had to admit that was a mature attitude and found himself half-wishing that she and Jamie *had* been involved after all, especially as this Eloise Beauman was an unknown entity.

But no, he reminded himself, he wasn't going to interfere in Jamie's personal life. He would simply support him and take more of an interest in him from now on. Whatever his brother wanted, Ben would do his best to be pleased for him if it worked out and help him pick up the pieces if it didn't.

He remembered about the coffee and opened the surgery door, just in time to see Jane and Summer at the reception desk, having an animated conversation.

His heart almost leapt out of his chest, and he gripped the door handle.

'Summer? What are you doing here?'

Summer's face lit up. He saw it as clearly as if someone had shone a torch under her chin.

'Ben! I was just telling Jane here that I won't keep you five minutes, but she said you're in surgery and—'

'I've finished for now,' he said firmly, giving Jane a

knowing look. He was well aware that she and Clive had been discussing his and Summer's relationship, and Jane had been as disappointed as her boss that the whole thing seemed to have fizzled out. Evidently she was holding Summer responsible for that.

'Come in,' he said, waving her into his consulting room. 'I've got half an hour,' he added, raising his voice a little to make sure Jane got the message.

His receptionist gave him a quizzical look, but just before he followed Summer into the consulting room she held up her hands showing crossed fingers on each. Ben grinned and shook his head, then closed the door firmly behind him.

'I wasn't expecting to see you here,' he said, but before he could say anything else, she spun round and pulled him into a hug.

Ben wasn't quite sure what had happened to bring on such a change of heart, but he was very glad something had. After a moment, he came to his senses and put his arms around her, holding her tightly.

'What have I done to deserve this?' he asked, bewildered but delighted. Clearly, if he *had* gone to The White Hart Inn after surgery she would have let him in after all, which was encouraging.

'It's an apology,' she admitted, gazing up at him. 'Well, half apology and half—well—half an *I'm such an idiot to let you go, because I know what a fabulous man you really are, and of course I want to be in a relationship with you, and will you give me a second chance* statement.'

Ben's eyes widened. 'Say that again?'

She wrinkled her nose. 'I don't think I could. I can't remember half of it. But surely you got the gist? I was an idiot.'

He shook his head. 'You weren't an idiot. You were right about everything.'

'No, I wasn't. I was horrible. I should have supported you, stood by you, not walked away from you like a coward.'

She stepped back and let out a big sigh before leaning on the worktop.

'It's my dad, you see. God, don't families screw us up? And when you told me what you told me, I panicked. I just thought, I can't live the sort of life Mum had with him. I can't be with a man who has all these emotional problems when I have no idea how they'll manifest in the future. I was being selfish. I should have stuck by you and offered to help you through it all, but I was thinking of myself.'

'You did the right thing,' he told her. 'Do you really think I'd want you to be stuck with someone as messed up as I was? I had nothing to offer you, Summer. Nothing at all. I wanted better for you than that. And that's why I—'

'But it's my choice!' she said desperately. 'And the thing is, Ben, I know what a good person you are. You and I, we have a lot in common. I've never met a man like you before— well, apart from Joseph, but there's no way on earth I could ever fancy him, bless him.'

'I'm very glad to hear it,' Ben said, amusement bubbling up inside him.

'Whereas you... well, I really fancy you.'

He smiled, half-embarrassed and half-thrilled to bits. 'You do?'

'You know I do.' Her cheeks were distinctly pink now. She looked, he thought, utterly adorable. 'But even more than that, I respect you as a person. I think you're the most amazing man I've ever known, with all the qualities I want and need from a—well, from a boyfriend,' she said, eyeing him warily, as if wondering how he'd react to the term.

'You're honest and loyal and unselfish. The truth is, you couldn't be less like my dad if you tried. And...'

She gulped, and Ben took her hand in his. 'And what?' he asked her gently.

'And I think I love you, Ben. The fact is, I know I do. And I'm sorry I hurt you, and I'm sorry I walked away and left you to it. But if you'll just give me another chance I promise I won't ever walk away again.'

Ben laughed.

'Don't laugh at me,' she said, stepping back. 'If you're not interested just tell me. Don't let me stand here making a fool of myself. Please, Ben.'

He put his arms around her and kissed her gently. 'Would someone as honest, loyal, and unselfish as me ever do that to you?'

She gazed into his eyes and the warmth in her own made him melt.

'No,' she said softly. 'I guess you wouldn't. Does this mean I'm forgiven?'

'There's absolutely nothing to forgive,' he said. 'You were protecting yourself, and so you should. And like I said, I had nothing to offer you. I only laughed because the idea of you asking for another chance just seemed so ridiculous. It's me who messed everything up, not you. But things will be different from now on, Summer. I promise.'

'You do?' She looked at him, hope in her eyes. 'Does this mean something's changed?'

'Oh, Summer, where to start?' He gazed up at the ceiling, wondering how to begin to tell her everything that had happened since they'd said goodbye in the churchyard. 'I have so much to tell you, you wouldn't believe it. But the main thing—the most important thing—is that I love you, too. I never dreamed I could be this happy. I don't want us ever to be apart again, because without you it's like all the colour in life fades away, and everything's shades of grey.'

She nudged him playfully. 'Well, you know what they say about shades of grey.'

He laughed. 'You see? You cheer me up all the time. You just told me what qualities you think I possess, but you possess them, too. You're the most warm-hearted, decent, honourable person I know, and...' he groaned as she drank him in with those stunning green eyes of hers, 'and oh hell, Summer, you're absolutely beautiful, and you have no idea how difficult it's been being so restrained around you.'

'Oh, Ben.' Summer shook her head and cradled his face in her hands. 'You really shouldn't have gone to all that effort on my account. I'd really love to see you when you're not being restrained at all.'

'Summer...'

Frustration bubbled up inside him, and he could feel it building within her, too.

'You know,' he murmured into her ear, his cheek grazing hers, 'I'm sure Mum would love to have Frankie over to stay tonight. She and Jamie could play computer games, and Mum would cook them supper, and in the meantime...'

'In the meantime, you could have a sleepover at my place,' she murmured back. 'And we could play games, too.'

Her arms went around his neck, and he kissed her hungrily, desperately, wishing with all his heart that they were in her room at The White Hart Inn right now, because being restrained was suddenly proving almost impossible.

'Just a few more hours,' she whispered.

'I'll be counting every minute.'

* * *

'We're home!'

The door banged open, and Summer, Frankie, and Ben looked at each other and grinned.

Rafferty and Sally walked into the living room, suitcases in their hands, and stopped, clearly surprised to see Ben sitting on the sofa between the two girls.

'Well, this is nice,' Sally said, dropping her case on the floor. 'Have you been here long, Ben?'

'How was Paris?' Frankie leapt to her feet and gave her dad a hug, then did the same to her new stepmother. 'Did you see the Eiffel tower? The Arc de Triomphe? Notre Dame?'

Summer stood too and kissed her mum on the cheek. 'And did you walk arm in arm along the banks of the Seine, whispering sweet nothings into each other's ears?'

'Speaking words of *amour*,' Frankie added, giggling. 'Sitting at a table in a Parisian restaurant, nibbling at both ends of a baguette?'

'Like *Lady and the Tramp*, you mean?' Ben suggested. 'But with bread instead of spaghetti?'

Rafferty and Sally exchanged bemused looks.

'What's got into this lot?' Rafferty asked. 'Should we be worried?'

'Not at all,' Summer said. 'Look around you. The flat's spotless, the pub's been running like clockwork, I've put clean bedding and fresh flowers in your bedroom, and there's a casserole in the oven that just needs warming up, so no need to cook anything for tea.'

'A casserole?' Sally's eyes widened. 'You made us a casserole?'

'Not me,' Summer said. 'Jennifer. You know how much she loves to cook.'

'Here, sit down, Sally,' Frankie said. 'You too, Dad. I'll put the kettle on.'

'Why would Jennifer make us a casserole?' Rafferty asked, clearly puzzled. 'I mean, don't get me wrong, it's very kind of her, but even so...'

'She's testing out recipes,' Ben explained. 'She wanted to get your opinion.'

'Testing out recipes?' Sally eased off her shoes and unbuttoned her jacket. 'Testing them for what?'

'For her new job,' Ben said.

Sally's eyes lit up. 'New job? Jennifer's got a new job? How smashing is that? Aw, I'm that pleased for her. It'll do her the world of good to get out and about, mixing with other people. What job is it?'

'Cook,' Summer said, rolling her eyes. 'Obviously.'

Rafferty looked impressed. 'Really? Whereabouts?'

'At the art school,' Ben said casually.

'Art school?' Rafferty stared from one to the other of them. 'What art school?'

'The one that will be opening in a few months' time. Ross Lavender's art school.'

'So it's going ahead? Excellent.'

Sally nodded. 'Fancy your mum getting a job there already, Ben. Where's the art school going to be?'

'Monk's Folly.'

Summer bit her lip to stop herself from smiling as Sally and Rafferty turned astonished gazes upon them.

'Monk's Folly?'

'Oh yes, Miss Lavender has bought Monk's Folly from Ben, and they're going to spend a small fortune on it turning it into a day and residential art school which, by the way, is going to be known as the Arabella Lavender Art Academy. Grand or what? There's going to be a gallery and a shop, and obviously they'll need food for the students, which is where Jennifer comes in. She'll have help, of course, but she'll be in charge. It's going to be amazing when it's done.'

'But—but where are you all going to live?' Sally asked Ben.

'That's actually a very good question, and one I've only just been given the answer to.' Ben turned to Summer. 'I haven't even had the chance to tell you yet, but Mum and I had a conversation with our old gardener, Mr Eckington. He's decided he's better off at his daughter's after all, and needs to sell his property, so we made him an offer and he accepted this morning.'

'Ooh, how fabulous! Whereabouts did he live?' Summer asked, thrilled for him that yet another matter had been settled.

'It's that little cottage on River Road. You know, the one with the blue door and roses growing up the walls?'

'Daisyfield Cottage?' Summer sighed with pleasure. 'Oh, that's such a lovely place.'

'It is. I reckon it's perfect for your mum and you two boys to have a fresh start, now you've got rid of Monk's Folly. Between you and me, love,' Sally confided, 'I don't know how you stood living in that house. Proper creepy place it looks to me, and just you three rattling around in there. I don't think it was good for you. You'll all be a lot happier at Daisyfield Cottage, I'm sure of it.'

'So am I,' Ben said. He squeezed Summer's hand, an action which, as she'd suspected, didn't go unnoticed by her mum. Not that either she or Ben minded that. Their days of hiding their relationship were well and truly over.

'Don't they look lovely together, Rafferty?' Sally asked, smiling fondly at them. 'Love's young dream, aren't they?'

Frankie returned to the living room, carrying a tray of hot drinks.

'You can say that again,' she said. 'Ben's stayed here every night this week.'

Summer flushed and Ben gave Sally an apologetic look.

'I'm sorry if that's a problem. I realise this is your home, and I wouldn't want to do anything to upset you. It's just—'

'Ben, love,' Sally reassured him, 'you haven't upset me at all. All I can say is, about bloody time.'

'We're very happy for you,' Rafferty said, smiling. He turned to Sally, shaking his head slightly. 'I don't know, we go away for a week and everything changes. What else are we going to find out, do you reckon?'

'You know,' Sally said, eyeing Ben thoughtfully, 'there's something different about you. You look—I don't know— younger. Lighter. As if a weight's been lifted off your shoulders. I reckon our Summer's done you the world of good. Love suits you.'

Ben laughed. 'You know what, Sally? I couldn't agree with you more.'

He put his arm around Summer's shoulders and her stomach lurched as she saw the look in his eyes.

How had she ever wondered if she could trust him? How had she ever worried that he'd turn out to be like her dad, or Ian? Ben was nothing like either of them.

He was reliable and honest and loyal, and she knew he would love her fiercely and devotedly, and never give her cause to doubt it.

And she also knew that she would love him back just as much, always, because how could she not? They were, she was certain, going to make each other very happy.

In fact, she would bet on it.

A Letter from the Author

Huge thanks for reading Summer in Tuppenny Bridge. I hope you were hooked on Summer and Ben's journey. If you want to join other readers in hearing all about my new releases and other bonus content, you can sign up for my newsletter!

www.stormpublishing.co/sharon-booth

If you enjoyed the book and could spare a few moments to leave a review that would be greatly appreciated. Even a short review can make all the difference in encouraging a reader to discover my books for the first time. Thank you so much!

The Yorkshire Dales market town of Tuppenny Bridge has been in my mind for a few years now, and there were two inspirations for it. The first was the market town of Masham, which I've visited many times and love. Its market square, and the beautiful church of St Mary's with its amazing churchyard, kept pulling me back, and I knew it would make a great setting for a series. The second was the artwork of Trevor Mitchell, whose website is full of paintings depicting rural England in bygone days. The village, farmyard, and shop scenes stirred my imagination, and I thought how I'd love to create a community like the ones he captures so brilliantly. You can visit his website and view the inspiration for so much of Tuppenny Bridge at www.trevormitchellartist.com

You can find out more about Summer and her backstory in my The Other Half series, where you'll also find the first mentions of Tuppenny Bridge.

Thanks again for being part of this amazing journey with me and I hope you'll stay in touch – I have so many more stories and ideas to entertain you with!

Sharon x

facebook.com/sharonbooth.writer

twitter.com/Sharon_Booth1

instagram.com/sharonboothwriter

Acknowledgments

I'd like to thank the team at Storm Publishing for taking a chance on me, and for all their hard work. Between them they've made this a book I can be proud of. It's been a very different experience, working with a publisher for the first time, but Kathryn and the rest of the team have been a joy to work with, and have made it all very easy for this nervous author! I'm so grateful to them all.

The person who pushed me into submitting to Storm Publishing in the first place deserves my gratitude. Thanks so much to Julie Heslington, aka Jessica Redland, who really is the best friend anyone could wish for, and thankfully has enough confidence for both of us. She is genuinely one of the kindest, most generous, and most caring people I've ever met, and I don't know what I'd do without her.

I'm lucky enough to be part of a writing community called The Write Romantics. We started off as a blogging group, but as our writing careers developed and we got busier, the blogging trailed off. We're still very much together though, and the nine other members of the group couldn't be more supportive. I'm looking forward to our next in-person meeting, but in the meantime big hugs and thanks to Jessica Redland, Jo Bartlett, Helen Phifer, Helen J Rolfe, Alys West, Deirdre Palmer, Rachael Thomas, Jackie Ladbury, and Lynne Pardoe.

Hugs also to my other writing family, the Beverley chapter of the Romantic Novelists' Association. The meetings are such fun, and the members so friendly and welcoming. Thanks for all your support and encouragement, and for all the laughs!

Huge thanks to my lovely husband, without whom none of this would be possible. Without his support and encouragement there's no way I'd have left my day job to become a full-time writer, and I'll be forever grateful that he showed such faith in me. He really is my rock.

Finally, I'd like to say a big thank you to you, my readers. To those of you who take the time to post reviews, respond to my newsletter, message me with lovely comments about my stories, ask questions, follow me on social media, or read my blog posts, I can't tell you how grateful I am. An author's confidence can be easily shaken, and it's your support that keeps me writing.

Stick with me. There's so much more to come.

Love Sharon xx

Printed in Great Britain
by Amazon